Sorrah

A Mirror of Blackmor Tale

Book one

Madison Thorne Grey

Other titles by Madison Thorne Grey

The Gwarda Warriors series

Magnificence
Sustenance
Recompense
Silence
Brilliance
Malevolence

Acknowledgements

*****

A special thank you to Ashley Vandenmeiracker, Gail Sanders, and my sister, Michele.

Dedication

To my husband and best friend, Jon

Prologue

San Francisco, March, 1868

"We're due at old man Ned's in an hour," Morris stated, wiping a trail of sweat off his brow with a dirt stained cloth. "I think we have everythin'." He pointed to a pile of items as he spoke. "Herbs, Metals, the special water... Where's the blasted wood? I know we got it."

He scanned the port, seeing many merchant ships and workers.

"Too many are coming in. They get wind of our deal, they'll be stealin' it out from under us." He waved his hand in the face of the man who stood in front of him. "Hello, George? You awake or what?"

"The wooo... wood is he... he... here." George stuttered, pointing off to the left of where they stood.

George was a hunched-over, short man, who had a permanently damaged right arm and one bad eye, but had worked the shipping yards since he was a kid and knew them better than anyone. He also knew the ins and outs of the *trade and swindle* business that regularly went on at the docks. It was the main reason why Morris had teamed up with him, for what he believed to be the deal of a lifetime. Times were tough, and men were even tougher, doing what needed to be done in order to survive.

Morris and George weren't the most upstanding citizens of their day, but they found work where they could, and when they couldn't, they'd steal. Anything to feed their aching bellies.

Morris looked to where George was pointing. There was a pile of fresh wood that had just come in on a ship. This wasn't any ordinary wood, but from a tree in the Tongass forest to be exact. It had taken two months for it to arrive, and hadn't cost them anything but a bottle of whiskey. Friends, who traveled the seas, were good friends to have.

At first, Morris had thought to trick the old craftsman he'd made a deal with, by giving him local wood, but the strange man insisted he'd know the difference, he'd know the age, and he'd know if it were from a Tongass tree. Morris believed him. It was never a good idea to trick people who were known to be into the dark arts, witchcraft and such, especially when they called you out on exactly what you were thinking about doing.

"The old man owes us some big coin for this stuff! We're going to be rich!"

Morris smiled, showing his missing front tooth. "There's no way the old keister could've managed to get these things himself. Looks like we have everythin'. Let's have a quick drink to celebrate, eh, Georgie?"

The men sat on crates and passed a bottle of whiskey between them.

"With all the talk about him and his family, I'm not sure many would've worked for the old wizard, but we did, didn't we, Georgie oh boy!"

"Yeppp... They wit... wit."

"Witches... yes. Right you are. But his family are all dead cept' a sister. I heard."

He took a hard swig of the whiskey. "She was smart nuff' to move far away. From what I hear, she doesn't want nottin' to do with her brother." Morris leaned closer to George, his breath heavy with the scent of alcohol and rotted teeth. "People say old man Ned is normal enough. Keeps to himself and such. Many love his craftsmanship, but his mother—she was a strange ornery goat. Evil lurked in her eyes, somethin' dark and malevolent. They say she could cast a spell with one gaze of her red eyes."

George grabbed the bottle and took a swig. Morris pulled it out of his hands and grasped it tightly. He glanced around for listening ears.

"I'm supposin' it ain't fittin' to talk poorly of the dead, especially with em' into black magic. Best we keep our traps shut, eh? Now, let's get these things loaded on the cart and get em' over to Ned. The sooner we get rid of this stuff and get our coin, the better."

*****

October 22, 1868, Clay Street, San Francisco

Ned stepped away and considered the completion of his complex work. With trembling hands, he clenched the stained and torn parchment paper.

"It is finished."

He had constructed the piece exactly as his mother had instructed long ago, with a carved-wood frame and a mirror in the center. Engraved in the wood were symbols and shapes, many of which looked like circles, stars, and odd lines. Ned hadn't understood the symbols, but that didn't matter. His goal had been to please his mother who had passed away years ago. He hoped she'd be proud of his accomplishment.

"It is finished right on schedule, Momma."

His mother, who had often times seen glimpses into the future, had been adamant about the timeline. The mirror had to be started specifically in March of the year eighteen sixty eight and finished by October twenty-second of that same year.

"It truly is magnificent. A piece fit for a queen. Helen doesn't deserve it, but I'll send it to her to please you, mother, because it's what you wanted."

He placed a note on the mirror and secured it with twine. He didn't claim to know why his mother insisted he ship the mirror to his sister Helen and certainly didn't know why she had him attach a note to it either. Ned and his sister hadn't spoken to each other in years, but he did as his mother instructed nevertheless. His mother had always said the true power of their family, lie in the women. But that hadn't always been the case. She had spoken briefly about her father once being very powerful in the arts and regarded as a prince in the craft of witchery. There was fear in her eyes when she mentioned him. Something epic changed in his mother's past, altering the abilities of the males in their bloodline and releasing much of it rather to the women of the family. She provided no details of the event, neither had she mentioned her father again.

He had to assume a curse had been brought upon all of them, making this mirror highly special. Perhaps, it was a way to break the spell.

The detail in the wood was not something Ned had done before, nor had he ever seen such intricate craftsmanship. It had taken him months to carve out each and every swirl, line, and shape. It had been as if his hand was guided by some force greater than himself. Once

11

finished, he burned the discarded shavings and scraps just as his mother had insisted upon in the instructions.

The mirror in the center was made with many layers, each containing melted down properties of herbs, silver, and bottles of special water shipped in from apothecaries all over the continent.

He walked to the small wood-burning stove and placed the instructions inside. "Just as you asked, Mother, it is burnt up now, gone forever. No one will ever be able to duplicate my work without knowing the specifics."

Unexpectedly, the earth began to shake, increasing with each passing second. Ned stumbled and tried to hold onto anything he could to stay upright, but this earthquake was too great a force for an old man to withstand.

As he lie on the floor, with the walls tumbling down on and around him, he kept his gaze locked on the mirror. His masterpiece mirror wasn't getting pummeled by debris and even the heavy fog of dust in the air seemed to avoid contact with it, as if it were magically protected. The note, which read the name and address of his sister, remained securely fastened. He believed his mother knew he would die this day and the landlord would see that the mirror was shipped as instructed. The man and his family, who owned the building, had been kind and considerate toward the family.

Ned struggled to breathe as the weight of the debris grew heavier on his chest. He thought of how he'd spent his last remaining days on Earth, creating something so extraordinary and laced with magic of his druid ancestors. A legacy. He somehow knew the mirror would never be destroyed and would survive him.

A wood beam fell from the ceiling, landing on Ned's back, and he grunted in pain. This was the end. As his eyes began to close, he noticed a shadow, moving inside the mirror. *What is that?* he thought.

The mysterious mist shifted and took on an unclear human form.

He knew no one else could possibly be in the building, certainly not in this room, which was crumbling down around him.

The form moved again and became clearer.

Ned's eyes widened from shock and astonishment. His lips parted as he breathed his last words. "That's impossible."

Chapter one

Walnut, Iowa – Present day

"Has she asked for me?" Sorrah inquired.

The nurse tending to her aunt didn't answer verbally but she couldn't miss the apologetic look on the woman's face. Whatever. What made her believe things would be any different today?

"I'll let you two have some privacy," the nurse said, leaving the room.

Sorrah took a deep breath. The feeling of death in the air was nearly too much for her to bear. She was always sensitive to these sorts of things.

"Who's there?" Kaye mumbled.

"It's me, Kaye," Sorrah answered, moving closer to the bed.

"Alaina? Alaina, is that you? Have you found it?"

Kaye reached her hand out and Sorrah took hold of it as she sat on the edge of the bed.

"No, Kaye. It's me. It's Sorrah."

Kaye closed her eyes then opened them abruptly. "Oh, Sorrah… you've returned from school."

"Kaye, I've been home for months."

Her aunt seemed perplexed. "Yes… yes, of course. I am very proud of you, Sorrah. You'll make a fine nurse."

Her mother was the nurse, not her. She'd thought of following in her mother's footsteps and getting into the medical field, becoming a doctor, but after only one year, found she wasn't cut out for it. She didn't feel the need to correct her dying aunt. *Let her believe the best of me.*

"I've tried to be good to you," Kaye mumbled.

"Shhh. You have been very good to me."

That was a bit of a stretch. She'd been cold and distant. But overall, Sorrah supposed her aunt had done an adequate job raising her.

Kaye wasn't really her aunt at all, but her mother's friend. Her mother died shortly after giving birth to her. Often times, Sorrah wished she had at least one memory of her mother to hold onto, a glimpse of her blonde hair or gray eyes. Kaye had described her, but oddly had no pictures. In fact, she had given Sorrah very few things of her mother's. A couple articles of clothing, a pretty hair comb with pearls inlaid in it that she used to pretend were the most priceless pearls from a far off kingdom. The truth was the comb had most likely been purchased at the local general store in town. From what she was told, her mother wasn't exactly wealthy. The menial items she possessed were nothing anyone would consider a keepsake of any great meaning but, she treasured them as if they were.

"I know I wasn't always the most attentive parent, Sor."

Always? Try never.

"Kaye, you haven't called me Sor since I was ten years old." Sorrah smiled even though she always detested the nickname. "You've raised me well. Be at peace."

"I know dragging you to all those antique shops and flea markets, wasn't much fun."

"I grew to like it. You always loved antiques which made me love them too." *Sort of.*

Sorrah liked some vintage things, mostly clothing and cookware. Mirrors on the other hand, she abhorred and not because it showed the reflection of her own plainness, but because her aunt was an outright freak when it came to them.

She glanced at all the antique furniture in her aunt's room. These particular items were actually quite beautiful. The craftsmanship alone was unlike anything in this day and age of put-it-together yourself furniture.

"You know that's where my appreciation for vintage things came from."

Her aunt harrumphed. "Won't do you much good in a hospital."

Sorrah took a deep breath. "You are *so* right."

What was the point in telling her aunt, again, that she had pursued a career as a doctor but never finished medical school? She had spent more time baking for her study partners than doing any real studying. It wasn't long before requests for muffins, pies, and tarts poured in from other groups. She loved to bake and thought pursuing a career as a pastry chef might be in her future. Now, she wasn't sure what she'd do with her life. She had always felt out of place, fumbling around life, trying numerous things but never mastering one.

"I'm an old woman, ten years older than your mother, but I loved her. You know that, don't you?"

"Of course."

"I searched. Sorrah, I did. You have to know that. I did what she told me to, but I failed. I told her I'd try to get you back home but I just couldn't find the right one."

Dear God, what meds did the doctors have her on anyway? She seemed delusional. Then it struck Sorrah what her aunt was going on about. It all came back to the mirrors.

"Don't be troubled. I have plenty of mirrors. You made sure of that."

The woman had been obsessed with mirrors for as long as Sorrah could remember. She'd spent many years searching antique shops all over the country, describing the wooden framed mirror she was looking for. She didn't even have a picture to go on and even the few images she had printed off the internet for examples, hadn't proved helpful.

She soon became frustrated with her lack of success. Later, when her health began to fail, she'd have countless antique dealers visit their home. They would insist that they found what she was looking for. They'd take her money and give her many mirrors, most of which were upstairs in the attic or were given away when they didn't meet her expectations in some way.

Sorrah remembered many nights she'd awaken from odd noises in the old rickety house. One night, hearing sounds coming from down the hall of her bedroom, she'd snuck to her aunt's room. She found the door a few inches ajar and peered through the gap of the frame. Her aunt was hitting one of the mirrors with her hand, spouting words of frustration. What did she think the mirror would do?

Just like a scene from out of a horror movie, her aunt suddenly met her eyes, catching her in the act of snooping. Even when she protested, her aunt yanked her inside the room and forced her to touch the mirror over and over, but nothing happened. Like all the other mirrors she'd been made to touch before. Nothing happened.

She had gotten over her aunt's bizarre touching-mirror-fetish, but she never could get over the strange, evil look in her aunt's eyes that night.

When Kaye had finally released her, she rushed back to her room and covered herself in the safety of her blankets and stuffed animals, which she lined up and down on each side of her for protection. They were her only weapon against the forces of Merlin or whoever cast the evil spell on her aunt.

For some months after, she'd watch animated movies and imagine Kaye as the woman who stole Dalmatian pups or transformed into an ugly, octopus witch of the sea. For the most part, she handled the oddities and eventually grew accustomed to her aunt's eccentric ways. Mostly, by avoiding her altogether. Funny, how well that worked.

Her aunt coughed a few times and grabbed Sorrah's hand once more. "There are things…" Cough. "There are things you do not know, Sorrah. I always thought I'd do them myself, you see… to protect you."

She was fading away, it was in her eyes. "I held things back. I should have told you, but…" She stilled and Sorrah thought she may have slipped away. Her aunt gripped her hand tighter, squeezing it hard.

"Auntie… Auntie, please." Her pleading got her nowhere. "Kaye!" she yelled.

Kaye blinked and softened her grip. "I have left you everything. This house, the money…"

Money?

She didn't think Kaye had much left. She had paid for medical school up until she quit, and said doing so had drained her life savings. Sorrah had protested the generosity, but Kaye had insisted. Now she wondered if Kaye had lied about her finances.

"Had I lasted, I may have been able to find Sorrah." She tsked. "I so wanted to go. Your mother described its wonder and beauty. I'm sorry I never found the way."

"Sorrah?"

"Yes. Your home. The home of your father."

"Kaye. My *name* is Sorrah, not my home, and my father died in the war."

16

"No. No he didn't. I lied. I thought it best, you see. The story your mother told me was outrageous and so unbelievable. At first. Many thought her crazy. She just showed up one day after being gone for ten years. What was I to think? All of her family was dead. I was all she had."

Kaye knew her mother from working in the hospital. They'd become friends.

Kaye's eyes drifted to Sorrah's shoulder. "Your mark."

"My birthmark?"

"Yes. It's more than a birthmark." Her breathing became shallow. "Your mother told me that your father had a similar mark but not exact. A symbol of his people."

The marking was nothing special really, not as simple as an ordinary circle, but one with two larger rings around it, almost looking like a planet, a sun or moon. As a little girl, she used to look at her shoulder, using a mirror, and imagine the circle bursting open and revealing magical gifts or transforming into a window that she could escape through and have great adventures. She may have watched Alice and her wonderland too many times.

"My home is here, Aunt Kaye."

The house was a two story colonial with six bedrooms, a formal dining room, library, kitchen, and maid's quarters. It had been passed down in Kaye's family for centuries, or so she was told. Sorrah was the last, not even blood, but the last remaining relative just the same.

Kaye's eyes grew weary. "There is a small trunk of your mothers, behind the—" Cough. "Behind the large mirror in the attic."

Was she serious? There had to be a dozen large mirrors up there. And why was she only hearing about this mysterious trunk now?

"There is a panel in the wall, an additional room." Kaye looked off to the side. "Do you remember playing in there, Arthur?"

Yeah, that was kinda creepy. Arthur was the name of her deceased brother.

She turned back to Sorrah. "Forgive me. I was selfish. I wanted to go. I deserved to go after taking care of her and taking you in."

Deserved? Sorrah thought.

"All the bright color and magic there. Oh, your mother told me such fantastical stories…"

17

Kaye smiled but it soon fell. "She was an adventurous one, your mother. I was always so envious of her." She got a faraway look in her eye which turned almost menacing. "There's a journal of your mother's in the trunk. I didn't even read it all, she always was too wordy. There's a small box of childhood pictures in there too of when she lived with her grandmother on Robush road. The fire took everything. And now I'm too old to keep searching for the mirror. I'm dying."

Journal? Pictures?

Sorrah slipped her hand out from underneath Kaye's hand. She was hurt. "Why didn't you tell me you had other things that belonged to my mother? Why would you keep them from me?"

Kaye's eyes turned dark. "*I* wanted to go! I wanted out of here!" she yelled.

Sorrah wondered how on Earth, Kaye mustered enough strength to scream like that. She'd had a frightful look of evil in her eyes, the same kind she had seen in her aunt many years ago. It caught Sorrah off guard.

She took a step back from the bed.

Kaye waved her hand in the air. "You… You were going to be my ticket out of here. I figured the symbol on your back was the key to get through the mirror. But no, I had to get sick. This is all your fault!"

"I don't know what nonsense you are talking about. I have loved you these years; please don't ruin it now in the end."

Her aunt's eyes cleared of the darkness somewhat, becoming weary once more. "I'm so sorry. I don't know what came over me."

She glanced to the corner of the room. "I must leave now. Goodbye my dear. Arthur is here to take me away and says we must leave now."

With those words, Kaye shut her eyes. A throaty rattle came next followed by a heavy release of her last breath, and Sorrah knew her aunt had died. Her eyes filled with tears that refused to fall when she recalled what her aunt had just laid on her. Apparently she hadn't known her very well.

Chapter two

Sorrah sat at the long, wooden table in the formal dining room, a room she used to play in often when she was a little girl. The room, which had been cleaned every day by Martha, their housekeeper, and was now filled with a strange emptiness.

The furnishings in the dining room, as well as all the rooms in the house, were old, antiques. The house had a nice aura about it due to the historical and vintage items, yet, always lacked the warmth she'd seen in magazines, others' homes or saw on television. The family shows where they gathered around the kitchen table at dinner time or watched movies together had always made her envious. She hadn't had that sort of life but knew those people who had were fortunate and lucky to be a part of something so special.

She loved Martha and Kaye as much as she could, all things considered, but Kaye had been gone a lot, traveling here and there... searching. Always searching. And Martha had been kind to her growing up and gave her some happy memories but still a void remained.

When other girls at school had spoken about returning home to their families, she'd just nod as if she understood but she really didn't. She had gone away for college for her basics, then later medical school. She remained at college for every holiday, knowing there'd be nothing special going on back in Iowa. At least not in her home. She had always possessed an earnest desire for a large family, lavish holidays, and a house full of loved ones. Inside her remained a hope that one day she'd have exactly that.

"I have many things to take care of. I hope this isn't going to take very much longer," Sorrah told Kaye's lawyer who had showed up the very day Kaye had been buried. There wasn't more than her, Martha, and a few neighbors who attended the small funeral. As soon as she and Martha had returned home, a knock sounded on the door and

Mister Farnsworth, attorney at law, was there.

"Kaye was most adamant about going over these papers as soon as she was," he cleared his throat, "in the cold ground. She changed some things just a week ago."

Sorrah knew the words, *in the cold ground* had to be from Kaye. She had always been blunt with her speech.

"Fine. Let's get on with it then."

As Kaye had mentioned to Sorrah, she had left everything to her, including the home which had been paid off over a century ago, two cars, three barns full of antiques, mostly mirrors, and three and half million dollars. And some change.

Sorrah nearly fainted. "I had no idea."

"She knew you'd be surprised. You are a very wealthy woman, Miss Blackmor. She also left me instruction to give you this unopened letter."

Sorrah took the letter from Mister Farnsworth, signed some papers and made arrangements for the money to be transferred into a new account. After saying her goodbyes and retreating to the library, her favorite room in the house, she opened the letter and read:

Sor,

If you are reading this, I am dead and have failed in finding the mirror your mother had spoken of countless times. It was my hope to find the courage to tell you about your mother's things, but if I didn't, they are in the attic room behind the mirror and panel in the wall.

Your mother reappeared out of nowhere after being gone for ten long years. She was pregnant, by only a couple of months. She had been assumed dead, and it was quite the shock to see her again.

Another strange thing was that after ten years, your mother had not aged. Not even a little. Not one wrinkle. Not one laugh-line on her face. Whereas, I was nearly ready to be a social security recipient.

Of course, her family, which at the time of her disappearance consisted of one grandmother, were all long dead. I was her closest friend. Her only friend.

I know this is terrible, Sorrah, but I grew exceedingly jealous of your mother. It started on that very day she returned so youthful. Please forgive me.

She had a small satchel with her, a strange-looking pouch (the pouch is among her belongings). Inside the pouch, were rectangular gold pieces, small bars. I was the only one she showed them to, the only one she trusted. In the end, she gave them to me, and begged me to look after you.

She told me marvelously shocking stories, and at first, I thought her insane. She named you after the very place her stories came from. A land called Sorrah.

When she knew she was dying, she made me promise to take care of you, but more than that, she made me swear to help you find a particular unique antique mirror, handmade with special wood, and laced with magic, from her ancestors who were druids. They were considered witches back in the day. This special mirror had been passed down through generations, through the females of the family.

Your mother described the mirror to me the best she could remember it, said she'd stepped through it after seeing it in the loft of her grandmother's barn. I assumed I could step through it too.

"Stepped through it?" Sorrah muttered to herself. "You're kidding me right, Kaye?"

While in Sorrah, she fell in love with a Sorrien man and gave birth to a boy. Years later, a war broke out and her love was killed, her son taken away and imprisoned by the enemy.

Sorrah's breathing hitched. "I have a brother?" she whispered.

Your mother panicked. She was the only one, apart from a trusted advisor and her son, who knew she was pregnant, she hadn't even told the father yet, and now he was dead. His enemies had gotten to him and she feared for your safety. She believed they'd kill her and that meant they'd kill you too. People there, encouraged her to leave, to go far away from Sorrah. By the time of her return, her grandmother had died and the barn had gone up in flames. From what we could find out, there was nothing left. Your mother believed the mirror indestructible, swore it was magical and that the mirror disappeared the moment she returned through it. This is when the search began.

This is a lot for you to take in. I am sure.

I felt the need to come clean with you, Sorrah, in the end, in hopes my soul will find forgiveness from the Creator and from you.

You need to return to Sorrah and find your brother. Your mother always believed he was alive.

21

I have enclosed a letter I received from an antique shop I sent an inquiry to. I know it may seem like just another fruitless lead, but you never know. The shop is in San Francisco. You had family there, on Clay Street, and legends say a family of witches lived on that very street. Maybe, the mirror found its way back to where it was created.

My hope is for you to succeed where I have failed. Go to Sorrah and find your brother, he's the only family you have left. And don't over analyze this, as you do with all things. Follow through for once in your life. Have an adventure and find yourself.

With love and affection,

Kaye

She folded the letter and stood. It was time she had some answers. If Kaye wasn't delusional and crazy, she'd certainly behaved that way for as long as she could remember.

Something called out to her, tugged at her very spirit and she couldn't deny it any longer. She dreaded entering the cluttered attic, but needed to see her mother's things.

*****

"What a mess," Sorrah muttered as she moved numerous items, mostly old, out of her way. There were cradles that looked like they'd been taken off the movie set of Rosemary's Baby, high-back chairs, civil war clothing, and mirrors. Lots and lots of mirrors in various shapes and sizes but all framed in wood. She remembered how Kaye had been specific about that in her search.

The attic was always a dusty place and in these older homes, pretty darn eerie too.

After a couple of hours of shrieking and being completely overwhelmed by debris and dust, she had finally made a clearing to the left wall which had a mirror hanging directly upon it.

All of the walls of the house had intricate molding from floor to ceiling. She touched along the side seam of the molding, looking for something which would trigger an opening to the panel and entry to another room.

She watched so many movies about secret panels and hidden castle rooms. The Secret Garden had been one of her favorite books when she was young, and when she saw the movie she'd made it her quest in life to watch it over and over again. At the age of eight, it had been a thrilling six months.

It wasn't like she had tons of friends to keep her busy, anyway.

Living in the rural countryside was pretty, with plenty of hills and fields of wildflowers, but it made it difficult to sustain any long term friendships with the kids at school. Even when she'd come out of her shell and spoken with them, the other children didn't seem to care for her very much. There was even a time when some bullies got in her face. Well, technically most had to look *up* into her face. She was consistently taller than most girls her age. She didn't back down from their threats but fear gripped at her heart. She never quite got over what that felt like. It angered her that anyone could make her or any other person for that matter, feel so small and meaningless with only the use of words. The tongue truly is a powerful weapon. Of course, she received a good punch to the face for calling the bully a 'poor excuse for a lizard,' but it had been worth it in the end. The girl had dandruff the size of a nickel and reptile-like peeling skin from sunburn. A lizard seemed fitting at the time.

Sorrah didn't know why she blended into the backdrop so well at times, and other times caught the attention of those more popular. It wasn't that she was particularly unpleasant or hideously grotesque. She was simple and plain. Tall and slender, especially in the early years. Her eyes were a bit too large for her face, her nose small, but normal enough and her teeth were white and straight. What more did kids want? She brushed her dark blonde hair that she left long and tied into a ponytail, and bathed regularly, but she was more interested in books and being whisked away by thrilling adventures they catapulted her into, than caring very much about what new dress she wore or what boy was the cutest. She wanted to bake, and thanks to a neighbor friend, climb trees and ride horses. Many days, when she had no one to talk to, she could be found sitting under a shade tree, reading fairytales and sci-fi fantasies. It was far more exciting than her own life and helped her stay out of Kaye's way.

Part of her was excited at the thought of a secret hideaway in the attic. The other part of her was thoroughly disgusted by the musty smell, the grime she felt under her fingertips and whatever hairy creature had just crawled over her foot. Gah.

She skimmed over a piece of metal, wire perhaps, then

backtracked and felt a hook. She placed her finger inside the loop and pulled hard. Sure enough, the panel to the wall popped out and with it, a load of dust shot out at her. Nice.

She sighed, brushed herself off and pushed the panel wider, squeezing through the small opening and making her way inside the secret space.

"Holy crap," she said, seeing piles of books, old clothing, and a tall coat rack with scarves and hats all over it. She moved things aside and noticed a brown trunk. Her heart skipped a beat. "Mother's trunk."

It was small as trunks go, and didn't look as old as some of the other things in the room, of which she guessed must have belonged to her mother's mom or grandmother.

Sorrah wondered if Kaye had been truthful about the things she said about her mother. If she'd lied about having money and these personal things, what else had she lied about?

The story of the mirror and a magical land inside of it, was far too fairytale-like, for her to believe, but there was that small imaginative voice within her that begged for it to be real.

How fantastic would it be if the bizarre and magical worlds we read about were real?

She lifted the top of the trunk and the hinges squeaked in protest. Inside, was a short stack of letters tied with twine, a broken black cord with an odd silver pendant on the end, and a small brown book. She hoped the book was the journal Kaye had spoken of, and sure enough it was.

She located a tipped over antique chair, straightened it upright, and tried to make herself comfortable. Old wood chairs apparently weren't made for comfort. Was everyone in history extremely narrow and thin? Not to mention very erect when they sat. Not Sorrah.

She wasn't considered fat, but then again, most females were told they were obese these days, and doctors everywhere referred to the evil charts they had in their offices. Conveniently enough.

Sorrah fit no molds in personality or in figure. She was a book fiend, fairly intelligent, and despite her thinner years of girlhood, had grown curves she wasn't so ashamed of. She liked to walk, had gotten used to it living in the country, so she was basically fit, active, but her hips were stubbornly wide, her breasts large, and she was more than a little fine with not fitting into the ideals society demanded.

The letters proved to be nothing, mostly correspondence inquires for nursing school and such. The journal was interesting. Most of the entries were about her time as a teenager being raised by her grandmother, Sorrah's great grandmother. She knew from what Kaye had told her, her mother, Alaina, lost her own mother to cancer at a very early age and that was what prompted her to become a nurse. The women in the family seemed to be cursed with early deaths or short lives, depending on how you looked at it.

She skimmed over her mother's words, feeling a strange sense of closeness to her. She wrote about life in the country, her summer rides on her beloved horse. Later entries when she was an older teenager were about neighbor boys and her first experiences with intimacy. Sorrah found the words oddly comforting, her own awkwardness, when it came to such things, was pretty much the same.

Sorrah lost her virginity during her first semester in college to a boy, which she will now and forever refer to as *Jerk*, because of the way he behaved afterward. She'd never seen anyone leave a room faster. Jerk had shown her a lot of attention, told her how pretty she was and how much he liked her. For weeks after he bolted out of her room and consequently her life, she believed she'd done something wrong, or wasn't very good at sex and had disappointed him. Later, after about two gallons of premium vanilla bean ice cream, and a trough of hot fudge, she brushed it off as his loss.

She hoped sex would be different with someone you really loved. She had honestly liked him, thought him attractive, but she hadn't been in love with *Jerk* and *Jerk* hadn't been in love with her either. He might not have even liked her all that much. And that part hurt. The deception of it all in order to get what he wanted.

She tried not to be too hard on herself. She did many things fairly well, but had issues with completion. What she really excelled at was Tae Kwon Do. There she rocked the world with her masterful moves. Well, she felt like she rocked the world, especially when she wore the outfit, until the day she was asked to show the rest of the class what she'd learned and ended up falling awkwardly, spraining her ankle and bruising a few toes. Who bruised toes?

She was a bit clumsy, but that damn Master Choo had it in for her.

Needless to say, she quit, gave up, but for six glorious weeks of semi-excellence, she had rocked-it-out.

Ever since the bullies circled her in grade school, she had wanted to learn to fight well, but it was yet another time in her life where she had started something and never finished.

She continued to peruse the entries of the journal, believing she was acquiring a small understanding of what her mother was like. Unlike her, her mother had set goals, worked hard and accomplished what she'd set out to do. She was adventurous and interesting. Sorrah admired those qualities and desired to be more like her mother.

She'd never be very interesting, in her own eyes, but suddenly, she had the strongest desire to be. She wanted to be the kind of person who finished what they started, took risks, and sought out new and exciting adventures. A person who endeavored to live the kind of life only read about in books.

Chapter three

Sorrah brought the journal downstairs to the library. It was her favorite place in the house to read. It was nearly midnight, but she couldn't stop. She observed her mother's handwriting, the way her impeccably executed cursive letters swirled up and around so beautifully. After a while her words became as her own, the letters fading into the background of the thrilling and interesting things she was learning about the mother she never knew. A glimpse was better than nothing.

She was over midway into the journal when she read this entry:

Today, I turn the ripe age of twenty six. Grandma, bless her heart, didn't remember it was my birthday, but that's okay. I tried to make a cake for myself, but I'm not very good at baking.

The rounds today with Doctor Sherman were horribly long and my feet ache. Still, I believe I was destined to become a nurse.

After getting Grandma some tea, she started talking about her death again. I hate that. She's been the only mother I've ever known. She's such a sweet woman. She wants me to look at things of her mother's to see what I want before she begins to donate. I want to please her and she's insisting her death is near so I'll go searching in the attic and in the loft of the barn, the two places Grandma always stored the things she no longer used. I remember when she had all of those things in the attic of the house. I never wanted to go up there; it was too dusty and creepy. She had some of the barn hands move some stuff to the loft. For a couple of days, old furniture and boxes were stacked in the center of the barn. Grandma had a trunk of old clothes among the things and I played dress-up for hours.

Second entry, same page:

I find myself again in my hideaway behind the barn. This place will always be my private oasis. It's where I do my best thinking and where I can read while listening to the sounds of nature. It calls to me.

I think everyone should have their own secret place to escape to.

Very relaxing. I think I'll close my eyes and get some rest.

Third entry:

I'm now in the loft and what a mess! I've found some interesting things, including an antique mirror I vaguely remember Grandma having in the attic. It's beautifully framed with amazing detail in the wood and the glass is in perfect condition. That's odd...

The entry ended abruptly. Sorrah flipped through the journal frantically but found no more writing, only blank pages.

"No," she muttered in disappointment. She tipped the book upside down and let the pages flutter open. Nothing was there. Wasn't there always an old flower or scrap of paper stuck in between the pages?

She was suddenly a bit more interested in giving the items in the attic a thorough going over. She headed back upstairs and started with the trunk. After touching every nook and cranny she found no secret spots or anything hidden. Lastly, she considered the pile of clothing. Most looked too old and vintage to be her mothers, until she reached near the bottom of the pile. There she saw the most beautiful light bluish-violet dress.

Contemporary in style, it was more like an elegant gown then an everyday dress, only it didn't look like anything she had ever seen. It shimmered and sparkled as if catching rays of the sun that weren't there.

She lifted the dress up to herself. It was long, cut low in front and back with the tiniest of crystals along the edges. The unique color and pearled effects of the material really made this gown breathtakingly gorgeous.

She smiled. "I think this would actually fit me." It was pleasing to know she and her mother were built the same way.

She lightly shook the dress out to see its fullness, and a small piece of paper slipped out from somewhere and drifted to the floor.

She picked it up and read the words written in her mother's handwriting: *Bethesda prison. Marcus.*

Marcus? Was that the name of her brother? Kaye said her brother had been taken off to a prison. God, was she really believing all of this?

"I think I am," she said. She smiled nervously. Like many of the mystery books she read, there were clues to be found here and she was determined to solve this mystery.

She had a lot of questions. Was there really a place called Sorrah? Could she really have a brother? Was there really something to this mirror business?

Sorrah spent hours looking through every inch of the secret room and beyond. The most she found was a small box of pictures. As she searched through them she saw pictures presumably of her mother as a young girl.

One picture in particular was of a young blonde-hair girl standing next to an older woman. Sorrah assume they were of her mother and mother's grandmother.

How sad was it that her and her mother shared the commonality of not being raised by their own mothers?

She went to place the pictures back into the empty box and noticed the corner of another picture poking out from a flap on the bottom.

"A straggler, huh?"

Had she not tossed things around during her search, the corner may not have stuck out.

She pulled the picture out from the confines of the box and she gasped as she gazed at the image of her mother dressed in extra-large clothing like she was playing dress-up. She stood inside of what looked like a barn. Around her were all sorts of old furniture and boxes of all sizes. But immediately her eyes went to the corner of the picture. The corner which showed a small portion of a wood-framed floor mirror.

Sorrah's heart was near to bursting. Could this be the mirror everyone had searched for? The mirror her mother supposedly entered through into a different land, an alternate universe? Her head was spinning from the thrilling thought of it.

"Well, Alice, I think we know what the rabbit hole looks like."

She laid everything out on a table in the library. The dress, the strange broken necklace, the journal, the picture, and the slip of paper. Like many investigative television shows, she wanted to make sure she wasn't missing something. Some things didn't make sense. Like why her mother hadn't wrote a letter directly to her. She knew she was dying, why not just explain everything in a letter and have Kaye give it to her? Unless... Unless she didn't fully trust Kaye. Had she seen the jealousy in Kaye's eyes and thought twice about writing a letter spelling out every detail? It was possible.

There was a good chance that picture had remained stuck inside the flap of that box for a very long time. Her mother probably hadn't even remembered it had been taken or that the mirror was in the picture, and as luck or fate would have it, Kaye had never seen it either, which made her believe fate was at work here and now.

"My mother was smart," Sorrah murmured. She wasn't a woman to quit things or give up. No, a woman like her would see things through, and darn it, if her mother was like that, she could be too.

As if someone whispered the idea in her mind, she thought about the journal and a specific entry, repeating it out loud to herself. "I find myself again in my hideaway behind the barn. This place will always be my private oasis... I think everyone should have their own secret place to escape to." Was it possible that her mother left clues in the very words she had penned in the journal?

The barn behind the house her mother had lived in had been burned up. She'd driven past it a few times; no one had ever rebuilt the property. She worried her bottom lip, grabbed her keys and a flashlight, and headed over there. If there was some secret place behind what once was in the barn at her great grandmother's house, she'd find it and hopefully find more clues.

*****

"One o'clock in the morning and I'm traipsing through a field," she said to herself. She knew there was no way she would be able to sleep. She had to find this secret place her mother spoke of. Kaye had said she didn't even read the entire journal. Chances were even if she had read it all, she wouldn't have picked up on this and certainly wouldn't have believed her mother would return to her burnt down home and leave any kind of clue.

Being an only child and living in the country you tended to learn your playground, and learn to make the simplest of things into something creative to play with.

With her flashlight out in front of her, she made her way beyond the broken wood remains of what was once her great grandmother's barn. The trees were quite large, mature, the branches long.

Sorrah used to love to climb trees and often times used broken branches she'd found on the ground to make forts. Could her mother have done the same thing?

She continued to walk and found numerous piles of branches. As soon as she decided to call it a night or morning as the case may be, she saw a very large tree with its trunk hollowed out. It appeared too small to fit anyone, but she walked closer and saw something more behind it, covered up by additional branches.

It was a makeshift room. The ceiling had been caved in by some thicker branches but it was there nonetheless.

Had anyone perused the woods behind the barn, they might not have noticed this at first glance. It could've been easily missed.

She lifted the branches blocking the doorway and saw two steps. "It's partly in the ground," she muttered.

She took a step down but heard something which sounded like branches snapping behind her. Instantly, she stilled. The thought of a burly backwoods man in overalls grabbing her from behind and taking her to some rundown farm where she'd be strung up and filleted like a fish nearly had her paralyzed in place. What was that Tae Kwon Do training she had? She really had to stop watching horror movies. Jim-bob farmer turned out to be a small animal probably wandering over to see who she was.

"Way to freak yourself out, Sorrah," she whispered.

She stepped inside, trying hard not to notice the spiders and their colossal webs. She'd been raised in the country, she was used to seeing mice and all kinds of insects but she still didn't want them burrowing and festering in her hair and making a home. Because that's-what-they-do.

There was a piece of a quilt on a handmade chair, an old lantern, and an empty wooden box. She couldn't help from feeling disappointed. As she turned to leave, placing her foot on the step, it creaked. It was more than an average, loose board sound. It was hollow.

She tapped on the board and moved it, revealing a large gap. Putting light on the area, she reached her hand inside, blowing out short breaths to stop from screaming when webs and tendrils covered her hand. She grabbed something that felt like leather and pulled it out. It was an envelope size leather billfold of some kind, tied with a cord.

She stepped outside and opened it. Inside were a folded paper, a silver ring, and three gold pieces with a symbol of an unusual star on them.

"Whoa. If these are real, they might be worth a fortune."

She unfolded the paper and saw that it was a letter addressed to her, and in her mother's handwriting. Her heart raced as she read.

My dearest Sorrah,

I am counting on you being an intelligent, curious girl. If I'm right, you have found this letter. There are some things I cannot tell you, for fear this letter could get in the wrong hands and your life be placed in jeopardy.

My life in jeopardy? she thought before continuing.

There are those who may be in our world who know just how valuable you are. I'm not sure of this, but I must warn you to please be careful. You are far more important than you know, not just to me but to the Sorrien and even some Borakien people. Find the mirror. Step through it but do not make the same mistake I have, know that once you step through, there is no going back.

I thought to make a sketch of the mirror, but again, it was too risky. We have a long history of druids in our family, Sorrah. They were considered witches a long time ago, and many were killed because of it. The mirror is special, created with great detail, including symbols of our heritage and enchanted elements of our people.

Kaye insisted I tell her everything but honestly, I purposely kept things from her. She was more than curious, and for your sake, I limited what I said to her. I didn't want her to use you.

"I was right," Sorrah muttered.

The mirror, I believe is indestructible. It survived the fire. I came back through it and when I turned back, it was gone. It literally vanished into thin air. I don't think it would've given me another chance to go through, to return to my true homeland. I cry even now. Had I not gotten ill, I would've taken you back there with me.

Sorrah is a place more beautiful than anything you could ever imagine. That's why I named you after it. You are beautiful.

I searched as much as I could. Kaye helped for a while and I believe she will continue to search. I don't think I was ever supposed to return here to this world. It will be my biggest regret.

My health is failing, and I am dying. I'm so sorry, Sorrah, not to have been here for you, but know that I love you with all my heart, and have every faith that you will make it to Sorrah and will unite with your brother.

Sorrah began to cry, her mother's words tearing a hole in her heart. She blew out a harsh breath and continued to read.

Your father has died, the enemy, a wicked alliance of some Borakiens, have killed him and have taken Marcus, your brother, to a prison in a place called Bethesda. He is special. My blood mixed with your father's, and together, it made Marcus something incredible. Some of the future was told to me by someone who could see these things.

Sorrah, I believe you too possess the same power, or possibly stronger. This power, I believe, will be unlocked when you are in Sorrah.

Sorrah and Borak have been at odds for a long time over some prophecy they hold sacred. There are those who seek to unite the two lands and stop the bloodshed, your father was one of them.

Be careful who you trust when you go there. I trusted the wrong people, believing them to be friends. They told me to leave. I should have stayed. I know that now. I fought an enemy as I entered the pond to leave, the same pond I emerged up from when I stepped through the mirror.

I could not bear for anyone to harm you. They never knew about your existence. I didn't get the chance to tell your father that I was with child, but your brother knew. I can guarantee his loyalty and know that he has told the rebel Borakiens nothing of you.

Your father would have adored his little princess. You can save Marcus and the Sorrien people and the good Borakiens; unite them as they should be.

I love you with all my heart. Be safe. Be well. Be strong. You will find all you have ever dreamed of and more in Sorrah. You will find your heart there.

Chills ran up and down her spine. Her mother's haunting words reverberated in her mind and in her soul. Sorrah. Marcus. The Sorrien people. The Borakiens. It was so much to take in. But what a thrilling prospect. Something wild and reckless stirred in her blood.

"I've never finished anything in my life, but my mother believes in me," she whispered.

She took a closer look at the ring. "Gorgeous."

The ring was silver with a large, bright blue stone in the center and carvings in the silver around it in the shape of a swirl. She used her flashlight to look at the engraving on the inside.

"My love. My life. My heart."

As she made her way back to her car, her heart flooded with emotion. What did she have here in this world anyway? She had no friends. She had no family. School was a bust.

Yet, far away in a land called Sorrah was a brother locked away in prison. A brother who needed her to rescue him. Then there were people, the Sorriens and the Borakiens. Her mother believed the Sorrien people to be honorable, even fell in love with one of them. Her mother had faith in her, believed she was someone special and could help these people unite and end their indifferences. Could that be true? Did she have what it takes to give the people of two lands, hope?

Determination filled her. She'd find this mirror and step through it like her mother had before her. She'd find her brother. She'd trust no one. She'd begin a new adventure and this time, finish it.

Chapter four

Sorrah contacted Cinder's Attic, the antique shop in San Francisco and asked them to send a scanned picture of the mirror in an email. Kaye had made it a point to mention this shop and include a letter of correspondence in her will. Maybe that wasn't a coincidence.

At exactly one o'clock in the afternoon, the email arrived with a ping, alerting Sorrah.

She took a deep breath, opened the email, and clicked on the attached image. Her heart sped when she saw that the picture of the mirror was a perfect match to the one in the old picture she'd found.

The shop manager was asking twenty-five hundred dollars for the mirror. With hands that now slightly trembled, she picked up the phone and purchased it without hesitation.

The antique shop offered to ship the mirror, via a local freight company, but Sorrah didn't want to wait, couldn't wait. What if something happened to the mirror during shipping? If the mirror was indestructible then it wouldn't get damaged, but what if it somehow got lost during the travel?

She wouldn't take the chance of missing out on this opportunity. She packed a few suitcases, making sure she placed the journal, the ring, the gold and other now very valuable keepsakes of her mother's in her carry on and headed to California.

Instead of a hotel, she made arrangements over the internet to lease a condo on the beach. It was outrageously expensive, but what did it matter? She was very wealthy now, and with any luck and a little bit of magic, she'd be gone soon.

She entered Cinder's Attic, and was instantly taken with the quaint atmosphere of the small shop. In nearly every corner the glow of small oil lamps and decorative strands of lights softened the otherwise shadowy main room. Every nook and cranny had a piece of time so long forgotten. She had always admired those who treasured pieces of history, those who took gentle care of antiques whether large wooden pieces of furniture or small accessories used centuries ago.

"Hello there. Are you Miss Blackmor?" a tall elderly man asked as he made his way closer to her.

"Sorrah. Yes. And you are Mister Gentry?"

"Yep! That's me. Nice to meet you," he told her.

"You have a very nice shop. Thank you for placing my mirror aside for me."

"You're quite welcome. If you'll follow me, I made sure it was carefully placed in the back room."

Sorrah followed him. "So many fine things here. My Aunt Kaye would've loved to peruse every inch."

"This shop has been in the family since it opened in the eighteen hundreds. You are fortunate to have made your purchase so swiftly; I've had numerous inquiries on the mirror. Even one from a gentleman from Iowa. That is where you said you're from, yes?"

"Yes. Walnut, Iowa."

"Yes, that's it. The same town. What a coincidence."

"I agree."

She wasn't sure it was a coincidence. What if someone had found out about the mirror or like her mother said in the letter, found out who she is?

Who am I really? she thought.

After twenty six years she still hadn't figured out who she was or where she fit in life, but something told her she'd soon be finding out.

She was more than a little anxious to see the mirror, touch it and know of its supernatural forces. There was a small bit of doubt that tugged at the common sense part of her, but her spirit sprang to life at the thought of this actually being real. To believe in druids, witches, enchantments and now, an alternative universe or gateway into another world was thrilling, but to see such a portal right in front of you? Insanity. And what if she were to enter into another land altogether? That would be nothing short of a miracle. She was crazy enough to believe in miracles.

Fueled by countless books and movies, she had dreamt of such magic, and imagined many fantastical things since as far back as she could remember. Why not believe this could be real? Her mother did.

The old man, who favored his left leg, led her to the storage room in back. The second she laid eyes on the mirror, chills ran across her body and the hair on the back of her neck rose. She knew immediately that this was *the* mirror.

"When would you like it delivered?" the man asked.

"Now."

"Now?"

Sorrah turned to the man. "I am not letting this mirror, my mirror, out of my sight. I will pay you six hundred dollars to take me and the mirror to my condo only two miles from here. I believe that's a fair offer."

She was certain she'd shocked the man. He didn't suppress his delight, looking like he was near to wetting himself.

Money really did talk.

Twenty minutes later, she was sitting on a bench in the back of an enclosed truck, the mirror securely to her right. Mister Gentry had begun to argue with her in regards to where she sat, but she reminded the man of the price she paid, and suddenly he found a heavy bench and had it placed in the back to make her more comfortable.

Sorrah was careful not to touch the mirror. She instructed the delivery men to carefully place it in the living room in her condo. After they left, she stood in front of it staring.

"So, you are the infamous mirror," she muttered. "Alright then."

She spent the next few hours going over and over everything she would take with her, how she would dress, including what shoes to wear.

The next two days she walked the beach, ate fast food, and like most things that threatened to change her life, she put it off, each day telling herself she'd do it the next and so on.

Until the fifth night after receiving the mirror. She packed her things including the fancy dress, two others, one of which she'd sewn the ring and the gold into the hem. Having a secret stash might prove useful and the ring looked too valuable to openly display on one of her fingers.

Having been in medical school for a while, she thought about bringing a bottle of antibiotics, but decided not to.

"It's not like I'm traveling through time. I'm sure they have their own medicine."

She glanced at herself in the bathroom mirror. She left her hair down, wore no makeup other than a bit of waterproof mascara and clear lip gloss. She wore a pair of yoga pants, which she only ever used to lounge in, and a simple t-shirt. Her mother made reference to going through a pond, but Sorrah didn't care how wet she might get; there was no way she was entering a new fantastical land wearing a bathing suit. She placed all items into waterproof bags and shoved them into one single bag. Traveling light seemed the smart thing to do.

"Okay. Underclothes, dresses, check." She looked at the pearl comb of her mother's but in the end decided against taking it and the journal, placing the items on her coffee table. She fixed the cord of the necklace and placed it around her neck, slipping the silver pendant underneath her shirt. It was kind of gaudy and manly, but if it had been her mother's necklace, she'd wear it. Maybe it would help her in the new world. *New world. Alternative universe.* Nerves were hitting her straight on, but there was no avoiding them.

She glanced longingly at her couch. She could just read a book, watch a movie, and curl up. After all, it was late. Who traveled to a new world at ten o'clock at night, anyway?

"Come on, Sorrah. Grow yourself some guts."

She lifted her hand and skimmed over the frame. "So bizarre," she murmured.

The skin of her fingertips began to tingle; a soft hum came out from the mirror as if it liked her touch. She became mesmerized by the shapes and details engraved in the wood.

Ever so slowly she glided her fingers to the glassy part of the mirror. Her finger instantly went through it. Not through it, but inside it.

"This is really happening."

Her heart pounded. She held the strap of the duffle bag tightly to her shoulder, inhaled deeply, and walked inside the mirror, disappearing out of sight.

Chapter five

Rohen surveyed his men and did a quick count of the casualties and wounded. This last run-in with a small team of Borakien soldiers of the Kingswatch had been tough on them and they couldn't take many more losses. The rebellion had to gain in numbers if they hoped to overthrow the self-proclaimed king of Sorrah, which just so happened to be Rohen's delusional Borakien uncle, Meserek.

"Let us bury our dead and head back to Castlemore," he told his second in command, Sevin. "We live to fight another day."

In these dark times, one could ask for little more.

Sevin nodded and proceeded to delegate to the others.

Rohen stood atop a tree covered hill which overlooked the village of Kegel. They had obtained five more men for the rebellion cause and lost two in the fight with the Kingswatch.

Rohen was the steadfast leader of the rebellion, but days like this, when the hope and spirits of his men were low, he had a difficult time providing them with the confidence they needed to carry on in this fight. His own hope wavered, but he knew it was in the face of adversity where the true heart of a soldier shined. And they were well overdue for a bit of shining.

"Rohen... the Borakiens? The soldiers?" Sevin inquired.

"What of them?"

"Bury or post?"

Burying them was the honorable thing to do, even in war, but there were times when hanging a dead soldier on a post and displaying them openly, sent a vital message to the king; a message that the rebellion army of the resistance would never give up and were still very much alive.

"Post. But only one. Make sure his pendant is visible."

The soldiers of the Kingswatch all wore a specific Borakien symbol around their necks, telling others of their allegiance and of their authority.

Sorriens, who once ruled the land of Sorrah, were now an oppressed people, over-taxed and in servitude, but their resilient spirits would not be broken. For the most part they were a people of faith, believing the gods would one day fulfill the prophecies of old, which spoke of a new leader rising from a foreign land and being the one true ruler of both Sorrah and Borak. This man, they believed, would lead them out from under the rule of the dark king and return them to the favor of the gods. Meserek claimed to be the fulfillment of this prophecy, but he wasn't, and hadn't successfully convinced many others in either Sorrah or Borak.

Rohen and his team of rebel soldiers mounted their horses and set out for their temporary home in the small village of Castlemore. He didn't look forward to telling the women belonging to the dead, the news of their mate's demise. He had no woman of his own and wasn't interested in ever having one for more than a night at a time. His sole purpose was to fight for the cause, fight for the Sorriens and the Borakiens, fight for those like him, who knew what Meserek and his soldiers, were doing was wrong.

Once inside the forest they stopped near a stream. Their water sources between here and Castlemore were few and far between, many having dissipated during a great and mighty storm long ago. They thought to refill their flasks while near clean water and take a short break while they could.

Out of nowhere, a largely built man, holding a sword, jumped out from the trees and toward Rohen.

"Rohen!" Sevin yelled, seeing the man first.

Rohen unsheathed his sword and swung around toward the man, their blades clanked as they connected. Soon he was in the heat of a fight, but the man had a slim chance in defeating him. Or so he thought. The man was giving him a fight he hadn't come up against from a commoner in a very long time. It was exhilarating. This man had skill, skill that not many possessed.

Rohen tangled with the man for a while as he gauged his skill but had about enough and moved left then right, disarming the man. Many who tried to beat him failed.

Rohen was muscular and tall, swift and fierce, a highly proficient and ruthless user of the blade.

He held the tip of his sword at the man's neck and looked him straight in the eye. "Tell me your name now before you are no longer able," he demanded.

"What does a name matter? Either way, you will kill me, rebel. What's one more among the thousands you've slaughtered? You are a notorious killer and a legend among many."

Rohen edged forward, forcing the man back.

"Now it's up to thousands?"

Sevin chuckled from behind him. "Like I said..." he told Rohen casually.

Sevin had been at Rohen's side for many years and kept him up to date on the latest news coming from Sandrin, the place where the throne resided. The throne and Meserek.

"Yes, you did mention the numbers were growing," Rohen answered while keeping his eyes on the man before him. He addressed the man once more believing he was seeing something more in this man. "The wild stories continue to gather steam. You are right in saying that I have killed but only those who have butchered the innocent in the king's name. Only the Kingswatch would spread rumors that say otherwise. So, I ask you again, stranger, have you set out to kill me or perhaps you are out to collect the bounty on my head?"

Rohen knew there were Sorriens and Borakiens who farmed the land and stayed out of the way of the king. The best they could anyway. The Borakiens sojourned to this land in the hope of a better future when many of their own decided to become a separate nation and were obsessed with taking over their neighboring land, Sorrah.

He couldn't blame the innocent, the nonviolent and peacekeepers for that. Little did they know the new king would greatly tax them along with the Sorriens he overthrew and impoverished.

The man spit off to the side and raised his chin. "I am Demetri of Hamish. I am a Sorrien of high-breeding, the son of a diplomat, but as you can see, that means nothing in these days of Borakien rule. Things were different when King Zarek was overlord of all. But now, I have lost my land, my wealth, and would rather die than kill for or follow that filth who calls himself king. Meserek is *no* king of mine."

Rohen's lips curved up for a split second. "Those words are likely to get you killed should the king or Kingswatch hear them."

"Yes. My risk to take."

This skilled man is willing to risk his life. Interesting, Rohen thought. He considered the man's clothing a bit more now. They were not in rags but had seen their fair share of labor. His boots were tall, that of a rider and made of fine leather. He assumed they too must have seen better days which told Rohen much about the man.

"So it is coin you are after."

"I have two sisters, one is unwell. I send money by courier to her when I can, but crops have not flourished as they should and the moon has depleted much of our water sources. I am not set to kill you, rebel." A look of shame crossed over his face. "But I saw a post of your bounty in the village and thought to—"

Rohen lifted his hand and pulsed it outward in the air to stop the man from finishing. "I get the idea." He lowered his sword, reached into his pocket and took out a gold coin with a Borakien seal on it. "What is my bounty up to these days?"

"Fifty Varkins."

"Fifty? Here are five." He tossed the coins to the man. "Send them to your sister."

Demetri, with a look of shock on his face, caught the coins. "Why?" he asked. "Why would you do this? You are one of them, a Borakien."

Sevin came to stand in front of the man. "What does it matter if he was born in Borak or Sorrah? Did your lineage save you? Our lands were long ago undivided."

"But they have been separated for a long time."

"Yes. But could you not find honorable and dishonorable men in either land? Even if you searched beyond into all regions of the world, could you not determine both exist there? Rohen is Borakien, eh, but fights for both Sorrien and Borakien alike. All people deserve a leader worth fighting for. Meserek is not the rightful king. Rohen and others like him know it. Including me."

"You are Sorrien?"

"I was born and raised in Sorrah, as were my parents."

"Yet you follow a Borakien?" A curious look was on Demetri's face.

"Have you not been listening? I follow that which is right whether Borakien or Sorrien. Those who follow because they claim their allegiance to a symbol or misguided prophetic sect, have no mind of their own."

Demetri seemed to consider what had been said to him. He nodded as he looked off to the side. "The heart of Sorrah needs to return. The only way that can be accomplished is if the evil which has rooted itself in Sandrin, is destroyed."

Rohen picked up Demetri's sword and handed it to him. "Take your weapon."

"I am free to go?" Demetri asked, sheathing his sword. "Just like that?"

Rohen shrugged his shoulders. "You are free to go or you are free to stay and join us, fight alongside us. You are clearly not a sympathizer of the current regime. Your skills with the sword are fair, but with some training you can improve."

"Fair?! Are you a blind leader as well as an arrogant one? Your arm marks where my blade made contact. How many get that close?"

Rohen smirked. "Do you believe yourself incapable of improvement?"

Demetri withdrew two daggers and flipped them around and around before sheathing them in their cases at his hip. "Do you?"

Rohen laughed heartily. "Fine then. You have a choice to make. What say you, Sorrien?"

Demetri's fingers brushed over the shadow of hair around his mouth and chin. "I will get pay?"

"You will take a share of what we gather from the Kingswatch we fight. You will have food for your belly and a warm bed. In return you will train and fight with the rebellion under my command. You will do as instructed. I offer you nothing more."

Demetri observed Sevin and the other men. "I say I shall choose the rebellion. Sir."

Rohen nodded. "Welcome to the resistance."

The men who were on horseback raised their fists in the air and shouted.

Demetri retrieved his horse from inside the trees and joined the men.

Chapter six

Sorrah's first cohesive thought was of the chilling water surrounding her. She held her breath and moved in the water like she'd been taught many years ago in the pond at the back of her home in Iowa. Struggling to keep her wits about her, she pushed herself upward. At least she hoped the direction she was heading was up. What if her sense of direction was wrong? She'd heard of that. People's brain being thrown off kilter to the extent that they didn't know which way was up or down.

As she continued to rise, the water became increasingly warmer. The moment she broke free from what she believed was the same pond her mother had come through, she gasped for breath.

She'd made it. She was alive.

She inhaled deeply. The air was noticeably cleaner smelling, purer. With her face lowered, she opened her water-logged eyes, noting the rippling, rich blue water of the pond which came to just above her waist. *The water had seemed so deep.* She moved her feet, feeling the sandy bottom beneath her. How odd that the distance in the water, had seemed much longer.

She lifted her face and glanced at her surroundings. "Holy crap," she muttered, pushing her wet hair off her face. "This certainly isn't Iowa, Toto."

All around the pond and beyond was vivid, brilliant colors. "Somewhere over the rainbow or possibly deep inside of it."

Even the sun was a bright orange with bits of red and yellow shining around as if flames were coming off it. Yikes. "No, I think those *are* actual flames." Yet the sun didn't seem to be projecting extreme heat, in fact, there was a chill to the air.

In the far distance from the sun, faint shadows of stars filled the sky. Billions upon billions. She wondered how spectacular they must appear in the dark of night. Two of the stars, from what were visible, seemed much larger than all the others. *Planets? The moon?*

Some of the tallest mountains she had ever seen scaled the horizon. From where she stood they appeared to be the color of blue. Her eyes shifted all around, trying to grasp the surreal landscape.

The leaves on the nearby trees were the lightest shades of green, the flowers dazzling red, yellow, blue, and violet. The grass was a forest green but even that had a striking boldness to it.

She scanned the pond, seeing multi-colored rocks around the edge and the smallest neon creatures about. She imagined all of these luminescent colors, glowing in the dark. Things were oddly different here and strangely more beautiful than the world she had just left. Could she be on a different planet altogether? It wasn't out of the realm of possibilities. What was at this point? *Alternative world. Right.* She had swum herself into the most ethereal fantasy world.

Just as she made a move to get out of the water, a dark-haired woman dressed in what could be considered a long tunic and leggings, approached with a large flask in her hand. Her head was turned as she watched something to her right, but the very second she saw her standing in the pond, she screamed. A blood-curling, high-pitched, saw a monster scream.

"Borakien guard!" The woman yelled, pointing at her. "The Kingswatch is here!"

"Wait, what? Guard? Kingswatch? No!" Sorrah called out. She looked down at her chest where the woman kept pointing in short thrusts in the air. The gaudy pendant was out from under her shirt. *Guard?*

Sorrah covered the pendant with her hand. Why does this thing offend this woman so much? Other women ran toward the screaming woman as if coming to her rescue. They too joined in the yelling, along with a few young men. They all had similar reactions to her and for the briefest of seconds she considered dunking herself underwater and finding her way back to her world. After all, that was what she did. No follow through, only quitting when things became too difficult. Something within begged for her to see this through, to be brave.

Sorrah sucked in a deep breath and exhaled. How bad could this place be?

She looked at the unmitigated horror on the face of woman number one. This woman hated her; it was clearly evident on her face.

Her eyebrows were down forming a v-shaped crease in her skin, her eyes were narrowed, and dear God the woman was clenching her fists. She didn't know her, but for some odd reason, this woman thought her an enemy. Great, she was already being rejected by the new world. How is that even possible?

I've been here for literally like a minute. That must be a record or something.

Soon, many large men arrived on the scene. They seemed to be some kind of soldiers. Their faces were fierce and enraged, which only fueled her nervousness and fear.

Okay, so... funny story, she thought, rehearsing some kind of story on why she mysteriously appeared in the pond. Why hadn't she practiced this ahead of time? Probably because she knew she would have to lie. She was never really any good at lying. No one would believe she stepped through a mirror. She barely believed it.

"Get out of the water!" two of the men yelled. Their hands were firmly planted on the handles of their swords and daggers. They spoke back and forth to each other, but she couldn't quite make out what they were saying. She did hear the word light head or light hair, something to that effect. They at least spoke English, which would hopefully be a plus.

She took a quick glance around at the woman, children, and men. Most had dark hair, brown or black. There was only one out of nearly twenty five which had a lighter tone to their hair, but even that color was still a lighter shade of brown. Were these people not used to seeing blonde-haired people? And why make such a fuss about it?

Sorrah swallowed deeply, held her duffle bag tighter and made her way to the edge. Was she in hostile territory? Were these people Sorriens? Borakiens? Maybe both. Much could have changed since her mother had been there.

The men yanked her up from the edge of the pond so roughly, her duffle bag dropped.

She wiggled her arms free and quickly bent to pick up her bag, catching a glimpse of her reflection in the water. She stilled, not recognizing herself.

Even though her hair was wet, she could still see that it was no longer a dark blonde but a bright yellowy-blonde, nearly white. How odd. She knew it would be even lighter once it dried.

Pushing someone's hand off her arm, she leaned down a bit closer to the water, trying to get a better look at her eyes which had transformed, going from gray to brilliant blue with the palest of white around the irises. Maybe that was what caused these people to fear her. She shifted her eyes around her, noticing she didn't seem to look anything like these people. To say she stood out was an understatement.

In fact, she looked more like the colorful landscape. Her hair and eyes resembled the illuminating brightness of the trees and flowers and looked just as strange and just as oddly enchanting. Now there was a first. She had gone from plain to extraordinary.

"How did this happen?" she muttered.

The soldiers yanked her upright, tore her bag from her, and pulled on her arm. The one man squeezed her arm, causing her to wince.

"Hey, that's mine!" she yelled, reaching and grabbing her bag.

The same horrid man, who gripped her arm so tightly, hit her shoulder then her arm so hard it nearly knocked her off her feet.

"Ahh!" she cried out as pain shot through her. She'd surely have a bruise. When she made a move toward her bag again, her only link to her world, the man lifted his hand as if he were going to strike her face. Reflexively she raised her arms and hands out in front of her face to shield it.

"No! Please stop!"

What had she gotten herself into? These rather large soldiers could pulverize her in minutes.

"Stop, you fool!" One of the soldiers hollered at the man who had been ready to hit her. "You strike her again, and I won't care that you fight beside me. And don't think the commander won't have you banished or worse. You've been warned too many times already. Reel in your rage!"

The soldier lowered his hand but gave her a shove right in the place where he had hit her.

"Bastard!" she hollered, stumbling back.

The soldiers looked at each other as if she had just spoken a foreign language. To them, maybe she had.

She clutched her arm as tears welled up, but she held them at bay not wanting to show just how much he had hurt her. She had to remain strong if she were going to last in this world.

Images of what it might have been like for her mother when she entered into this strange and unusual place, came to mind. Her mother had come through the pond too. Had she been manhandled? Had she been thought the enemy? She hadn't mentioned any of that. Whatever the case, she had survived, even found love.

Suck it up, Sorrah, she told herself. *If mom could do it, so can you.*

With a group of people following, some even yelling ill words to her, the soldiers led her through some kind of fortress. On each side were stone one-story buildings in rows. A village. Farther out, as far as she could see, were large elaborate tents.

The pungent aromatic smell of food filled the air as they continued to walk and had her stomach growling.

At the end of the town was an enormous wall with iron gates. They passed through the gates onto a cobblestone walkway, which led to an impressive three-story, gray, white, and pale rose stone castle that looked like it had been plucked out from the pages of a medieval novel. Four towers of the castle were cone-shaped with iron grids at their peaks. The gigantic wooden doors in front were dark and iron trimmed.

She half expected the owner of this lavish abode to be named Arthur.

They entered and Sorrah's mouth nearly dropped open. The inside was even more majestic-looking than the outside. It was immaculate, with rustic, yet, fine furnishings in nearly every area. To the left was a long, winding wooden staircase with rails carved with meticulous detail. At the ends of the rail on each side were carved dragons.

To the right was an enormous sitting area which could have been the perfect backdrop for a photo in Medieval Living Magazine. If there were such a thing. The fireplace filled the center of the far wall and had a roaring fire burning inside its hearth.

She trembled. What she wouldn't give to feel the fire's warmth. Somehow, she didn't think her comfort was a priority for these men.

"Where are you taking me?!" she asked as they began shuffling her to a lower level.

The steps were made of cold stone and she could feel the cool air hit her wet body as they descended below.

Her nerves were on edge. This was all too frightening. *God, what will happen to me?*

They entered a dismal corridor and her heart sank.

"Am I to be imprisoned? What have I done?"

"Don't worry, beautiful. You'll be just fine."

The man, who had hollered at the other man, spoke as if his words would settle her. Highly unlikely. Not with the lustful way he had said them. And what was up with the beautiful comment? It was a foreign reference to her to be sure; she'd never been described as such.

On each side of the gray corridor, were rooms, some having their doors ajar, allowing her to catch a glimpse inside. There were beds, lanterns and even fireplaces in each of these rooms which apparently were bedchambers.

"Please! I'm only here to find Bethesda prison. Let me speak with whomever is in charge and we can clear this up!" she pleaded. "I only seek help."

The soldiers didn't answer her. They stopped at a room on the right side, unlocked it, and pretty much threw her inside. Well, they pushed and she kind of tripped on her own feet. Typical.

Without giving the room a quick look over, she abruptly swiveled on her feet, turning back to the open door. The soldiers were staring at the area of her chest. She glanced down to her shirt and noticed her hardened nipples. She felt her face flush. *Sheesh, I'm wet and it's cold outside. Give me a break. So much for the eighty dollar padded bra she had on.* She crossed her arms over her chest. "Please give me my bag. I have dry clothes in there."

One of the soldiers opened her duffle and pulled out one of the larger bags which had her two vintage dresses and underclothes in them. The other blue dress was separate. He examined the bag with odd curiosity.

"What is this covering?"

"Covering?"

He lifted the bag higher.

"Well, now... that's a *plastic* bag." Duh.

The man pulled one of her garments out of the plastic and tossed them to her and took her duffle bag with him as he left.

She heard the sound of clicking as someone locked the door from the outside.

She hit the door. "Bastards! That means idiot… losers… ass… people." *Ass people?* Whatever. She was never very good with quickly comebacks or coming up with curse words other than the occasional obscenity when she tripped or fell.

She turned around to see what kind of horrendous prison she had to endure. Were there chains hanging from the walls? Maybe whips in the corner for later interrogations? No. There was a modest bed with a quilt and a pillow on it, a small table with a lantern and a large pot on the floor by the narrow window. Okay so overall, it wasn't terrible, as far as prisons went.

"I hope they don't expect me to use that pot for a bathroom. Yuck."

The room was small but clean and in a strange way, it kind of reminded her of the dorm room in college, only sadly enough, this was bigger.

She quickly removed her wet clothes, wrung them out, shook them and hung them over a chair. Grabbing the dress the man had flung to her, which had the sewn-in gold pieces and the ring, she slipped it over her head. Using the corner of one of the blankets she began to dry her hair, noticing the bright blonde ends more clearly.

A few hours later, she heard voices outside her room. "Please!" she called out as she hit the door repeatedly.

The voices stopped and she heard a noise at the bottom of the door. Someone lifted up a hatch and slid a plate of food into her room. On the plate was some sort of meat, a chunk of bread, and an apple. She was grateful for the food but wanted desperately to speak with someone. Anyone.

After she devoured the food, she lay on the bed, pulled the blankets over her, and drifted off to sleep. Traveling through a mirror into a new world was quite exhausting.

Chapter seven

"A fairhead? Here?" Rohen asked the soldiers who had approached him immediately upon his return.

He handed off the reins of his horse to the stable boy, and started for the main gate at Castlemore. It had been a grueling past few days and he was exhausted. The only thing he wanted to think of was food, wind, the comforts of a warm fire, and his bed.

However, it seemed the soldiers had captured a stray, and not just any stray, but a rare fairhead.

The majority of people in Sorrah and Borak were dark-haired, some with a fair complexion; others had skin which varied from light to dark brown. Very few had hair the light tones of fairheads, the term used for yellow haired people. These fairheads were rarely seen in either Sorrah or Borak. It had been said that fairheads were blessed of the gods, who had kissed the heads of these people which explained the blonde hair and pale features, and also explained why fairheads were said to be of noble blood, as were former kings. Until Meserek. Meserek was from Borak and Borakiens as well as common Sorriens were notoriously dark-haired people. Meserek had only a lighter shade of brown which he tried to pass off as a fairhead but it wasn't.

"Where was this fairhead man when you found him?" Rohen asked as they walked.

"The fairhead is no man at all, but a woman. A very—" The soldier stopped when the other shot him a look.

"A *very* what?" Rohen asked with irritation to his voice. He needed a break.

"She is attractive. Beautiful even. Many soldiers speak of wanting her and Alexander has had to keep guard. Many insist she is a spy. She wears the emblem of a soldier, a Borakien Kingswatch."

"There are no females in the Kingswatch. No female Borakien guards at all or soldiers that I know of. I highly doubt Meserek has changed his mind in this regard."

51

He considered the possibility that these men were right about this female being a spy. Perhaps, Meserek planted her in their camp, but why send her in openly bearing a symbol of the Kingswatch? What kind of trickery was Meserek up to now?

"She has not been touched?" Rohen asked. He would never tolerate any soldier to remain in his army, who had lack of honor. Taking a woman by force was a crime punishable by banishment and flogging, even death if they had also lifted a sour hand to them.

"No. She has been placed in a lower room. Gerta has already sent food to her."

"Good. I need to wash and eat. Have her sent to my quarters in an hour. Her womanly beauty will have no effect on my interrogation. If she is a spy, I will find out, and she will be put to death just as all other spies Meserek has sent our way. No mercy."

The men nodded and took their leave, well knowing how efficient Rohen's interrogation skills were. He was the best and highly regarded among the rebellion. Over the last five years and a few deaths later, he had risen to the position of leader. Commander.

Rohen entered the main house at Castlemore, his temporary home, and the current home base of the resistance. Years prior, the massive stone structure had been the home of a Sorrien nobleman who lived there as a guard and overseer of one of the sacred caves known in existence.

Rohen and his army of the rebellion claim Castlemore as their landing place, for now, and have remained in this location longer than any other prior.

It was a dangerous thing to stay in one place, doing so made them vulnerable, but many feared the sacred cave and few would risk coming close. One of three sacred caves, the legends stated the feet of any who dared to walk inside would burn and the eyes of any, who looked upon the writing on the wall, would lose their sight. And those who lasted long enough to touch the drawings? Instant death. Many spoke of death, disease, and even maiming of those who thought to test the accuracy of the tales.

But Rohen wasn't very superstitious and didn't scare easily. He cared nothing about being close to the cave, but took advantage of the fact that many stayed away because of it.

Besides, the area had fields of grain nearby and contained a clean water supply for them, the pond. The clean water of the pond was used for drinking water, and the stream which ran from it, used as bathing water for body, clothing, and dishes.

Rohen himself didn't stay in Castlemore for more than a week or so at a time. He and a handful of select rebel soldiers, known to all as his elite, searched and recruited men for their army. They had plans to storm the castle in Sandrin and end the reign of terror his Uncle Meserek had placed upon Sorriens and Borakiens alike.

After feasting on food in the kitchen below, Rohen went upstairs to his chambers, which was the largest and most extravagant in the main house. They assumed his chambers had been that of the nobleman who had once resided there.

His bath had already been poured, a slow mist of heat rose from the water. The large basin, customized to his build, was in front of the fireplace which looked as if it had recently been lit.

The people of Castlemore treated him well. He had provided them with protection, coin, and let them farm the fertile land. These particular people of Sorrah ignored the warnings of the king and his men, and dismissed any reservations of living near the cave, in return for a better life, a life Rohen and his men provided for them.

He thoroughly washed his body in the basin and splashed water over his short beard, then bent back to relax in the warmth. The cold endured in traveling had a way of getting straight through to the bones; it was surely a luxury to soak in a warm tub. He tilted his head back along the edge of the basin and nearly drifted off to sleep. The sound of knocking at his door startled him out of his rest.

"Enter." The second the words left his mouth he remembered about the fairhead woman. Fortunately for him, it was the head housekeeper and cook, Gerta. She had a large towel in hand and splayed it open in front of him while she turned her face to allow him privacy.

"I knew you'd be ready by now. Some men are making a fuss over the fairhead, said they'd be bringin' her up to ya' in a few minutes."

"What do you mean a fuss?"

"They were fighting and carryin' on about who would be escorting *her ladyship* up here to ya'." Gerta always did have a way with words.

Her sarcasm was spoken bluntly. Rohen appreciated that about the woman.

"Well, having a fairhead is unusual. I'm sure the excitement will die down soon."

Gerta tipped her head a bit to the side. "You haven't seen this woman yourself, have ya' now?"

"No. But I'm guessing I will soon enough."

Gerta held back a smile and turned to the door.

He moved to his armoire and dressed as Gerta opened the door to allow some men to help with emptying the bath and moving the basin.

Soon they left and another knock came on the door.

"Enter!" he called out. Before making his way to the door, he poured himself a goblet of wine and left it on a wooden table used for strategic planning. He had rolled up some of the maps and purposely left the rolls on the table. A temptation of sorts. If this woman was a spy she'd be sure to have herself a look and he'd be sure to catch her. It wouldn't take him long to detect lies and deception in her. He was sure of it.

Chapter eight

"Let go of me!" Sorrah said as she tried yet again to yank her arm free from the soldier's clutch. That hadn't worked very well. What was with these guys anyway? Why did they find it necessary to have six soldiers escort her anywhere, it wasn't like she tried her Tae Kwon Do moves on them. Instantly, an image of her clumsy-self getting hurt at Master Choo's dojo drifted through her mind. Yeah, probably not a good idea to test her fierce skills on them. With her luck, she'd end up with another wounded body part.

The soldiers knocked hard on a large black door and answering from behind it, she heard the sound of what had to be a beast of a man. Probably a barbarian of some sort. His voice was deep and authoritative, bringing a shot of chills through her body. She couldn't help but picture a tall man with a gold tooth and extended brow bone, like a hit man.

She stiffened her resolve. Whoever was beyond the door, she'd courageously face him. She refused to be intimidated. After all, she only wanted to find out how to get to this Bethesda prison place. Was that asking too much?

She thought to find the prison, rescue her brother, and perhaps they could return to her world. It didn't seem like she fit in here anyway but then again, she never quite fit in back home either, which was both a bit sad and terrifying, depressing even. What if she didn't fit in anywhere? She had no family left other than a brother she'd never met—suddenly, she felt more alone than she ever had in her life. But loneliness was just another place to reckon with. She was due for a reckoning.

As one of the soldiers moved to open the door, she took a step back only to feel a hand on her arm. She winced. The man surely didn't know he had touched the exact area of where she had gotten wounded the day prior. She whirled around to face the soldiers, not wanting to be manhandled again but before she could voice her objection, she was gently pushed inside the room. Still, she gave her escorts her best reprimanding look and rubbed her arm. "Gee thanks, boys."

They actually had the nerve to smile at her which simply unnerved her.

She lifted her eyes to the vaulted ceiling, noticing exquisite artwork worthy of Michelangelo himself, painted directly above where she stood. A gorgeous black-haired male angel was strikingly depicted with spectacular detail. The angel's body was muscular, toned, his face stoically handsome, having bright blue eyes and statuesque features. His massive shining black and blue tipped wings were stretched out high and wide. He gripped a sword in his raised hand as if fighting off an enemy.

Mesmerized by the angel, she turned to follow the tip of the sword but looked instead at *mister brow-bone.* She nearly stumbled back. The man in front of her was nowhere close to what she had imagined, other than the tall part… and maybe the fearsome part. Holy crow.

He was by far the fiercest, most ruggedly handsome, yet, formidable man she had ever laid eyes on. She couldn't stop staring at him. He had dark brown hair which skimmed his shoulders, a short-haired beard around his lips and chin, and gorgeous greenish-blue eyes that reminded her of the sea.

She reflexively let out a soft sigh as she gazed into his eyes. She never wanted to be lost at sea until this very moment. She let her eyes slip lower. His lips were inviting, the bottom a bit larger than the top. His build was robust and she immediately detected a leadership quality about him. There was something dangerously wicked about the look of his face, and she half expected him to yell for his men to *batten down the hatches* or *swab the deck.* Which would've been perfectly acceptable phrases had they been on an actual ship. Her mind seemed to be mysteriously stuck at sea.

She considered him further and decided he could definitely pass for a pirate. *No,* she thought, correcting herself. More like a sea captain, a younger version of the captain from that old movie where the pretty woman rents an old sea captain's house only to find the place haunted by the sea captain himself.

She let out a heavy breath. Man, she loved that movie. Unfortunately, she never could remember the name of it, only the ghost and the hauntingly eerie old painting of the sea captain on the wall.

Reading adventure stories and watching movies really made the imagination soar, and hers was no exception.

"Ghost?" he asked. "Movie?"

Had she said that out loud? She meant to look away, but couldn't seem to pull herself from his gaze. Besides, he really didn't look like he understood what she'd said anyway. She was spellbound, intoxicated by his sea captain stare. Her mind had set sail on a vast sea. Where was a life jacket when you needed one?

After she had stumbled inside and turned, he'd been leaning back against a table with his arms crossed over his chest but now he was standing formidably... and... and staring, possibly ogling, but then, so was she.

God, I'm ogling. What's wrong with me? Great first impression.

His brows furrowed as he roamed her body with his eyes.

Her face flushed from the intensity of his scrutiny. She never really had a man, let alone one that looked like a sea god, looking at her the way he was right now. He looked intrigued, pleased, hungry. For her.

An image of a ferocious lion came to mind, a predator. Suddenly, she envisioned herself as a juicy steak, the lions prey and next meal.

Sadly, she was *very* all right by the idea of being devoured by this brawny man, even though she always saw herself more as a stalk of broccoli or leafy green of some sort.

"Leave us," he told the soldiers without taking his eyes off of her.

The men, who had lingered at the door, nodded.

"Oh," one of them said. "She arrived with this."

He tossed the captain her duffle bag before leaving the room, taking the other smiling men with him.

He opened the bag and withdrew part of the blue gown. His eyes went from the dress to her. "Yours?" He eyed her again from top to bottom. "Not exactly a dress of a commoner."

Commoner? Was that supposed to be an insult?

"It was my mothers."

He shoved the dress back into the bag and tossed it on a chair.

Sorrah shifted on her feet. She flattened out her dress and wondered why he continued to stare at her as though he could see right through her. She must look a mess. Her hair had dried but she didn't have a mirror to see herself. Was her hair sticking up in various places, giving her Alfalfa-bedhead? It was her typical waking-up look.

Well, no time like the present to ask about Bethesda. "I was won—"

"What is your name?" he asked sternly, cutting her off.

Was it necessary to be so rude? Sorrah cleared her throat and lifted her chin slightly into the air. "Sorrah."

"Your *name* is Sorrah?"

"Yes. That's right."

The man nodded but she could tell he didn't believe her. He came closer and began to circle her. "You are a fairhead."

"Excuse me? What's a *fairhead?*"

He stopped behind her and leaned closer. "You want to play the innocent?"

"I… I'm not *playing* anything."

"Your arm?"

She hadn't realized she had gone back to rubbing it. "It is sore from earlier today."

"Show me."

"Wh… what? Show you? Show you what?"

"Lift your sleeve and show me the hurt you are caressing. Unless you'd like me to do it."

The last part of his sentence had an unmistakable heat to it.

He waited at her side, staring… hovering. She had the distinct impression this man wasn't used to being disobeyed. My, but he was an irritating sea captain.

She sighed and pushed her sleeve up, revealing the area of her skin that was black and blue. "It's nothing really. I'm fine."

He lifted her arm, gently skimming his fingers over the bruise. Goosebumps formed on her skin. "Clearly it is not *fine*. Tell me how this happened."

For a split second, she thought to tell him how one of his soldiers had hit her, manhandled her and raised his hand to strike her face, but she couldn't do it. Not if in the future she might need help from the soldiers. No one liked a tattletale.

"I'm kind of clumsy. It's just what I do. I trip a lot and knock into things. I must have done this by accident. I really don't remember how exactly."

She watched his expression and how the muscles at the back of his jaw flexed. She didn't think he believed her explanation and for some reason that bothered her. Even if she was withholding the truth from him. Would he believe anything she had to say, even when she spoke the truth? She noticed the tautness of his face. Was he angry?

He released the gentle hold he had on her arm, walked to the door, and opened it.

"Gerta!" He stepped back from the door. Within a few seconds a hearty, fair skinned, red-haired woman came into the room. Her face was flushed and her apron dirty.

"Yes?"

"Prepare the Marseilles room. Make sure there are blankets and amenities, a warm bath, and a fire lit."

"Food?"

"She will be dining with me tonight."

"Very good, sir." The woman glanced at Sorrah before leaving.

Was all of that for her? Why was he being so nice to her?

"You may sit, Fairhead."

Sorrah took a seat at the table and without thinking about it, began tapping her fingers down on the wooden table while she glanced around the room. The warm colors of amber, gold, red, and cream really did blend well with the tapestry drapes and elegant medieval-looking furnishings. She knew she hadn't traveled to another place and time on Earth, but things in this alternate universe could be compared to pictures out of historical books from her world. Her aunt always had books on artifacts and such in the library of their home.

"Would you care for some wine?"

Well, that seemed friendly enough. Maybe this wasn't going to be so bad after all.

"Yes, thank you."

He brought her a goblet of wine, sat to her left, pivoting his chair so he was facing her. He was close. So very close. He crowded her space. Overpowered it.

She leaned away, giving him a fake, yet, polite closed-mouth smile before lifting her glass and taking a good swig of her wine and nearly choking. She coughed. "Whoa. This is very strong."

"Strong? How do you mean?"

She didn't want to be impolite, but what she wouldn't give for a diet cola right about now. "It's fine." Cough. "Can I ask—?"

"Why are you here?" he asked, his voice taking a sharper tone.

She raised her palm and scooted an inch away from him. Haven't these people heard how rude it was to get into someone's personal space?

"Wait. I would like to ask a question."

He leaned closer to her. "Let me be clear. This is how this is going to work. *I* ask the questions and you answer them honestly. If I feel at any time that you are lying to me, your time here becomes... less comfortable."

Oh, is that right? God, bullies really were everywhere. She leaned closer to him and mocked the intense look plastered on his steely face, not willing to cower under his attempt at intimidating her.

For a split second she saw what looked like a stifled grin and amusement cross his face which only made her mocking fierce-look, gather steam. She narrowed her eyes, her nostrils involuntarily flaring ever so slightly as she breathed in his alluring masculine scent. *Damn, he smells good. Was this his natural scent or did they have cologne in this place? Eau de sea captain toilette?*

Her mind was ever so prone to wander. *Okay, Sorrah, get a grip. Focus.*

"I can see that you want answers. Honest answers," she lowered her voice to a near whisper and turned her face a bit to the side before continuing, "but I'll let you in on a little secret... kindness goes a very long way with me." She'd be no pushover.

Her voice returned to normal as she straightened in her seat. "Demand what you will, but I will choose what I want to tell you... or not."

His eyes widened and he sucked in a small portion of his bottom lip as if trying to control his temper which she had no doubt was brutally savage. He didn't back off, only let out a short puff of air.

"Oh, I'm good with brats. I've broken dozens of them."

Did he mean what she thought he meant? "Why you arrogant—"

He stood and towered over her. Leaning down, he rested his hands on each side of her chair.

"Ask your question."

She tightened her lips, looked down momentarily then stood, freeing herself from the cage of his arms. She lifted her face to him.

"I just wanted to know your name."

He blinked a few times fast, seemingly thrown, shocked even, by the simplicity of her question. What did he think she was going to ask?

"I am Rohen. The leader of the rebellion forces here in Sorrah."

"Rohen," she repeated. He gave her that weird look again, as if she'd wounded him or irritated him somehow. "There. Now that wasn't too hard was it, Rohen? There's no reason why this can't be civilized."

His eyes drifted over the plains of her face. "The way you speak. The way you say my name."

"And what way is that?"

He lowered his brows. "You are a strange female."

"If I had a dime for every time I've heard that..."

"What's a *dime?*"

"May I have my things? They can't mean anything to you, and between you and your soldiers, it has been thoroughly ransacked. I can assure you, I have no weapons."

"No, weapons? You give yourself far too little credit, Fairhead," he said, raking his eyes over her once more.

Again, odd comment.

He grabbed her bag, looked inside it once more, this time pulling out a pair of her lace panties. She might love the outdoors and nature but she also had a bit of a fetish for pretty, lace things. Especially undergarments.

He gazed at the panties with an intrigued expression while he strung them out between his hands. It must have dawned on him what they were because his eyes lit up and shifted between the panties and her.

"Those are just my... my, well, they are my—" Why couldn't she say the word panty? Maybe her mouth didn't work right because he was staring at her as if imagining her wearing them.

She recalled how the soldiers kept smiling at her. *They must have seen them too.* She felt her face warm.

He quickly shoved them back in the bag before tossing it to her.

"Tell me why you are here."

She assumed he meant why she was here in Sorrah. The captain couldn't possibly know she had come from another world. Probably wasn't the best time to throw that little bit of information out to him. She could only image how that would go. Better to start slow and build.

Don't trust anyone, she thought, recalling her mother's words in the letter.

"I have come to find my brother and hopefully free him. He is in a prison in Bethesda."

"Bethesda?"

Sorrah didn't miss the look of disgust on his face.

"You are a long way from Bethesda, Fairhead."

"Oh. I hadn't realized."

She glanced around as she thought about that. She'd need a horse and possibly a guide to show her the way. How was she going to rescue her brother once she got to the prison? What if the captain refused to help her?

It finally sunk in that she might have to do this on her own without the help of anyone. But wasn't she used to that? She'd been nothing but alone her entire life. She'd survived alone in her world and figured she could make it here alone too, if she had to. It would be simple to make her way to the pond and return to her world. Her empty, shallow world where she had no family and where she rarely finished a thing. Not here. She had the opportunity for the new beginning she had wanted. She had to see this through. But first, she needed a plan.

Glancing at the far end of the table, she noticed rolls of paper. The end of one of them was slightly unrolled revealing what looked like a map of some kind, and a map sure would come in handy if she needed to find Bethesda. It was the start she needed. The beginning of a plan.

"Oh? Do you not know the lay of the land?" he asked with sarcasm to his voice. He eye-balled her suspiciously.

"No. I'm not from around here. I had hoped the prison was close."

Not thinking anything of it, she made her way around the table and began to unroll the paper. Before she knew it, her back was plastered against the wall and Rohen's body was pressing against her, pinning her in place.

"So, you think to spy on me and give Meserek information on where the rebellion troops are and will be next?"

If he meant to scare her, he was doing a pretty fair job. She regarded his face and relaxed a little. She wasn't sensing the harmful intent she had with the soldier who had hit her. Rohen's eyes were completely different, showing no malice in their depths only mistrust and... something she couldn't quite detect. Yet.

She tried to move, her hands twisting against his torso. She wasn't getting very far. She kicked the wall behind her out of frustration which only jerked the upper part of her body.

He let out a groan and pushed away from her only far enough to grab her wrists and position them against the wall over her head. There, he secured them with one massive hand.

"Go ahead and kick all you want. I have you now. Spy."

It was right then and there, when she changed her mind about him. Surely, no self-respecting sea captain would do this to a lady. He may not intend on really hurting her but there was an unsettling wildness in his eyes, undoubtedly coming from a wicked, restless spirit.

She scrunched her eyes, deciding right then that she had successfully figured out what she detected in him. This man may portray himself as a fierce sea captain on the outside, but inside... he was nothing short of a wolf. An overbearing, foreboding, alpha male wolf.

"You're hurting me!" She may have exaggerated that a bit.

He leaned in, coming within inches from her face. "You're lying. I can tell."

She swallowed deeply. "Whoever this Meserek person is, I do not know him." *If he's so good at knowing lies then maybe he could detect the truth as well.*

He put more distance between their faces.

She was tall enough to only need to lift her face a bit to look him in the eye, and that was exactly what she did. She looked him in the eye and boldly told the truth. She wasn't a liar. She might not freely tell him every detail of her intent, but she didn't trust him any more than he trusted her.

He held her gaze and there was an awkward, lingering silence between them. He slowly shook his head as if clearing it, then seemed

63

to regain his focus.

"Meserek is the self-proclaimed King of Sorrah and Borak but you already knew that didn't you?" His voice was harsh. He lifted his free hand to the top of her dress.

"Wha… what are you doing?"

Why did her voice sound so shaky? And why did he seem amused by her stammer?

He suddenly, and most likely deliberately, captured her gaze as he slowed the movement of his fingers, skimming her skin with his finger as he lifted the cord of her necklace up from her neck.

He lifted the pendant higher. "Do you see this? This is the medallion of the Kingswatch. The enemy of the rebellion."

What? How did her mother have a necklace of the enemy? It just didn't make sense.

"No. No, that can't be. I know nothing of the Kingswatch or the king. Please believe me."

"Know nothing of the king? You are his spy!"

"I am not!" she yelled.

He yanked the cord, breaking it free from her neck. He clenched the pendant tightly in his fist and shook it once in front of her eyes. "This tells me otherwise!"

"I found that among my mother's things. I had no idea what it was." Immediately the words her mother wrote played through her mind 'I fought one of them…' Could the necklace of been around the enemy's neck and her mother grasped it before she fled? It was a good possibility. Here she thought she was wearing a Sorrien necklace in an attempt to blend it. Terrific.

"Your mother was close to the Kingswatch and you know nothing of them? Then she must know Meserek, yes?"

This was all too confusing. Tears threatened to fall. "What? No. My mother is dead."

For a brief moment, she could see in his eyes that her words had affected him. But his face let on no emotion, remaining as steel.

"You tell me the blue gown was hers; a gown that unmistakably had to be owned by someone with great wealth. And now you tell me the pendant was hers…"

Sorrah knew how it looked and it wasn't good. She deliberately calmed her voice, softened it. "Listen, I'm not here as a spy. Why would I wear something plainly marking me as such? My mother is gone and I have no father. I've come to free my brother. He's the only family I have left. Please, Rohen. I need for you to believe me."

With his free hand he threw the pendant across the room. "Oh, you'd like me to believe you, wouldn't you? That's the plan, isn't it? He sent you here to entice me… to tempt me with your beauty and then betray me."

"No! Not at all!" *Wait, did he say beauty?* She quickly regained her thoughts. "I only seek your help. A horse. A guide. I only want to make it to my brother. Will you… Will you help me?" The desperate plea simply slipped from her mouth. Intuitively, she believed inside this sea-captain-wolf, although terrifying in his own right, was someone who had honor.

He swallowed, turned his head partway to the side, as he continued to observe her from sideways. His eyes roamed over her again, scorching her nerve endings with the exploration. His expression went from angry, to interest and if she wasn't mistaken, a bit desirous. The latter was far more unsettling. She felt the spark between them too.

He once again faced her straight on. "A female in distress, hmm? That's the way you're playing this?"

"No. I mean, I may be in distress at the moment, but trust me, being distressed is perfectly normal for me. Eventually, I figure things out though. I've had to do things alone all my life, so if you won't help me, then I'll be on my way. And I'm not *playing* anything."

When he spoke again, it was nearly a whisper. "What are you doing here? What is this?"

He still had a hold of her wrists but lifted them off the wall, then pushed them back on it. It seemed as if he was struggling with whether or not to believe her, but also… something more. He lowered his face toward her once more, his eyes shifting between her eyes and lips. His lips parted but he quickly retreated, moving his face away.

"What is *what?*" she asked, her voice sounding much softer than intended.

"You have cast some sort of spell on me."

Then the spell must have overtaken them both. The tension he had on her wrists lightened, but he continued to hold them in place, or was she leaving them up there on her own? She didn't think he knew it, but his thumbs were skimming over her skin. Oddly, it comforted her more than it should have.

A warm flush started from her head and gradually drifted downward. She wriggled a bit as the sensation stimulated her, and he swiftly reacted by pressing his body a bit more firmly against her. The evidence of his excitement lay firmly against her belly.

She had learned some things from her self-defense classes, how to be aware and gauge the actions of others. There were no warning signs alerting her of ill intent where he was concerned and he certainly wasn't causing her pain. She didn't feel trapped or helpless. In fact, thoughts of getting free from his hold were far from her mind. On the contrary, if it were possible to get closer to him, to possess more of this mysterious, handsome man, she wanted to and how.

This gorgeous man, this wolf, heated her, lit her up as if it were Christmas morning and she were the tree. Every inch of her burned for more.

A bit startled by her own reaction to him, she meant to lower her gaze completely but landed instead on his incredible mouth. His lips were parted and his breathing heavy. Why she imagined this stranger, from an even stranger land, kissing her, consuming her, was crazy.

That must be it, she thought. She must have slipped through the rabbit hole, aka the mirror; landing in a place of sheer insanity or worse… she was only dreaming. *Please don't let me be dreaming.*

She licked her lips. If this was a dream, that meant she could control it, that meant before she awoke, she'd make sure she kissed this wolf.

"Rohen…"

"Hmm?" he asked, watching her mouth.

"My wrists." *What?* She had no idea why she said those words when what she really meant to ask for was a kiss. *Wait, what?* Was she a complete loon? She didn't even know this wolf. Maybe he was the one with special powers. Her brain was too foggy around him.

He immediately released her and stepped back as if he'd been struck. He pushed his hand through his hair, lingering it behind his head.

"What… what are you doing here?"

"I really am here for my brother. That's all. I'm not a spy."

His eyes went from her head to her toes, returning up and pausing briefly at her breasts. "Go to your room. Whatever your intent I cannot allow you to leave. Not yet. For now, you need to leave my sight."

"But I need—"

He ground at his jaw and gave her a look of warning. "No. Do not speak to me of need. Not now. What you *need* is to leave this room."

He walked briskly to the door but didn't open it.

"I had Gerta prepare you a room on this floor where I can keep an eye on you. I will consider you a guest here for the time being. We will talk again soon after my head has cleared and I get some sleep." He turned to face her. "You will tell me all I need to know, only then will I decide if I am to help you or not. However, you will need to earn your keep while you are here."

He crossed his arms over his chest, and took a wider stance. All looks of desire and prior heat gone from his face.

"What can you do, Fairhead?"

Earn my keep. That sounded reasonable enough but she didn't plan on being there very long. She thought about the things she could do well, Ride horses, climb trees, which probably wasn't the handiest skill at this present time, read, and bake. She assumed he wouldn't allow her to tend to the horses fearing she'd slip out and reveal great and might spy secrets or something.

"I can bake."

"Fine, I'll let Gerta know you will be helping with dinner. Everyone has a purpose here."

"Fine," she said, straightening out her clothes once again, this time feeling for the gold pieces and the ring in the inseam, one of the few things she owned. She relaxed a little when she felt them. If she were going to make a getaway, she'd need a way to pay for things.

She had seen the stables, knew she could get a horse if she could make her way outside. There were many things to be thankful for in all situations, right now she was glad she knew how to ride a horse and bake.

He opened the door. A guard in the hallway stiffened his shoulders. "Sir."

"Take the fairhead to the Marseilles room."

She made her way to the door, but before leaving fully she turned on him.

"Oh, and Rohen?"

His back was to her. He clenched his hands when she spoke. He looked partway over his shoulder. "What is it?"

"My name isn't Fairhead, it is Sorrah."

For a brief second, amusement drifted over his face. "I'll see you at dinner... *Sorrah.*"

A smile tugged at her lips. She tipped her head to him and left the room.

Chapter nine

Rohen closed his eyes and exhaled as the door closed. "You are good, Meserek, I'll give you that. You're trying to knock me off my feet and it's certain she'd be the one to do it. If I let her."

The only explanation he could come up with regarding the fairhead's surprising presence was the evil king must have sent this beautiful female, this temptress, to cause a disturbance for him and his men. She was certainly disturbing in more ways than one. Disruptive, but also stubborn, strong-willed and strikingly gorgeous. It took everything in him not to run his fingers through her golden hair. And her eyes? He had the strongest desire to see her eyes grow hooded from passion and to be the one to make them so.

He wasn't the only one affected by her unique beauty; he saw the lust plainly on the faces of his men. *Six* soldiers to bring one woman to him? Right. His men apparently needed some down time. Time to be with females. *Because this one is off limits.* He knew the thought was too possessive and that only meant Meserek's plan had started to work.

He strolled around the room, finding himself skimming over the chair she had sat in before heading around the table to where the maps were. He picked up the roll of paper she had touched and threw it across the room

"She's a spy!" he yelled out, not caring if anyone heard him. It was the only reason why this fairhead enchantress was there. To stir him. To stir up trouble.

"She's trouble all right."

He had to hold back his desire, the immense want that flared inside him. He had pressed his body against her and when she wiggled, he had nearly covered her mouth with his. The craving in his soul for this woman was unlike anything he had ever known. And why was that? Had the gods decided to pay attention to his life? They never had before as far as he was concerned. So, why now?

He had certainly bedded more than his fair share of females. Many were either too eager to please, awkwardly trying too hard, or they would lie there stiffer than a board. The act had been satisfying for the females, he'd made sure of that and even though he enjoyed the relief himself, he ended up with a void afterwards. The females had wanted more affections, especially afterwards, but he wanted none of it. He'd been clear and upfront right from the start but still they seemed to expect more when it was over. They wanted more of him but he could not give what wasn't there.

Sorrah didn't strike him as a woman who fit any female molds, but as someone altogether unique, piquing his interest and more.

The bed chamber he had set up for her was two rooms down from his, only now he thought he should've placed her in the room next to him. The closer she was, the easier for him to keep his eye on her. He wanted her close.

His uncle knew the resistance was gaining ground with their numbers, and also knew he and the rebellion troops were the kingdom's strongest threat. No doubt his uncle had felt the effects of their work and had planted this mysterious woman in his camp.

Rohen rested on his bed, willing his heart to calm its rapid beat. Sorrah, if that was even her real name, had roused him in more ways than one. She caused his blood to heat and his mind to cloud. She was a vixen, a siren to be sure and had a good deal of brat in her as well. The combination was incredibly enticing. Perhaps, she was an enchantress with power to cast spells over him.

He recalled her bright blue eyes and how he hadn't seen deceit in their depths, but mistrust. She was a stranger and was being held in a rebel fortress; of course she didn't trust him. But what if she did? What if he turned this around? Instead of Meserek using this spy to gain secrets, what if he could gain her trust and obtain secrets regarding the king?

This plan might work. He had been intimate with enough females to know when they were aroused. He watched her carefully, how her lips parted, her breathing became shallow. She had found him attractive. She must have felt the air around them grow thick with tension, the sizzling heat between them. He could use their attraction against her.

Images of covering her mouth with his possessively, touching her soft skin, and running his fingers through her bright blonde hair filled his head.

In the few moments he had allowed his mind to wander, he'd become aroused once more.

"I have to control my want of her," he muttered as he adjusted himself, allowing his hand to remain on his erection for a few seconds more. *I can do this.*

Was he lying to himself? Did he really want to remain close to her for the right reasons? He had been completely absorbed in the rebellion and couldn't risk losing all they had gained.

It was possible that Meserek's only intent was to throw him off, cause him to make mistakes. The wretched king knew enough to know that when soldiers lose focus they become weak. If there was one thing Rohen hated, it was to show weakness of any kind... to anyone.

He'd been beaten down too much in his younger years. What remained of his Borakien family had taken one road and he another. Taking a nobler path when his own blood took a dark one, had been difficult but in the end made him stronger because of it.

Many times over the course of recruitment travels, he had been jumped by those who wanted him dead. The worst was his own cousin, his half-brother, Ian, son of Meserek. For a brief time, he believed they could be true brothers, but in the end, Ian chose to follow his father.

No... He trusted few. The strong didn't blindly follow the masses, they were the ones who stood against the majority in the name of what was right. Weak men were those like his cousin, those who dropped to their knees before unworthy kings, pledging loyalty.

That would never, could never be him. He'd remain strong and continue to build the resistance. The rebellion army fought many small battles over the years but a war was coming and soon they would rid Sorrah of the evil dark king or die trying.

Remembering the cause strengthened him. Sorrah made him weak. He couldn't allow himself to become what he abhorred. He'd place armor over his lust, over his heart, and contain his primal needs. He'd take up with females, nightly if need be, anything to rid his mind of this beautiful female named Sorrah. *Yes.*

Determination filled him. He was the leader, a soldier. He had killed many, fought for both Sorriens and Borakiens. Surely, he possessed what was needed to bring down one fairhead woman.

He released a short breath. "Sorrah."

Surely his enemies could've come up with a better, more believable name than that. He would not flatter Meserek by using the name he'd given her. She was Fairhead to him. She was a means to an end. She was wreckage.

Satisfied with his plan and renewed purpose, he drifted off to sleep.

Chapter ten

Sorrah scanned her new room, noting how warm and inviting it was. The stone fireplace in the right wall had a fire already started and there was a basin of water in front of it. A bath sounded heavenly but before rushing to undress and submerge herself, she made her way around the room. She raised her hand to one of the four thick posts of the massive bed and drifted her fingers over the intricate detail in the wood. She dropped her hand and skimmed over the pile of thick white quilts on the bed. So soft.

The far wall had three large windows extending from floor to ceiling. Enticed by the surreal look of the land, she made her way closer to the windows, and pulled open the heavy drapery to have another look.

It appeared to be early evening. The last remaining bits of sun continued to spread brightness on the numerous mountains and treed hills on the horizon. The odd yet pretty colors of yellow, red, and bright green of the environment, brightened with onslaught of sunshine.

High in the sky and to the left, as if waiting their turn, was not one moon but two, the largest lingering behind the smallest, seemingly in an attempt to make their glowing presence known.

In Sorrah's eyes, the moons were fighting for the sun's territory, illuminating their own areas of the sky where darkness slowly treaded behind, ready and willing to smother out the light. Soon, the moons would win, claiming their domain, casting shadows upon the land and beyond. Sorrah was curious to know all which resided below their radiance.

"How incredible," she murmured, observing the mountainous landscape of this wondrous placed called Sorrah. She smiled, envisioning her mother seeing the same sunset and grandiose view.

Flying out from behind the closest hill, a flock of at least fifty birds rose steadily into the air. They stilled, seeming to hover while facing her. Even from a distance and with the backdrop of the sunset, she could see the birds were the color of bright blue and quite substantial in size.

As if her thoughts had cued them to move, they flew in a circular pattern before forming a straight line and moving closer to the window.

Mesmerized by their unusual behavior and unique look, Sorrah didn't even consider backing away from the glass pane. She wasn't frightened by them at all but rather intrigued.

The closer they came, the clearer she could see how peculiar and exotic they were. Their blue feathers were extra thick, their eyes a shocking bright yellow. She'd never seen any kind of bird like this before, but then again she was no longer in her world. What other bizarre animals and strange anomalies would she encounter here?

The birds slowly brightened, illuminating right in front of her eyes. They circled again and returned outside her window.

"Well, hello there," she whispered.

She lifted her hand to the window pane, and immediately, the birds formed a perfectly synchronized circle, and then oddly shot into different directions before forming yet another shape.

"A star?" she whispered. "Am I imagining this?"

Did the birds really just show her symbols?

She shifted her eyes lower as she considered what she'd just been shown. Two soldiers, including the one who had hurt her, were peering up at the window. How long had they been there? Did they see what the birds did?

The birds suddenly let out a frightful screech and flew off toward the mountains.

Catching the eye of the burly soldier, she stepped back into the shadows, out of view. That soldier, above any others she had come in contact with, gave her the creeps. There were some people who emulated evil. He was one of them.

She pulled the heavy burgundy drapes shut and lit some oil lamps in the room. Turning, she grabbed her duffle bag and laid her things out on the bed. She was glad that they didn't keep these things from her.

Even though she never felt at home in Iowa, these meager belongings spoke of her mother and the place where they both had lived.

She glanced around the room again. "But Sorrah was your home too, Mother. And father's home." If her mother had chosen a life here, she must've grown to love this place. After all, she had fallen in love with a Sorrien man and made a life here.

She held the edge of the blue dress, allowing the silky material to slip off her fingers.

Like Rohen mentioned, the dress was extravagant. Her father must have had money in order to have provided her mother with such a dress. So far, she hadn't seen any women here in this place wearing such fine things.

She brushed her hand over her check. "You have to make this work, Sorrah."

Near her bed was a dark wooden vanity, complete with a large mirror. She hadn't seen herself since the glimpse in the pond and was more than a little eager to have a better look.

Rohen had studied her, and if she wasn't crazy, she thought she'd seen a look of desire on his face, in his eyes.

She moved the chair out from underneath the vanity table and sat down. She closed her eyes before she could see her reflection in the mirror.

"No time like the present. How bad could it be?"

She opened her eyes and instantly felt her mouth drop open. Seeing yourself in the reflection of a pond was one thing, seeing yourself clearly in a mirror was quite another. She hardly recognized herself. Her hair was bright blonde as she had thought, but it being dry now, looked far prettier than she imagined it would be.

"Fairhead indeed."

She touched the ends of her hair which lay near her chest. "Blonde. Blonde."

Her hair, now being closer to a yellowy-white tone, could no longer be described as dirty or sandy blonde. She leaned in, getting a closer look at her eyes. They were still her eyes, circular shaped and oversized, but the irises were brighter blue with a hue of violet almost matching the color of her mother's blue dress. Even her lashes appeared longer and darker.

"No need for mascara here."

She skimmed a fingertip across her lips which had a darker pink tone to them. Her pale skin, she noticed, had an almost opalescent appearance. It was so unreal, how much her appearance had changed.

So many women used multiple cosmetics to achieve this kind of look and now Sorrah had it naturally. Good thing. She'd never been over zealous regarding makeup.

Even though she had been plain and simple, she had always thought herself fairly attractive. She wasn't one to degrade herself because of her curvier figure or simplistic style. However, for the first time in her life, she believed herself to be truly beautiful and had to admit, it felt outstanding.

She tried to recall the women at the pond and in the village. They didn't seem to display the same coloring as she did. She thought of the woman Rohen called Gerta. She was red-haired, pale skinned, and didn't display any of the same brightness of color in her hair or her otherwise.

"Okay, so my look is probably not a Sorrien trait."

She didn't understand why her appearance would have altered so severely here in Sorrah, and wondered if the same thing had happened to her mother. Or, she thought, maybe she had transformed this way because her blood wasn't fully human of the Earth kind, but was a mixture of human and Sorrien.

Her mother's ancestors were known as druids. Witches. There was a good chance that druid blood had mixed with Sorrien and created, well, her.

She lifted her eyes to the mirror again. "Powers," she muttered.

Her mother spoke of powers here in Sorrah. She lifted her hands, turning them palm side up. If she had powers, they hadn't surfaced as of yet.

Glancing at the tub and the water which was most likely turning cold, she undressed and slipped inside the basin. She washed, dried herself and her hair in front of the fireplace, and put her vintage dress back on. If she was going to bake, she'd probably make a mess. Even though she baked well, that didn't mean she wasn't a sloppy, clumsy baker.

She dozed off to sleep and woke to the sound of someone at the door. Opening it with a yawn, she saw a young woman, wearing a dirty apron over her dress.

"Gerta has sent me to fetch you. It's time to start dinner and you'll be helping."

"All right," Sorrah said. She followed the young woman downstairs and to the kitchen.

Sorrah entered the impressively large kitchen and glanced around the room, witnessing at least ten women running around in an apparent frenzy.

"I'm hearin' you know how to bake?" Gerta asked, coming to stand in front of her.

The woman didn't appear to be overly thrilled to have her there. Apparently more people other than Rohen, had their doubts about her, which explained the look of mistrust Gerta and the other ladies in the room had on their faces. So be it.

"Mostly sweets."

"Whatcha meanin' by sweets?"

"Pies, cakes, muffins, tarts."

"We have meat, bread, and consous. We make cakes but not every meal."

"Consous?"

Gerta pointed to what looked like a green vegetable. Evidently, some things had different names here.

"I can make a dessert, if that's all right with you. I know plenty of recipes, many are my own. I can make an apple streusel caramel tart or something else. A streusel maybe."

Gerta once again gave her a confused look.

Sorrah thought it best to start with the basic ingredients. "Flour?"

She saw a large bowl with a white powdery substance, dipped her finger in and tasted it. Flour. "Flour," she said, pointing.

Gerta nodded and pointed to it. "Peufer."

"Poo-fur?" What a horrible name for flour. Although Gerta could be saying the same thing about the word, 'flour.' She might think it strange it had the same name as a flower. Come to think of it... that was kind of weird.

Gerta wore a stern look. "Eh, Peu-fer."

Like I said. "Peufer."

Okay, now they were getting somewhere. Sorrah lifted a red apple. "Aaapppllle," she said, sounding way too much like the teacher in the movie about Helen Keller.

Gerta placed her hands firmly on her hips. "Eh, I know what an apple is."

"Oh. Okay, good. What about sugar?"

Gerta seemed lost on that one.

"We are speaking the same language but not the same words," Sorrah told her.

"Come this way," Gerta replied as she walked toward the back of the room. The workers intuitively stepped out of her way. Simultaneously she opened two large wooden doors, revealing a walk-in pantry. It was a chef's dream pantry.

"You should find everythin' you'll be needin' in here."

Sorrah quickly located what looked like sugar stored in a clear glass jar, opened it and took a small taste. "Sugar."

"Grans," Gerta replied. "I think we be stayin' at this all day if we like. But we've got a dinner to make. Bake whatcha like," she said, leaving Sorrah to work on her own. It was probably best. They could've gone back and forth with words, both getting frustrated, but Gerta had better things to do, and Sorrah would rather just bake.

She made a mental note to herself. Words weren't the same, plants, trees, and flowers were, safe to say, different, a whole lot brighter. There was an anxiousness building inside her, a curiosity to see more, learn more about this land and its people. If she could fit in a little better with these women, perhaps, she could gain their trust and get a more thorough tour of the castle and surrounding area before she left. She was curious as to what else in this foreign place was different from her world. Could she stay here with Marcus and call this place her home? After all, it was her brother's home. He might not want to leave. How fair was it to suggest they leave and go to her world? But the king wouldn't act too kindly, she imagined, toward anyone breaking someone out of prison. She hadn't thought about that.

"First things first," she muttered.

Home. How odd to consider Sorrah that way. In the back of her mind, she believed one day it might not seem so odd, one day she might come to love this place as her mother had.

She'd have to consider that later. She was here now, had walked through a mirror and stepped inside a dream. Only, it was unlike any dream she'd ever remembered having. The fantasies in the books she read had somehow combined to make one unique world.

She cleaned off a spot at the end of one of the long tables and got to work making crusts for her tarts. She'd make a simple caramel sauce from brown sugar, if they had it, honey, and cream and hopefully find some pecans or almonds to add to the top. Many in her study group in college favored this particular recipe and it was simple enough, yet, required some skill.

From what Gerta told her, there'd be nearly twenty five mouths to feed at dinner, all soldiers and a few of their wives. Before she got started, Silva showed her the dining hall in the next room. Dinner guests had begun to arrive so they simply peeked around the corner. Silva pointed to each soldier in attendance and told her their names, including mister-man-handler himself, Foley. Sorrah repeated the names over and over in her mind with the hope that she'd remember them later, believing that knowing them might be useful in the future.

She was relieved to find that the cooking crew ate their dinner in the kitchen after the work was finished and the dinner had been served to the others. Rohen had mentioned that she'd be dining with him, but that all changed and it was more than fine by her. The last thing she wanted was to sit among the soldiers, including Rohen. He intimidated her, but also stirred up desires she'd long forgotten existed in her. He was a stranger, yet, oddly enough, she sensed a connection to him.

She put together six pie-size tarts with the help of Silva who was the only one besides Gerta who was half way decent to her.

An hour and a half later the kitchen had a coat of white *peufer* all around but smelled scrumptious. Many of the women, who had finished serving the main meal, hovered close to the huge ovens waiting for the dessert to be done.

"All done!" Sorrah beamed, opening the oven.

"They smell like a lot of grans are in them," Gerta commented.

"They are supposed to be sweet and smell sweet. It's dessert."

"I guess we'll soon find how well they be a tastin'. Rohen has requested for you to serve what you've baked. So get on with it and get them out there."

"What? Me? Why me? There are so many of you, someone else can do it."

"I do not question his requests and neither should you if you know what's good for ya'!"

"Well, you can tell him I refuse his request. Tell him that I've done what I was supposed to do."

Gerta shoved her hands on her hips. "Rohen will not be refused. Now get!"

The stern woman looked at her like she was crazy, and maybe she was, but the last thing she wanted to do was go out in that dining hall and serve those soldiers. But then again… she'd wanted some or at the very least two of the men to help her get to Bethesda. Dang. By the steel-cold look he often had on his face, she didn't believe Rohen would be one of them. He seemed bound and determined to prove she was a spy.

"Fine. I'll serve the dessert." She meticulously cut each tart into six pieces, giving the diners a hearty slice with enough left over for the hard-working staff.

She placed each slice on a plate then onto two separate carts, rolling out one while Silva rolled out the other.

The very second she entered the dining hall, the men and the other guests fell silent. The weight of their stares and soft chuckles of laughter unnerved her, which she naturally assumed was the intent. She was considered a spy under the watchful eye of the rebellion. Nevertheless, she held her head high and proceeded to help Silva serve each person a slice.

From the corner of her eye, she could see Rohen's observant stare. The others had started to speak to one another, ignoring her for the most part, but not Rohen. His attentive gaze caused her to tremble, not from fear but from what he awakened within her. She bet he would love to know he had that effect on her. Although a man like Rohen, was probably used to women reacting that way to his attention.

She noticed that none of them lifted their forks to take a bite of their tart. *What?* Did they think the *spy* poisoned them?

Clearly to make a point, she grabbed an extra plate and a fork, broke a piece of tart off, making sure she coated it with caramel before putting it in her mouth. It was delicious.

The diners mocked her action and soon smiles of delight were on their faces as they ate up the fine dessert.

"They love it," Silva said, leaning toward Sorrah.

"Of course they do."

Sorrah turned her cart and started back for the kitchen. She couldn't get out of there fast enough.

"Sorrah," Rohen called out in his commanding sea-captain manner.

She stiffened and slowly turned, her eyes meeting his.

"Sit with us."

Dread filled her. He had obviously given her an order. She looked around the table, the soldiers and others were all watching her, probably anticipating her reaction. If she denied Rohen, it would embarrass him and show her lack of respect for leadership. She wasn't an idiot.

"As you wish."

Silva didn't even make eye contact with her. She simply turned her cart and headed for the kitchen. *Traitor.*

Sorrah held her plate of unfinished dessert and went to an empty seat at the farthest end of the table, away from Rohen. Apparently, he didn't care for her choice.

"No. Not there. Here." He pointed to the chair next to him and waved at the soldier to his right. One by one the men stood and moved down one chair to make room for her. Of course.

She smiled wryly and somehow knew he was enjoying her discomfort far too much. Her apron was a mess and her dress had flour, Peufer, or whatever, all over it. She wiped her hands, one at a time, on the cleanest part of her apron and took a seat.

"What do you call this?" he asked, taking another bite of his tart.

"It's a caramel apple dream tart. My own recipe. They can be made with many different kinds of fruit."

"I see."

I doubt that.

"What did you say?" he asked quietly.

Did I seriously say that out loud? Good thing she muttered or he wouldn't have asked what she said.

"Hmm? Nothing."

Sorrah took another bite of her tart before he could ask her anything else and casually glanced across the table. The newest soldier,

Demetri, which many of the women in the kitchen were clucking on about his good looks, signaled to her that there was something on her cheek. Mortified, she lifted her hand to her face, nonchalantly wiping.

A huge grin came over Demetri's handsome face but he quickly looked away when Rohen cleared his throat.

What did his grin mean? Oh God, she'd made it worse didn't she?

She quickly downed another bite. If she could keep her head bowed maybe others wouldn't notice her. She was used to not being noticed. But she looked different now. Everything was different. Her stomach did flips at the thrilling idea of it all.

"You bake well," Rohen commented.

After a few seconds of silence, he said her name.

"Sorrah."

She knew what the tone meant. He wanted her to look at him. She obeyed, lifting her eyes. "Thank you," she replied.

She glanced at the men across from her then slowly drifted her eyes down the table. They were once again watching her, observing every move she made and listening to every word she spoke. Suddenly, she was once again Sorrah plain and tall, as she used to call herself, the awkward girl who stumbled into third grade late as usual. She was in the spotlight.

No way was she reverting back to grade school where she used to hide away and sink into her own personal oblivion. She wasn't going to let these people see her frazzled either. Things always got worse when she seemed affected.

She dismissed the notion to hide her face. Lifting her head high, she purposely cut off a huge bit of dessert and shoved it in her mouth. The most important thing here was that she had rocked the apple tart. Boo-yah.

Just as she swallowed, she caught another signal, this time from Rohen's second in command, Sevin, and on a different area of her face than where Demetri had showed her. This time it was the nose. She couldn't tell if these men were deliberately trying to be funny or were actually trying to help her.

However, Sevin didn't strike her as the humorous kind. Each time she had seen him, his face had been stern. He was attractive in a dark way, she decided, with his steel blue eyes and black hair, but unlike

Demetri, Sevin seemed more closed off, more like... Rohen, actually. The fact that he signaled to her at all, seemed out of character which meant she should probably pay attention.

Trying to be nonchalant, she quickly wiped at her nose and looked back to Sevin. The corners of his mouth twitched but his expression soon returned serious as his attention went elsewhere.

As far as she was concerned, Rohen by far out-shined all who sat at the table, in the area of good looks. In a sea-captain wolfy kind of way.

She hadn't really noticed the women seated at the table, but now she did. They were all brunettes, all very attractive, but with an air of haughtiness about them. Of course these types of women wouldn't gesture to her, letting her know she was a mess. Fine. Even though she tried to dismiss their stares and now, subtle giggles, she was slowly sinking down her chair as old insecurities threatened to surface.

With what had to be a forlorn look on her face, she turned to Rohen and leaned in as if wanting to tell him a secret.

He bent his shoulder and offered her his ear.

"Please," she whispered, breathing in his enticing scent. "Do not humiliate me any further. Let me go."

He turned to her and drifted his eyes across her face before penetrating her with his intense gaze. And there it was. The attraction, the chemistry, the possibility of ruin. Men like Rohen crushed women like her. They might take a curious taste but then they fled out the door and didn't look back.

His lips rose into the subtlest smile before his eyes slipped away from her and took a hardened glance at the others around the table. His jaw clenched again, and she swore there was anger in his eyes toward those who had caused her discomfort. But why should he care? He believed her a spy. He soon nodded, agreeing to let her leave but then whispered for her ears only, "It was not my intent to humiliate you."

She looked at him with all sincerity. "I do a fine enough job of that myself."

She cleared her throat and stood to leave. "If you'll excuse me." Foley, the soldier who had manhandled her earlier, rose abruptly from his seat. "I shall escort the spy back to her room," he told Rohen.

Good God, no! she thought, cringing. Rohen had to see the

horrified look on her face. He instantly shot Foley down.

"No. Gerta will see her back to her room. She still has duties to perform in the kitchen. Sit, Foley."

Foley's face reddened as he shot her the evilest glower. He certainly didn't seem to appreciate Rohen telling him no and probably didn't care very much for the relieved look on her face either. He didn't seem the kind of person who did well with authority.

Relief flooded her as she hurried back to the kitchen. She removed her apron and ate a small portion of dinner with Silva. Gerta and some of the other workers really didn't want anything to do with her, aka, the spy.

With Gerta behind her, she sluggishly climbed the stairs to her room. She was exhausted, feeling almost jetlagged. Acclimation to this new world, was apparently taking its toll.

Entering her room, she went to the mirror and shrieked. Her hair was a mess with small clumps of dough in it. Her face didn't fare much better. Peufer was smudged all over.

She chuckled. What else could she do? "I've been peuferized." Apparently, she wasn't the tidiest baker in this world either.

She cleaned up with the pot of water and cloth that were left for her and brushed her hair. On the bed lay a white cotton nightgown, and she was pleased someone had thought of leaving it for her. *Probably Silva.* While slipping the garment over her head, she slowly moved to the bed and climbed under the warmth of the covers. Soon after, she fell into a deep slumber. For what seemed like hours she dreamt about mountains, valleys, vivid color and a wickedly handsome rebel leader.

*****

Sorrah's first thought as she teetered restlessly between sleep and reality, was what an odd dream she was having. She was lost inside a cave, moving left and right through a maze of walls. Fear suddenly gripped her as her body became paralyzed.

She couldn't move as snakes slithered over her body, moving first on top of her clothes then slowly trying to make their way underneath to her skin. A frightening chill hit her, a warning of some kind, as if a fire alarm had gone off urging her to wake up. It was so intensely real.

Her breathing became erratic and tears threatened to fall.

No, she thought, gaining enough mobility to try and pull the quilts back over her. But the snakes wouldn't allow it. They were on her skin now, rubbing their scaly skin on her.

"Stop," she muttered.

"Shhh, now. I'll just be havin' me a bit taste," a burly voice said.

Sorrah's eyes flew open. "No!" she screamed before a large hand covered her mouth.

Wide eyed, she met Foley's eyes straight on.

Within seconds, his hands were all over, touching her skin and pulling her nightgown up higher.

She twisted and turned, but he pinned her with his heavy body. The stench of beer mixed with body odor assailed her.

She had to think fast. *Tae Kwon Do.* Even though she'd quit, the few weeks had been about self-defense. She relaxed her body and faked a softer look with her eyes. She even forced herself to wiggle her hips. The change seemed to work.

Foley lifted his hand off her mouth and quickly replaced it with his finger, shoving it inside.

"That's the way, dearie." He ground himself on her. "You like that, don't cha'?"

She shifted her face away. "Help! Help!" she screamed before shoving her knee to his groin as hard as she could.

She remembered the instructor telling her that you don't have to be a black belt to get out of situations; you have to be smart and try not to panic. You have to do anything you can to free yourself. In this case, she did enough to gain some space and give herself the freedom to scream.

His body no longer had the tight hold over her. She pushed and fought her way off the bed and with a hard thump, landed on the floor.

"Someone! Please help me!" she hollered, putting as much distance as she could between herself and Foley. Her training, albeit small, kicked in. She searched the immediate area for anything she could use for a weapon against her attacker.

He was right on her heels.

"You'll pay for that!" He grabbed her leg and pulled her along the floor toward him. He slapped her, jolting her head to the side.

The door burst open.

"Unhand her!" Rohen thundered. He had the tip of his blade to

Foley's neck within seconds. He was undoubtedly seething from anger and only but glanced Sorrah's way. "I swear it; I'll spear your heart without a second thought. Get up!"

Foley rose from the ground, releasing her. "You really gonna do this over a fairhead frolic?"

"No. *You* are. You're through here. Done."

Sevin and Demetri, half-dressed came charging inside the room with their weapons drawn.

Sorrah crawled to the wall and curled up in a ball, still in shock over what happened. She clenched her eyes shut, silently thanking the heavens she hadn't been raped.

Tears slid down her cheeks.

"Get him out of here! Take him below and lock him up!" Rohen yelled to Sevin. He looked at Foley. "You will be punished at first light. You're done."

"You're gonna regret this," Foley chided.

"All I regret is ever taking you on here with us in the first place."

"You bring shame to the Borakien people, Rohen. They will never follow you!"

Rohen shoved him against the wall and this time held a black-handled dagger to Foley's throat. "You have no honor. You have no code. You are henceforth banished from the rebellion and from Sorrah. You will be escorted to the borders of Borak in the morning but not before a public flogging." He leaned closer to Foley's ear. "I should cut your throat out right here for even placing your disgusting hands on her."

"That's the real reason why you're so enraged. You're angry because you think she's yours! And what's yours no one else touches... isn't that right, commander?" He laughed mockingly.

Rohen tossed his dagger and punched the vile man in the face. "It's because you are a worthless piece of filth! Get him out of my sight."

Sevin and Demetri left with Foley still murmuring obscenities under his breath.

Rohen slammed the door shut behind them. His chest was still heaving when he turned and met Sorrah's gaze.

With apprehension, he made his way closer to her, kneeling down so he was eye level.

"Are you all right, Fairhead?"

Sorrah nodded and wiped her tears. With a shaky voice she answered, "Yes."

She tried to stand on her own but began to slip. Rohen was there to lift her up, and before she knew it, had her cradled in his arms. Immediately, she felt a warmth of safety encompass her. The tears continued to fall.

"To think of what…"

"Hush, Fairhead. You are safe now. You will have a guard, an honorable one, outside your door from this moment on. I'll be moving you to the room next to mine. There is a door on the inside that separates the two rooms. If you call out, I will hear."

He tenderly stroked her hair.

Her heart did a little flip, and she couldn't help but lean her face into his neck. She'd never felt so safe, so protected, so cared for.

He seemed to be taking his time reaching her bed and she was fine with his hesitance.

"Are you certain, you are not wounded anywhere? I could call for a healer." As he lowered her on the mattress, his intense gaze drifted over her.

Was he wondering if Foley had been successful? Did it make a difference to him? She couldn't leave it be, for whatever reason, it mattered to her that he know the truth.

"He… he didn't. I mean, *that* didn't happen. Thanks to you."

How would she ever be able to thank him? A full-fledged hero was inches away from her, and not just any knight in shining armor, but her knight, her hero.

The features of his face visibly softened. "I'm pleased."

As if it were the most natural thing to do, he brushed some stray hairs off her face. His fingers lingered on her cheek.

His own behavior must've been a shock even to himself, he nearly propelled off the bed. With his hands clutched behind him, he began to pace, his face tightening into what looked like a forceful frown.

"You will tell me the truth right now! I will not hear lies from you!"

The ghost of the sea captain was back in the house.

Chapter eleven

"Where did you come from? I need to know and you *will* tell me."

He really wants to do this, now? She sighed. *So much for the strong silent type.* Oh well, it wasn't like she was going to fall back asleep anyway. Not tonight. Maybe not ever.

"I'm from a world, a place, I'm sure you've never heard of." *From a galaxy, far, far... Whatever.*

"Try me." He stopped and crossed his arms over his chest.

She slid her legs over the side of her bed, stood and considered his determined look. "So, a minute ago I was fragile and now you are sure I'm strong enough to answer your demanding questions?"

He pushed his hand over his forehead and back through his hair. "Something like that. If I am to protect you or believe you in the least, I need to have some answers."

"And then you'll believe me?"

He shrugged his shoulders.

"Yeah, that's what I thought. You've already gotten it in your head that I'm some sort of spy. I'm not sure you'll trust anything I tell you."

He tightened his lips. "I guess that's what I need to find out. So, tell me your story and I'll decide to believe you or not."

Fine. If he wanted the truth, she'd give it to him. Brace yourself captain, you're about to set sail for fantasyland.

"My name is Sorrah. Sorrah Blackmor. I'm from Walnut, Iowa, that's a place far away from this place—" She didn't finish.

How absurd her words must sound to Rohen. They even sounded absurd to her.

"I'm from Iowa, a really small portion of my world."

"Walnut."

"Yes. It's a place where corn comes to grow and dreams go to die."

Rohen raised a brow.

Sorrah smiled. "Walnut is known for its quaint village, farms, and eclectic charm. I read that saying on a sign that sat inside a shop window. I guess it stuck with me."

More likely than not, the reason why the saying had remained with her was because she always believed otherwise. No one should ever stop dreaming. Dreams were a funny thing, changing, altering as time passes. But even the smallest dream can come true if you believe in the power of magic. She silently sighed. God, she really should've sent that line to Disney.

"I don't know much about this place, the land of Sorrah, or this world, because no one from where I come from has ever heard of it."

"But *you* have?"

"Yes. No. I mean, my mother once lived here."

"Then obviously someone has heard of it," he said in a correcting voice.

"Where am I? I mean… Where does Sorrah exist?" She asked the question haunting her spirit, begging to be answered long before she ever traveled through a mirror. She couldn't explain the sensation rising within, as if the question was personal and the answer all around her. Where does Sorrah exist? Where shall I belong?

"Sorrah, Borak… they are on the plains of Kortah, a vast firmament here in the world, as you say, of Aaru."

He answered as if the words didn't sound foreign and of course, they didn't. To him. But to her, well, he might as well have said this place was the planet Mars. Actually, according to a book she'd read, men were from Mars… and women were from… she didn't remember, but some other planet. She chuckled at the inside joke she knew he'd never understand.

"Your mother is Sorrien, then?" he asked, pulling her out of her wandering thought.

"No. I mean, yes, but by marriage. Before I was born, she came through, quite literally a mirror which I can only tell you was a gateway into this world.

My mother rose up through the cool water of the pond here at Castlemore, just as I did."

"A mirror?"

"Let me explain. If I can. This is no ordinary mirror but a floor-length one, with the most intricate designs hand-carved in the wooden frame. The entire thing was meticulously handcrafted by an ancestor of mine, a druid ancestor."

"I don't know this name *druid*. Explain."

"Druids are people who possess special abilities, powers even."

He nonchalantly looked her over. "And you possess these powers."

"No."

"It wasn't a question."

"Well, I have no powers that I know of."

He let out a huff and she continued. "A long time ago druids were considered to be witches but not any longer. They were enchant—"

"Enchantresses..." He looked at her suspiciously with a note of teasing.

Sorrah ignored his comment. "While my mother was here, she fell in love with a Sorrien man and they had a son. My brother."

Rohen pulled a chair out, turned it around so the back faced forward, and took a seat facing her, watching her.

Her gaze immediately fell upon his legs, noticing how the muscles strained against his black pants. Damn, but she adored thick thighs on a man. In fact, if she were honest, from what she'd seen so far, she liked many things about Rohen. She sensed stimulating warmth, a heat stirring in the air between them. Even now as she spoke she was acutely aware of his presence as if they were meant to be here in this place... in this world, destined to meet in this time.

Silva said Rohen was unmarried and often times went off on his own. Without a doubt, she believed him to be much like herself, well acquainted with loneliness.

As if an apocalyptic alert went off in her head, a steel clad barrier rolled over the window to her heart. As much as she desired not to be alone, she didn't want to be used by a man again. Protection in place, captain.

Still, her determination to fight the growing attraction seemed to clash with her ongoing appreciation of the physical attributes of the male in front of her. She involuntarily roamed her eyes over him. He wore a loose white shirt that had come free from the confines of his pants during the fight with Foley. Ties were at the top, hanging loose and showing a good part of his smooth upper chest. She drifted her gaze to his enticing sea-green, come-for-a-swim-the-water-is-warm eyes. And there she treaded while the waves rose.

His brows lowered, his face looking as if he were confused by her attention. She quickly tried to rein in her seemingly raging hormones. *Stop looking. Stop looking.*

She blew out a breath and he smirked.

"So there you have it."

From what she could tell, he was definitely trying to determine whether or not she was telling him the truth, or trying to think of a good sanitarium he could place her in. Did they have such places here? A room with a mountain view might be nice.

His lips parted as if he were going to say something then closed. The man was surely dumbfounded.

Her last comment had been about witches. Perhaps, in Sorrah the definition of a witch meant... well, witch. Black hat, point nose, wart of face, witch. She didn't have any of those attributes but nevertheless she hoped they didn't torch witches here.

It wasn't like she didn't know how utterly wacky all of what she said sounded but she needed, wanted, Rohen to believe her and it wasn't only because she needed his help.

"This brother you speak of... this is the brother who is in the prison on Bethesda?"

"Yes. My mother came back to my world."

"How?"

"Hmm?"

"How did she return? Through another mirror?"

She followed his eyes as he glanced to the mirror over the vanity. Was he not listening to her? Special mirror. Floor length.

"No. Back through the pond."

He nodded as if attempting to take this all in.

She continued. "A war had broken out, her husband was killed and her son taken from her. She was pregnant with me and feared for my safety. No one knew she was with child but my brother. My father died before she had a chance to tell him."

Rohen's face was stoically somber. This was the look of those familiar with loss.

"Which war? Pendulum?"

"I'm not sure."

"Could have been the Sacrum War. It's the last big war we have faced. Many called it a spiritual war. Far worse than Pendulum as it altered the state of Kortah. Much loss. King Zarek perished in the war along with many Sorriens and Borakiens. In the end, Meserek took the throne."

"No war ends without casualties." Even though Sorrah commented, inside Rohen's words regarding King Zarek gnawed at her. "Why did the people call it a spiritual war?"

"Borakiens and Sorriens have their differences but come together in agreeance regarding the ancient renderings given to us by the gods."

"Renderings?"

"Prophetic drawings given to the people of Aaru. They are on the ancient walls and are viewed as sacred and ultimate truth. Although the people may agree on their divine nature, the interpretations of them are enough to start wars."

"Where are these renderings?"

"Sorrah has two caves of prophecy but only because the very first ones to appear are located inside the kingdom of Sandrin, on the cavern walls beneath the castle. Have you been there?"

She knew he was testing her. "You know I haven't."

"They are beautiful. Mysterious. The images of trees and symbols take up a great deal of space. The castle itself is built within and on the side of a mountain."

"A mountain?"

"Yes. The largest mountain in our world. *My* world." He stood and lifted his hands as he continued. "Much of the royal castle at Sandrin looks like this stone one but on a far greater scale, grander. It's magnificent. There are caverns throughout it, leading deeper inside the mountain and many other rooms, chambers and such. All built, formed, inside the mighty rock itself. Below the castle is where the first renderings appeared along the cave walls. The area is sacred."

"You've been there many times?"

"All people of Kortah learn of Sandrin and the royal kingdom early on in their teachings. My father told me many stories. I journeyed there with my family once, a very long time ago. I haven't returned and

92

won't until it's for war."

There was an undeniable sadness in his eyes at the mention of his father and Sorrah's heart went out to him.

"Where was I? Oh, the caverns. There are many beneath the castle, gold coins are forged, only it's corrupted by a corrupt king. Back in King Zarek's day, the symbol on the coin was of Sorrah. Now, it bears the mark of the Borakiens."

Sorrah gave him a questioning look. "Why should Borakiens, such as you, not be pleased by that?"

"Pleased? No. When Kortah was governed by an honorable king, the mark was of Sorrah. Many believe the prophecy where the change of a bar to a coin and the mark itself would be symbolic of the king who successfully unites Sorrah and Borak."

"But this King Zarek you speak of, the one before Meserek, did he not unite Sorrah and Borak?"

"It is true he was a fair and good king. But the prophecies spoke of a time of tribulation. A time when chaos would be prevalent resulting in a great divide and inevitably... war."

"Meserek caused all of it so he could look like the prophetic king?"

"Yes. But not many in the beginning saw him for what he was. He called himself a crusader who wanted to branch out and said Zarek was preventing the advancement of Kortah. He slowly began to cause discourse in Borak and turned the loyalty of many away from the king." He clutched the chair.

"Meserek is not the fulfillment of prophecy, not the rightful ruler and had no right to ever change the bar to a coin or the mark upon it."

"What are the marks?"

"Sorrah's symbol is of a star. With one longer, exaggerated point in the center. Many believe the gods brought down a star from the galaxy and placed it on our world."

She instantly thought of the gold she had in the seam of her dress. There was a strange star symbol on them. Seven points, with the bottom point elongated.

"And Borak's symbol?" Sorrah asked.

"A ring."

"A simple circle?" she murmured nervously. There was something about this history, specifically the symbols that made her spirit thrum.

"There is nothing simple about an endless ring of infinity."

She recalled the flames rising off the sun here, spewing color in hues of orange, red, and amber.

"The Borakien symbol is said to represent an infinity of resilience, heat, fervor of a people and nation. The symbol is a circle with two larger ones around it, some say depicting the rays illuminating out from the mightiest of stars. The sun."

Sorrah's heart dropped. Her birthmark. It was as Rohen described. One circle with two outer rings going around it. How? If her father was Sorrien why did she not bear the mark of a Sorrien, but of a Borakien? Wait.

"Does anything other than the renderings and coin bare the symbols?"

"That's an interesting question. Like what?"

Sorrah did her best nonchalant gesture. "Oh, I don't know… a person?"

Rohen stood. "Why would you ask that?" Suspicion was in his voice and on his face.

"I'm just curious. What's wrong? Have I said something to anger you?"

He exhaled and calmed. "These symbols are highly regarded. It is forbidden to either give or obtain a mark and those who have done either are put to death."

Put to death? "So severe."

"Yes."

"So, are there any who have them naturally?"

He stared at her for a minute before answering. "Babes who are born with a mark are judged by holy men. Some believe they are either cursed or blessed by the gods. Depending on the interpretation. But a natural born mark is very rare. When it happens, the babe is immediately listed in the archives at Sandrin so they don't get mistaken for a lawbreaker." He paused. "And the royals need to know if they have competition."

"Competition?"

"What if the child grows to be a fairhead like you, considered favored by the gods? They may overtake the throne one day."

No worries of that here, she thought.

If she told him that many had markings on their bodies where she was from, he might ask if she did. She didn't want him to know of her mark. Not yet at least. Maybe never.

He started to show signs of the whole close-himself-off thing she already picked up about his personality. Maybe he was suspicious of her questions. In any case, she thought to get him back on track with the caves. She climbed back into bed.

"Tell me more."

"Are you sure you're not too tired to continue? We could speak again in a few hours. You've had a rough night."

"No." She snapped that out a bit fast. She didn't want him to leave. She didn't want to be alone.

"Morning will soon be here. I won't be sleeping, anyway. Where did we leave off? A cave with these hieroglyphics on its walls is part of the Sandrin mountain-kingdom thing, right?"

"Heiro…"

"Special drawings. Renderings."

It really was fascinating to hear history of this world. It couldn't hurt to familiarize herself.

"Yes. The prophecy, as I said, was written by the gods along the walls of the enormous cave below the castle. Long ago, two priests, twins, were the only ones to enter the cave where the symbols were miraculously and meticulously engraved. These special, sanctified priests spent many hours, days, weeks in the cave, lighting candles and praying for the gods to give them insight on the prophecy. Soon, the priests became advisors of the king, and many believed the gods blessed the king because of the priests' loyalty and service."

He grew silent.

"Please go on. I really want to hear this."

"All right. One day, the priests suddenly went missing. As you can imagine, rumors swiftly unfurled with the news of their disappearance. There were those who believed the priests were killed and disposed of in act of anarchy against the royal kingdom. Others spoke of the priests venturing outside the gates of Sandrin, and traveling in separate directions, never to be seen of again. Many stories continued to rise and the caves of Sandrin were closed off to all but the king himself.

Years later, a cave here in Nemis, now known of Castlemore, and a cave in Jakus, a remote area of Borak, mysteriously bore the exact renderings of the sacred cave of Sandrin. A replica but no less profoundly sacred."

"Just showed up out of nowhere?"

"Yesssss. Don't tell me you of all people don't believe in these kind of things."

She smirked. "Of course I do."

"Many people were able to see the drawings for the first time. Multitudes flocked to the caves in Borak and Sorrah, standing in line for weeks, waiting for a chance to see them, and much to the dismay of the king, do their own interpretation of what they meant.

Brutal fights inevitably broke out. Great and horrible things happened during this time."

"Like what?" Sorrah asked, wishing she had a tub of popcorn in her lap.

"Lightning strikes, land shifting, strange illuminations exploding out from the caves, and some even heard voices and screams. These things frightened the people greatly. Many formations grew larger on their own accord. Mountains formed where there were none, separating the two lands even more. Many bodies of water disappeared. Our world changed forever."

"The reigning king, fearing the caves were becoming idols of the people and allegiance to the throne weakening because of it, decreed the caves a holy place, forbidding the average citizen from entering. By that time there wasn't much need to stop them. Fear had taken root in an already superstitious people."

"As years passed, rumors of vagrants sneaking into the caves and mysteriously dying, surfaced throughout all regions of the world. Myths and superstition grew, as you can imagine. To this day, you will rarely find either Sorrien or Borakien willing to enter one."

"And you have such a cave here? You said Castlemore was once called, Nemis."

"You were paying attention."

He seemed pleased by that and she was happy to please him.

"Yes. The cave is not far behind the pond you were found in."

"The pond I came through from my world."

He conveniently ignored her comment and continued with the history lesson.

"People from both lands claimed the prophecies irrefutably showed them as the rightful ruler and king of the land of Sorrah and Borak. The one true ruler of both lands."

It was a story heard often when referring to wars and battles of people and rightful land ownership.

"So both countries believe they hold the rights to both lands," she commented.

"Yes, but there's much more to it than that. Meserek claims he is *the* fulfillment of the prophecy."

"Ah. I would think it hard to live up to a prophecy fulfillment. Awfully big shoes to fill."

Rohen chuckled slightly. "Some believe him even to this day. Meserek was the head of the governing council in Borak so he had influence there. Influence he took advantage of. Like I said, he started the revolution and discord, then rose himself up as the solution."

"How horrible."

"The priests spoke of how the Sorriens and Borakiens would go to war against each other one day but one great ruler would arise from the ashes of battle and would unite the people forever. Meserek claims to have done that, yet, here we are... far from being united. Some of us have since united in a small way, but only for one cause. To dethrone the wicked king."

"*You* have united them. I know you have both Sorriens and Borakiens in the rebellion. You've brought them together to fight for their freedom, to stand against Meserek. Perhaps, *you* are the fulfillment of the prophecy."

"I am no king, Fairhead. And I am no ruler. The prophecy is clear. The rightful king will be a fairhead to be sure and come from a rare bloodline, an ancient lineage of the god of Mercury, the purest line of royalty and will possess great power. I possess neither."

Sorrah noticed his expression turned dark and shielded. She was ever so curious about Rohen and his life.

She got out of bed again and made her way to him. "You may not be from a rare lineage of royal blood, Rohen, but you are not without power. You are foolish to think otherwise."

A slow sly smile lit up his face. Her courage seemed to be gaining in strength and from his reaction; he seemed to like her boldness. His appreciation pleased her more than it should.

He stood and pushed the chair away. Even though he only had a few inches on her, he seemed to once again tower over her. He swallowed hard and narrowed his eyes as he held her lingering gaze. "Power can be a dangerous thing, Fairhead, especially in the wrong hands."

"Yes. I agree. With great power comes great responsibility or something to that effect."

"Those are true words."

"I know." She had heard that in a movie or somewhere she couldn't quite remember at the moment.

Silence lingered between them until she couldn't take his stare any longer. She slipped her eyes away from his.

"Is Meserek of royal blood?" she asked, her skin cooling from the loss of his gaze.

Anger clouded his former pleased expression.

"No. But he says as much. He is Borakien, brought up in the ranks of the council. He made claims of a royal bloodline and took the throne by force, killing King Zarek and claiming prophetic falsehoods."

He touched the ends of her hair and dropped his fingers away. "Only fairheads are believed to be of royal blood. There has never been, nor will there ever be, a king who does not possess light hair. Many believe fairheads are sanctified, the chosen of the gods."

"Does Meserek... Is he—?"

"A fairhead? Yes, that is partly why people believed his false claims. His hair is a far darker shade of yellow than yours. Yours is quite brilliant."

"So, do you believe *me* to be of a royal bloodline?" She teased.

"No, but I'm still in the early stages of figuring you out. Perhaps, if I study you long enough, I shall unveil many of your secrets."

Their eyes locked once again and for the briefest of seconds she lost her train of thought. "I was told Meserek is your uncle."

"People are telling you things?" he asked, his voice a bit deeper. He studied her face.

She gave no reply only shrugged her shoulders.

"The answer is yes. He is my uncle. I am ashamed to be related to such evil."

"You can't choose your relatives. And you are nothing like him."

"You do not know me."

"But I know evil."

He nodded slowly. "I'm sorry that you do. I should have done more to protect you."

"More? You did everything. You saved me."

She rubbed her arms as the memory of the evil in Foley's eyes came to her.

"Meserek may call himself a fairhead but it's not likely. No one in my family line has light enough hair considered bright enough to be a full-fledged fairhead. My father denied Meserek's claims to the end. He watched his brother rise in the ranks of the council and become filled with conceit. At one point Meserek urged him to join the council but my father hated politics and stayed out of it as much as possible. But when called upon, my father used his skills to fight for Borak. He was loyal to his homeland, to the King and to Sorrah."

"Long before any of us, in the days of the priests, there were no Borakiens, only Sorriens. When the people separated into two lands, they took upon them the symbols which were taken from the drawings in the cave."

Sorrah understood. "It's all very interesting. I can see why you fight so hard."

Sorrah could see how personal this was to Rohen. Meserek had somehow personally done wrong by him, she could tell.

"I've kept you awake long enough. Get back in bed."

She did as he told her.

"Rohen?" she said as he turned toward the door.

"Will you stay for a while longer? Until I fall asleep?"

He sat on the floor next to her bed and leaned his back against the wall. "Try to sleep, Fairhead. Nothing will harm you. You are safe."

She was sure of that. She yawned. "Tell me some more."

Without her seeing, Rohen's lips quirked up in half-smile. "Close your eyes. I'll tell you more of the castle."

She smiled and closed her eyes.

Chapter twelve

Rohen had tried to fall asleep on the floor in the Marseilles room after Sorrah drifted off to sleep, but it had been no use. His mind reeled with thoughts of her and the story of how she came to be here. He didn't believe the wild tale but she did. He could see it in her eyes, hear it in her voice.

He'd been rambling on about Borak and was close to disclosing personal things regarding his upbringing and the death of his mother and father. He hadn't shared his past with anyone other than Sevin and had withheld things even from him.

The way Sorrah looked into his eyes as if she could see clean through to his soul, kept him in a constant state of unease. When she spoke, it was with such liveliness and animation, unique only to her. He'd never come across such passion. Had he searched the world over for such a creature, he'd inevitably fall short. She was far too special.

She roused his body, stimulated his mind, and touched his spirit.

It wasn't until he heard the faint sounds of her deep breathing and noticed her stillness that he believed she'd slipped off in sleep. Before returning to his room, he stood next to her bed, watching her for a brief moment, appreciating the soft plains of her face and silently thanking the gods for her mysterious entrance into his life.

His prayers had shocked him. He hadn't spoken to the gods, hadn't meditated, in a very long time. Not since before his parents died. After their death, when he found himself alone in the world, he had all but disowned the notion of a higher intelligence, of gods who watched over the world. They seemed too cruel and unjust.

She slept with a contented look on her face, fully trusting in the safety he now provided.

He was pleased she felt safe, but he was still angry with himself for not seeing the enormous threat Foley had been to her. He'd be sure not to make the same mistake again.

She was genuinely grateful that he saved her from the deranged soldier. Although pleased she wasn't hurt worse, part of him rejected the idea of being anyone's hero. He and many of his men strived to save many from the evil workings and injustices brought upon them by the false king. He tried most ardently to make up for not being able to save his own family. It was foolish to hold so tightly to guilt. He'd been too young to stop anything from happening. But inwardly he bore the scars of their deaths and held onto self-judgment and condemnation for not saving them. The trauma of his youth remained a heavy burden in his spirit and on his heart.

He spoke of honor to his men yet at times his feelings toward Sorrah had been less than honorable. She was incredibly beautiful, even more so when her vulnerability showed. He was attracted to her in the most primal way, wanting her with every ounce of his being. Of course he'd never take anything not freely given in these matters but had she been just another attractive female, he might have tried to charm his way into her bed. But he didn't. He couldn't. Not with her. She was something far greater, far more unique and exceptional than the average woman. With great ease Sorrah conjured up immense passion and projected it to him. Even thinking about her now, stroked his spirit, spurring a memory from long ago. He crossed his arm over his eyes and took a deep breath as a vision of his younger self came into his mind.

He was a mere boy, sitting back, listening and watching his father and mother converse. So very often, they would laugh and openly display affection, showing their love for one another. They were his example of what two people could share in his life, and it was one more thing he'd wanted when he grew to be a man.

At least, it started out that way. Unfortunately, later in his life, those same memories, along with the ones of their deaths, caused him to vow never to take a wife, never to open his heart to a woman. There was too much darkness there, too much loss at stake, too much risk.

He'd seen too many men fall weak in the name of love and one too many women mourn the death of their mate.

What was the use of this kind of love, if all it provided was heartache and agony? He had worked diligently to put off a strong veneer, placing an invisible shield of protection over his heart, never allowing any woman to penetrate it. A tender heart only took a man into a valley of darkness and left him with a pit of sorrow.

He rose from bed, giving up on any attempts to sleep, pulled open the drapes from the massive windows and saw nothing but gray sky.

"Fits my mood," he muttered.

He began pulling fresh clothes from his bureau and once again recalled the long conversation he had with Sorrah.

She seemed genuinely interested in what he was saying, as if she'd never heard the stories of Sorrah and Borak before, which left him even more curious about her, more intrigued.

She was a distraction which was probably Meserek's intent. But she was also a beautiful surprise that had appeared out of nowhere. No matter the intent, the gods had allowed it to happen. He wasn't a spiritual man but knew the gods placed obstacles, challenges and tests into the lives of people so their worth might be measured. As if his life hadn't been one great big challenge in and of itself.

He blew out a huff and turned to the large bowl of water on his table.

He'd have to give it time with this one. Time for her to get comfortable here and let down her guard. It was possible she'd reveal her true intent if she believed attention had eased off her. A person's nature eventually shows itself. She was either highly skilled or very well believed her own story. He'd prefer the first because if the latter was the case, it meant she had a loose mind, ridden down with craze… and if there was one thing he was sure he didn't need was a crazy woman on his hands.

He cupped water in his hands and rinsed his face. The cool water seemed to help him become more alert but did nothing to calm his nerves. It seemed Sorrah kept him in a constant state of restlessness.

Now he had to deal with Foley, the infidel. When he thought again about what might've happened had he not reached Sorrah's room, outrage and possessiveness toward her overtook him. It was a reaction he thought best not to consider too thoroughly.

He finished washing up, dressed and stood in front of the floor mirror in his room, noticing the inordinate frame for the first time.

"An ordinary mirror," he muttered, placing his fingers along the edges of the frame and then onto the reflecting glass. Was he honestly starting to believe her outlandish story? No. She was a ploy set to destroy him. The fact that Meserek knew of his weakness for females in trouble, ground at him. But of course if anyone knew this about him, it would be the one who harmed his mother, put his filthy hands on her.

"Meserek," Rohen muttered in angst.

A memory from Rohen's past once more assailed him.

He was only a lad in Borak when his father, Kleypas, died. A Borakien soldier, Kleypas fought in the name of King Zarek but under the guidance of the governing council of Borak. The leader of the council was none other than Meserek, his uncle.

His father had been sent to the front of battle on the outer regions of Borak to help secure their land, running off many insurgents from the neighboring country of Noreh. It was a small war for Borak, one they proudly informed the king they could handle and all but blatantly refused Sorrah's aid in fighting. Borakiens always were a pride filled people.

Many believed it was then, that Meserek conspired to overthrow Sorrah.

From what his uncle told him, an enemy from Noreh drove a blade through his father's heart during the heat of battle. But to this day, Rohen remained steadfast in his belief to the contrary. His father was the strongest man, the fiercest with the sword. Many of his fellow Borakiens believed the same. Besides, the soldiers of Noreh weren't exactly known for their exceptional fighting skills. Overtaking his father would not have been easy, unlikely apart from an all-out ambush.

As a child, Rohen had watched his mother severely mourn his father's death. She was inconsolable and had separated herself from him. He knew why but her departure both physical and mental, hurt nonetheless.

He looked like his father, the spitting image and he reminded her of what she'd lost. He eventually withdrew as well, not finding comfort or consolation for his loss from his own mother. He withdrew farther, throwing his efforts into training and alleviating his pain by fighting and plotting to avenge his father's death. Later, he discovered the soldier from Noreh wasn't the culprit, but instead his own uncle was.

Meserek had taken upon himself to aid in his mother's recovery, summoning her to his estate on many occasions. Being her husband's brother, and the head council of Borak, she obeyed. Nine months later, his brother... his cousin was born, his mother, dying giving birth to him.

Rohen wanted only to remain with his advisors and trainers but was forced to live with Meserek until he became of proper age to be on his own. He loathed his uncle and stayed as far away from him as possible.

While everything in Rohen's world seemed to crumble apart, many admired how surprisingly strong he remained. But inside he burned with hatred and suppressed his grief. He told himself he wouldn't allow bitterness or sadness to consume him but rather would use it to the best advantage, allow it to mold him into the kind of man his father would be proud of.

As he grew, he buried the anger and pain even deeper. Lingering in the far-reaching depths of his heart was the courage and the strength of his father. It was the one thing, the constant he could rely on, the thing which would never falter, never fail him, never abandon him.

In his dreams he spoke with his father and told him of his life and quest to overthrow Meserek. He saw pride in his father's eyes and that pride renewed his strength over and over again.

Before he died, his father had started to teach him the sword and the importance of knowing who the real enemy is. It was a lesson that remained with him as he grew.

Rohen rubbed his chest with the palm of his hand as he imagined Meserek traveling to the front of the battle and killing his father, leaving him to die alone. It was an image singed into his mind, haunting him.

He knew his father's final thought had to be of his wife and son, thoughts which drifted away with the blood-tainted wind of the battlefield.

"If you are the enemy, Sorrah. I will find out."

His train of thought dissipated with the fervent knocking on his door.

"Enter."

Sevin opened the door and entered the room. "You're not going to like this." Thunder rolled and lightning filled the dark morning sky.

"What's wrong with your eyes?"

"I didn't sleep much last night. What do you have to tell me?"

"Two things. First, the infamous Murtagh has struck again. He and his band of knights have taken out a group of ten Kingswatch two nights ago."

"This is why we need to get back on the road and find these men, get them recruited so we can unite with one allied purpose. We need to train as an army should train and not as soldiers who are no better than the Kingswatch. We need to schedule a meeting with this stranger as soon as possible and see where his head's at."

"If we can locate him."

"I know he hasn't made it easy. I'm sure that's on purpose. He has skill, so I've heard."

"There are other rumors."

"I've heard them," Rohen said, cutting Sevin off. "Raised and trained by renegade assassins. Dangerous armored knights who dress in black. Those kind of men would have found us by now if they wanted to, which warrants the question of whose side they are really on. Have you received a description of what Murtagh looks like?"

"No. I'm told he wears a hooded cloak and pulls it forward so much of his face is covered. But there is something else."

"What?"

"He bears a unique emblem on his overcoat."

"Emblem of what?"

"A red-handled sword. It's attached to his cloak. There's some kind of sentiment behind it. No one knows for sure what it is. He neither calls himself a Borakien or Sorrien."

"Great. That's all we need... another mystery. Trust me. Everyone's from somewhere. He stems from one plain or the other in Kortah or maybe even Noreh. What else do you need to tell me?"

"Foley is gone."

"What?" he asked, pinching the bridge of his nose. "Probably should've led with that one, brother. How did this happen? Who was guarding him?"

"Rev. But he was knocked out and when he woke, Foley was gone. From what the barn hands tell me, two horses are missing. Foley's and Edgar's. Revel's pissed. He wants in on any plan to find

Foley."

Rohen shot Sevin a look.

Sevin lifted his hands up. "I'm just relaying a message."

"Yes, well... His ego is bruised. But Rev will have his chance. We'll go after him. Foley will be making his way to Meserek and there's no doubt in my mind what he'll tell him. He'll betray us in a heartbeat. I held back information from him because I didn't trust him. I should've listened to what my gut was telling me and gotten rid of him a long time ago."

"It was a smart thing to do, keeping Foley out of the loop. The man is a fool and Meserek will pick up on that fact, quickly. He'll probably believe half of what Foley tells him, if anything at all."

Rohen swiped his hand over his face and through his hair in frustration. "I should have killed him last night!"

Rain poured out of the sky, hitting the panes of the windows in Rohen's room.

"And in this weather, I doubt we'll catch him."

"Eh," Sevin agreed. "But I know you, brother. We will try nonetheless."

"Yes. The longer we wait, the greater distance he gains and the closer he gets to Sandrin. We've tracked in worse conditions."

A burst of thunder rolled in the sky momentarily interrupting Rohen's words.

"Find Alexander and tell him to prepare the horses. Then tell Demetri and Rev they're going on a hunt with us. I have only to leave instructions concerning the fairhead and then we are off."

Chapter thirteen

Sorrah came awake to the sound of booming thunder. She stretched as memories of last night played through her mind. *Rohen.* He'd come to her rescue just as many valiant men had done in the romance and fantasy books she had absorbed many times over.

She went to the windows and pulled back the drapery, seeing the heavy rain and not much else.

The memory of Rohen and her talking last night, even laughing at times... played through her mind. He thought she was nuts, of course, but he'd listened which was more than most men would do. He'd been kind and seemed genuinely concerned for her. It was refreshing. But even as valiant and considerate as he seemed, she didn't believe he'd allow her to leave. She'd have to do this on her own.

"Gerta says Rohen gave her instruction concerning you," a female voice said behind her.

"God, Silva!" She glanced at the door then back to the young woman standing in her room. "Why didn't you knock?"

"I did. You didn't answer, and I assumed you left your room."

Wow, she really must have been lost in thought not to have heard the knock. "Oh, sorry. I was somewhere else in my mind. I'll find my clothes."

"Here, I brought you these. Your dresses are fine, but if you'll be cleaning, you'll need to wear some britches." She laid a small pile of plain clothes on the bed and began fixing the blankets and pillows.

"Britches. Pants. Right." She imagined herself riding a horse in a dress. Not a nice picture. She had the yoga pants she came with, but they were super thin.

She touched the edges of the clothing. "These are your things, Silva?"

Silva continued to fluff pillows and straighten. "Yes. They are sufficient?"

"Of course. It was very kind of you to loan them to me. Thank you. Others wouldn't be this way with me, believing I am a... well, that I'm the enemy. Why are you?"

Silva stilled and turned to Sorrah.

"I know what the enemy looks like. You're not one of them. And I know what it's like to feel like a stranger in a strange place. But all of us are people, no matter where we've come from or what we look like. We breathe, we bleed and we feel pain." She gave Sorrah a closed-mouth smile.

"You are Borakien," Sorrah said. It wasn't a question.

Silva nodded. "We are all Sorriens now."

"Still, I'm sure you miss your home."

"I do. Sorrah has the majestic mountains and the royal kingdom in Sandrin, things which are obviously beautiful, but in Borak, well, there are several smaller things that contain beauty. My family and I became refugees when troops invaded our farm."

"Troops?"

"Meserek's Kingswatch were once just a bank of rebels. His army grew so fast. They took anything of value to sell and fund his insurrection and told us to leave. We had nowhere to go. We lived just inside the border and decided to believe that the new king would provide for us. We were wrong."

"Is your family here in Castlemore?"

Silva shook her head. "No. My mother, my father... all of them. They are all dead. I have no family left."

"What? I'm so sorry."

Sorrah could relate to Silva. They shared an awful commonality. Her family had all died too. All except for one. In a prison in Bethesda, sat the brother she never knew existed up to a few weeks ago. Hopefully, he was still here. Hopefully, he was alive.

"Meserek had his eyes on my father and brothers. For months he tried to recruit them into his army. He wore them down by kicking us off our own land, making sure we were desperate for food and necessities, even offered to pay them. They had no other choice. Or at least they felt that way. After a few weeks of training, Meserek started to require more and more from them. His troops invaded lands and made my family... he made them do things they didn't want to do."

"Like what kind of things?"

"He wanted them to kill anyone who wouldn't join his uprising. Forced them to kill and..." Her voice shook.

"Oh, Silva. I'm so very sorry." Sorrah touched Silva shoulder.

"My youngest brother was killed by Meserek's men when he refused to kill anyone else. My father and eldest brother, so filled with rage, turned on the troops and fought them. Killed some. They rode home to my mother and I as fast as they could." She looked off to the side, lost in thought. "They were wounded but rode all the way home to get us. Later, after we fled, Rohen found us in the mountains."

"And he brought you and your family here?"

"No. He and his men buried my dead family and brought me here. They all died at the hands of Meserek's men. We were marked as traitors, you see, and Meserek ordered for us to be killed. By then they were known as the Kingswatch. They tracked us and found us barely surviving in the mountain caves. They butchered us all." Silva covered her stomach and her arm as if remembering a wound in her torso. "I remained still, lying beneath my bleeding brothers. When Rohen came inside the cave, he fell to his knees and screamed out. He saw us... really saw us as people... as if we were his own family. I could see in his eyes that he really cared. I mustered up enough energy to cry out and he saved me. He found me covered in blood. He wrapped up my wound and took me straight to a healer here in Castlemore. I owe him everything."

"You are very courageous, Silva, a survivor. I'm sure your family would be very proud of you." She gently squeezed Silva's shoulder and gave her a comforting smile. "I'll finish making up my bed. I certainly don't expect you to do it."

Thoughts of the rebellion and all the good they must have done for these people, caused a swell of emotion to rise in Sorrah. She admired these men and had gained a respect for them and for Rohen. She'd been right. Rohen might be a tough leader and cold as ice at times, but he was a good man.

"Oh, I'm used to starting my chores early. It makes me feel useful. Been up since before dawn. Already finished with all the rooms on this floor. Besides, I'll be moving your things, few as they be, to the room next to Master Rohen's."

"Is he awake?" She knew he was a busy man, but they had stayed up talking till almost dawn. When exactly had she fallen asleep? She didn't remember him leaving the room. She had felt safe near him and not just because of what happened with Foley. He had a protective presence about him.

"My yes. Master Rohen has risen and has left Castlemore." Silva looked nervously to her then away as if she wasn't supposed to tell her that last part.

"He's gone? To where?"

"Gerta will have my hide for telling you, but we've heard about what Foley did to you. I'm sorry. I for one am glad he's gone."

"Foley is gone?"

"Yes, he escaped the room below and he and another left some time during the night. Master Rohen was filled with anger at learning he slipped away unawares, mind you, but he's a good tracker. He'll be having Foley's head for sure when he gets a hold of him."

Rohen is gone. A shot of adrenaline raced through her body and instantly her plans changed. This was a sign. An opportunity for her to leave.

A hollowness settled in at the thought of Rohen. Would she ever see him again? He could be gone a long time and he'd left without saying a word to her. She knew it was ridiculous, but she felt hurt by that. Last night's event with Foley had brought them together and she honestly thought there was a moment, maybe more, when they had bonded because of it. She could tell herself she didn't care one way or the other if she saw him again but the truth was, she did. How had this man come to be important to her?

"I'll change and head downstairs to report to Gerta for work."

"All right then. And just so you know, Master Rohen has appointed you a guard. For your safety."

"Oh... how thoughtful." And conniving, and... and alpha wolf-like. He didn't trust her. Of course not. He was a smart sea captain.

After Silva left she quickly washed, brushed her hair, and dressed. She had to get inside Rohen's room, steal the map, get to the stables, and get a horse. That was the plan, how she'd execute it... well, she'd just have to figure that out as she went. One thing was for certain, when Rohen returned to find her gone, he'd come after her and he'd never believe she wasn't a spy.

The thought of him chasing her sent a thrill to her spirit until the image of him turned into a wolf with large pointy teeth and wolfy paws. God, if Rohen did catch up with her, there was a good chance he'd devour her.

Her lips curled up into a soft smile as she walked out the door and met Kehgen, the soldier and her guard for the day.

"I have to stop by Rohen's chambers for a minute," She told him as they walked down the hall toward the staircase.

"No. I have strict orders to bring you straight to the kitchen."

She turned on him. "Kehgen, please. I left my paper there and I need it to sketch, you know when I get a break. It's the only thing I really like to do."

She gave him her best pitiful plea and even batted her eyes, attempting to be flirtatious to obtain her way. Her altered appearance was now more appealing so why not use it to her advantage?

"Your eyes are twitching. What's wrong with them?"

Apparently, mastering the art of flirting took time.

She briefly raised her eyes to the ceiling. "Whatever. Please just let me grab my stuff. You can step inside with me while I gather it. Rohen was so nice to give it to me. He did say I am a guest here. That hasn't changed has it?"

Kehgen seemed to be giving her speech some thought. "Fine. One minute."

They entered Rohen's room and both stopped dead in their tracks. Lying on his bed was a half-dressed woman.

"Rohen... I was... Oh..." the woman said.

Oh? Yeah, oh. As in... Oh, I could've gone my entire life without seeing her bare parts. Who was this woman sprawled out in Rohen's bed? Had she been there all night? Had Rohen been with her after he slipped out of her room?

Sorrah's face flushed at the embarrassment of it all. She'd been such a fool to believe there'd been something special between Rohen and her. She thought she'd detected something unique between them, soul mate kind of thing but it had only been a fleeting moment of lust. That was it. That was all.

Instantly, an image of *Jerk* came to her mind. She'd been wrong about him too. She remembered watching the back of his retreating body after they had sex. Her dorm room door slammed shut behind him and she had been faced with the reality that he'd only used her to get what he wanted. Once he had gotten it, she no longer existed. She hadn't realized it until now, how deeply that one event in her life had altered her perception of romance and love. How sad that reality wasn't anything like how it was depicted in the books she read because evidently women craved that kind of once-in-a-lifetime kind of love, and apparently she had too.

Even though she'd probably never see Rohen again, the fact that he was with this... this skank after they had shared hours of talking, of staring at each other in silence, grinded at her. God, she really felt like an idiot. Had last night only been about gaining information?

Jerk had more than likely been cloned, leaving many little mini-me *Jerks* out there, even in Sorrah. *Don't glorify this place or it's people, Sorrah,* she told herself. *Smarten-up and remain focused. You mean nothing to Rohen.*

"Alba, you know not to be in here without Rohen. Now get up and get to work. You have chores to do today, I am sure," Kehgen told her.

Sorrah used the distraction to make her way to the wooden table and to where the maps were. She looked back over her shoulder, and when Alba flirtatiously wrapped her arms around Kehgen's neck, holding his attention, she opened one of the rolls of paper. Seeing a smaller version of the map in the far corner, she tore it off as quietly as she could and placed it in between a few blank sheets she saw on a shelf.

"I have my paper," Sorrah said, waving the sheets in the air, careful not to dislodge the map she held between them.

As they left the room, Sorrah quickly folded the sheets of paper and tucked them in her back pocket. She was more determined than ever to remain focused on her goal.

Where her plans blurred becoming foggy and allowing for the briefest of hesitation lay an image of Rohen, the sea captain, the wolf who maintained a presence in her mind and called out to her spirit.

Chapter fourteen

For the next few hours, Sorrah worked hard cleaning the dining hall, mopping every crevice and tight corner and dusting nearly every item. She knew how to clean. Even though growing up, her aunt Kaye insisted on having a live-in maid, she also insisted Sorrah learn to take care of herself. At least that was Kaye's excuse when she wanted to go off on a search and leave Sorrah to fend for herself.

The first maid Kaye hired was cranky but for the most part quietly performed her duties. In just short of six months, Kaye fired her when she noticed things had gone missing.

No one touched Kaye's things.

Then there was Martha. The strongly built woman was a bit younger than what Kaye had intended on hiring, but was a hard worker and after a few months under Kaye's careful scrutiny, proved to be loyal. Martha was a sweet woman and had taken Sorrah under her wing, teaching her much. In many ways, she'd been there for her, when Kaye had not.

Sorrah smiled, remembering the woman and the final meeting she had with her lawyer before she left. She'd placed the house and a good portion of money in trust to Martha and her family. She could just imagine the look on Martha's face when she realized how much money she was inheriting. She'd never have to work again.

Earlier, Kehgen had taken a brief break from watching her, stating he'd be back after he relieved himself. The man was simply bored. How exciting could it be to watch a woman clean? She was grateful for his brief absence and had taken the short window of opportunity to run upstairs, grab her bag and quickly hide it behind some nearby bushes.

Nearly finished with her chores, she leaned against the long, wooden dining hall table and wiped her forehead with a clean cloth. But her break was short-lived when an ear-piercing cry coming from the kitchen, startled her. She instantly dropped her cloth and ran into the room.

113

One of the younger kitchen workers stood over a large basin, holding her hand while blood slowly but steadily flowed out. No one seemed to be helping the poor girl. Maybe they didn't know how to help, but Sorrah did, having had some training.

"What happened?" she asked, edging her way closer to the girl.

Gerta was visibly upset. "She's gone and cut herself. Fool girl! You don't ever touch the knives again. What were ya doin'? They ain't your job!" she scolded.

"I can help," Sorrah offered but Gerta seemed to ignore her.

Just when she thought she'd reach the girl, a woman with a horrible scowl on her face, stepped in front of her, blocking her way. "I think it best that all spies stay out of our way."

Spy was it? Of course. More bullies.

"Spy? Well, Rohen wants me here so unless you want to talk with him about that, I think it best you move out of my way so I can help the girl."

The woman crossed her arms over her chest and didn't budge.

No one else was paying much attention to the run in she was having with this ornery woman who had the ugliest black mole on the left side of her face. She really should get that looked at or hacked off or something.

"Look, however you feel about me, there's a girl over there bleeding. I know about treating these sorts of things."

"Get me a cloth!" Gerta told Silva. "Enough, Miranda. You'll be mindin' your own business," she told mole-woman. Miranda lowered her arms and nodded in a huff before walking away.

Sorrah quickly made her way to the girl and gently touched her arm. "May I have a look?"

The girl nodded and winced as Sorrah lifted her arm. The cut was deep.

"You'll need stitches. But first we have to stop the bleeding."

"I'll send for the healer," Gerta offered.

"I can do this. She'll bleed out bad before any healer can get here. Now, fetch me the cleanest, coldest water you can find and get me some white thread and a thick, sharp needle. Put a flame to the end before you give it to me."

"I have some cold water here!" one of the workers said, lifting a latch on the floor, exposing the below-ground cellar. She pulled out a glass jar of water and brought it over.

Sorrah, applied pressure to the wound and held it in a bowl of cold water. The girl was shaking horribly probably from shock.

"What is your name?" Sorrah asked, trying to calm the girl.

"Hethel."

"That's a nice name. How old are you, Hethel?"

"Fourteen."

Sorrah smiled, deciding she needed to talk with the girl, who was growing paler by the minute. "When I was your age, Martha, the housekeeper of the home where I lived, baked me a cake for my birthday. It was the most marvelous cake I had ever seen. It was two-tiered and had white frosting and flowers of every color on it. There wasn't a spot that didn't have some kind of decoration. She knew I loved the outdoors and had covered it with trees and nature. She even placed a bright green candle on the top. Green is my favorite color."

Hethel looked around at the other women in the room, and Sorrah was sure she had said something they didn't quite understand but she continued with her story anyway.

"You were of importance then? From a family of nobility?" Hethel asked.

"Hmm?" Sorrah didn't understand.

"You had a housekeeper in your home?"

"Oh. Well my Aunt Kaye, who raised me, couldn't do very much." Couldn't. Wouldn't. Didn't want to. "She was gone a lot. Ever so busy."

"And what of your mum?"

"I had no mother. Or father for that matter."

From the corner of her eye Sorrah saw some of the women edging closer.

"Anyway," she said, continuing to tend to the wound as she spoke. "I told myself not to touch that cake until my birthday but late at night, I snuck downstairs and put a fork into it and tasted it. It was delicious. Better than anything I've ever tasted in all my life. A sweet bite of heaven."

"Heaven?"

"It was a good cake."

She held the wound together and dried the surface.

"And then what happened?" Hethel asked curiously.

"Just as I was putting my fork into the cake for another taste, Martha came into the kitchen and caught me in the act."

A few of the women in the room, chuckled.

"Did ya get a beatin'?" Hethel asked.

"Oh no. She told me I had to stay there in the kitchen, in the middle of the night and bake a cake exactly like the one she had made and if it didn't taste the same, she would cancel my birthday celebration altogether and feed the cake to stray dogs."

Each year, Martha called her birthday a celebration but it really wasn't. No friends came over and no family attended because she had neither. Even Kaye took no part in it. Her birthdays consisted of herself, Martha and their cat, primarily, but it was all she had ever known.

Sorrah began stitching Hethel's wound with thread and needle Gerta had given her.

"Did ya make the cake then?" Gerta asked inquisitively.

"I baked all night, trying and failing miserably at reproducing the same delicious cake Martha made me. I only succeeded in making the kitchen look like a tornado had come through it."

The women shot glances to each other and Sorrah heard the word tornado being repeated.

"That's it? You had no birthday then?" Hethel asked.

Sorrah smiled. "Martha came into the kitchen the next morning and tasted my failure as I stood off to the side, exhausted, knee deep in flour, *peufer,* and with tears in my eyes. Then she took me inside her arms and held me."

"What kind of punishin' is that? I've never heard such a thing!" Gerta went on.

"Martha knew she had taught me a great lesson and she did. She taught me how difficult baking truly can be. I loved her for that. Still do. I learned to love baking even more because of her." Tears continued to well up in her eyes at the memory. "Martha and I spent the entire day, my birthday, baking and laughing. It was the best birthday I ever had."

Hethel's eyes lit up and a wide grin spread across her face.

116

"Now. Keep this clean and dry," Sorrah told the girl as she wrapped her wound with a clean cloth and tied it together.

"Thank you."

"You're welcome," Sorrah replied. She placed the cloths and needle on the table and turned to see many of the workers still peering at her.

Funny, she hadn't noticed that many people in the room earlier.

Gerta approached, her stern look softening as she spoke. "You did well, Sorrah. Most well." She smiled and Sorrah got the distinct impression she'd received a rare gift from the ruley housekeeper.

Gerta turned on the gawkers in the room. "Back to work!" The women quickly scattered about, returning to their chores.

"If you don't mind," Sorrah started. "I would like to get some fresh air. Would that be all right?" She looked over at Kehgen who was leaning against the door frame, then back to Gerta.

Gerta eyed Kehgen. "The rains have let up a bit. I can't see what it would hurt to let the lass take a few minutes."

"Fine. Come on," Kehgen said, conceding.

Sorrah nodded and left the room, escorted by Kehgen. This could be her chance. The opportunity to make her way to the barn and out of this place. She didn't want to start caring for these people but feared it had already started to happen, especially toward Rohen. She just needed to get out of there.

She stepped out onto the wide front porch. The afternoon had given way to more clouds but just as Gerta mentioned, there was a reprieve from the rain.

"May I take a walk?" she asked Kehgen.

"Walk to where? You'll be knee deep in mud before you blink your eye. It's too muddy."

"To nowhere in particular. To anywhere. You don't have to follow me."

"That's where you're wrong. I do have to follow you."

"Fine. If I can stand the sludge on my shoes, you can handle a bit of mud while wearing those boots."

"Here," Gerta said from behind her. She held out a pair of boots and an overcoat.

Sorrah's heart warmed. "Thank you."

"Best you don't be takin' too long. We'll be startin' dinner after a while and I'll be needin' ya." She turned away quickly, leaving Sorrah stunned by the kind gesture. Gerta was all business when it came to running the staff at Castlemore but Sorrah suspected inside the brazen woman was an enormously warm heart.

She put the boots on and tossed the coat over her shoulders, covering them before heading for the barn.

"Where are you going?" Kehgen asked suspiciously.

"The barn. And you don't have to worry, it's not like I know how to ride in the mud, let alone know where I'm going." She lied. She'd become a liar. *Oh well,* she thought. No way around that if she were to get to Bethesda. *My brother comes first.* She'd offer up forgiveness for it later.

After a few minutes, a woman called out for Kehgen. By the way he smiled at her, Sorrah got the impression Kehgen was soft on the young woman. She couldn't have been a day older than eighteen. Come to think of it, where were the elderly? No one she saw so far looked very old. Rohen, she guessed, was around thirty, his men about the same. Silva must be around her age, twenty six or so. *How odd,* she thought. She hadn't thought about asking Rohen last night but wondered now if people aged differently here. Even Gerta couldn't be much older than forty. Did they hide the elderly away somewhere? She'd have to remember to ask someone about it at a later time. Right now, she needed to escape.

She took out her paper and began sketching one of the horses. When she was sure Kehgen wasn't looking, she looked at the map. She hadn't lied about liking to sketch. It was more of a hobby than anything else. And right now, it was the perfect cover.

The woman, who had called out, ran into the barn and smiled at Kehgen. They kissed and Kehgen looked nervously over to Sorrah.

"Do what you like. I'm sketching. Gerta will be hollering for me in a few minutes."

"I'll be right back," he said, moving out of view with the woman.

Sorrah could hear giggles and kisses coming from around the corner. He wasn't far from her. She quietly led the farthest horse out of the stable, and placed a saddle on it. As soon as she tightened the strap, the rain began coming down hard again but she knew this was her chance. Perhaps, her last.

She walked the horse farther out into the rain and draped its reins on a tree branch.

"Stay," she whispered as if the horse were a dog. She ran back to the house, grabbed her bag from the bushes then headed back to the trees. She mounted the horse and took off, all the while hoping the rain masked the sound of the horse's hooves.

Chapter fifteen

"He couldn't have gotten much farther," Sevin commented to Rohen who seemed bound and determined to ride fast and hard to catch up with Foley.

Sevin, as always, rode on the left side of Rohen, Alexander, to his right. Behind him were Demetri and Revel.

Demetri had displayed great skill during sparring, or so Rohen was told by Sevin, who trained all new recruits.

Rohen's elite soldiers, those whom he trusted the most, had spent many hours over the course of the past year, discussing politics and battle plans. It hadn't taken them long to conclude that their latest recruit, Demetri, had much of the same views which were in line with the rebellion and their focus.

Rohen believed that Demetri, being a former nobleman and advisor to some of the hierarchy during King Zarek's reign could become a great asset to the regime and assist in the transition of the throne once they rid Sandrin of Meserek. A new king would be needed to govern the people and restore democracy. Having key people surrounding them would be beneficial.

Rohen was good at reading people, all except Sorrah. He knew he had made a mistake when he overlooked Foley's shortcomings in order to have another exceptional fighter in his army. The fact that Foley had shown his stripes in such a horrendous way, ground at his nerves. He'd made a great error in judgment. Had he gotten rid of Foley when he should have, Sorrah would not have been touched. He shuddered at the thought of anyone touching her. She was his. It was a possessive thought, one he dismissed quickly. Besides, Sorrah was in need of protection and he merely had the desire to provide her with safety. He didn't want to consider the alternative too thoroughly.

The dark rain clouds seemed to move with the four men as they rode, settling themselves in large gloomy masses over their heads.

They had ridden for hours, moving forward on the pathway leading through the mountains and in the direction of Sandrin, periodically stopping to consider even the faintest marks in the ground. Many tracks would be completely washed away by the rain but Rohen and his men were certain Foley and his cohort, Edgar, would head straight for Meserek and that motivated them to keep moving forward. Foley would betray Rohen and the rebellion forces giving Meserek their location and whatever evidence of future plans he had found during his time at Castlemore.

Rohen put his hand in the air, signaling to the others to slow. He gazed down to the ground and once again scoured the terrain for any tracks or signs Foley had passed through the area. With the rain, it was an opportune time for Foley to gain his freedom, well knowing he'd be difficult to track in the adverse weather.

He let out a growl of frustration and raised his voice over the sound of rain. "All right. We take a break in the northern caverns."

The caves along the mountain side were widely known to those who traveled through the rocky peaks. They often safeguarded many from the frigid weather and added dangers.

Quickly finding a cave that would shelter them, the men held up inside. An hour later, the rain still hadn't eased which made Rohen exceedingly restless.

"I know you're anxious to get your hands on Foley—" Sevin started.

"We aren't quitting. Not yet. I'm going to take another look for tracks. There is no way Foley rode straight through to Sandrin. My guess is he is waiting out the storm, just like we are. The rain is a bit lighter now," he said, making his way outdoors.

Demetri stood at the entrance, watching the rain pour down. "Lighter? He's kidding right?" he asked Sevin who sat against one of the walls.

"No. He's just determined and angry with himself for not killing Foley when he was still at Castlemore."

A few minutes later, Rohen returned. "Let's move out."

The men followed Rohen as he backtracked. The muddied ground provided little in the way of clues to where Foley and Edgar might have stopped, but the rains finally began to diminish which meant more people would be on the move. Including the would-be traitors.

Rohen held his hand up, signaling for the men to stop. "Listen. Do you hear that?"

"What is it?" Sevin asked.

As soon as Sevin asked, they heard the sound of raised voices and whistling that were distinctly male.

"Could be the Bervous. They must have cornered someone," Rohen answered.

"Or the Kingswatch?" Sevin added. "It doesn't sound like Foley's voice though."

Rohen wasn't sure. "He could be with others. Let's go around them and take a look for ourselves. There are a lot of Bervous in these mountains. They could have come across a lost traveler."

He waved his fingers in the air, motioning in different directions. They'd leave their horses behind and try to be quiet while they surrounded the mountain men, gaining the advantage by approaching unaware.

Rohen believed, if this was Foley they were about to come up on, and he was in the company of the Kingswatch, he'd likely be trying to talk to his way into their favor, or giving up Rohen's location, in hopes of reward. The price on Rohen's head continued to grow. Whatever they were about to face he hoped for another chance to kill Foley before he betrayed the rebellion to Meserek.

*****

Sorrah was surrounded by burly men dressed in worn clothing. She'd never been faced with scoundrels in dark alley ways but assumed if she had, they'd look something like this.

She had ridden for what seemed like hours, not letting up even while the rain pummeled her face and body. She didn't know how far behind Kehgen was, but knew the man wouldn't leave her be. She had a rebellion soldier following her and now wished he'd hurry and catch up. He'd be upset with her for tricking him, but she'd take that any day over these vile men who stood in front of her.

She was no guest of the rebellion, but a prisoner who now, because of her trickery and escape, looked more like a spy than ever before. If she were caught, there'd be no explaining herself out of this one. There was no way Rohen would believe her now that she ran off.

She had counted on rough terrain, but nothing would've prepared her for running into these mountain men who strangely reminded her of the toothless men on a short-lived television series about a young woman who went to live at a mission in the Appalachian mountains, Dirty backwoods mountain men. Yikes.

Was she even going in the right direction? She thought she'd read the map well enough but everything looked so foreign to her. Because it *was* foreign. She was in a different world and you couldn't get farther from familiar than that.

"Get off your horse, Fairhead," one of the men commanded.

The sound of the nickname she'd grown accustomed to hearing from Rohen, sounded horribly wrong coming from this stranger.

She moved her horse one way and then the next but they blocked her in every direction. Suddenly, three of them rushed her and yanked her off her horse. She had thought quickly and pulled her bag down with her, tossing the strap over her shoulder as she stood face to face with one of them. Meanwhile one of the men led her horse away. Great.

"What is a fairhead doing here and alone in our territory? Are you lost?"

Yes, she was lost but she sure wasn't going to tell them that. "Of course not. In fact, I rode up ahead. My escort is not far behind me," she answered with a confidence she didn't feel.

The man circled her as he spoke once more. "Is that right? And who might this escort be? A husband? A lover?"

"If you must know—"

"Ohhhh, yes. I fear I must."

The men laughed. The man placed his dirty hand over his chest. "Such fine speech. Not one of a commoner but not completely Sorrien either. Hmm. Where are you from, beauty?"

She wasn't going to go there. It's not like they'd understand. "A land far, far away."

"Come on, Gil, enough with the talkin'. Let us have a taste of her," one of them called out from off to the side.

"My escort is a soldier of the rebellion!" she blurted out. She hoped these men knew of the fierceness of the rebellion and of Rohen.

They laughed and came closer to her.

"You? With the resistance? With the rebellion army?"

"Yes. I am a guest of Rohen."

The man named Gil looked skeptically at one of the other men. "A fairhead in the hands of the rebellion? I don't think so. Now, take off your clothes and let us take our fill of you and then we'll be off."

"Wh... what?" She backed away. "I will not!"

"Then if you aren't willin' to offer it... we'll be a takin' it."

What? Dear gods, no. She began to pray for a miracle or at the very least for doctor MacNeil to ride in and save her. In her state of fear, her mind easily wandered to other things, this time it was back to the mountain series she'd watched.

And didn't the fair doctor have the same first name as his last? *Yes!* she thought. *His first name was Neil.* Who did that to their kid? Naming him that way. Didn't they know how torturous kids at school could be? Bullies were bad enough, why give them added ammunition? You know, had he actually been a real person. She sighed. Clearly, she'd watched too much television.

Who was she kidding? She had fooled herself into believing she'd make it here in this world on her own but only because she'd been accustomed to doing so much by herself. Still, her own mother had come to this place alone and survived. Surely, she could too.

My mother, she thought. *My brave, courageous mother.*

She changed her stance to a defensive one, ready to put up the fight of her life.

"I should warn you, I will not be taken easily."

She turned to run and heard them laugh behind her. She hadn't gotten far before they'd taken hold of her and began grabbing at her body.

She elbowed one, kneed the other in the groin and scratched and punched her way out of any solid hold over her. Overall, she was fighting them off. Sort of. Until one of them hit her across her head. Hard. She fell to the ground.

As the men began pulling at her clothes, she screamed loudly and continued to punch and kick as much as she could.

One by one, the mountain men were leaving her side, nearly being plucked away by some powerful unseen force.

Then she heard it. The wonderful sound of the most fearsome and unmistakably dangerous voice she'd ever heard. The voice of her sea captain wolf, the very one which brought a thrill to her soul. Rohen.

"Step away or lose your head!"

Directly in front of her stood Rohen tall and brooding while holding the tip of his blade at the neck of the last standing man who tried to attack her.

"Mercy. I thought she was jesting when she said she was with you." The man tried to apologize. "Let us go. All is fine now."

Rohen took a firm hold of the man and punched him across his face. He shoved him away while he and his soldiers formed a protective circle around her. Their backs remained to her and their weapons out in front of them. She was safe and once again *he* had saved her. Even Kehgen had showed up and joined Rohen's men.

Sorrah rolled to her side, the mud clinging to her clothing and boots. She positioned herself on her knees and grabbed a hold of her bag before trying to stand. She slowly rose but soon learned trying to remain upright was a mistake.

Feeling light-headed, she began to sway, seeing the ground becoming closer once more. The hit on her head must have done more damage than she thought.

Strong, muscular arms came around her waist before she hit the ground. She didn't have to look to know who had helped her. His touch was unmistakable, their attraction undeniable.

"Easy now, Fairhead." Rohen's breath drifted across her ear, spurring ripples of delight and a steady flow of warmth within her.

For the umpteenth time she found herself needing to offer an explanation. "Rohen... Rohen—"

"Later," he said, gripping her firmer and closer to his body. "You will listen to me now." His voice was stern, his hold possessive. He moved his free hand to her head, and she could tell he was searching through her wet hair, probably for a wound.

She nodded at his command, too tired to protest. She let her head fall back against the upper area of his chest, finding incredible relief in leaning on him.

Who was she kidding anyway? She'd never make it here in Sorrah or the plains of Kortah by herself, but maybe she didn't have to. Maybe being strong wasn't always needing to do things on your own, but realizing your need for help. All this time she'd thought about her mother making her way in this world alone but what if she hadn't? What if she was strong and brave yet found the right people to trust? There was certainly strength in recognizing your weakness. Wasn't there?

"Sevin, Revel, make sure these men get on their way—far away from here."

His trustworthy men nodded and with their swords still drawn, escorted the mountain men to the path where they, no doubt, would eagerly flee.

The rain returned in sleek downpours, and Sorrah hoped it would cool off the fury she sensed in the wolf.

Chapter sixteen

Rohen couldn't believe what he'd witnessed. Fairhead... Sorrah had once again found danger, this time by the likes of the Bervous who made their homes in the caverns of the mountains. These men were recluses, immoral savages for the most part. Everyone from Sorrah to Sandrin to the farthest reaches of Borak, knew of the Bervous' existence and the dangers of traveling the mountain sides, yet, Sorrah had chosen to take the journey and alone. She really must have been desperate to leave Castlemore, to leave *him* that she'd risk her life to do it. The latter bothered him more than he wanted to admit.

He walked to the nearest cave with her still firmly against him, their bodies moving as one. He turned to Alexander before entering inside. His breath creating a light fog in the cool air as he spoke.

"No one disturbs us. Take shelter in another cave but remain close. We head back to Castlemore shortly."

"All right. And what of Foley?" He shifted his eyes to Sorrah then back to Rohen.

Rohen's face tensed. "I will live to fight Foley another day. And now, most likely a great deal of the Kingswatch as well."

Alexander nodded, leaving Rohen and Sorrah alone.

Once fully inside the cave, he leaned her against the wall, making sure she could stand on her own before he stepped back.

With great effort, he peeled his wet overcoat and threw it off to the side. "Are you all right?" His voice sounded more angry than intended.

Sorrah nodded. She seemed more alert but her rain-soaked body trembled from the cold air common to the mountain range. She mimicked his actions, peeling off her wet coat.

"One of them hittt... mmm my head," she stammered. "But I'm ffffine."

She tried so hard to be brave. And she was. First Foley and now the Bervous men. She could've been killed. Didn't she know how much he wanted to keep her safe? He would accept no excuse for her being out here alone.

"The wound is not bad but you'll need to rest until you get your bearings."

He glanced around the cave, irritated that there was nothing he could use for a fire.

They'd have to return to Castlemore soon. She'd be warm there. Safe. He wasn't concerned for himself, he was accustomed to such frigid conditions, but Sorrah was obviously feeling the effects of the rain and cold. Her teeth were chattering, her body shaking. Everything inside him screamed to comfort her, warm her, but he could do no such thing until he gave her a thorough speaking to.

"You're fortunate a hit on the head was all you suffered! What in the gods name were you thinking, leaving Castlemore?! he yelled.

She lifted her teary eyes to him in challenge but he wouldn't let her win this one. She looked fragile, innocent even, but he wouldn't succumb to her wiles again. She had fled the safety of Castlemore, placed herself in danger and had exposed her traitorous intent in doing so. She was a spy and he had her just where he wanted her. Images of them in desire-filled play entered his mind, many of her beneath him in his bed, writhing in ecstasy. All right, he didn't exactly have her where he wanted her.

She crossed her arms and rubbed. Her voice elevated as she answered. "What was I thinking?"

She cleared her throat and stood a bit taller.

"I was thinking that you didn't believe what I told you last night! I was *thinking* that you'd never believe that I wasn't a spy! That you weren't going to help me and that I needed to get to Bethesda on my own. I was thinking my brother is all I had left in *this* world or *my* world for that matter!"

Her voice shook. "I was th... think...," she stammered again and all self-restraint fled him. He pulled her inside his arms and held her, lowering his mouth near her ear.

"You're freezing. I have to get you someplace warm."

Her body seemed to melt against his. Her mouth rested against the top of his chest where his shirt separated, exposing his skin.

It was sufficient enough that she accepted the warmth of his body.

128

For now. Yet he craved so much more. She drove him to the brink of insanity.

"You are someplace warm," she whispered, her lips grazing his skin.

He wasn't sure he heard her correctly. She'd spoken so quietly and his body had gone on high alert from the feel of her tender lips.

"Hmm? What was that?"

"Nothing. I said nothing."

She wasn't fighting his embrace, the warmth of their connected bodies seeming to calm her. He was warming too, both inside and out. A slow mind-wrecking churn of heat. He ran his hands up and down her back as he continued to speak. "I saw you—I saw you and all I could think of was what if I hadn't gotten to you in time? What if something horrible had happened to you? Gods, Fairhead—why did you leave Castlemore?" He took a hold of her shoulders and pulled her slightly off of him. "You were safe there! I made sure of it! Why did you leave?"

She lifted her face to his, her blue eyes, mesmerizing him. "Be honest with me. Would you of helped me?"

He sighed. "For gods' sake. I asked you a question first. Why did you escape the safety of Castlemore?! We would have spoken when I returned."

"Answer my question, Rohen. Would you have helped me get to Bethesda? Would you have helped me find my brother?"

He searched her face and decided to tell her the truth. "Yes, Fairhead, I would have helped you. Gods help me, against my better judgment—I would have." He wiped away a stray tear that had fallen down her cheek.

"All right. That was then. What about now?"

He didn't answer. How could he? All evidence pointed to her guilt. She was a spy. Only now the thought of her being one didn't anger him like it had in the beginning. If she was Meserek's spy, maybe the wicked man held something over her. And maybe, he could help her and keep her near at the same time.

"But now you won't help me. Will you?" she asked softly, pushing away from him. She leaned against the cave wall and wrapped her arms around herself. *"Now,* you're sure I'm the enemy."

He stepped forward, leaning in and getting even with her. He placed his hands on the wall behind her, caging her between his arms.

"The only thing I am certain of is that seeing you away from the safety of Castlemore and in the clutches of the Bervous frightened me like nothing else! And you can be sure that I don't fear much. You should've trusted me then and you should trust me now."

How could he make her see reason?

"Why?" she asked, looking at him wide-eyed. "Tell me why I should trust you?"

When she looked at him this way, like she could see clear through to his soul, it set him afire, astounding him. No one had this kind of effect on him. No one.

He sighed as he shook his head. "I know you sense whatever this is between us. Think. Did you honestly believe I wouldn't help you?"

She quickly brushed wet strands of hair off her face. Her lips stiffened and her eyebrows furrowed. If he didn't know better, he'd think she was angry. He huffed internally. What right did *she* have to be angry with him?

"Sense something? Before you left without saying anything, you gave orders to Gerta to put me to work. Again. The only thing I sensed was that I was becoming a new housekeeper or cook at Castlemore. Don't misunderstand. I don't mind working, but you gave me no reason whatsoever to believe I was going to have an escort to Bethesda anytime soon or ever for that matter."

She fell silent and studied his face. "Come to think of it, I did *sense* something after seeing your lover in your bed this morning. I *sensed* that the two of you had a really good time." She paused then added, "I'm surprised you had the stamina after such a long night."

He pushed himself away from the wall, folded his arms across his chest and tilted his head as if he weren't hearing her right. "Say that again? My *lover?*"

She shrugged. "I assume you're familiar with the word."

What a brat. "We'll get back to that in a minute. What reason did you have to be in my quarters?"

She ignored his question which only fueled his anger that much more. And his curiosity.

"Her name is Alba or something like that. Does the name ring a

130

bell? Or… wait. Maybe you don't care to remember the name of your lovers, I'm sure there are so many of them. God, I didn't even think of that. Maybe you don't bother to ask their name before you take what you want and then toss them aside."

Rage churned within but he held back from lashing out. Still, his voice was harsh when he spoke. "You question my honor? I can assure you, Fairhead, all my lovers, and there have been many, are left extremely happy," he leaned his face closer, "highly satisfied. They know up front that I promise them nothing more than a time of immense pleasure. Still, none of that is any concern of yours." The second he uttered the last sentence he regretted saying it. But he had nothing more to offer any female. Even her.

She lowered her gaze and her cheeks pinked in color. Had he embarrassed her? Angered her?

"Now, tell me why you went to my room."

For a split second he hoped she'd gone to his room to be with him. They had some moments the night before, times where their mutual attraction was undeniably evident. They could deny it all they wanted but still the sexual tension between them remained.

"Kehgen took me to your room so I could get some paper for sketching, and we saw, well, we saw Alba half-dressed and lying on your bed. But like you said… It's none of my business. You talked about sensing something between us but I'm sorry… I don't sense a thing. There is nothing between us."

His heart ached. "You speak falsehoods!"

She blew out a defeated breath and gently shook her head. "Just forget this. Forget about me. Let me go and you'll never have to see me again."

"Stop it." He clenched his jaw. He was enraged at her for speaking lies. What was between them was real. He knew it. She knew it. To hear her denial was a travesty.

Her chin shook. "Just let me go," she whispered.

Everything about this felt wrong, was wrong. His guarded heart went from coldness and distance to closeness and want within seconds. Forget? How could he ever forget anything about her?

She turned her face to the side, away from his gaze.

"You know I can't do that."

"Yes you can. You can forget."

It was clear that she was lying, mostly to herself. There was an awkward uncomfortableness about her when she lied. It was a subtle change in her demeanor and in her stance, something many wouldn't likely notice, but he did.

"No. And I won't allow you to leave. Look at me when I speak to you."

"Do not give me orders like I'm one of your servants! You don't have the right to keep me. You don't have the right to tell me to do anything!"

"Yes I do!"

He threw his hand out to the wall, hitting close to her head and making a startling sound. Undoubtedly, it was not an action to harm but meant to shock.

There was no way he'd let her get away with this. Was she seriously trying to turn this back on him? As if he were the one who did something wrong? There was only one way to prove her wrong and stop this madness.

She let out a frustrated grunt but lifted her eyes to his. Gods, even dirty and wet, she was the most beautiful thing he had ever seen in all his life. Betraying his resolve never to allow a woman into his heart, the fact became crystal clear. She was irrefutably his. Whether or not he acted upon this truth, she belonged to him and was his to do with and what he pleased. She just didn't seem to realize it yet.

He gently cupped the back of her head with his free hand and brushed his lips against hers, withdrawing and remaining a few inches away. Causing more agony for him.

When he spoke this time, all harshness was gone from his voice.

"Does it bother you to think I may have been with a woman after I left your room?"

He repeated his action, gliding his lips over hers, restraining from kissing her fully.

"Fairhead... Answer me," he whispered against her lips.

His teasing seemed to work. As he moved his lips away again, she leaned toward his mouth, trailing after him, seeking more. Of course, her reaction pleased him immensely.

"Bother me?" She swallowed hard planting her head firmly

against the wall away from him. "I don't even know you."

If that were only true. Strangely, he believed she had a keen insight into his soul, an attribute reflecting a bind rarely shared between people, but not unheard of in Borak or Sorrah. She could deny their bond, he could too for his own reasons, but denial did nothing to eradicate the absolute certainty that she was created explicitly for him and him for her. The priests of old preached of such rare unions, his parents were the evidence of their speech.

And there lie the conflict of his heart.

Images of war, of his mother mourning the death of his father plagued his inner spirit. The thoughts of his uncle's ruthlessness, and the finality of his parents' deaths were enough to squash any sentiment or idea of ever completely belonging to anyone. Ever. He would fight what lie between them.

Even though he and his men had diligently strived to build the resistance, to train the rebellion army, fitting them for battle, the Kingswatch still far outnumbered them. Yet, he would never quit, never yield or surrender to Meserek's rule. His men held the same unrelenting resolve. He made sure of it. There was no room for question or doubt in the rebellion and certainly no room for pleasantries past a night or two with a lover.

What was wrong with him? He knew better than this.

Sorrah would be more than a lover, the feelings he had for her made that clear. And that's exactly why he couldn't take her as one, because he'd never have enough of her. The desire for her would never be quenched. He must remember that. He must remember his destiny was one of an early death. He knew that when he rose in the ranks of the resistance and became their leader. He was committed, bound and determined to overthrow Meserek and made a vow that he would die trying to rid Sorrah and Borak of their evil ruler. He'd come to terms with his inevitable death in this war a long time ago. He'd make no female a widow or bring mourning upon her. There was no place in his life for the complications of love.

However, his mouth, so close to the lips of the temptress before him, didn't seem to want to stay in line with his unwavering resolute.

"You know me as much as I allow. I have probably shown you too much of myself already, yet, you still believe I could be with a woman

133

after—"

He stopped himself in an attempt to suppress the overwhelming need for her swelling within.

He reminded himself that Meserek sent her. But what would he really do if she turned out to be a spy? What punishment could he give? What penalty would she pay? Even the thought of banishing her, having her thrown out of Sorrah and placing vast distance between them made him insane. It was too late for that now. He couldn't rid himself of her. He couldn't stop thinking of her, couldn't rip her out of his spirit or his soul. This bond between them was of the inseparable kind. He would continue to fight it but it seemed like the more he did, the stronger it became.

"Are you *jealous,* Fairhead?"

She shook her head but her eyes settled upon his lips before lifting to his, taking them prisoner.

"I... I... I am not jealous."

"No?"

"No. And you can wipe that smug look off your face. You're far too amused."

He leaned his body against her. "Yes, Fairhead. I am amused. And completely enthralled by you. You have the strangest effect on me. What have you done?"

She slowly shook her head in denial. "Nothing."

"You've bewitched me."

"No. I've done nothing. I haven't—"

His lips involuntarily twitched.

"Oh. You're making fun of me, is that it?"

Appearing wounded she turned her face from him, trying to get away.

He blocked her. Again.

"Stop. Let me go."

Never. "I can't."

*****

Was he playing some sort of game with her, toying with her emotions or just another curious man who would leave after quenching his desire?

Sorrah felt the same way he did, bewitched by some unseen force, as if she were held captive by an unbreakable spell. This was all too much. She was cold, wet and weary, and on the verge of dispensing yet another humiliating downpour of tears but she forced them back with unwavering determination. Treacherously, one or two tears slipped past her internal forces, her diligence weakening from all she'd gone through.

Rohen remained within inches of her mouth. She couldn't seem to figure out if she was the one edging closer or if he was. She wanted to leave, but at the same time, wanted to stay and taste him, be with him, let him hold and comfort her. God, she couldn't seem to gain full control over herself.

Like usual, built up anxiety demanded she spew out the first nonsensical thing that came to mind. "I'm not your enemy. I'm not a spy," she said, staring at his lips. *What did I just say? Way to kiss-block, Sorrah.*

As if mentioning the 'spy thing' wouldn't be the angel-of-death to the pending kiss. And sure enough, death's sickle appeared, determined to kill the fire, burning between them.

Rohen lowered his gaze. He clenched his jaw, his features tensing as he seemed to place a guard back over his heart. It was an attribute of his that she'd picked up on right away. He struggled with allowing people to get too close. Apparently they had that in common.

He started to back away, distancing himself, clearly, in his mind, he was having second thoughts about kissing her. And that bothered her. A lot. She immediately took a step forward and placed her hands on each side of his face, stopping him. His eyes instantly captured hers, shock over her bold move evident on his face.

"Careful, Fairhead. You tread on dangerous ground."

The moment her hands made contact with his skin, an intense hunger rose to the forefront. Her face flushed, her mind swam with sensuous thoughts. She had instinctively reacted to his withdrawal, not being able to stand the thought of him walking away. It was irritating that she needed him, wanted him and in more ways than one.

Exhausted from taking this journey and mission on by herself and from enduring loneliness year after year, she felt her strength falter. She was so tired of never having anyone in her life who truly gave a damn about her.

She scanned his face. "Don't—please don't leave—don't—"

He covered her lips with his, stealing her words, devouring her senses and kissing her like she'd never been kissed before. His passion spoke of more than lust but of intense possessiveness, and she never wanted to be taken, never wanted to completely belong to someone so much. Not like this. This was an intensity unlike anything she'd ever known and like a plant neglected of water, she'd soak up everything he offered.

Their tongues met and tangled together with a fervor that inflamed her spirit, fueling a throaty moan and igniting a great fire.

Their clothes were soaked, clinging to their bodies, the wet material a slippery barrier between them. But still they wrapped their arms around each other as if holding and clutching onto something they knew wouldn't last, knew was but a fleeting moment, because that's what happens to these spontaneous and desirous acts, they come in like thunder and leave much the same way, scorching their victims like a lightning strike.

Nothing lasts forever, so she'd learned from her past, but she was going to absorb every shred, every ounce of these precious few moments with him. Forever be damned.

Chapter seventeen

Had he lost his mind? Sorrah was a spy and that fact should be clearer than ever before but something primal snapped with the magnificence of her flavor. She tasted as sweet and delicious as nectar gifted from the gods themselves.

He took a firm hold of her shoulders and pushed away before taking a few steps back. The departure was numbing, the loss of her warmth terrifying. Lifting the back of his hand to his lips, he wiped, unsuccessfully removing the taste of her kiss, a kiss he'd not soon forget, perhaps, not ever.

Her expression went from hurt to anger and instantly he regretted his abrupt actions. What she must be thinking. She most likely assumed he didn't like the kiss but nothing was farther from the truth. He'd only meant to stop his mind from spinning and stifle the need to devour her, ease her down to the cave floor and sink inside her. But stopping the whirlwind in his mind was an impossibility while her lingering scent drove him to madness and her delectable taste was frozen in state on his lips and in his mouth.

Now that he'd gotten a true taste of her, nothing would erase the want and yearning for more of her. What had he done?

He deliberately withheld any clarification of his actions. Offered no explanation. Better she think badly of him. Better for them not to act further on their passion. There was no time, no place for the two of them.

"You will ride with me."

"Ride? To where?"

"You have to ask? Back to Castlemore."

"Back to Castlemore? No! I will not go back there. I'm going to Bethesda."

He stepped closer to her and she stiffened, raising her chin defiantly.

"You. Are. Coming. With. Me." He clipped out each word. *You are mine.* He pointed nowhere in particular. "Those vagrants you came up against? They are the Bervous and have grown in numbers, but they aren't the only dangers in these mountains. If they don't get to you, you must realize the Tarrigen would reach you by nightfall. Your attempts to reach Bethesda are futile."

He could see she didn't fully believe him. "You are so headstrong! I speak the truth, Fairhead!"

"The Tarrigen?"

"You're going to stand here and tell me that you don't know about the Tarrigen? How far are you willing to take this?" *She doesn't trust me.*

"Tell me about them. These Tarrigen."

"Enough! Better you admit your deceit now and beg for forgiveness. You have my protection. I give you my word."

She neither offered argument or an apology.

"Why do you continue with this? You know that I will protect you from Meserek."

She folded her arms and tilted her head to the side as if stubbornly waiting for him to answer.

He grunted in disapproval. "Fine. I'll give you another lesson. The Tarrigen are predators. There are only two of them but they are deadly creatures that have existed here in the mountains of Sorrah for a very long time. They come out at night, flying high above the mountainous terrain in search of any living thing to feast upon."

He slowly moved around her as he continued to speak.

"They circle their quarry and with their mighty talons, pierce their prey's flesh, relishing in the sweet scent of their blood. They don't dig in quickly but tauntingly play with their meal before sinking their sharp teeth into their victims' bellies—" He lifted his hand in front of her and snapped it into a tight fist before continuing, "devouring them up then licking the ground with their coarse tongues until every last drop is consumed."

Sorrah's eyes widened and she swallowed deeply, clearly shocked by what he had told her. Did she really not know of the creatures?

"I know what you're doing. You are trying to scare me."

"No! I'm trying to warn you! There is a big difference!"

"If these creatures... these Tarrigen, are so vicious and deadly, why haven't they devoured all people then? Wiped them out of existence? It sounds like they've had the time to do it."

He returned in front of her, fixated on her beauty as always. Her enormous eyes were wide and bright, her yellow hair nearly glowed even through the muck on it, and her lips continued to call to him, beckoning his own. But still he fought the ever-growing desire for her.

"And eliminate their food supply? No. They allow reproduction so they can continue to thrive. They remain in these mountains only, existing at the highest peaks, making large caves their home. Some believe they are the Sandrin priests I told you about. Transformed, cursed and trapped in these mountains for disobeying the gods and leaving the sanctuary of the castle. Maybe, a spell was cast upon them by... *druids*. Relatives of yours."

Sorrah shot him an annoyed look. "Funny."

"I'm not trying to be funny, Fairhead. I'm trying to get through that willful head of yours. You do not belong traveling in these mountains—"

She turned her face away. "Well... I really don't *belong* anywhere," she muttered. "Never have."

"What did you say?"

He heard what she said, but wanted to hear it again and ask why, more importantly, who. Who could have made her feel this way? Could that be what Meserek had over her? Family?

Even if his thoughts were wrong and Meserek had nothing to do with it, anger burned within at the thought of anyone neglecting her. Desertion, abandonment was, at times, the worse kind of abuse, leaving a victim lost and alone. How was it possible that this beautiful female, full of wonder and passion... How was she ever made to feel this way?

He wanted to scream to her right then and there, 'you belong right here! You belong with me! You belong *to* me! I will protect you and I will never leave you.' But how could he make her a promise he wasn't sure he could keep? Instead, he choked down the words, keeping the barricade in front of his calloused heart upright and secure. While triumph raged in his insistent mind, sounds of sorrow cried out from his damaged spirit.

She shook her head dismissively and worried her bottom lip. "Never mind. It's not important."

It's important to me, he silently answered. *You are important to me.*

"If I am a witch or a spy, as you say, then let me go now while there is still light."

He shook his head no. He couldn't allow that. "You haven't been listening."

"Yes, I have but hear me out. You can follow me to see where I go. I guarantee you'd be following me to Bethesda, not to the Kingswatch and definitely not to Meserek."

"No."

"Fine."

She edged toward the opening of the cave and before he could grab her, she bolted outside into the rain.

"Sorrah!" he thundered.

He quickly gained on her as she ran toward the path leading across to another rock formation, only she veered toward a cliff. He didn't want to hurt her but he'd do whatever was needed to save her from herself. She clearly did not know the terrain, the dangers, the shifts the mountains made. Just as the thought entered his mind, he felt the mountainside tremble. Perfect.

He glanced to the sky as he called to her again, "Sorrah! Stop!"

She listened this time, turning to face him as her body shook from the motion of the ground.

"Wh... wh... what's happening?"

"It's the Aurora Shievitous."

She looked confused. "The shift of the firmament."

Her look was genuine but how could that be? She should know about the Aurora. The same time every day, the two moons of Aaru provoked a gravitational pull and subsequent shift in the firmament which was predominantly felt in the mountains. It had always been so from the beginning of time. She didn't seem to know of the Bervous, the creatures, and now this. Could it be that she'd been telling him the truth all along?

Doubt that she was indeed a spy filled him. He hated this. Hated how he couldn't seem to figure her out.

She was slowly backing up, taking one step at a time. He stopped moving toward her, not wanting her to continue to move back.

"Fairhead, you must listen to me!" he yelled loudly above the rain. "Do not step back any more. The mountains are moving and you *will* fall." *Gods, do not let her fall.*

As if his words of caution provoked her to do so, she looked behind her just as the ground shifted again.

Rohen thrust his body forward to catch her but he was too late, landing hard on the ground as she dropped out of sight, sliding with the mud and broken rock down the side of the mountain, taking his next breath and heart with her.

*****

The treetops whipped by Sorrah as she continued to fall at a frightful speed but her mind slowed as numerous thoughts plague her all at once.

Why hadn't she listened to Rohen's warning? He was right. She was stubborn and headstrong and had reflexively looked at the danger. Maybe that was why acrophobic people who were told not to look down, inevitably did exactly that... just before losing their footing and falling.

She'd always been that way. As soon as someone, like Tommy, the boy who lived at the farm not too far from where she grew up, told her not to follow him, she did. He was crossing old man Henry's property to get to the pond and she had to follow him.

She wasn't sure why, in this most troublesome circumstance Tommy came to her mind. He'd been her only friend in the early years. In most years. Maybe ever. Could it be the reason why she never got very close to anyone in grade school or high school? Maybe. Maybe her experience with Tommy had a lot to do with why she kept to herself.

Tommy was two years older than her and they'd spent two glorious fun-filled summers together. His parents were divorced and each summer he came to stay at his father's farm. The two of them were inseparable but not as invincible as they once thought as they hung like monkeys from the highest tree limbs they could find. He'd taught her many things like how to climb trees, how to catapult your body off a rope into the deepest part of the pond and after he died, he'd taught her about death. He was the first boy she ever loved and he'd left her. Just like her mother had.

She was an infant when her mother died and of course remembered nothing about her. Not a lingering scent. Not the faintest of image. Later in life, her absence was felt more clearly, especially when Kaye wasn't there for her. Ever.

She closed her eyes and thought about her mother, her journal, and the letters she'd written. At least she had something. She'd been a wanderer and alone her twenty odd years but was she also destined to die alone, without ever experiencing the kind of love she'd only dreamed of having one day? An image of Rohen brushed through her mind and her lips turned up in a smile. She *had* experienced it. Even a little.

Thank you God or gods. Whoever is listening. Her life had been no 'Little House on the Prairie,' but it didn't make sense to seem ungrateful. Not in the end.

Her eyes flew open as her body unexpectedly veered off to the right, dangerously close to the trunk of an enormous pine tree. The branches of the tree, shifted, elongated beneath her as if reaching out for her, catching her.

Must be a ponderosa pine, she thought, remembering reading about a huge ponderosa pine tree somewhere in Oregon. Many came to see the ancient tree, believing it mysteriously relinquished its life flowing essence to those who were worthy of receiving it.

Her body broke through numerous branches but the speed of her fall slowed as the limbs continued to move and shift beneath her and, if she wasn't hallucinating, forming a cradle of sorts. The amount of limbs increased at a rapid pace, taking on her weight with ease. Thanks to the now thick shield of protection, her body finally stopped its whirlwind descent. She was cocooned inside at least a hundred branches and surrounded by thousands of brilliant green pine needles. The needles were strangely soft and comforting. She was safe and protected in the boughs of the pine tree.

The tumbling rock, which had followed her down the mudslide, hit the top of the barrier of the branches, but nothing made its way inside to her. When the pummeling of rocks finally stopped, the branches opened, stretching their shielding limbs wide.

She lay still, her heart racing. "Well, that was something," she muttered.

Noticing the rain had finally ended, she gazed upon the gorgeous teal blue sky which held two faint moons and a flaming sun in suspension.

"You truly are one beautiful sky. And I cannot believe I survived to see you again," she said, overwhelmed that she hadn't fallen off a mountain to her death.

In her excitement and unbelief, she shifted, poking her foot out between some of the branches. As if the limbs were fearful of her breaking through and falling again, they began to move beneath her. Nervous and astonished, she pulled her foot back, watching the foliage cover the hole where her foot had been.

"It's helping me." Her eyes widened as she watched the tree adjust around her as if it were filled with an enchantment. "Wait. The *tree* is helping me?"

Just like the event with the birds, she wasn't sure her mind wasn't playing tricks on her. But the more she thought about it, the more she recalled how the branches wondrously appeared and captured her in their net of safety. "It was real. I know what I saw."

This ginormous tree assisted her. It had reached out and caught her.

"Thank you," she murmured. It only seemed fitting to express her gratefulness.

After what seemed like only minutes, she heard Rohen's voice from below. He must have climbed down the mountain the moment she left his sight. How long have I been here? Time was still a blur.

"Sorrah!" he called up to her.

How long had he been down there? Had he seen what the tree did?

"I'm all right," she answered, turning her head to peer through a small gap between the limbs. She put her hand through some branches and waved then quickly pulled it back in and watched in awe as the pine needles covered the hole up.

"Good," he called up to her. "Now get down here so I can throttle you!"

His words caused the strangest flutter in her stomach.

She poked her face through the limbs again.

"Really? Do you even know any kind words?" she asked loudly. "I just escaped death!" She watched him place his arms across his chest

143

and shake his head. He didn't seem to be paying attention to anything she said.

He started for the tree. He was coming after her. The thought made her smile and a soft chuckle escaped her. He was climbing well, but not as fast as she could of course. He apparently realized that she was in no hurry to come down to him. But really… was it necessary for him to come after her? If she wanted to climb down from the surprisingly alive, in a Lord of the Rings sort of way, tree, she could manage it by herself.

She watched Rohen climb from limb to limb then noticed Sevin and Demetri standing on the ground below her, smirking. Apparently they hadn't climbed down from the mountain as fast as Rohen had.

Whatever, she thought, turning to look at the sky again. Why should she be in any hurry? Rohen was only going to take her back to Castlemore, and she'd be no closer to getting to Bethesda or her brother.

"Oh, yes by all means, let me hurry down there so you can scowl and thunder at me with your," she deepened her voice and spoke mockingly as she continued, "sea captain-voice or pierce my retinas with your angry alpha-wolf eyes. Maybe… I'll just stay right up here with my new friend Mister Tree…" she muttered on.

With a loud crack, an area of the branches suddenly broke apart.

"Ahhh!" she screamed, seeing Rohen appear with a reprimanding frown on his face.

"Alpha-wolf eyes?"

Chapter eighteen

Rohen rode his horse toward Castlemore with Sorrah sitting across his lap and a blanket he was thankful he remembered to pack in his satchel, snugly around her. His men followed closely behind on their horses while pulling the horse Sorrah had taken from the stables. There was no way she could've rode the horse back herself. She was exhausted and besides, he wasn't going to let go of her anytime soon. With trembling hands he hoped she didn't notice, he'd pulled her against his body for warmth and tied the blanket around his back. He had an undeniable need to touch her and repeatedly assure himself that she was all right. He'd continue to do so until he was satisfied or until his nerves calmed down, which at this rate might take days.

After watching her fall off the cliff of that gods-forsaken mountain, his heart had nearly stopped and continued, even now, to pound hard in his chest. How she survived such a fall was nothing short of a miracle. Truly the gods had found favor in keeping her alive, and who was he to question the gods? Actually, he did question them more often than not.

His life had changed drastically, turned upside down, by the recent turn of events. Sorrah had swept into his life and quite possibly altered it forever. More like catapulted into his life from out of thin air. Since the very first time he'd laid eyes on her, he thought of little else than to be near her, hear more of her wild stories, see more of her animated expressions and hear her speak words and phrases he had never heard before. His life would never be the same and he didn't want it to be. Besides, it wasn't like he could return to his daily schedule of recruiting and training.

He glanced to his shoulder where she peacefully lay. She'd fallen asleep so quickly after getting as comfortable as she could in his lap. *She looks so calm and innocent when asleep.* He knew how different she was awake. The thought made him smile. She was fiery and vivacious.

She destroys me, he thought. How was she able to tear down his guard so easily?

Earlier, he'd forgone his temper and kissed her. She'd reached out to him, touched him, and his restraint snapped. He shook his head in disbelief and briefly smiled in sweet remembrance. The desire to kiss her again and more flared within him.

She genuinely didn't know about things here. The mountain men, the creatures, the shift in the firmament. Not many could deceive him and he highly doubted she was the exception.

You may just be telling me the truth, Fairhead, he mused, glancing down at her again.

The way the trees reached out as if they recognized her was incredible. Deep down he never really believed like others did, never had the kind of faith they held. But today, he had to rethink much because surely the gods intervened on Sorrah's behalf. But why?

Little by little his faith was returning. He hadn't truly trusted in the gods since he was a young boy and his father taught him things about spirituality. One lesson was the teaching of trees. If he hadn't seen them move beneath Sorrah, he might not have ever believed in their enchantment and the gods' use of them.

He recalled how honest-to-goodness surprised she was by so many things. She was in awe over the forest and marveled on and on regarding the size of the trees, their color, how many of them there were and more. She'd even touched the trunks and giggled, swearing she felt the tremble of singing beneath her fingers.

After hearing ancient stories of such happenings, he'd tried to feel the same thing, but never did. Sorrah had behaved as if it were the first time she'd ever seen Silvermist Forest. And just how could that be? Silvermist was enormous and span regions far beyond Sorrah. Much of the world of Aaru was covered with forests just as lively and mystical as Silvermist. After all, trees in the world of Aaru were considered more than a growth by which wind wrestled and filtered through, but were fruitful entities to be respected and revered, symbols of life and set apart by the gods for their use.

Her reaction had been real. He'd bet his life on it. His beautiful Fairhead may be stubborn, outspoken and peculiar but she was no charlatan.

He took a deep breath and exhaled harshly, deciding right then and there to stop looking for deceit in her and simply trust her. Believe her. The best he knew how.

He shifted his eyes to the path in front of them, then back to her once more.

"What are you looking at?" she said quietly, opening her eyes.

With his mouth closed, he smiled at the sound of her sexy, raspy voice and how her blue eyes shined up from her dirty face. She was an adorable sight to behold and excited him like none other.

"What am I looking at? Well, I'm looking at *you,* Fairhead."

She smiled back at him and his heart turned over. *What she does to me.*

"What's changed?" she asked suspiciously. Her eyes drifted across his face.

"Changed? Hmm, I can see you still don't trust me. I'm wounded."

"Uh huh." She narrowed her eyes. "What are you up to?"

"Nothing. I've decided to believe you. I will help you, Fairhead."

"You have? You will?" she said excitedly, bumping the top her head into his chin as she repositioned herself. She looked beyond the horse's head. "But we are still on the way back to Castlemore?"

"Yes. You need to rest. You need food. We all could use a bath. And my men and I will need a day to figure the best route to Bethesda and devise a plan to get inside the prison and find your brother."

Sorrah smiled widely and threw her arms around his neck, hugging him. "Oh, thank you, Rohen. Thank you!"

He couldn't help but smile at her pleasure. Making her happy felt good. Right.

They continued on the path carrying on conversation about both of their worlds and bits about their personal lives.

"You have another question you hesitate to ask."

"How can you tell?"

"You tug on your bottom lip and your eyes, they drift away to an unknown place. If I dare ask what you think about in those moments, I would likely hear the word nothing."

He could tell by the surprised look on her face that his assessment

147

was accurate.

"My mind is prone to wander. Yes. Sometimes I feel as if I've lived a hundred different lives... but here in this world with you I wonder if I've ever really lived at all."

He smiled weakly. His own spirit feeling quite the same way until she entered his life. "Is there a question on your mind, Fairhead?"

"What is your age?"

He chuckled. Her question unexpected.

"Will you tell me your age first?" he asked.

"I am twenty six. Now you."

"Twenty six? How long do—"

"Rohen!"

"I am two hundred and thirty eight."

Sorrah's mouth fell open. "That's impossible. You don't look a day older than thirty."

"Thirty? I'd look like a boy." He sighed. "But if I'm to believe you fully, Fairhead, then I would have to concede that nothing is impossible. You of all people should believe this."

She stared down in deep thought. "How long does the average person in Aaru live?"

"We've had females who exceed nine hundred eons. But it is rare. Typical life expectancy for a male is eight hundred and ten. For females, the number is slightly longer."

"Wow. How long have you looked the age you are now?"

"For a long time. Clearly we age differently. How would someone from where you are look if he were my age?"

"Ash."

He smiled. "Different. Yes."

"The times of our worlds must not sync. Maybe it even alters when passing through the gateway," she said quietly as if trying to figure it out.

"For now, let's concern ourselves with the present. Yes?"

Sorrah nodded, and Rohen gave her a gentle squeeze.

"To the west!" Sevin yelled, unsheathing his sword and riding to the side of Rohen.

Rohen pulled back the reins of his horse and veered to the right behind a large boulder. He set Sorrah on her feet before dismounting.

"Stay behind this rock. No matter what you hear or see, do not move. Understand?"

Sorrah nodded.

Sevin, Rohen, and the other brave men of the rebellion, stood in a circle with their swords drawn, ready for anything.

Six men of the Kingswatch charged in, attacking. They hadn't stopped to inquire anything. They seemingly recognized Rohen and his men right away.

Rohen raised his sword, the blade connecting with his opponent. He swiftly swung left then right, focusing on the top area of the soldier's blade, hoping to dislodge it from his enemy's hand.

This particular soldier was skilled but Rohen could tell his training had to come from schooling of nobility, whereas, his own had come from raw teachings of the craft.

He swung around and gained in force, knocking the sword from the soldier's hand. The knight stumbled back as Rohen descended upon him.

He glanced to Sorrah, pleased she had obeyed him. Her eyes were observing the fighting men but met his briefly. Even in the muddy conditions, his men seemed to have the battle under control.

"Tell me, Kingswatch, did you come searching for us?"

"I'll tell you nothing, Rebel! King Meserek will be rid of you all soon. His army has a far greater number than you'll ever have, Borak traitor."

The man spit on the ground at Rohen's feet. Imbecile.

"The false king may have blind followers and have the allegiance of murderers but calloused hearts and bloodied hands is all that the Kingswatch will ever be. You fight without honor and enforce laws created by a wicked leader. What the rebellion army may lack in number, we make up for in skill and decency."

Rohen lifted his hands, his blade coming off the man. "As you can see by how quickly we've overthrown you."

In the second he'd raised the tip of his blade from the enemy's chest; the man had taken out a dagger and moved toward Rohen.

"Rohen!" Sorrah yelled.

Rohen's heart sank, fearing she was in danger. He quickly turned her direction and the soldier took full advantage of the distraction,

149

lunging toward him with his weapon.

"Behind you!" she cried.

Rohen spun around just in time to stop the man from making contact with his gut. He shoved the soldier's arm away and buried his blade into the man's chest. The soldier dropped the dagger and fell to the ground, blood pouring from the wound.

No kill was ever easy, a person's life ought not to be thought of as inconsequential but the fact remained that this Kingswatch soldier had given him no choice.

The small battle yielded no rebellion casualties and soon they were back on their horses and heading to Castlemore once more.

Sorrah settled herself on his lap. "I'm sorry for distracting you, but I saw the man grab for his weapon and—" She started to say but he didn't let her finish.

"I should not have lifted my blade off of him for even a second. It was my mistake. I underestimated my opponent."

He hadn't done something like that in a very long time. His mind had been too absorbed by all that had happened. By her. "And you cannot help from distracting me, Fairhead, even when you do not speak."

He tucked the blanket back around her as they once more set out on the path back home.

When they reached the gates of Castlemore, many were gathered, seemingly awaiting their arrival. News of Sorrah's quick departure surely spread. Many, believing Sorrah a spy, wouldn't be concerned so much with her welfare, only that she might've given the enemy their exact whereabouts and spoke of weaknesses in the rebellion camp. Many would fear that Meserek in turn would dispatch an army of the Kingswatch to demolish their homes or worse, kill them all.

They'd assume, from past experiences, Rohen and his men would find Foley and silence him before he could make it to Sandrin. Sorrah... well, it was likely that the people of Castlemore eagerly waited to hear of her demise. They clearly underestimated her ability to survive.

Rohen had too.

*****

"They hate me," Sorrah said, climbing down from Rohen's horse.

150

"You escaped them."

"And now they are certain I am a spy."

"Oh, you were always a spy, as far as they were concerned. Your escape only confirmed their belief of your deceit, I'm afraid. News of your sudden appearance in the pond spread quickly. They've always believed you a spy, a sorcerer, or daft."

Sorrah didn't miss the slightly amused look on his face.

"You're enjoying this," she told him.

They walked through the gates and started for the castle.

He turned, taking her by the shoulders. "Make no mistake, Fairhead, there are those who would disregard my orders and take it upon themselves to rid Castlemore of a spy if they believed their families were in jeopardy. I've told you that I will help you but do not betray me or defy me again. You will obey my every word from this moment on."

She lifted her eyebrows in question.

He sighed. "You are the most stubborn female."

She opened her mouth to speak but his fingers landed on her lips stopping her speech and drawing her attention to the torment in his eyes.

"Shh. I can see that I—" He stopped talking.

His tender touch rendered her speechless. Well, almost.

"I want to—" Her lips moved beneath his fingers.

"Hmm?" he muttered before his jaw muscle did that flex-thing again that now drove her insane but in a good way... That's if there is a good crazy.

His eyes were intensely focused, for the most part, on her mouth. He moved his fingers, but not withdrawing them, skimming them across her bottom lip, making it nearly impossible for her to think straight.

Background noise suddenly silenced. Her thoughts were overtaken with images of his touch, his kiss, his consumption. Sensations rocked her as before when he'd kissed her.

Why... how did Rohen have this astounding effect on her?

He swallowed deeply. "You will listen to me, for your own protection," he said, abruptly removing his fingers and scanning the immediate area. He had to notice the many eyes watching them and no doubt silently questioning what was going on between them.

Still, she resisted pouting from the absence of his touch.

With a look of frustration, Rohen took a few steps back and placed his hand over his mouth, sliding it over his chin and off his face.

Sounds returned full force and people seemed to be everywhere, hovering and crowding to such an extent that chaos broke free in Sorrah's mind. She was overwhelmed, feeling like a trapped animal, surrounded by strangers who probably wanted to poke and hit her with a giant stick or something.

She quickly moved forward, more anxious than ever to get inside and to the safety of her room. She was tired, hungry, and needed a bath to rid herself of the mud caked on her and the grime others figuratively placed on her with their frowns.

If Rohen really did believe her story, he'd have to sell it to these people. But if he openly displayed affection toward her, favored her, would they trust his judgment? Probably not. Her presence placed the entire rebellion at risk.

She understood Rohen's discretion but didn't have to like it. Between them was more than a mere mutual attraction, at least she felt that way. However, she'd been wrong before.

"I want to leave as soon as possible," she said, walking briskly ahead.

"I know you do," Rohen answered.

She believed he did. Like before, he'd noticed how others treated her and read the change in her with pinpoint accuracy.

They entered the castle and stopped when they saw Gerta standing in the foyer with her hands on her hips.

"Master Rohen."

"Gerta."

Sorrah remained silent and averted her eyes, not wanting a confrontation. She couldn't handle it right now.

"I was told you were headin' back. A bath has been set in your room."

"And Sorrah's room?" Rohen asked, using her given name and not the nickname he had for her. She liked the note of tease accompanying his voice when he called her Fairhead. It was sarcastic in an enduring sort of way, but the way he said Sorrah spoke of passion and strength.

The next time he said her name, she hoped it would be directly to her, and accompanied with another kiss.

"As you requested she is set in the room adjacent to yours. And yes, a bath is ready there as well. I'll have some supper on the table soon."

"Good. Thank you, Gerta."

Gerta nodded and stepped in front of Sorrah.

Sorrah lowered her head but Gerta placed her fingers on her chin, lifting it. "The tears in your eyes canna be faked. I shall give ya' another chance. Go clean. You have duties in the kitchen."

Gerta walked to where Miranda the mole-lady stood with other workers and began dispensing orders.

What had she really expected from the housekeeper? She knew Gerta had a tough exterior but seemed to have a good heart. Sorrah hated that she let the women down. She couldn't help but think of her mother and how disappointed she must be in her fruitless efforts and meager results thus far. She hadn't gotten very far in Sorrah and was no closer to her brother. But thanks to Rohen's new found trust, things were looking up.

She walked to the staircase without looking at anyone else, even at Rohen who seemed to be in conversation with his men. At least *he* believed her now. Having the sea captain on her side was a definite plus and she was stronger because of it. With renewed fervor she took to the stairs with greater purpose. She'd soak in a tub of warm bath water and think about the future. A future which now held greater promise.

From the top of the stairs she glanced back to Rohen, hoping she had him on her side for a very long time. His touch and kiss had her hoping for even more. There was something special between them, something she could no longer deny. She may not have found her brother yet, but she just might have stumbled upon something else here in this surreal world. Something tangible… Something that looked and felt an awful lot like love.

She entered her room which was just as large and extravagant as the Marseilles room. She glanced at the closed door separating her and Rohen's rooms. As if on cue, she heard him enter his room and close his heavy door.

She began disrobing and wondered if he were doing the same. Leaning down, she felt the tepid water which welcomed her. She preferred her bath to be a lot warmer but didn't mind as she slipped her naked body inside, keeping her back to the main door of her room. She washed herself thoroughly, including her hair, and before the water could become any cooler, leaned her head back to relax.

She closed her eyes, feeling herself on the edge of sleep. Moments later she heard the sound of the main door to her room unexpectedly open.

"What in the—" she said, sitting straight up and turning her eyes to the door behind her. For a split second she was happy her bare breasts were facing the opposite way. Then she remembered her birthmark on the uppermost part of her back, high near her shoulder. The mark which was no longer concealed by clothing.

"I knew it!" Miranda hollered, standing behind Sorrah with a huge towel in her hand. "There'll be no denying it now, Spy!"

Miranda ran out the door, leaving it wide open as she flew out into the hallway, taking the towel with her.

Sorrah glanced frantically around the room, searching for dry clothes. She heard Miranda pound on Rohen's door. She probably didn't want to use the connecting door inside because she was going to tell Rohen of her mark. A mark which was forbidden here. A birthmark could mean she was cursed by the gods but more than that, her symbol represented the Borak people. How could her story hold up when she was branded with such a mark?

Rohen would feel betrayed. Again.

She bolted out of the basin and ran to the bed where her white cotton nightgown lay and quickly slipped it over her wet body. Instantly, the soft material began to soak up the water from off her. She only had time enough to turn before the door between her and Rohen's room flew open.

Chapter nineteen

"Leave us!" Rohen roared to Miranda who had lingered behind with a haughty and curious expression. At Rohen's command the ornery housekeeper immediately high-tailed it out of the room, closing Sorrah's door behind her but not before shooting her a wicked smirk over her shoulder.

Rohen's hair was wet; his clothing barely on him and the pain in his eyes was enough to choke her words.

"I can exp—" Sorrah began but was stopped.

"Do not!"

He wore a savage expression but Sorrah could see the betrayed look beneath the anger. She'd hurt him by keeping her birthmark from him. Half-truths were still full lies.

He took one step toward her and she took one step back toward the bed.

His fists were clutched at his sides, his jaw set and his nostrils flared, but even through the rage she sensed his passion. His eyes fell upon her breasts, and she knew what he saw. Her wet gown clung to her bare body in many areas, showing much of her shape and leaving little to the imagination.

With long, hard strides he reached her, grabbed a hold of her shoulders and gently shook her.

"I told you not to betray me!"

The intensity on his face with his furrowed brows and stiff lips, matched his immense presence over her.

She was nearly in tears and helpless to prevent her jaw from quivering.

"Rohen. Rohen, I didn't..."

"No. No more!" he bellowed before gripping her shoulders a bit harder and taking her lips in a punishing kiss, a kiss that nearly broke her heart in two. A nip of pain registered as he continued to kiss her but quickly melted away as his touch softened and passion ignited between

155

them, throwing her body into a fever pitch. Without a doubt she knew he was chastising her, giving her a taste of what could have been.

"How far," he murmured against her mouth before sliding his lips to her neck and sucking on her skin, leaving a trail of heat as he moved to another spot and then another. His arms came around her and within seconds she was pinned against the corner post of her bed.

She moaned, her body surrendering to the desire, as he lifted her off the floor and pressed himself against her core. His muscles were tense, his body hard and aroused. He moved as a man with deliberate intention but beneath his touch were subtle hints of malice and inner torment. She wanted things to happen between them, but not like this, not while he believed her a betrayer.

"Please, Rohen—"

He placed her down so her feet touched the floor and pulled the back of her hair, lifting her face to meet his.

"You would've taken to my bed... taken me inside of you... all in the name of Meserek."

He kissed her hard once more, and an abyss of tears broke free, flowing down her face, his anguish a spear to her heart. He must have felt the evidence of her weeping on his face. He broke apart only far enough to shove her nightgown off her shoulder, revealing the mark on the uppermost part of her back. The circle with two outer ones, the symbol of Borak, the mark she'd had since birth.

"You are filled with deceit," he chided, pushing himself away from her. "And I have been played the fool."

"No—no—it's not what you think."

He shook his head. "What I think... *female,*" he said with guile, "What I *know* is that you are Borakien and somehow, somewhere, you received this mark. Meserek planted you here. Did he mark you so others would believe you favored by the gods? You know nothing of this world? Lies. All lies."

She shook her head no but words failed her. All hope seemed lost. He'd never believe her now. What a nightmare all of this had become.

Relinquishing all, she dropped to her knees, cupped her face and openly wept.

"Let's see what the gods think of you. Your tears will no longer work on me. Now stand and get dressed. You're coming with me."

She wiped her tears and rose.

"What do you mean? Go where?"

"Does it matter? You are now a prisoner. You will do as you are told!"

"Let me tell you—"

"No! Now get dressed or I will dress you myself."

"Then at least tell me where we're going, Rohen. Where are you taking me? What will you do to me?"

He huffed. *"Do* to you? You believe I'd hurt you? How many times will you question my honor?"

She knew he would never hurt her and could see how his own words of protectiveness betrayed his anger. He was trying so hard to guard his heart and she got the distinct impression he had valiantly done so his entire life.

"I will allow no harm to come to you."

She thought of what he'd said earlier about there being those at Castlemore who might want to harm her if they felt threatened.

He drifted his eyes over her face then slipped them down and away from her body. "It is true the people will be convinced of your treachery." He turned his face away. "No matter what I tell them," he muttered. He looked off into the distance with a look of deep thought.

"What did you say?"

He ignored her and began pacing the floor. He definitely looked like his wheels were turning a mile a minute.

"We must go to the cave and take our chances with the gods. You will not be able to lie to them."

"I thought you said people are forbidden to enter and are thought to die for going inside?"

"I don't fear death."

Coincidentally enough, she didn't either.

"Now get dressed."

He turned his back, allowing her privacy. She quickly pulled on a loose shirt, a pair of pants and boots. Silva provided much of her clothing and she was grateful.

Rohen was calmer now, she thought, but unnervingly so. Losing his trust so soon after gaining it, tore at her heart which made her realize just how important he'd become. He was gorgeous, honorable, and brave. A virile sea captain who had sailed his way straight into her heart.

If he wanted to go into the sacred cave then fine, she'd go. She'd go anywhere with him. She didn't buy into any of this superstitious stuff anyway. She wasn't from this world, didn't follow or believe in their gods. According to legend, the spirits of these gods existed inside the sacred caves. It was time she met these feared gods of Aaru. She could use some divine intervention right about now. Besides, part of her wanted to see the mysterious drawings on the wall. And if the stories were true and death found her, here in this land of her namesake? Well, she was glad not to have to die alone but alongside the one she loved. Loved? She and Rohen would have each other, an end before a real beginning, and just how tragic was that?

He led her by the elbow, down the steps of the castle, through the group which had gathered in the entryway. They parted, making it possible for her and Rohen to get out the front door but they followed closely behind.

She could no longer speak of her world, not here, for in the eyes of Rohen and these people, she was guilty. The Borakien symbol on her body had irrefutably marked her as someone familiar with this world. Her carelessness in exposing it was a mistake on her part to be sure. She had planned on telling Rohen about her mark... eventually. And after he proclaimed his belief in her, she'd thought to tell him soon. Their relationship had increasingly become more heated and she wasn't stupid. If they became intimate, he would see her mark. But things had happened so fast and now the opportunity to be forthcoming was lost.

How easily one event can alter things, she thought. No matter her intention, she'd blown it with Rohen. Big time.

She had gone her life never really fitting in anywhere, never belonging, but she never felt more like an outsider, a foreigner, than in this moment.

"I'm coming, you don't have to pull me!" she cried out.

He turned on her. "I'm not letting go of you! I'm not letting you out of my sight!"

Even though he spoke angrily, she couldn't help but be pleased by his choice of words. She didn't want him to let her go. Not ever.

There would never be a time she could reveal her feelings for him.

Not after this. In his eyes she was nothing more than a liar. But somewhere in the midst of all the madness, she'd fallen in love with the sea captain and even admired the wolf.

He turned his apparent frustration on the group behind them. "You are here to watch me kill her?"

A roar erupted among the people, a calling out in agreeance of her death. It was the most horrible sound she'd ever heard. The cries of pure unadulterated hatred.

"I will do no such thing!" Rohen hollered. "The gods will decide her fate."

And there it was, she decided, the real reason behind the trip to the cave. Her heart swelled. Rohen didn't believe in the gods curse, she could tell that the moment he told her of the tales, but he knew many others did believe it.

When the two of them came out of the cave, alive, the people would accept the gods' decision and she'd escape harm from the people of Castlemore. Rohen was trying to save her from anyone who might go against his orders and harm her. He was once again protecting her. He cared for her and knowing that, made her heart soar.

He softened the grip on her arm but his eyes stayed on the crowd. "We are going into the cave. Sevin is your leader should I not surv—return."

Sevin stepped forward from the crowd. His steel eyes shifted between Sorrah and Rohen.

"Rohen," he said. "You cannot go inside the cave."

"I don't fear the gods, brother. I trust them to make the right decision. They will tell us all if she speaks the truth. There is no other option. Should the gods destroy me and the fairhead, you know what to do."

Sevin nodded. "Then I accept nothing less than your survival, my brother, and will remain at the entrance, awaiting your safe return."

Rohen nodded and moved Sorrah forward. A few minutes later, he lifted a burning torch off a pedestal just inside the entrance to the cavern.

"Stay behind me," he told her, slipping his fingers down her arm to take her hand in his. He tenderly squeezed, confirming to her, his unrelenting protectiveness.

She knew in her heart that he couldn't possibly believe the gables of deaths and disfigurement regarding the cave. If he did, she would be far from there. All he has ever done was save her, care for her, comfort her. My God, maybe he even loved her.

She squeezed his hand in return and felt him stiffen then relax. She affected him. Her eyes welled with tears as hope renewed.

He used the light of the torch to see their way through the stark darkness and the many twists and turns.

There were no foul smells of mustiness or dampness, as one might expect from a cave. On the contrary, a crisp clean scent drifted to greet her, a prelude to the aroma of jasmine, lilac and honeysuckle that followed.

She tugged on Rohen's hand. "Where is that smell coming from?"

He turned. "What smell?"

She closed her eyes as he placed the torch above her. "The heavenly smell of flowers. Don't you smell that?"

She opened her eyes and instantly met his attentive gaze.

"You smell flowers in here?"

"Yes." She nodded. "Very much so."

She glanced down the cave floor.

"Oh, look… I don't remember seeing these a minute ago."

"You didn't see them, because they weren't there."

As if they had been deliberately scattered on the cave floor, fresh flowers and flower petals were beneath their feet and beyond, seeming to be paving their way.

"How beautiful and strange."

"Let's keep moving, the main cavern can't be far."

A glowing light shimmered in the distance. As they made their way closer, they saw a golden archway illuminating a particular area.

"It's a room," she uttered beneath her breath.

This place seemed vaguely familiar as if she'd dreamt it or read it in a fantasy book. Her stomach fluttered, giving way to her nerves.

Rohen placed the torch in an empty socket on the wall beside the arch, withdrew his sword and filled the doorway with his body as he scanned inside the room.

"This is it."

She maneuvered herself left then right, trying to see inside, but his massive body blocked her view.

"It's all right." He moved out of her way, allowing her to go in first. "Let's have a closer look."

Before entering, shivers which could only be described as spiritual flowed through her body. This was far from an ordinary room. There was something or someone worthy of humbleness in this place.

She bent down and removed her boots. It just seemed a fitting thing to do. The bottoms of her feet stepped upon the soft flower petals, eliminating any harshness from the gravelly ground. She entered the room solemnly, reverently.

Candles which burned in each corner of the room flickered before the flames swelled and abruptly soared higher. Flowers filled the space, lying on small rock tables and covering the floor.

"I didn't expect it to be so beautiful." Or did she? "Who lit these candles?" She skimmed her fingers over some of the flowers closest to her. "And put these flowers here?"

"Who indeed," Rohen answered.

"These drawings," she whispered, lifting her hand.

"Wait!" he shouted.

Her fingers had already begun to skim over the engravings which seemed to glow beneath her touch.

"What?" she asked Rohen who stood to her left staring at her.

"All who are in the world of Aaru, especially those of Sorrah and Borak know of the threat and of the tales. They know touching them could mean an instant death."

"But I didn't know this because I'm not—" She stopped herself, smiling half-heartedly and shrugging her shoulder as she continued to glide her fingers on the markings. "They really are masterfully carved and do you see how the renderings shimmer? So magical. So unique. But yet they are somewhat…"

"Somewhat, what?"

"Familiar. I've seen these somewhere before. Please tell me what they mean. I must know."

"I can only tell you of what I've learned from my father. Some of these, the tree of life, here…" he said, pointing to but not touching a large drawing of a tree. "As you came to see in the Silvermist forest, trees are full of life. They are a symbol of vitality and strength of life

161

itself."

He moved his finger over the limbs of the tree in the drawing but still didn't touch them. "You see how the branches here are intertwined, forming a circle, a representation of infinity, a life never-ending or possibly two lives. There has never been an absolute consensus on the interpretation.

"Infinity... I can see that. Everything is so detailed. The symbols, the branches. Every line and mark makes them appear alive. What are some of the interpretations?"

"There are those who believe this particular symbol is not only the life of two but of all life in general and how each of us are bound to the other since the beginning of time."

"That's an interesting one. Any others?"

"There are those of a more romantic variety, which say the first tree represents the prophetic king, bound forever with his queen, even after death."

Sorrah liked that interpretation best. As she skimmed over the branches, they shifted beneath her fingers, rising up and changing to three-dimensional. "They moved... changed. How is this possible?"

"I do not know."

"How extraordinary," he repeated, looking at her in awe. "Here." He pointed to more of the drawings but again, didn't touch them. "These next images are also part of the history of Sorrah and Borak. From what I've been taught, this depicts one mighty firmament, the land of Sorrah. Then see there, it splits into two separate lands. Over here represents the great castle in Sandrin and mountainous terrain."

"And these creatures?"

"Believed to be the Tarrigen. Of course, this part of the prophecy came true when they appeared in the mountains. They are the creatures I warned you about."

"Dragons," she stated because that was exactly what the beasts looked like. "Like the ones carved on the ends of the staircase in the castle."

"Drah... gons?"

"Yes."

She traced the drawing of the creatures and it moved beneath her fingers, lifting off the wall. She backtracked, moving back over the now three dimensional skin of the dragon.

"It's moving as if it were coming to life. How bizarre. It's like I can feel it breathing."

She moved to another drawing feeling a vibration. "This is trembling beneath my touch. And look, they've all started to glow even more brightly. What's happening? I can't seem to stop touching them. I can feel a vibration traveling into my body—Rohen—"

His arms were around her waist in seconds, pulling her back from the drawing and against his steel clad body. A despairing coldness settled over her. The gods didn't like the removal of her hand. She knew this without a doubt.

"No," she said, trying but failing to break free from his hold. She turned in his arms and reflexively placed her hands on each side of his face.

"Please, Rohen... you must allow me to continue, no matter how frightening things become. It's the only way you'll believe what I've been telling you. I also know that the gods have something here for me. I'm meant to be here."

After a few seconds, he conceded, releasing her. "I can only allow so much. I don't want you to be harmed. Proceed cautiously."

She nodded and moved closer to the wall, lifting her hands to the engravings while Rohen continued to tell her what he'd been taught the interpretation of the drawings were.

Sorrah swayed as another strange sensation, assaulted her. This one was much stronger, rocking her body. Before Rohen could insist on her stopping, she caught her footing and continued. "I'm all right. I'm supposed to be here. I've seen this... And this—"

"The symbol of Sorrah. The star."

"Yes," she muttered as she outlined the star. Beneath her fingers the star seemed to breathe, swelling up and back down while shimmering and glowing.

"How very odd. Magical."

She was mesmerized, completely enthralled with each detail. She stilled her fingers as the star moved, shifting to the right then back again. She could barely hear Rohen calling out to her in muffled tones. How long had she been standing there touching the star? Time had seemed to have stood still.

She turned to look at him, all the while keeping her fingers on the wall, fearing the loss of the magic.

Why does he look so panicked? she thought, before realizing a clear barrier stood between them.

Rohen was hitting the transparent wall, pounding on it hard with his fists but his efforts were in vain. The clear wall was impenetrable.

She shook her head.

"Stop. You'll only hurt yourself!" she yelled but he couldn't hear her. She lifted her hand, signaling him to stop. She knew she had to continue tracing the drawings, she had to finish, believing with all her heart that there was a message here in the caves, meant only for her. *Message? For me? Dear gods,* she thought, acknowledging, with great certainty, that a deity of multiple gods from this bizarre new world had a message for her.

A breeze came out of nowhere, rising to the force of a gale, whipping through her hair, carrying with it, a soft subtle voice which drifted calmly into her ears.

"Sorrah—"

Sorrah, turning to her left, saw an image of a woman, looking as if she was standing on a pedestal or platform.

"Mother?"

She knew with certainty that this was her mother. She'd only seen the picture from when her mother was young, the one with the mirror in the corner, but knew this woman was her.

Tears filled her eyes.

Her mother smiled but it was short-lived, her expression turning serious as she stared down at her. While moving her lips, speaking words Sorrah could not hear, she held a long white paper with drawings on it. The same drawings from the wall of the cave.

"I can't hear you!" Sorrah cried out in frustration.

She moved forward to touch her mother but her hand passed right through as if the image were a hologram.

Where was the volume? She needed to turn her mother's voice up so she could hear what she was saying. *Please, gods, turn it up, let me hear my mother.* The moment she silently uttered the plea, she could hear her mother's voice.

"One day, Sorrah, you will see these drawings, the drawings

marking your destiny. If you are seeing me now it is because you have made it to Sorrah and have entered one of the sacred caves. Nothing will hurt you here, in fact, quite the contrary. You have triggered this memory by touching one of the drawings along the wall which means you are well on your way to becoming very powerful. I was told of this future, of *your* future.

"War broke out and your father, King Zarek, insisted your brother and I be taken to safety in special chambers in the lower part of the castle. There were many people there, mostly noblemen. It was there that I spoke with a sweet woman, a Hendrin, druids of this world, her name was—"

Her mother's voice cracked and her eyes glazed over before shifting behind Sorrah.

Sorrah followed where her mother was looking, seeing Rohen standing behind the wall, his hands pressed against the now shimmering partition.

"I didn't think I would have this capability... it must be our druid heritage. Oh, Sorrah... he is a leader, strong and valiant. Your father would be so pleased."

"You can see him? You can see Rohen?" Sorrah asked but her mother couldn't hear her. In fact, her mother seemed to be speaking to Rohen now, and once again her mother's lips moved in silence.

Sorrah's curiosity flared. What could she possibly be saying to him? She shifted her eyes between her mother and Rohen. He seemed to be hearing her and even answering back. His lips turned up into a partial smile as he listened. He looked warmly at her mother then to her. His fingers splayed on the shield between them and his eyes filled with tears as he continued to stare.

"What? What is it, Rohen?"

After a minute or so, her mother's attention returned to Sorrah.

"I don't have much longer."

She closed her eyes briefly then murmured, "Rohen. I remember that name. Shay, the Hendrin I told you about, spoke of him." She glanced once more to Rohen. This time when she spoke, Sorrah could hear what she said. "Take care of my Sorrah. Take care of your queen. Keep her safe."

"Wait—what? Queen? That can't be true."

"You are special, Sorrah. Your mark will change but don't be afraid. It is, you are, the fulfillment of ancient prophecy. Kortah, this world, needs you to save it. Another great war is on the horizon and only you can prevent it from happening. Only you can unite Sorrah and Borak for good. It is your destiny. Their fate is in your hands. In you. In your heart. It is only the beginning. The beginning of the life you were truly meant to live. You belong here."

Sorrah swallowed deeply. It was as if deep down she'd always known Sorrah was her home. But to be the queen? To be the only one able to unite a people and keep them from war?

"Dear gods," she muttered suddenly feeling like Leia had just told her she was their only hope.

Her mother began to fade. "Be sure to touch every drawing my child. Find Marcus. Once you gain your powers, you will have an easier time locating him. You will sense his presence and he will in turn be able to sense yours. You both are connected forever. Give him a hug from me. Tell him I love him so very much. Our time has ended. Trust your heart, Sorrah. I love you."

Her mother was slowly drifting away, fading back into the surface of the wall.

"No! Wait! Don't leave! Don't leave me!" Sorrah reached out her hand, extending it to her mother as her mother outstretched her hand as well, seeming to see her in the here and now. Her mother smiled widely as the tips of their fingers connected momentarily, startling the both of them.

"There you are…" her mother said with tears flowing down her cheeks. "My gods. You are so beautiful. Sorrah—remember—Sorrah, remember once you step through, there is no going back. I wanted to so badly."

The truth of her mother's words hit her straight on. Her mother wasn't referring to returning to Earth but to Sorrah. Just as her mother's letter stated, once she'd entered the pond and returned to Earth through the mirror, she couldn't go back. Clearly, it was a decision she'd deeply regretted, and Sorrah made a mental note not to make the same mistake. No matter how tough things got here, no matter how crazy powers and being a queen sounded, she could never return to her former world. She meant to make her mother proud and face this, fulfill her purpose, finish this and live her life, however long that might be, right here in this place of her namesake.

Courage filled her.

"Goodbye, my baby girl," her mother said, fading farther and farther away, until there was nothing more of her. The bitter loss was indescribable.

"Mother!" Sorrah cried. "My mother."

Tears continued to flow. Her mother... believed in her. Loved her.

She spun around seeing Rohen, standing with a look of shock and awe on his face. She raised her hand to the clear partition between them and Rohen raised his hand to meet hers. Even with the pane separating them, a soft quiver was detected. No one stirred her like he did and in this mystical place, the bind between them was stronger than ever. She raised her lips in a closed-mouth smile. She wasn't sure how much he heard.

"Be careful." He mouthed the words to her.

Sorrah nodded, wiped her eyes and once more placed her fingers on the drawings in front of her. This place was truly special, sacred. She'd never believe otherwise from this day forward. Making her way around the room, she made certain to touch each drawing and tried her hardest to make sense of it, although the feat seemed impossible. She had much to learn. Some symbols she recognized from the drawing her mother showed her, others she recalled seeing carved into the wooden frame of the now infamous mirror.

And then she saw it. The symbol of Borak, the mark identical to the one on her skin.

She traced the outlining circles, feeling a vibration strumming low at first then gaining in intensity. The walls shook but still she left her hand on the wall, strangely unafraid.

A light shot out like a rocket from the Borakien symbol, traveling out from beneath her hand and between her fingers, rising and gathering into the center of the room. From the corner of her eye she saw another light, a beam streaming outward from the wall where the Sorrien star was glowing and projecting the same intense illumination.

Without warning, the two brilliant beams of light projected farther, colliding together high above before landing directly on her birthmark, setting her aglow. She was helpless to move as an invisible

167

power filled her body, rocking and shaking it, spiraling her out of control. On the verge of unconsciousness, she gave herself up, submitting to the gods and surrendering to her destiny, but it wasn't like she had much of a choice. She was completely and utterly taken over.

Remaining a steady stream of light on her and the wall, the beam ricocheted into all corners of the room, cascading down over the engravings, covering every square inch of the cavern. As it gained in brilliancy and force, the walls and ceiling quaked, causing the shield between herself and Rohen to burst into a million pieces. A veil had been lifted from the cave, from this sacred room and from the two of them.

Debris continued to fall from above as the cave began closing in on them.

The last thing she saw before darkness completely took her over was Rohen's frantic green eyes. The sea, she decided, was a wild billowing storm.

Chapter twenty

"Sorrah!" Rohen cried, making his way to her through the rock and debris which had fallen between them.

His mind still reeled from all that had happened, all that had been revealed. Sorrah was the fulfillment of the prophecy and the repercussions would be monumental, changing the plains of Kortah, changing Sorrah and Borak forever.

No one, not even the priests long ago spoke of the possibility that the rising leader could be a woman. It had never been considered, not even once. Everyone spoke of a king, a man, coming out of a foreign place, rising up and uniting the Sorriens and Borakiens forever.

My gods. "The Queen."

Marcus, the son of King Zarek had to be Sorrah's brother. Is it possible that Marcus was still alive? The rumors over time have certainly said otherwise. But Sorrah seemed to think he was alive and after all that had taken place, he knew anything was possible. *Gods.* He hadn't even thought about asking her what her brother's name was. Would he have believed her to be King Zarek's daughter? Probably not. He had no inkling of her connection to the throne or to Sorrah. And now he knew why. The gods, working in their mysterious ways, didn't want him to find out who she was until now. He still couldn't wrap his mind around it. The protectiveness he felt for her was strong before, but now? Now... she would have her own Queensguard, knights of the highest degree appointed personally by her. But after the way he'd treated her, would she pick him? Would she want him to be one of her most trusted guards?

Images of him putting her to work in Castlemore, his anger toward her, kissing her so forcefully while lust and passion raced through his mind. The more he thought about it, the more he cringed at how he'd behaved. He deserved her scorn or worse... exile.

He reached her and took her safely into his arms as he carefully scanned her body for injury, checked her pulse and watched as she calmly breathed in and out. She was alive and well. The gods had protected their chosen one.

In the area of her mark, the material of her shirt was completely shredded and hanging off her shoulder. Singed deeply in her delicate skin was not only the Borakien symbol, but the Sorrien star which had joined in the center of the Borak circles. Underneath the newly updated mark was an intricate tree, its branches elongated up the sides, cupping the conjoined symbol protectively, identical to the way the branches had protected her in Silvermist. The mark glowed and glistened, swelled and relaxed, its vibrancy breathing the very essence of life. Even the rich green leaves of the tree moved, swayed as if a constant breeze filtered through its leaves.

Sorrah. Borak. The infinity tree. Together it was the perfect symbol of life, unity and strength.

He peered at the drawing on the wall, seeing the same prophetic symbol Sorrah now had on her body. The rendering of a new leader. As if that weren't enough, the drawings were alive like Sorrah's mark, three dimensional, vivid and bright, shifting and moving as a living organism. Right then and there he wondered if the cave in Sandrin, and the one in Borak changed as well. Nevertheless, the people in all of Aaru would soon know things had changed.

There could never be, would never be, any doubt who this beautiful, enchanting fairhead was. She was the Queen of Sorrah, the Queen of Borak and the Queen of the plains of Kortah, the fulfillment of the ancient prophecies which had been in existence for many eons.

His tear-filled eyes fell upon her ravishing face.

"Sorrah."

The prophecy spoke of the leader having powers and he couldn't help but wonder what powers Sorrah possessed. Even without any, she was magnificent.

When the ground began to shake once more, he knew it was time to leave.

Knowing Sevin was true to his word, he'd be waiting outside at the entrance of the cave and couldn't have missed the powerful light, pouring out from the cave. The light along with the quake was surely a sign to all the people of Castlemore.

They'd believe he and the fairhead were dead but nothing could be farther from the truth.

He moved through the maze of the cavern seamlessly, noticing how the debris from the quake lay off to the side. The petals of flowers were still visible as if laying out a clean path for them to part.

As he approached the entrance, he saw Sevin's face.

"Rohen! My gods, man, what happened in there? What—"

"Step aside, Sevin, make way for your queen."

"Queen?"

Rohen stepped out into the light, purposely leaving Sorrah's shoulder exposed for all to see. The moment Sevin and Alexander saw the prophetic mark moving and radiating light off her skin, they got down on one knee, bowed their heads and in unison said, "Your Majesty."

"Follow me, my brothers," Rohen told them. "Stay close and watch for ill intent. You protect the Queen of Sorrah now."

People parted, making a clear path for Rohen and Sorrah. Seeing their miraculous escape from the cave and the glowing mark of Sorrah's shoulder, many bowed their heads murmured words of reverence and honor. Others stood in shock and unbelief.

Rohen's eyes lifted off into the distance where men rode out of Castlemore, surely on their way to spread the tidings perhaps right into Meserek's ear.

Sorrah was a threat to the crown, a threat to Meserek and from this moment on, in danger of losing her head.

Upon entering the castle Rohen observed Gerta, standing wide-eyed and welcoming.

"We thought you dead, My Lord. Plenty came to tell me of the light and great quake. And even now, I've heard the most shocking news—I," Gerta's eyes landed on the mark on Sorrah's shoulder. "So, it is truth they spoke."

"Sorrah is the fulfillment of the prophecy," Rohen told her as he looked out at the servants, the staff of the castle. "She is the queen."

Gasps and murmurs were heard all around.

"Rohen," Demetri said, breaking through the gathered crowd with Kehgen and Revel behind him. "She's... she's the—"

"The Queen and the one you are to protect with your life. Vows will be taken as soon as she chooses her Queensguard."

Demetri, Kehgen and Revel nodded, turned their backs to Rohen and faced the crowd. They spread out, taking a wide stance in a show of protection.

"Get on with your work!" Sevin commanded.

"Alexander!" Rohen called out.

"Here."

"Go below and get me a weapons count from the armory. And I need to know an exact count on how many men we have."

Alexander nodded and set off.

Rohen once again looked to the head housekeeper for help. "Gerta, I want the finest of everything we have here in Castlemore. The finest robes, linens, clothing, anything else you can think of. Send someone to the butcher for food and to the winery. I want the best food and wine brought back. From this moment on, she shall have the best Castlemore has to offer. That includes the best room. My room."

Gerta nodded. "As you wish. Is she... is she all right?" She lifted her head to look at Sorrah's face.

"Yes. Her breathing is steady. I'm putting her in bed." *My bed.* "When she awakes, I want the room to be transformed, fit for a queen. See to it. I'm taking the room adjacent to hers."

"Of course." Gerta turned to the staff, instantly giving orders.

Rohen took a few steps up the stairs then turned back to Gerta once more. "Oh, and Gerta?"

"Yes, My Lord?"

"I need you—and bring Silva... I want you both up here as soon as possible with a basin of warm water and fresh clothing. Oh, and be rid of that one," he added, pointing to Miranda. He turned and continued up the staircase.

There was no need to give explanation, he knew Gerta wouldn't question him. Besides, many knew Miranda had been nothing but temper and troubles for a long time. It was time to clean house.

He continued up the steps and into his room which would soon be altered to better suit a female occupant. The Queen Sorrah.

He gently placed her down on top of the quilts and turned to Sevin. "Either you or Alexander are to be outside this door at all times."

"Understood," Sevin answered, making his way out the door.

Gerta and Silva entered at the same time.

"How is she?" Silva asked, holding a stack of cloths and bottles of lotion in her hands.

"Her mark glows," he whispered, still in shock over all that had happened.

He cleared his throat. "The gods light burned her clothing, altering her mark, altering her but I see no signs of blood or wounds. I need you both to carefully wash her from head to toe and change her clothing. Position her comfortably in bed."

He moved to the hearth and stoked the fire, adding another log as he spoke. He turned to see Silva and Gerta watching him.

"If you are waiting for me to leave, don't. I'm not leaving. I'm not leaving her side. Begin."

Gerta nodded. "I will call for food to be brought up for the both of ya then. But may I off a bit of suggestion?"

"What is it?"

"If ya don't mind me sayin' you may want to do some fixin' up of yourself before she wakes."

He hadn't considered himself not even for a moment. He glanced down to see black soot on him and his clothing burned in places.

"As soon as you finish, I will tend to myself." He turned around in a show of respect as Gerta and Silva began disrobing Sorrah.

Nearly an hour later, Gerta and Silva left, leaving Sorrah cleaned, clothed, and under the warmth of his blankets. She looked vulnerable yet so perfect, lying in his bed. Just looking at her pulled at his heart strings.

Her blonde hair appeared as fine as silk; her skin nearly shimmered with an opalescent glow, given to her by the gods. If he believed her beautiful before, she was exquisite now.

He went into the adjacent room, leaving the connecting door open so he could watch if anyone came inside or if she woke. He washed and changed before making his way back to where Sorrah lay. Soon after, others made their way inside, changing things and leaving food and other pleasantries for their sleeping queen.

One of the servants moved a large tapestry chair by the bed before leaving, and Rohen knew it was for him. He was exhausted but his mind was consumed with the future and with the beauty lying in his bed. He remained alert and seated for hours up against her bed, watching for signs she was regaining consciousness.

Her breathing was still steady and strong, her chest gently rising and lowering. He watched and listened as the steady rhythm lulled him, soothing his anxiousness. His eyelids became increasingly heavy but he continued to fight to stay awake.

He rested his forehead down on her bed, meaning only to close his eyes for a few minutes but within seconds he was fast asleep with his head lowered at Sorrah's side and his hand on her arm.

Chapter twenty one

Sorrah lifted her eyelids. *Where am I?*

Raising her eyes to the vaulted ceiling, she saw exquisite paintings of beautiful bright blue-eyed male angels both with black and white wings in the heat of battle and knew she was inside the castle of Castlemore. More specifically, Rohen's room. *I'm in his bed? How did I get here?*

Images of Rohen and the cave and—

She sucked in a breath. "Mother."

She clenched her eyes shut as she recalled her mother's face and the words she had spoken. All at once the event in the cave came racing back. The flower petals, the scents, the room of light... the gods, the future, and the prophecy. Her mother had come to Sorrah and the man she'd fallen in love with was none other than King Zarek. She was his daughter and now the Queen of Sorrah.

I'm the Queen of Sorrah.

But what of Marcus? Surely the crown goes to the male first.

A sensation, a soft burn heated her, strumming her from inside, provoking her heart to pound.

"Marcus," she said, closing her eyes.

As if a beacon of light was signaling her, she honed in on an invisible rope within. She imagined herself taking hold of the rope, allowing it to guide her.

An image of a blond-haired man appeared. He wore a black cloak and was armed with a black handled silver sword. His back was to her as he stood alongside other men.

Even though she couldn't see his face, she knew beyond a shadow of a doubt that he was her brother. This was Marcus. Her mother had been right. She could sense his presence. Marcus was alive and well, only he was in no prison.

The man began to move forward, away from her and toward another group of men.

"Where are you, Marcus?" she murmured.

The man in the image stopped in his tracks but didn't turn around.

"Sister," he said. She could hear his voice clearly as if he stood right beside her.

Sorrah's eyes flew open. The connection was lost but the information of his whereabouts was not.

"He's alive and I know where he is." Kind of. She still didn't know the layout of the land surrounding her.

She suddenly became more aware of herself. She was different. Power filled. But what abilities did she possess?

She wiggled her toes and took a deep breath. She was rested, clear headed. She went to move her arm and felt someone touching her.

Turning, she saw Rohen sitting beside her bed, his head down and his hand on her. What must he think of her? Surely, he was disappointed in the gods' choice. These people all expected a mighty leader, probably male to rise up and save them.

Inwardly, she felt a soft stream of power flow through her blood. She might not have all the confidence a queen should have but it was there for the taking just the same.

Not wishing to disturb him, she gently removed Rohen's hand from her arm before moving off the bed.

She stretched feeling once more the energy churning within. She'd never felt better, stronger in all of her life. Life. Her new life had begun the moment she'd come up out of the water of the pond. She needed to embrace it and know now that the gods of this world had a purpose for her. Perhaps that was why she never fit in her world, why she never finished things she pursued. Perhaps, it was because she had a future, a purpose far greater than the confines of a small world where the people neither believed in fantastical places, nor dreamed them possible. But she did. She always had.

Her former world was never her home, just a temporary place where she passed through, quite literally, to where she belonged.

Sorrah was her home.

She smiled at the thought of it. She went to the windows and kneeled on the bench. Pulling the drapes open she was greeted by two moons, brilliantly glowing in the sky. Just as she bent forward to crack open a window she heard a man's voice bellow.

"Stay away from the window!"

Sorrah felt herself careening backward, her waist encompassed by two muscular arms. Rohen.

"What in the world—" She started to say, falling on top of him as they hit the floor.

In seemingly slow-motion he moved her off of him, guiding her as if she were made of glass.

She pushed his hands away. "What are you doing?"

Rohen quickly rose and shut the drapes.

She stood. "I know it's cold but I just wanted to get some air. What is wrong with you?"

He turned to her, dragging his eyes up and down her body. "Are you all right? I woke and you weren't in bed then I saw you by the window."

He stopped speaking, instantly dropped to his knees and bowed his head.

"Forgive me."

"Rohen… you're frightening me. What's the matter? Why are you acting like this?"

She didn't like any of this. Where was her sea captain?

"I ask for your forgiveness for everything I've done. For everything I put you through. For not trusting you. For not believing you—"

"Stop this. Stand up."

He stood but kept his eyes to the floor.

"Can't you even look at me?"

He lifted his eyes to her and instantly her heart skipped a beat.

"Nothing has changed."

Anger graced his face. *"Everything* has changed!"

"No. I mean… I know it has. But I'm still me. You are still you."

He nodded.

"Why did you pull me from the window? What did you think would happen to me?"

His jaw clenched and she loved that she finally could recognize him again.

"Your life is in danger. We are not very high from the ground. An expert marksman with a bow and arrow, if using a steel tip, might have been able to get to you."

Talk about a long shot. She appreciated his concern and liked that he felt protective of her. Still, she wanted Rohen back.

"Before anything more is said. Tell me if you accept my apology."

"There is nothing to forgive you for. Anyone in your shoes, having a woman suddenly appear out of nowhere in the village of the resistance, the place of the rebellion, would have acted the same. Far worse, I imagine. If anyone is to ask for forgiveness it is I... of you."

He dragged his hand threw his hair. "Do not talk like that. You are the queen now. You ask forgiveness of no one."

She moved closer to him. He almost backed away but as if thinking better of it, he moved his foot back in place and stood his ground.

"I don't... I don't know how to be. I am ridden with guilt for not believing you. Gods, I made you clean." He inhaled deeply and blew out a harsh breath.

She lifted her hand to his face and cupped his cheek.

"Sorrah," he said, covering her hand with his own.

"I know why you brought me to the cave. You wanted to protect me just like you did when I first arrived. You protected me again in the mountains and at dinner the night before. You have only looked out for my welfare from the very beginning. I could not have asked for a better protector. I know I wasn't the easiest... I know I was a brat."

His lips twitched ever so slightly.

"I don't want you to act differently toward me. I'm going to need your help. I'm going to need you. I *do* need you. Even now."

"Tell me how." He leaned his lips into the palm of her hand and kissed. "Tell me what it is you need."

Her heart sped up. "I want you to... what I want is for you to—"

She stopped herself again, listening to her own voice and how it cracked. She forgot her words as his kisses drifted to her wrist and arm. She desperately wanted him.

Suddenly, he stopped and lowered her arm. "I need to hear it."

The look in his eyes heated, his jaw shifted, his actions completely throwing her for a loop. He was so sexy standing there with his dark brown hair disheveled from his sleep, his face so serious yet his sea green eyes filled with desire. For her. Filled with desire for her. It was unmistakable. Many things had changed for her over the course of the past few weeks, including meeting this man who knew all the right buttons to push. He was frustrating, infuriating to be sure, but he could take her from icy to boiling hot in the matter of seconds.

She lowered her gaze to his lips, thoughts of kissing him swam through her mind until it was all she could think about. Like many times in the past, her thoughts had a way of escaping her big mouth.

"I want you. I want to kiss—"

His mouth was on hers in a flash and for once she was glad she'd said the words out loud. He kissed her deeply and unlike the gentle way he treated her moments ago, there was something urgent about the way he pulled her inside his arms and dragged his hands over her body. He made a trail of kisses from her lips to her neck. There he stayed. There she melted into his sensual assault.

He could stroke her desire in a way no one else could and she melted into him so easily.

She was just as ravished for him. She pulled on his clothes, not wanting any barrier between them. She wanted this, wanted him.

"Sorrah..."

"Shh. You'll ruin it. I don't want to stop." Not ever.

She could feel him smile against her neck as he continued to plant kisses along her skin. He brought his mouth back to her lips, kissed her and placed a few inches between them.

"You have to have sustenance. After all you've been through. The cave and—"

She broke free from his arms. *What? Why did he stop?*

"All I'm hungry for right now is you. I can't explain it but when you touch me it's as if you are clutching my heart." Her inner voice was there telling her she was making a fool of herself. Back off Sorrah. His near refusal hit her hard. Could she have read him wrong? "But if you don't—I mean if this isn't something you want. If I'm not someone—I mean..."

"Stop it."

"I've stopped. Forget I said anything."

His eyes widened and she could see the anger in their depths. What did he have to be angry about?

"Stop it, Fairhead! Stop this right now!"

179

"No. I don't want you to do something because the queen has commanded it."

There. She blurted it out but it wasn't at all what she'd been thinking. If she were honest with herself she was thinking about rejection. The age old worry many women were freaked out about. Not good enough. Men didn't stay or really want to be with her. Not her. Her own thoughts were cringe-worthy. She thought it was still a positive that she said something.

Until he laughed. At her.

Apparently she could leave her former world but her former world could not leave her. It wasn't a robust laugh but it was a laugh all the same and the sound of it hurt her ears and wounded her heart. She turned her face away and backed up slowly, grabbing a firm hold of her nightgown and pulling it closed at the top where her skin had been exposed.

"Leave me alone. I'll eat."

"No."

"Leave me alone!" she shouted.

"Never!" He had her against him with her hands behind her back in seconds. "Why do you always believe the worst of me?!'

He was right. She had thought the worst. But it wasn't him. It wasn't anything other than an annoying habit.

She had known her fair share of disappointment from the people she had expected more from. The truth was, her expectations were far too high. But she internalized everything. Admittedly, it was the reason why she became an introvert and loner. If she never took the chance on people, then they could never hurt her. For a short time she'd opened herself up to *Jerk* but that too proved to be the wrong choice.

"In time, Fairhead, you will learn to trust me." He brought his lips to her ear. "I did not mean to hurt you and I would rather die than ever humiliate you."

She struggled but not much. Wildness stirred within.

He moved forward, backing her and stopping when they hit the back of a nearby table.

"You only made me laugh because you are so beautiful. To even consider I wouldn't want to make love—"

"Make love?"

"Yes, Sorrah. Make love. You are my queen, there is no denying that. But I'm no servant to command. I've wanted you from the moment I laid eyes on you and have thought of little else."

"Really?"

"Yes." His lips skimmed her cheek. "Thoughts of you... of touching you, kissing you, have robbed me of sleep. I need you to trust me."

"I do trust you."

He dragged his lips near her mouth and remained a frustrating few inches away.

She watched his mouth, silently beckoning him to kiss her.

"Sorrah." His voice sounded like a warning. He gripped her hands tighter behind her which caused her chest to arch, bringing her tighter against him. He planted his lips firmly on hers, sucking in her bottom lip then her top, swiping his tongue along the edge until she opened for him. Their tongues met and tangled in slow drawn-out movements.

"I want you more than my next breath. I would die to have you."

He released her hands and she lifted them to the back of his head, threading her fingers through his hair.

She gave the strands a firm tug. "And I you. I guess we both die together then. Stay with me, Rohen."

"Hmm. Anything else?" He nipped at her lip.

"Don't lie to me. Ever."

He edged back a few inches and looked her square in the eyes. "I won't lie to you. Not ever. I promise."

He lowered one of her hands, turned it over and kissed the palm then repeated the action with her other hand. With his eyes locked with hers, he lifted her in his arms and carried her to the edge of the bed. He slid his fingers across her collarbone, tracing the contours of her body, lowering his fingers to the edges of her nightgown. With assistance from the other, they slowly undressed and faced each other naked, vulnerable, and aroused.

Sorrah could feel a steady warmth rise to the surface of her skin. She was more than ready, and even a bit anxious to join with him in the most natural, primal, sensual way. He had made his way into her heart and spirit, now her body cried out for more of his touch, to be possessed by him, bound to him.

Rohen's lips parted and his brows lowered as his jaw slowly shifted to one side. "My Gods, you are so beautiful, Sorrah. So—"

He didn't finish his sentence seemingly awestruck. He was no slacker in the physique department either; in fact, she was pretty sure people sculpted statues resembling such perfection. Apart from the scars. He bore the marks of a warrior.

Even as she admired his toned body, she couldn't help but warm under his scrutinizing scan of her own. How incredible it was to be looked at the way he looked at her with hunger, admiration, and want.

He swallowed deeply, placing the palms of his hands on her shoulders. His fingers splayed, a hesitation which only sparked a greater yearning for more. If that were possible.

Her skin was still hyper-sensitive to touch, the soft stirring of power an unrelenting presence in her blood, igniting her nerve endings.

She observed the way he tenderly touched and stroked her body. His eyes returned to hers then back to where he explored. With a delayed response, she lifted her hands to his body and did much the same to him, touching the hard curves and muscles. His skin was surprisingly smooth considering the amount of marks which had once pierced his flesh. His broad shoulders and rigged chest weren't overly huge, which she liked very much. Her attention leisurely slipped past his abdominals to his heavy arousal. He was well built, thick, and her face flushed thinking of him buried deep inside her.

"I... I..." she stammered.

Before she knew it she was lying on the bed with Rohen over her.

She chuckled. "I was going to say that you are equally pleasing to look at."

"Not even close, but I'm pleased you like what you see."

How could she not? All of his masculine attributes came together perfectly and formed the most attractive male she'd ever seen. Even with the scars, which oddly were as appealing as the rest of him, he was exceptional.

She lifted her lips to his but before she could kiss him he spoke. "Tell me again that you want this—that you want me."

She gently shook her head. "I do. I do want this. I want you," she murmured. She lifted her face to his and skimmed her lips against his. "More than you know."

He nipped at her upper lip and moved across the side of her cheek to her ear. He pushed down gently, his hardness a tease of what was to come.

"And what part of me do you want, sweet Fairhead?" he whispered, his warm ragged breath drifting across her skin.

She threaded her fingers in his hair and once again pulled on the strands. Their faces met. "I want all you can give and more. I want all of you, Rohen."

He licked his bottom lip, and tugged on it as a low guttural growl escaped him. His mouth descended firmly on her, taking her lips in a demanding, tantalizing kiss. The edge of his knee came between her thighs and gently nudged her legs apart. She willingly complied, feeling him hard and ready at her entrance. She wasn't the most experienced lover but knew he was.

Even though a brief flicker of trepidation ran through her, her body reacted to his, pivoting upward, seeking more.

He slowly and gently glided his arousal up and down against her folds, further stimulating her most sensitive area. The contact was a warm tease, the friction arousing and maddening at the same time. She wanted him inside, filling her, stretching her.

His breathing became increasingly heavy and hot against her neck as he rocked gently. He lifted away slightly, leaning the majority of his weight on one side while he cupped her breast, circling and skimming over her hardened nipple with his warm fingers. He lowered his mouth on the peak, taking it into his mouth and sucking. She arched up, delighting in the sensuous wetness of his tongue and the slight pull from his lips. He paid equal attention to her other breast before dragging his lips down her body. He touched her core, using his fingers in tender exploration and eliciting her soft moans.

She nearly came unglued.

"Rohen, please."

She was craving so much more, but inwardly, she loved the slow build of fire he was coercing. Her sexual experience in the past had been rushed and one-sided. Rohen was eager and wanton, yet thorough and giving. His passion seemed to rise with her heated response. When his mouth replaced his fingers, her hips bucked and she thrashed beneath his assault. He reached his warm hand to her hips, steadying her while he relentlessly pleasured her.

"Rohen!" she called out, shattering into a million pieces.

"I'm right here, Fairhead."

He returned over her with eyes fierce and aflame.

Her breathing was erratic, her languid legs lay open in invitation. She gripped his back, gently scraping her nails on his skin. His reaction was swift, his hungry eyes lighting up, his expression turning desirously savage. He had steadily heated her, stirring and stroking the coals of desire, triggering a slow-building blaze and setting her heart afire. She wanted nothing more than for him to claim her.

He groaned in her mouth as he thrust deep inside. All of his prior restraint had fled. He kissed her deeply, dominating her, tangling his tongue with hers while he moved fervently inside her. She was right there moving with him, savoring every second of their intimate connection.

This was what she'd imagined making love was like with someone you cared for deeply and wanted to be with, quite possibly, forever. Making love was this. It was periodically locking eyes with your partner and watching their reaction as you touched and kissed. It was gaining pleasure while giving pleasure, each having their distinct reward.

She hadn't known him very long, but time made no difference where her heart was concerned. She loved this man. She had left a world where she never belonged and tumbled into the receiving arms of a most virile man. She had never felt so feminine or wanted.

She allowed her eyes to close as an extraordinary mixture of heat and purity filled her. This was right. They joined together more than just their bodies but their spirits and hearts. She belonged to him and him to her, even for this small fragment of time.

He withdrew one hand at a time and raised them above her head, holding them with one hand against the pillow.

"Open your eyes, Sorrah. Look at me."

She did as he asked and their eyes locked.

"We fit perfectly," he murmured. "Fairhead... You were made for me."

He slowly thrust upward then nearly pulled out before thrusting deeply again.

"Yes."

"Yes what? Tell me."

"We fit perfectly."

"That's right. You belong to me now, Fairhead. You are mine."

His movements became more fervent but their eyes remained locked on each other.

She nodded.

"Say it."

"I'm yours. I belong to you. And you... you belong to me."

No truer words had been spoken. He had voiced them first when she had been helpless to, but the belief, the knowledge, had sifted through her mind as if the gods were confirming the absolute truth of it. They were one.

She gasped, giving into the sensations rocking her as his actions increasingly became more urgent, building up another monumental release within.

Her head fell back and she arched, as she careened over the edge, as he thrust deeper and faster. He found her lips and swallowed her cries of ecstasy, kissing her as he too fell into blissful euphoria.

Their bodies may have stilled and somewhat relaxed, but their breathing was heavy and deep.

He tucked his face into the crimp of her neck and tenderly kissed her. "I have no words," he muttered.

She knew the feeling. She placed her hand on his head and leaned into his kiss. Her eyes began to fill with tears but she stifled back the overwhelming need to release the emotion swelling inside her. They had bound themselves together, possibly forever. In the back of her mind where buried scars and insecurities remained, she wondered if it was the same for him. After all, he was the more experienced one. *You are in love with him. Knee deep. Taken over. Lost. Quicksand with nothing to hold on to kind of lost. Captured by a sea captain wolf.* She couldn't deny her heart. She was in love with Rohen. A single tear slipped out of the corner of her eye and slipped off into the crumpled quilts. Knowing he couldn't see, she smiled. This was a moment of all moments, a time she'd never forget. Greed became her friend. She wanted more of him. She wanted his body, his heart... his love. She wanted an always. She wanted the fairytale.

He rolled off her breaking the connection and ending her intimate thoughts of love for the time being.

"Come here," he said with a raspy voice.

He guided her to him, and she rested her head on his chest, hearing the lulling sound of his heartbeat. *Home.*

*****

Rohen shifted on the bed as he began to wake. Before opening his eyes, he smiled as images of the night played throughout his mind. He and Sorrah had woken up periodically throughout the night and made love several times. They couldn't seem to get enough of each other.

Queen. She's the queen. She's in danger. Meserek will want her head.

His eyes flew open. There was much to do. She had to choose her Queensguard out of nearly two hundred men in the rebellion army.

They needed to speak about Marcus and pin down a location. She'd told him about her connection to him and how she knew he wasn't in prison. Then of course there was the siege of Sandrin and the overthrowing of Meserek. Yeah, lots to do.

He turned to speak with her and found the bed empty. He flew out of the bed and looked anxiously around.

"Sorrah!" he yelled, seeing the door ajar.

He had given Sevin explicit instructions, and knew he, of all the men, would never disobey a direct order. Had Alexander been on duty? Something had to of happened. He was sure of it. Now frantic, he hurried his pants on and nothing else before grabbing his sword and running out the door and down the staircase. His heart was racing, pounding hard in his chest while he tightly gripped the handle of his sword. Had she been taken?

Before he called out her name again he heard the sound of her laugh coming from the kitchen. His fear turned into relief then anger in three seconds flat.

He placed his sword down on a nearby table, shoved the door to the kitchen open, his jaw nearly dropping from shock.

Alexander and Demetri were sitting at the long wooden prep table. They stilled the moment they saw Rohen. Alexander was in the middle of shoving an enormous muffin in his mouth.

"Woo-ren," he muffled as he chewed.

Sorrah turned around with a wide grin on her face. "Rohen... Good morning. I baked muffins," she chimed, holding out a platter of baked goods. "Uh oh. I know that look. What's wrong?"

She wore a silky robe over her nightgown but with the sun shining through the window you could make out the subtle curves of the body. The light accentuated her opalescent skin given to her by the gods. The men in the room had to of noticed her. He might just have to kill them.

Swallowing hard, Rohen forced down the lump in his throat. *Dear gods.*

Her hair was loosely gathered and secured on the top of her head while stray strands hung low around her face. Peufer was blotted on her cheeks and scattered on her clothing but it didn't matter. She was an angel. She was his.

"What's *wrong?*" he asked with a bitter tone.

"I... I wanted to make you breakfast."

"Breakfast?! My gods, woman, have you no idea what it did to me, waking up to find you missing from our bed?!"

"Rohen," Sorrah muttered. Her face flushed.

"And you!" he yelled pointing at Alexander. "We'll speak about this later."

"What? I'm watching her. She's really good at baking. These muffins are awesome."

On his way to Sorrah, Rohen walked by Alexander and flipped his plate of food onto his lap.

"Hey!" Alexander exclaimed, standing abruptly as food fell down his legs. Demetri chuckled.

"Clearly you're not a morning person," Sorrah stated. "Good to know."

"You are the queen. If you wanted food all you have to do is ask for it. Any one of the servants in this castle would be more than hap—"

"You're right. I *am* the queen. So, I suppose that means if I want to bake something myself, I can."

Gerta let out a short giggle then swiftly turned away and began cleaning up the mess.

Rohen clenched his teeth, took the platter out of Sorrah's hands and set it on the table. "Yes. Of course. As your appointed guard, I ask that you proceed upstairs and get dressed. We have much to accomplish today."

"All right. I want to leave as soon as possible. I need to look at a map. I'm sure I can locate Marcus."

Rohen nodded and looked to his men. "Meeting in one hour. Just the six of us and the queen. Have Sevin gather as many of the men as possible and get them ready to present themselves in the courtyard. Our queen will be selecting her guard. Or at the very least a unit to accompany us on our travels."

Alexander and Demetri spoke in unison. "Yes, sir." They made their way out of the kitchen and out the front door.

Rohen made certain they were gone. And as soon as Gerta walked out, he gathered Sorrah in his arms and kissed her.

"I change my mind," she said breathlessly. "You *are* a morning person."

Before she could protest he hoisted her up and over his shoulder.

"Rohen! What are you doing? Set me down!"

He smacked her behind a good hard whack. "No."

"Ow!" she said with amusement in her voice.

"I warned you that I'm good with brats. Even when the brat is the queen."

He carried her up the stairs and to her room then pushed the door closed with his foot behind him before setting her on her feet.

"Was that necessary?" she asked.

He pulled her inside his arms. "Yes."

He kissed her until her breathing became shallow and she softened against him. "This is where you belong. Right here. With me."

She smiled against his mouth. "Right here? Ahh!" she squealed as he picked her up and nearly threw her on the bed.

"Actually. Right here."

He climbed on the bed and positioned himself on his side while he untied her robe and spread it open. He cupped her breast through the thin fabric of her nightgown and spoke while he caressed. "You are short on time to do what needs to be done."

"And what is that?" she asked.

"Beg for my forgiveness."

"Me? A queen... beg a commoner?"

She was right of course but he knew her well enough to detect the teasing in her voice.

She sighed dramatically. "However, never let it be said that I am not a humble queen. Please forgive me."

"Hmm." He narrowed his eyes. "I'm not convinced your apology is genuine. Let's try a visual. Show me that you are sincere."

"A visual?"

He nodded and quickly kissed her. "Show me just how sorry you are for scaring me."

She giggled as he kissed her neck.

When he lifted his face to her, his expression turned serious.

Possessiveness reigned supreme in his spirit while thoughts of her with another man bombarded his mind. He couldn't handle the idea of a man being intimate with her, touching her, kissing her. Gods, he'd really fallen for her. What was he going to do?

It was not uncommon for a ruler to marry immediately after their coronation. Meserek hadn't chosen that route but instead had many lovers, sometimes at the same time.

Sorrah wouldn't be like that. Her mother had married King Zarek so their future children, Marcus and Sorrah were legitimate heirs. As far as Ian, his brother… he was a bastard but lived in the castle and received benefits of his station.

As queen, Sorrah might choose to marry, even be advised to do so. Noblemen would be presented to her. The male, either from Sorrah or Borak, even elsewhere, wouldn't have to be of a royal bloodline but still a member of the hierarchy of a kingdom. An honorable, worthy male. The queen would give him a higher title and together they would present a strong united front.

He and Sorrah had bonded and if she chose to marry, he knew she would pick him.

Only he wasn't a nobleman but a soldier. A leader of armies. Besides, he'd told himself he would never marry, never risk his heart in such a way, so many times he believed it through and through.

Imagining Sorrah with anyone other than himself, whether an honorable man or not, drove him insane with jealousy and filled him with rage.

"Rohen?"

"Hmm?" His eyes met hers.

"You were somewhere else."

"Yes. But I'm back now."

"Tell me about what happened in the cave."

He kissed her collarbone. "Which part?"

"There was a short time when I couldn't hear what my mother said. When she spoke to you."

He'd been kissing her neck but abruptly stilled and lifted his face.

"The Hendrin in Sandrin told her things regarding the future but Hendrins are fickle, their visions can be accurate but there is always the power of frecwill, a gift given to every one of us, and choice has the power to change everything. Nothing is set in stone." He paused. "I can tell you this… your mother spoke of tribulation but also of hope."

He hesitated, not wanting to elaborate. Her mother had asked him if he'd sacrifice his life for her daughter. His answer was swift. Yes. She'd been happy with his reply. She also told him they'd soon face a dark time, perhaps an event, where their lives would linger in the balance. She said the outcome was unclear to those who saw the future. He cringed even now, recalling her warning. To lose Sorrah would be certain death to him.

"What she told you… it disturbed you then and still disturbs you now."

"Some of it. Yes. You read me too well, Fairhead."

He brushed some strands of hair off her face and tucked it behind her ear. "Your mother has faith, and asked me to remember mine. Whatever lay in store for you, for us—know that I will protect you with my life."

Sorrah gave him a half smile. "I know."

She touched his face, her fingers lingering on the side of his cheek. Her eyes searched his and she smiled, seemingly satisfied with what she saw.

"You are so beautiful, Sorrah. Your heart as well as your face," he stroked her cheek, "and your body." He slowly slid his hand down the front of her.

Her smile widened, provoking him to grin.

Logic and habit told him he should back away and pull the shield of indifference over his heart. They had a dangerous journey ahead of them. And no matter what Hendrins had foreseen, the truth remained that only the gods knew the future.

One thing was certain, by now Meserek not only wanted his head but Sorrah's head too. He would protect her with his life, but the Kingswatch were fierce and many. He didn't want her to go through what his mother had, mourning her husband's death so severely.

If anything happened to Sorrah, he'd prefer punishment be swiftly brought upon him. He no longer desired to live in this world or any other without her.

He pushed the thought aside. For now he'd linger in the light of her pleasure and enjoy being with the one he loved. *I do love her.*

They made love to each other again, slowly and thoroughly. With a growing silence emerging between them, they washed, dressed, and made their way downstairs for the meeting.

Chapter twenty two

"You will need to choose men, most trusted guards. I know you haven't been here very long," Rohen stated.

Sorrah and Rohen were in a room on the first level of the castle and were joined by Sevin, Demetri, Alexander, Revel and Kehgen.

"I have no time to cypher through so many men and choose. So, if your men here are willing then I choose them."

The men stood nearly in unison.

"Are you certain?" Rohen asked.

Sorrah lifted her head a bit higher. This was the first decision she made as queen and knew it was important. These men had risked their lives for her early on. Rohen especially. If she were to put her life into anyone's hands, it would be theirs.

"Yes. I'm certain."

"After the official coronation in Sandrin, you will need to choose many more men. Or else place someone in charge of the Queensguard to choose for you. Men will be needed to come with us when we go to find your brother."

"I have already chosen such a leader."

Rohen lifted his eyebrows in question.

"You. There is no other."

His eyes flinched for a second. Was it such a surprise? She wasn't sure how to read his reaction. "You are in charge of the Queensguard followed by Sevin, Alexander and so on."

The men briefly bowed their heads as she said their names.

"As you wish," Rohen answered.

The men formed a straight line in front of Sorrah. One by one they dropped on bended knee and pledged their loyalty to queen and crown. Rohen did likewise.

In the past day since they made love for the first time, things seemed to be going fairly well with Rohen. They seemed happy but made no promises to each other regarding their future nor did they profess confessions of love which both pleased and bothered her. Rohen was all business now, as he should be, but there were things left unspoken, things which left a strange void between them.

What would happen to them once she was on the throne? *The throne.* There was so much to think about. For the time being she would set aside her concerns regarding their relationship or at least try to.

While a map lay sprawled out on the table, Sorrah closed her eyes using her new gift from the gods to locate Marcus. This time when she saw him, he was wearing armor, a silver chest plate and knight gear, training with other men who were dressed likewise. Once again she saw only the back of him. Still, when she opened her eyes to the map she was able to locate his whereabouts. He was in a rural land between Sandrin and Castlemore. A place Rohen and the others called Shendora. On horseback it would take them nearly two days.

"They won't expect us to leave the safety of Castlemore. Meserek must know of Sorrah by now," Rohen stated, addressing the men in the room.

"They may be on their way here as we speak," Sevin added. "Although the men we have watching the outer perimeter have seen no signs of the Kingswatch. Yet."

"That's why we leave so many men behind to protect these walls and all who inhabit Castlemore. We meet Marcus and his men then send word for more troops to join us once a plan has been set."

"Then we storm Sandrin?" Sorrah asked.

"Yes. And you take your rightful place as Queen of Sorrah and beyond."

They were all in agreement but Rohen still seemed on edge. But for the next hours or so, they packed and made ready for travel. As Rohen instructed, Sevin gathered an additional twenty soldiers to accompany them to Shendora and had the remaining soldiers prepare for the battle to come either at the gates of Castlemore or Sandrin.

With a full day behind them, Sorrah continued to take comfort in having such a fearsome group of men looking out for her. Also knowing she had the things of her mother's safely tucked inside one of her bags provided her with strength and courage.

She wore a thick, dark blue cloak with a hood that upon Rohen's insistence, had to remain up in order to cover her bright blonde hair. Underneath the cloak she wore a white peasant style shirt with numerous laces up the front which gave her waist a nice corset held in shape. Her gray skirt was long and she wore tighter fitting pants beneath it along with high black boots. Wearing pants made riding a horse far more enjoyable. Between the way she was dressed and how her hair was adorned she looked every part a medieval lady. Having attended a few renaissance festivals, mostly walking around admiring the garb and settings, she believed she nailed the look pretty well. But nestled at her hip was a black-handled dagger that her sea captain gave her. The weapon was a reminder of the seriousness of their journey.

The first night they made camp under the coverage of the trees in Silvermist. Rohen had said the forest was large but it really appeared to be endless. She was thankful to be far from the mountains, having no desire to see the Tarrigen creatures.

Rohen had set up a tent and the two of them had slept next to each other. Well, she slept but Rohen seemed to be up every hour, keeping watch. Periodically, he would lie next to her and pull her inside his arms but she knew it was more to provide her with warmth than anything else.

The next day as they headed onward through Silvermist forest, the sun filtered through the thick trees, making the trees and foliage seem to explode pieces of brilliant color like a kaleidoscope. She marveled at all the beauty and magnificence of this most enchanted forest. The majestic landscape was just another piece of the glorious world Rohen and others had existed in but for Sorrah this was nothing short of magical.

She chanced a quick glance Rohen's way, noticing his grave expression. "Is everything all right?" she asked, riding alongside him.

"My only worry is for you. I'm not sure this is the right decision."

"What decision is that?"

"At Castlemore there are nearly two hundred men or more to keep you safe. Beyond this forest is a valley, a long stretch of land where we will be riding out in the open, crossing terrain familiar to many."

"And you fear they've heard about me and I'm in danger."

"Meserek and Ian. They—"

"Ian. Your brother."

"Yes. He has recently been given charge over the entire Kingswatch army."

They had spoken briefly about their families during their time alone in her chambers. He had lost his parents. So had she. He had one half-brother who he had rarely seen since they were younger. She had a brother she'd never met. Even in worlds so far apart from each other they had things in common. But where she was excited to meet her brother, Rohen was hoping not to see his. They were enemies. The son of his enemy, even a brother, was his enemy or something like that.

"Believe me, Sorrah. Everyone in Sandrin knows about you by now. News of this magnitude travels fast. People have been waiting and praying for the fulfillment of prophecy for a very long time."

"But many believe Meserek is that fulfillment."

"Many will say anything when their lives are in danger and follow him regardless of the evil he has done. There are people in Sandrin and beyond who will be curious to see if their prayers have truly been answered, others, who align with Meserek, will want your head."

"That's why I have you and the Queensguard with me. I am confident you will protect me."

Rohen slowed his horse as he looked at her. "It may not be enough. I may not be enough. But I will lay my life down for you."

"I know that."

"We could've easily sent word to Marcus. He could've come to you."

She slowed her horse even more and Rohen followed suit. She looked at Sevin and the men of her Queensguard. "Give us a minute will you?"

Before moving off to the side, Sevin glanced at Rohen and received an affirming nod.

"Rohen, I didn't ask for this."

"No, you didn't. But it has been thrust upon you nonetheless."

"Listen to me. I know you want me to remain safe. I get that. But I cannot... I will not hide in a village. I was chosen as the queen and I need to be one. We need my brother and his men. My mother spoke of powers. Powers that are in Marcus and me. But I'm not foolish. I've spoken to Sevin and others. I know we need all the power we can get to take down Meserek and I know that you have believed you die in an end battle with the Kingswatch."

"That was before you were here, Sorrah. You have changed everything." He ground his jaw. "And Sevin needs to learn to keep his mouth shut."

"He doesn't talk very much as it is. I had to pry it out of him. Don't tell him we spoke about what he's said. I may never get him to speak openly again." She smiled wryly.

Rohen nodded.

"Going to Shendora is the right choice. I needed to go to Marcus not the other way around. I know it. I feel it. No matter what hesitation you feel now, will you trust me?"

"Fine. In return I ask that you do as I say in regards to your safety. Can you do that?"

"Yes," she said, nodding. "You know I will. I need you. She positioned her horse to the side of his, getting closer. Wanting nothing more than to be reassured, to feel his lips on hers, she leaned toward him in invitation and placed her hand on his arm. But instead of meeting her halfway, he covered her hand with his and gave it a gently squeeze, before moving his horse ahead of hers.

She felt the twinge of hurt as though she'd been slapped. Was she reading into things? Maybe. She knew it was ridiculous to be so sensitive but his action coupled with the way he'd been acting… it was different. *He* was different.

"We'll take another break in a while. Let's make up some time."

She nodded, following him back to the road while the men fell in line behind them. Why hadn't he kissed her? Her intent was clear when she leaned toward him, yet, he'd held back. She loved him and had thought he felt the same way even though neither of them had spoken the words. He was shutting her out and she didn't know why.

"We will be to Shendora by nightfall," he told her. "The valley is just ahead. I want you to remain close."

"Fine."

"And if we make safe passage through the clearing and get to Shendora, I want you to wait behind me until I check out Marcus' camp and his men."

"He won't hurt me, Rohen."

"Sorrah."

"Fine. I'll wait until you check it out. But he is my brother."

"A brother you don't know." He narrowed his eyes. "My own uncle wants me dead. All men whether blood related or not prove themselves in the same way as all others. Loyalty."

The evening was quickly falling upon them and she knew Rohen wanted to make it to Shendora before nightfall. They continued to ride through the valley, with mountains and forest on three sides of them. The cold winds from the east suddenly kicked up, whipping Sorrah's hair into a frenzy and carrying with its gale the vicious sound of a beast.

Sorrah slowed her horse, oddly recognizing the sound for what it was. A Tarrigen. It was a sound she'd never heard, yet instinctively knew that it came from one of the two creatures of the mountains. The strumming vibration of power within her spirit began to gain in intensity, nearly taking her over.

"Sorrah! Can you hear me?"

"Hmm?"

Her mind had been focused only on the sound of the beast. It was a cry… a warning.

"What is it? What's going on?"

She stopped, jumped down from her horse, and began walking west toward the forest, stumbling and moving erratically.

"Sorrah!"

Rohen, who had dismounted the moment she did, took a firm hold of her.

The beastly cry came to her once more this time much louder.

She clutched her ears, cupping them with her palms. She wasn't trying to end the beast's cry but attempting to block out all other sound so she could try and interpret what it was trying to tell her. "Stop!" she yelled, struggling in his arms. "Wait."

He let go of her.

She closed her eyes, trying to hone into the sound of the Tarrigen. "It's a warning. Something is wrong."

"What? A warning? Talk to me, Sorrah."

The winds whipped around them, lifting twigs and dirt off the ground, blocking their view. When the dirt and debris finally settled, Rohen's men spotted a line of soldiers riding toward them from the east. They didn't have long.

"Kingswatch!" Sevin yelled. "At least fifty. Maybe more!"

Four of the twenty soldiers who had rode slightly behind them, came forward as if waiting for Rohen's command.

Rohen grabbed her arm and hauled her back to her horse. "We ride to Shendora. There are more men there to help us fight."

She didn't argue but inside she felt bad for bringing the fight to Marcus' door. What a fine hello. Rohen and his men could fight a band of Kingswatch, possibly more. They were highly skilled and fierce with a blade but an entire army? Rohen may have stayed to fight, taken the chance had she not been with him. He was looking out for her, she knew that.

"They've split up!" Sevin called out. "They mean to surround us!"

They rode forward fast and hard but before they made it to Shendora, a band of Kingswatch soldiers appeared closer and heading straight for them.

"Stay on your horse," Rohen ordered, jumping down from his horse. "The first chance, ride hard and fast to Marcus. Sevin, you will get her there and assure the queen's safety."

Sorrah's heart dropped. Had he lost his mind?

"No! Rohen, no!" She argued, abruptly dismounting. Earlier she had seen Rohen and Sevin speaking discreetly. Now she knew what it was about. Rohen had made his second in command promise to keep her safe even if that meant, riding off without him.

Rohen turned on her. "Get back on your horse. Now!"

"No. No, I'm not leaving. I won't leave you."

He took her by the shoulders. "Listen to me, Sorrah. Sevin is an exceptional fighter!"

"Then let Sevin stay and fight. *You* take me to Shendora."

Even in the short time they were speaking, additional Kingswatch soldiers had surrounded them but still kept their distance.

"Rohen!" a familiar voice hollered out to them.

"I know that voice," Sevin commented.

Rohen nodded. "Foley."

"The king requests an audience with you! Come quietly and your men can go free."

Rohen didn't turn around.

"Foley is with them?" Sorrah asked nervously.

"Yes. The fact that he is only confirms our belief that Meserek and the Kingswatch know of your claim. Now do as I tell you, Sorrah, go with Sevin."

He spoke with such urgency but she wasn't in a hurry to leave him, in spite of her new found title. It dawned on her what he really was going to do.

"My gods... You're turning yourself over to him aren't you? You knew this might happen. Nothing has changed, has it? You still are willing to die in a war with Meserek and the Kingswatch."

"No. Not for the cause but for *you*. I'm willing to die for *you!* So that you live!"

The Kingswatch edged closer. With their weapons drawn the rebellion soldiers formed a protective circle around Rohen and Sorrah.

"You made me a promise. You promised to keep me safe. To protect me."

"And I'm keeping my promise to you the only way I know how. Foley is dying to get his hands on me and it's likely my uncle offered him a lot of money for my head. Quite possibly for your head too. He would not have sent so many soldiers otherwise."

"Make your choice or let us fight and be done with this!" Foley yelled. "Perhaps the fair maiden will be my first kill."

Rohen clenched his eyes shut then opened them. His jaw tightened. "They are not here to take us alive. Trust me. He will obtain his reward whether we are dead or alive."

"Then if he's here to kill us, let's get far away from this place," she pleaded.

"He'll only follow and bring an army along with him. No. I need to keep Foley here. If I prod his desire to fight me, if I fight him then I pull his attention off of you." He shrugged off his heavy overcoat and tossed it off to the side on the ground. Sorrah knew he was preparing to fight, losing anything that might restrict his movements. "You will leave and allow me to do whatever it takes to protect you. You gave your word."

"Don't speak to me of *my* promises while you break your own!"

Rohen shot her a cold look. "I said a lot of things to get what I wanted." He searched her eyes as if waiting for his meaning to sink in.

She could feel her heart pounding hard in her chest. He said the one thing that would hurt her the most; the one thing that might make her leave. Either he was using her insecurities to his advantage or he really meant what he said. Part of her believed wholeheartedly that it was a lie but the other part, the part where scars lay deep within, said he spoke the truth. Either way what he'd said hurt. How could he do that to her?

"I… I don't believe you." She cursed herself for stuttering.

"No? You need to grow up if you're to be queen. I don't know what men are like where you come from, but in this world, they will say just about anything to separate a female from her knickers."

She slapped him hard across the face as tears pooled in her eyes. "You promised me no lies."

"Yes I did. So what does that tell you?"

His jaw was flexing, his breathing heavy and his hands were clenched into tight fists.

Not being able to look at him for a second longer, she slipped her eyes away while her face contorted in agony. "Please don't do this. I know you are strong enough to win a fight against Foley, but what of all the men he has with him? There are too many. It's suicide, Rohen. I will not let you sacrifice yourself for me. I just won't." *I won't leave you.*

"My only sacrifice is for the greater good, Your Majesty. As the commander of the Queensguard, I insist the queen get to safety."

His voice was proper, his face cold as ice. "Meserek knows he's not the rightful leader. And soon all will know the truth. You have changed everything."

"No. You're wrong, Commander. I haven't changed everything," she said, interrupting him. *Not your heart.* By the way he briefly cringed; she knew he understood her meaning. Still, he displayed little emotion and made no remark regarding her words.

"It is crucial for you to survive at all costs. We are up against a heavy battle. I have no choice but to face Foley and you have no choice but to leave."

"I don't accept that, Rohen."

Rohen looked to where some men of the rebellion had already begun to fight those from Sandrin. Foley, however, wasn't partaking.

His eyes were glued on Rohen. The battle would soon be upon them.

"If sacrificing my life ensures your safety, then it must be done! I will speak no more on the matter. Sevin—take her."

She briskly shook her head.

Sevin urged her. "I don't want to touch you, Highness. But I will gather you against your will if need be. Let us go."

"There's got to be another way. There has to—"

"There is no other way!" Rohen hollered. "Go!"

Before Rohen could turn away to fight, Sorrah lifted her hands to each side of his face, prompting him to look her in the eyes.

"I cannot do what needs to be done without saying one last thing to you. No matter how you do or *do not* feel about me..." She shook her head. "Sometimes the greatest wounds inflicted on a person are words which are left unspoken. When death finds me, my heart will be lightened knowing I spoke honestly what lie inside. I love you, Rohen." Her chin involuntarily trembled. "I love you so much."

If she wasn't seeing things, she detected a look of regret in his eyes, but for what?

Rohen nodded to Sevin, looked her in the eyes one last time, and then proceeded to walk away, meeting a Kingswatch soldier who had broken through the front line and gotten close.

Sevin quickly dismounted and grabbed her around the waist. "Get on your horse."

Alexander held the reins of her horse as Sevin helped her to mount before returning to his own horse. This was it. She was really leaving Rohen.

Rohen called back to her after quickly defeating the soldier. "Align with Marcus and use whatever power it is the gods have given you to survive. You must live, Sorrah. Whatever the cost. You must take your place as queen."

It didn't escape her attention that he hadn't said anything regarding his heart even when he had an opportunity to voice it. This could be the last time they seen each other, yet he'd chosen to remain silent which led her to believe what he said earlier must be true. Maybe she'd only been as all the other women had been to him.

He was breaking her heart into pieces. But in the back of her she was relieved she'd had the chance to tell him her heart. She wouldn't stop loving him.

Before she knew it, Alexander smacked his hand down on the behind of her horse and her and Sevin were off, riding hard and fast, away from the fight and away from Rohen.

He can survive, she silently told herself, and believing, hoping, destiny would bring them together again.

Destiny, as it turned out, came sooner than she thought it would as four Kingswatch soldiers came out of nowhere and rushed her and Sevin.

They had to of been watching us, she thought.

Sevin clanked swords with one of the soldiers while another pulled him off his horse.

Before she could get away, big hands reached up and yanked her to the ground.

"Stay right where you are!" a Kingswatch soldier commanded. He placed his boot on her side and pushed down hard. Her right hand was at her hip and when the soldier looked up to the action, she stabbed him in the leg with her dagger.

"Ahh! You wench!" he cried, kicking her in the stomach. Her dagger dropped out of her hand and the hood of her cloak slipped off, revealing her bright blonde hair.

"She's the fairhead all right!" one of the men yelled.

"Foley is waiting for you, love," the soldier who kicked her said. "The gods would never allow a woman to be ruler. We have our king. This is trickery. The resistance will do anything for their cause." He reached down and grabbed her hair in his fist, pulling her to a standing position. "I'd kill you myself right here and now, but you are important to Rohen and that makes you important to us."

She couldn't breathe, the hit to her stomach stealing her voice. *Please gods, help me,* was her silent prayer. In an instant, a jolt of adrenaline shot through her. She curled her fingers and drove the palm of her hand upward hard into the soldier's nose, following up with a swift thrust of her knuckles into his esophagus. Now he was the one who couldn't breathe. The soldier stumbled back, falling to the ground.

She turned to see Sevin, fighting off two soldiers. Where did the fourth one go? she wondered.

"I'm right behind you."

A blade appeared at her throat. She really needed to control what she said out loud.

"Put down your weapon, rebel!" He yelled to Sevin. "Or the fairhead dies. I don't care about keeping her alive."

Sevin immediately dropped his sword.

She thought the soldiers would kill him right then and there, but instead they pushed them both forward, keeping a blade aimed at her neck and one at Sevin's back.

When they returned to the battlefield, the soldier turned her over to Foley who used the same threat against those who continued to fight. "Rebels! Put down your weapons or the fairhead dies!"

Many of the rebellion looked to Rohen who had been fighting two Kingswatch soldiers.

Rohen signaled for his men to do as Foley ordered.

All soldiers, both of the Kingswatch and rebellion, stood in silence as they watched the scene play out before them. These men were both Sorrien and Borakien born yet had been at odds with one another for so long. Had Meserek been the true king, he would've been able to unite them as one, just as the gods had prophesized. They could have become one enormously strong and fearsome army.

Foley, pulling her behind him, pushed through groups of men to get to Rohen who was heavily surrounded by Kingswatch soldiers.

He pushed her into the arms of two soldiers, pulled his fist back and punched Rohen across his face.

Sorrah turned her face away, hating to see him hurt.

"How did you ever convince Meserek to allow you to command these Kingswatch men?" Rohen asked with guile.

"I made him realize my importance when I ran my mouth off about your puny rebellion. I promised him the head of the traitor against the throne. Then just like that, I became important." He snorted but continued to stare at Rohen. "It's a pity the king wants me to bring you back alive. As for the lass, I believe he's wantin' to place her head on a pole just outside Sandrin for all to see."

Rohen came at Foley but soldiers held him back. Foley laughed sadistically.

"It gets much better than that. I'm thinkin' he wants to personally see you suffer. I have that in common with him."

Foley nodded to the two soldiers holding Rohen back. They held him in place while Foley proceeded to punch him repeatedly.

"No! Stop!" Sorrah cried out. She could hear Sevin, Alexander and the other men of the rebellion, calling out in rage. The Kingswatch had blades to all of them, rendering them helpless to aid Rohen or her for that matter.

Rohen fell to his knees, his mouth bloodied and torn. The soldiers bound his feet and hands with thick rope.

Foley yanked back Rohen's head. "Don't be passing out on me, you have a show to watch." He thrust his knee into Rohen's face.

A show? she thought. Her mind was reeling with ways to get out of this. It seemed hopeless.

"Just let him go! You have me now!" Sorrah screamed as tears streamed down her face. "Bring me to Meserek but leave him alone!"

"Bring the witch closer," Foley ordered without looking at her. He leaned down and got in front of Rohen's face. "You should have shared her when you had the chance."

Rohen struggled for his breath but conjured up enough energy to spit in Foley's face, a mist of blood splattered over Foley's face.

Foley reached into his pocket and removed what looked like a black bag. He swiped it over his face before tossing it to one of the soldiers standing behind Rohen.

"Don't bag em' till I kill the wench."

"No!" Rohen yelled, seeming to have gotten more of his bearings. "Take me to Meserek but leave her alone. She means nothing to you, Foley." Rohen jerked and pulled as soldiers restrained him further.

"Oh, how sickening, yet intoxicating it is to listen to you both beggin' for the life of the other. You are right. She means nothing to *me* but," Foley leaned in closer to Rohen, "she means much to *you.* And since I'm ordered to bring you back alive, you're gonna watch her die." He punched Rohen in the face again, the hit made Rohen's head to slump down.

"Lift his head," Foley commanded.

The soldier behind Rohen yanked his hair back, lifting his face.

Rohen was breathing heavily. His face was red and swelling more by the second, his eyes barely able to remain open.

"Gag him," Foley ordered.

"Fairhead!" Rohen yelled with a gravelly and rough voice. "I lied! I lied, Fairhead!"

One of the soldiers shoved a black cloth into his mouth and pulled it tight behind his head before tying it.

Sorrah nodded. "I know!" she answered loudly then whispered, "I know." Deep down, she'd known.

Sorrah and Rohen locked eyes. Her heart sank into her stomach. 'I lied,' he'd said. Two small words, yet they entered her ears with tremendous strength and truth, burrowing themselves deep into her heart and warming it. How could she ever of doubted? And how had it all come to this?

This cannot be the end. This cannot be all there is. Where was all the power her mother spoke of? She was able to summon a portion earlier but now felt nothing.

Rage burned in her spirit. She was the rightful ruler, the chosen of the gods. Surely they didn't mean for her to be powerless. They would not have chosen her, yet made her helpless and weak. Would they?

As Foley reached for a sword and turned to her, Sorrah took a deep breath.

"Gods, empower me," she muttered.

"Pray to them all you like, wench, there are no gods." Foley laughed.

The winds suddenly hurled around them kicking up dirt and loose foliage, whirling it in a circle. It wasn't much but she'd use the distraction. If she died so be it, but perhaps a battle would allow Rohen the opportunity to escape.

"Queensguard!" she yelled out. "I command you to fight!"

The Kingswatch and rebellion soldiers commenced once more into battle. The distraction didn't stop Foley or lessen the tight grip the soldier had on her arms. With a nod from Foley, the soldier holding her back grabbed hold of one arm while the other soldier took hold of the other. She thrashed about but could not break free from their hold.

Sorrah's eyes shifted between Rohen and Foley while she tried to strum up a harsher weapon. She knew progress had been made when the force of the gale nearly knocked her off her feet and disrupted those who were fighting. The more fiercely intense the wind grew, the weaker she became. The use of the power was draining her ability. She needed to control any power she had but there'd be no time for learning right now. Death was at the door.

"Any last words?" Foley asked, standing in front of her with the tip of his blade at her heart.

Her focus remained steadfast on Rohen.

"I didn't think so," Foley chided, before she could open her mouth.

She didn't really believe he was allowing her any last words. But everything seemed to happen in slow motion.

"Murtagh is here!" a rebellion soldier shouted.

Sounds of horses and battle cries drifted away from Sorrah's ears. In her mind and heart, all who remained were only her and Rohen.

Tears spilled down her face. This was truly the end.

Rohen was struggling against the ropes binding him. She knew he likely had never been in such a vulnerable position, never been so helpless. Or had he? He mentioned the loss of his parents and the agony of his mother's mourning. She wished him not to suffer. The revival of old wounds and buried pain did nothing to change the past, only bringing to the heart the worst sorrow has to offer. Her heart went out to him. Even though she faced death, she ached to comfort him.

She knew if she spoke, he couldn't hear her above the noise of what seemed to be a storm erupting around them. So, she hoped he could read her lips.

"I love you," she mouthed just before Foley shoved his blade through her skin, piercing her heart and going straight out the back of her.

Chapter twenty three

Everything happened slowly, then all at once. Foley withdrew his blade, and Sorrah's still body jerked with its retraction. Her body went cold as she fell to her knees and dropped over on her side.

Rohen went berserk, thrashing about and roaring behind the cloth in his mouth. Just as his anguished, rage-filled tears fell, Kingswatch soldiers slipped a black bag over his head and knocked him out cold with the handle of a sword. They lay his unconscious body on the back of a horse and fled the scene with him in tow.

Foley stood over Sorrah's body more than a little pleased with what he had done. "Just another powerless woman," he said with guile. "Throw her body over my horse," he told Edgar, one of his cohorts. "I'm taking her to Meserek myself. The reward for this will make us wealthy men!" He observed the fighting going on around him. "Let's get a move on."

Before Edgar could touch her, Sorrah's body jerked.

"She's still alive!" Edgar said.

"I pierced straight through her heart. She's dead," Foley answered, lifting his foot back to kick her. When he was within an inch of connecting, Sorrah thrust her hand forward, faster than any mortal eye could see, stopping Foley's foot.

Foley lost his footing and stumbled back.

Sorrah rose with blinding fast speed. Her head remained down, her blonde hair an effervescent glowing light.

"No," she stated matter-of-factly.

She inhaled and exhaled, taking deep breaths. She lifted her face and with her eyes burning brightly, touched her chest where Foley had thrust his blade into. She pulled her hand away and saw there was no blood. In fact, there was no wound. She was very much alive and power filled. *I'm immortal,* she thought. *But that's not all.* She was highly aware of the power within.

Her eyes shifted to Foley who seemed paralyzed in place. *I did that. I made him immobile.*

"Kill her!" he shouted to nearby soldiers as he attempted to move his feet but failed.

Soldiers of the Kingswatch started to rush her. She raised a hand in front of her, and one to the side, palm facing out. An invisible force field projected outward, stopping the men. With another jerk of her palms, the men flew backward, far away from her.

Men in black cloaks, who didn't appear to be either rebellion or Kingswatch soldiers, were coming closer. She made eye contact with Sevin who was making his way to her from the side of the battlefield.

"Sevin. Kill Foley."

Sorrah placed her hand near her mouth. What was that? A faint light had accompanied her words. Sure she felt different but did she now possess a built-in flashlight? Her voice sounded strange as well. She hardly recognized it as her own. It was oddly melodic yet held great authority. She had changed. She had obtained her powers.

Shouts of awe and wonderment rippled through the battlefield and slowly both sides began to cease fighting. Phrases like, 'She's alive' and 'She is the chosen,' could be heard among them. However, there were those of the Kingswatch who mounted their horses and sped off in the direction of Sandrin.

"This is impossible!" Foley said, wobbling on his feet. With the greatest of effort he raised his sword and with a trembling hand aimlessly swung it in the air while soldiers of the rebellion approached. They kept Foley away.

"Stay back, Highness," Sevin stated. "I will kill him."

"Wait."

"What is it?" Sevin came closer but didn't touch her.

"I'm all right, Sevin. More than all right. Foley shall never touch me again. I know this." And she did know it with tremendous certainty. The gods were working through her. "He will die this day for all he has done and especially for harming Rohen but you are not the one to kill him."

This time when she spoke she'd controlled her voice and the light was gone.

She took a single step closer to Foley and concentrated on keeping him set in place. Sevin remained at her side.

"How can you be alive?" Foley strained to move. "I killed you. I killed you. This is impossible."

Sorrah tilted her head observantly, knowing if he lifted a hand to her, she could stop him.

The rebellion soldiers behind and around Foley suddenly parted. Coming out of nowhere, one of the knights dressed in black appeared behind Foley. He was eerily still, his head slightly lowered, the hood of his cloak extended forward enough that she couldn't make out his face but there was something strangely familiar about him.

When he finally moved it was swiftly, just as she had been only seconds ago. She tilted her head partly as she watched a sword with a bright silver blade materialize in the air high and to the side of Foley. It hung on its own, suspended in the air. The cloaked man raised his hand and in the blink of an eye the sword was in his grasp.

He hadn't grabbed it at all. Was this familiar stranger a sorcerer?

The man, who reminded her of a knight, briskly and masterfully swooped the blade sideways at Foley's neck, instantaneously severing his head. His headless body dropped to the ground.

"Fool. *Nothing* is impossible," the executioner stated.

He sheathed his sword at his hip and gave a quick bow to Sorrah. "Majesty."

Sorrah's gaze went to the emblem pinned on the man's cloak. On the silver piece was a red-handled sword just like the one worn by the man Rohen had spoken about. The man called Murtagh.

Sevin must have noticed the symbol at the same time. "You are Murtagh?" he asked the man.

"Yes and no," Sorrah answered for the man knowing now who this man was and why he was so familiar to her. "He is my brother. My brother Marcus."

Marcus pulled his hood down, revealing bright blond hair, similar to Sorrah's. He had a very handsome face and undeniably the eyes of their mother.

Sorrah heard many murmur Marcus' name. How long had he been out of prison? He had taken on another persona, that of Murtagh. How long had he needed to hide?

"Hello, sister," Marcus said with a warm smile. He lost his smile and appeared almost sad. "My Sister... I have waited a very long time for you." He spread his arms open and without a second of hesitation, Sorrah flew into his embrace.

"I saw what you did. I knew you'd be special," he said, holding her tight and resting the side of his face on the top of her head.

"How did I not sense our connection like I have before?" she asked.

"Your mind was clearly on other things. When in heightened situations, you are caught up in the power. But in time you will learn how to masterfully wield what the gods have bestowed upon you. I promise."

All around the field of battle, both Kingswatch and rebellion soldiers bowed their heads in reverence to the children of King Zarek. Some dropped to their knees.

Sorrah lifted her face to Marcus then to her right as more Kingswatch soldiers rode quickly away.

"Shall we stop them?" Alexander asked.

"No. I noticed others rode off when they saw that I survived," Sorrah said. "Let them tell Meserek."

She stepped away from Marcus but kept her hands on his arms. "I need to find Rohen."

"Yes. I know."

"How do you know?"

"We are connected, sister. I know how you feel about him. Had you not come, I would have joined Rohen and the resistance. We will formulate a plan of attack. I am in contact with someone on the inside of Sandrin Castle. There is much to talk about." He looked around them. "But not here out in the open. You and all who are loyal to you may join us in Shendora."

"All right, but I need to ask you something first, Marcus."

Marcus smiled wryly. "You are wondering if I am after the throne of our father." It wasn't a question.

"You are his son. The first born."

"Yes. This is true. I am his son and I voluntarily abdicate the throne. Allow me to show you something."

Sorrah nodded. "All right."

Marcus addressed the men who gathered beside them. "For all of you to see so there will be no question from this day forward."

He removed his cloak and the chest plate beneath, tossing them on the ground. He untied the top of his black shirt and pulled it down off his shoulder, unveiling his birthmark. The Sorrien star.

"Do not be afraid. Our father had the same mark as I. Now, sister... If you'd be so kind as to show your mark which I believe is quite different from that of mine or our father. It is necessary."

"Of course," she replied.

She did likewise with her clothing, only when she exposed her unique mark, it flared to life, moving, shifting and shooting out a brilliant light which spread far and wide across the land. The only two people remaining upright were she and Marcus. All others, were on bended knee with their heads bowed once again. There was no question who the chosen one was, the prophecy of the gods had been fulfilled by her and her alone.

"So you see... the choice is not ours but has already been made. Predetermined if you believe in such things. It is clear, Sorrah. The prophecy trumps any tradition of the first born son being the heir to the throne. The moment I was old enough, my father... *our* father, took me down to the cavern beneath the castle. The most sacred of the three caves."

Sorrah knew the cave below the castle was regarded as the most holy. Rohen had told her as much.

"With witnesses present, he had me touch the etchings on the walls. Each and every one of them. He had many Hendrins as advisors and had been told ahead of time that because of our marks, we were able to touch them without consequences."

Sorrah instantly recalled how crazy Aunt Kaye had her touching mirrors over and over again. She knew what it was like to be forced to do such a thing.

"The Hendrins told the king that although I am marked and somewhat gifted, I was not the fulfillment of prophecy. But he was stubborn and had to be certain with his own eyes."

Sorrah nodded as she fixed her clothing.

"Long ago, even before he became king, Hendrins informed our father that his blood was of an ancient bloodline, one that one day would mix with the rare blood of a daughter of Mercury. And together a child would be conceived. A child who would one day fulfill the prophecy and rule the kingdom."

Marcus shrugged his shoulders. "Only the child wasn't me. Later, before I was taken by Meserek's men, Mother told me she was pregnant and I knew right then that you were the one. The chosen. She knew you were female and had already chosen a name. The Hendrin, Shay, who advised her had something to do with that."

With a sincere expression he continued to look her in the eye.

"There is no mistaking who is the rightful ruler. And I'm all right with that. You have my loyalty, Your Majesty," he said, bending down on one knee.

"Stand up. Please. I need you to help me, Marcus. And I want you by my side."

Marcus stood and took her hands into his. "You have me. I am your brother and we are family."

Tears welled up in Sorrah's eyes. *Family.*

Sorrah surveyed the bloody scene before her and was horrified by what she saw. Many had given their lives for what they believed was right, she understood that. But there was something more in the eyes of the men who stood motionless and in shock from what they witnessed here today. Beyond the brutality and rage of war, lay courage and hope for a better future. These men, whether Sorrien or Borakien, wanted nothing more than to live peaceably and honorably. Meserek could never bring them prosperity or give them peace because he hadn't been the rightful successor to King Zarek. She was.

She was determined to make her parents and these people proud. But she'd need help. She lifted her voice when she spoke to the men.

"I look at this battle scene and see no Kingswatch soldiers, people of the resistance or rebellion army. I only see those who love Sorrah. And those who love Borak and the plains of Kortah. I see the greatest potential in this most beautiful land."

She had changed so much since arriving in Sorrah but much of her personality remained and she was grateful for that. Those who lost themselves could wander without ever knowing who they were. She finally did.

She came from a world where epic movie scenes and long heroic speeches were a part of its culture. Especially for her, who relished in imagination and romance. This moment reminded her of such a time.

She pushed aside the thoughts of such scenes playing through her mind and hoped she didn't inadvertently scream out the word freedom. *Gah.*

Instead she listened to her heart.

"Meserek sits on a throne of falsehood and proclaims he is the chosen of the gods. But he mocks them. He laughs in their faces and has made many of you his accomplices in deceit and tyranny. But I tell you today that all will be forgiven of any soldier who chooses to leave Meserek's army. You have a voice. You have a choice. I offer you one right now. Follow me. Follow the one whom the gods themselves created for this time. I believe it. I believe them. I know in my heart there has always been a greater purpose for my life. *This* is my purpose and this place? This place is my true home.

"I come from a faraway land that is all too familiar with war. A vast wasteland of forgotten values and dreams. Sorrah. Borak. The plains of Kortah do not need to follow that same destructive, deserted road. This war among us can end. We can live in peace with dignity and honor. All who follow me," She glanced at Marcus before continuing, "and my brother, into Sandrin and into war against Meserek, are the Queensguard. I will take my rightful place on the throne where my father once reigned! All who stand opposed, you are free to leave. No harm will come to you here. You are free to return to Sandrin and to Meserek, but know this… We will meet again soon and judgment will come upon you and upon the false king. My father shall be avenged. The people of Sorrah and Borak shall be avenged."

A few claps started, sparking an eruption of cheers.

A light coming off the horizon caught Sorrah's attention. It shone down upon the ground, illuminating a black overcoat. Mesmerized, she edged her way forward, making her way around dead bodies.

"Rohen," she murmured, bending down and lifting his coat. She clutched it to her body as tears edged their way out from her eyes, tumbling down her cheeks. She raised the top of the coat to her face, closed her eyes and inhaled. A familiar masculine woodsy scent assailed her senses, a scent which tugged at her heart and set off in her mind a reel of images of her sea captain.

"Sevin," Sorrah said.

Sevin instantly came to her side. "Highness? Are you all right?"

She hadn't cared how it looked to the numerous men who continued to watch her. She opened the coat and put it on. It was big, of course, but she didn't care. She was reveling in the essence of *him* lingering in the fabric.

"You, Alexander, Demetri, Revel and Kehgen remain my most trusted guards. I want all of you to remain close to me."

"Of course."

She hugged herself, pulling the coat around the front of her and running her hands up and down her arms.

"He is strong. He will survive Meserek," Sevin offered with confidence.

"I know he will. He is stubborn and willful... and,"

She stopped, giving Sevin her best determined look. "Make ready to send word to Castlemore. We are not only going to fight for the kingdom but for Rohen's life. You will not lose your leader, and I will *not* lose the man I love."

She looked him square in the eyes and firmly patted his arm. "We are going to get him back."

Sevin smirked. "Yes, Majesty. And if I might add..."

Sorrah lifted her brows.

"He isn't the only stubborn one."

"Best you remember that." There was a subtle note of teasing to her voice. "Oh, and send another request to Castlemore. I want Gerta and Silva to be brought to me. I want women around me that I can trust. They will remain in Shendora until Sandrin is secure."

"As you wish."

Sevin turned to leave, but Sorrah stopped him.

"Wait. Sevin... My gods, you're wounded," she said, noticing blood coming through his clothing at his side. "Why didn't you say anything?"

"It's nothing."

"There are healers in Shendora. I assure you, we will find him the finest," Marcus offered.

"The way he's bleeding, he might not make it to Shendora," Demetri added as he approached.

"I'm fine," Sevin insisted. He glared at Demetri.

"Sit and show me the wound," Sorrah commanded.

Sevin didn't move and gave her a stubborn expression similar to one Rohen might give her.

"That wasn't a request, soldier. I gave you an order. Am I to believe that my second in command of the Queensguard means to disobey me?"

She won. Of course.

He reluctantly sat on a nearby rock and lifted his shirt, exposing an open slice where a blade had made contact. Blood steadily leaked out.

"Demetri is right, I'm afraid. I don't think you have time to wait."

"I'll have it wrapped," Sevin answered. "It's really not that bad."

"No. It will bleed right through any cloth. It's deep. Let me see if I can help."

Sorrah wanted to try to use her power again. Everything was so new to her and she desired to know her full potential. Her gifts. With a greater ease than before, she summoned the power within, strangely knowing it had been lying inside her dormant, awaiting her call. She believed using the power would come with a price, as it had earlier and would deplete her body's energy but what did that matter when a life was at stake? She lifted her hand to his wound and closed her eyes in concentration while imagining the flow of power extending out from her and touching the wound. At first an odd sensation rippled up from Sevin's skin. She opened her eyes but left her hand on his wound.

"This... this can't be true," she muttered, confused. "This cannot be right."

She lifted two fingers off his skin, noticing his blood on her.

Sevin met her gaze. He looked just as confused as she did but said nothing.

"There is the faintest sense of familiarity. Kind of the same recognition I have with Marcus... only much lighter. How odd. How could I know you, Sevin?"

"You don't," Marcus commented from behind her. "But it is likely Sevin's ancestry might've somehow crossed Father's bloodline."

"Royal bloodline?" she asked.

"Perhaps. I sensed it in him as well, but we are both highly attuned to these kinds of things. His blood makes it that much more evident.

We may have family all through the plains of Kortah, family we don't know of."

Marcus' words, although sparking her curiosity, didn't seem to ring as fully accurate. What she sensed in Sevin seemed more similar in nature to that of her mother. Even though she'd only had a small amount of time with her in the cave. She considered her druid heritage and thought somehow Sevin was linked in that way.

Because she hadn't discerned any familiarity in Sevin on the onset of meeting him, she could only deduce her sensitivity to such a thing, came with his blood, as Marcus said, but also the onset of her power.

She closed her eyes to concentrate on healing him.

"I know nothing of this," Sevin told her in a whisper.

Sorrah opened her eyes to look at him. "That doesn't mean it isn't true."

Joy fluttered in Sorrah's spirit at the thought of having more family. She had been alone for far too long.

"You need to be healed," she told him quietly as she closed her eyes once more. She thought of Sevin's loyalty to Rohen and her. He was quiet and kept to himself but from what she had seen and heard, he was a worthy male. Worthy of life. Worthy of the gods healing. This truth rang through her with great certainty.

"Careful, sister. Such efforts will exhaust you or worse," Marcus cautioned.

Marcus already seemed to know what using the gift of power did to the body which made her curious about the abilities he might possess. She could learn from him.

A steady aura of light came out from her hand, and slowly Sevin's skin began to alter into a healthier state, changing color and mending together. She swayed from the endeavor but persevered until the wound was fully healed.

She lowered her hand and began to slump off to the side.

Marcus was there to catch her. "Easy now, Sorrah." He lifted her in his arms and whistled for his horse.

"My bag," she muttered.

"I've already retrieved it for you. Along with the others," Demetri said, handing the bag which contained her mother's things to Marcus.

"You know how much it means to me," Sorrah murmured,

offering him a weak smile. "Thank you."

Demetri nodded before joining Rohen's men. They mounted their horses and watched as Marcus lifted Sorrah onto his lap.

"She's going to make an exceptional queen," Demetri commented to those around him.

"She already is," Sevin added.

"Marcus," Sorrah mumbled as she felt her eyes close in exhaustion.

"Yes?"

"My men?"

Sevin answered before Marcus could. "Are right beside you, Your Highness. We will not let you out of our sight." He leered momentarily at Marcus.

"You are already a queen, sister," Marcus stated with a smile. "You've already managed to secure trusted guards and loyal subjects."

Sevin and the other five men of Rohen's elite rode on each side of Marcus. Marcus' men were behind them followed by a new army of the Queensguard which consisted of men of the rebellion and former Kingswatch soldiers.

Silently, as her strength slowly increased, Sorrah lifted prayers to the gods.

Please watch over Rohen until we can get to him. Please don't let him die. I love him.

Chapter twenty four

"You did not see what I did, Father!" Ian exclaimed. "She has—she is very powerful. She is blessed by the gods. The rumors are true. You must accept her claim."

"You dare question your king? I accept nothing. By giving way to this female's false profession, you speak treachery against the throne. The only thing clear to me is that she is nothing more than a Hendrin. A witch who receives payment from your brother for her hypocrisy! Rohen has been after my throne for how long now?!"

"That's not true. And she is not a Hendrin."

"She is someone who has received reward for being a fairhead and her ability to perform sorcery. If that isn't a Hendrin I don't know what is. Why I... I..." Meserek picked up a book. "The spine on this book needs to be restored."

Ian blew off his father's last comment and took a defensive stance. "We have always spoken plainly. When you've allowed me to speak that is."

Meserek looked aimlessly around. "Where are my plums? I asked for plums," the king mumbled as he frantically pulled on a tapestry cord hanging near the wall.

As of late, Meserek had been losing control over his thoughts and tongue, speaking absurdities and at times, uttering nothing but complete nonsense. Some of the servants reported strange behavior to Ian but he had already been a witness to these times. Nothing diminished the man's evil tendencies. It was unfortunate he didn't lose his wicked nature along with his sanity.

"I will listen to no more! You are an ingrate! A bastard. Questioning your king!"

It wasn't the first time his father had resorted to name calling. "I do not question the king, but I do however, question my father! Can't you see how your lies have come back to haunt you just as I've

218

warned? This needs to end now before more innocent people die."

"Insolence!" Meserek proclaimed. "You have done nothing but scowl and whine in my ear. A constant thorn in my side! How you are my son I do not know!"

Oh, I'm sure you can figure it out. "For the sake of Sorrah and Borak, Father," Ian pleaded. "Do what's right for once!"

Just as in times past, Meserek hardened his heart to the truth.

Ian knew the gods had a plan for the female named Sorrah. She was the one they'd chosen to unite the people and rule the plains of Kortah. That fact was clearer than ever before. He just wished the king would see his wrongdoings and surrender before it was too late. But deep down he knew his father was filled with arrogance and beyond hope of reconciling his soul with the gods. He was lost, his mind sick and twisted, held in servitude by evil.

"I have done nothing but serve and cater to these wretched whining people!"

"My gods, listen to what you're saying, Father. These people? Wretched? Whining? They are your subjects. Many of which started out loyal to you. They wanted so badly to believe the prophecy had come true. They wanted to believe in you so much that they backed your claims but now? Now they flee from this land in droves! They sojourn to regions far beyond your reach and hide in fear of your wrath because of it. You have over taxed them, starved them and grossly abused them."

"They whine! I give them meat, they want bread. I give them water and they want wine! There is no pleasing them! I give them protection!"

"Protection from whom? You? Because that's what they're desperately in need of. Protection from the king they refer to as the king of death."

Meserek sneered. "What is in a name?"

"A name is everything. Not that it matters to you but I'm glad my mother named me."

Ian's mother had told some of the elder Hendrins that the baby in her belly was a gift. She hadn't known he was a boy but had chosen the name Ian because the name meant gift of God. Her faith had been an example for his faith.

"Those who were slain were traitors and offenders of the realm!" Meserek insisted.

"Why because they hunted on land you claimed belongs solely to you? Or because they couldn't afford to pay the taxes to have a cart in the marketplace?"

"Bleh!"

"You chose the vilest man and made him the Kingswatch commander. You knew what would happen."

His father's grin grew wide and wicked. "Ah. Burdish. Now there was a true Borakien soldier. He was a legend."

"Burdish was notorious that's for certain but it wasn't for his morals or honor. Still, you gave him liege over the Kingswatch and approved his methods. I know where Burdish's orders came from."

"Oh, you don't give the man credit. He had many ideas of his own." Guile was in his voice.

Ian never really did consider Meserek to be his father. Not with the way he treated not just him but others as well. So many others.

"You disgust me."

"Feeling is quite mutual. Son."

His father had considered Burdish more like his son. Probably because they had similar wicked hearts. Evil didn't beget evil through blood, Ian was nothing like his father, but evil most certainly attracted evil.

"It is fortunate for the people of Sorrah that Burdish finally lost his head at the hands of Murtagh."

"Murtagh? Fables. Untruths. The dark knight? Bah! Murtagh is nothing but a myth!"

"A *myth?* Well, the myth successfully broke through your defenses and killed the commander of the Kingswatch. You don't fool me. Murtagh and his black-clothed knights are people you've come to fear."

And I have come to admire. From the first time Ian had heard of Murtagh's escapades he'd wanted to join the knights. But after in depth councils with his Hendrin friend, Shay, and others, he decided he could do the most good from the inside. Influence others to choose a different path other than murder and wickedness. It had been difficult for Ian to remain in the castle, taking the beatings and knowing of the filth his father continued to perform, but he was steadfast in the knowledge of the greater good. The big picture.

The king flipped his hand in the air dismissively. "I was able to capture the leader of the rebellion and it's only a matter of time before I catch Murtagh too. If he truly exists."

Ian shook his head in disbelief. "You're so absorbed in darkness. You'll never see light."

"Enough! No one cares more about this land or Borak than I!"

Ian pounded his fist on the table in front of him. "Then you should have been a good king! People would have fought for you. Bleed for you. But it is far too late for that now! If you truly care about the welfare of Sorrah and Borak, then step down! Return to our homeland. Return to Borak—return to—"

Their voices overlapped.

"Never!"

"Surrender! Let them have their rightful ruler! The gods have been telling you to give up this farce for how long?!"

"Ahh. And there we have it once again. The gods. The gods you have spent so much time conferring with. They've made you soft!"

"Soft?" Ian stood straight. "I am more of a man than you have ever been or will ever be."

He was taller than his father, and much broader in the shoulders. He had worked over time, on strengthening his build, working in nearby communities, helping them rebuild homes and stables, the ones his father and former army destroyed upon taking over Sorrah.

"Where are these precious gods who rule from above?" Meserek said, lifting his hands in the air. "They have no say in Sandrin. They have no voice here."

"There are so many things wrong with what you just said. If you aren't hearing the voice of the gods, it is because your ears are blocked by evil. The gods should be in every part of ruling a kingdom. They are in everything. You have turned your back on them and they have left you to your devices. But now... now they are coming to collect. It is your penance. Judgment is at your door and you don't even see it. The gods will destroy you and all who remain at your side. You can be sure I won't be one of them."

Meserek charged Ian who firmly stood his ground. But the king stopped abruptly before touching him.

Ian jutted his chin out and kept his eyes on his father. "Go ahead. Strike me. I dare you." He leaned closer to his face. "Only don't forget, I'm no longer a child you can whip. I've trained with the finest. You will *never* touch me again."

The mad king walked to the window and abruptly turned back. He tilted his head to the side and blinked speedily. "Camden. There you are. Finally I will get my biscuits."

What? His father's behavior was worsening but Ian felt no empathy toward him. His sickness didn't excuse the heinous acts he had done. "Camden is not here."

"I know who you are!" The king's face reddened and he clenched his fists. "I could have you put to death over the words you speak to me."

"Don't you think I know that? I've always known that. I know there are those in the castle who remain loyal to you. But don't mistake loyalty for reward. I know you pay them well to watch me. But if you send any one of your executioners after me, by the time they lift their swords, there'd be a hundred soldiers at my side to defend me. There are more Kingswatch who are loyal to me than you realize. I have trained, ate, drank, and laughed with these men. They are my brothers."

"I should have disavowed you. I should've killed you myself at your birth when you came screaming out of that whore!" He pointed his finger at Ian. "You are and will ever be a bastard."

Ian bared his teeth, clenching them. He thrust his hand forward and took a firm hold of Meserek's throat. "Careful, *Father.*" He could kill him; snap his neck for calling his mother a whore. There were no witnesses after all to see him commit the deed. But even as the thought entered his mind, the notion to do such an act, was snuffed out by the honorable side of him.

He released his father with a slight shove.

Meserek heaved as he caught his breath. "Perhaps… there is hope for you yet. You are more like me than you think."

"I am *nothing* like you."

The king was not the true sovereignty but he was unfortunately, his father. The gods didn't look well on those who killed their own father, he imagined. Even an evil one.

All in due time. The gods will weed out the evil. Their voice will soon be heard by all.

Ian continuously attempted to overturn laws the king set in place, those which infringed so heavily on the rights of the common people, trying his hardest to use his position in the kingdom for good. He meditated daily in the sanctuary near the great sacred cave below the castle and wanted to do that which was right in the eyes of the gods, but his father fought him every step of the way.

There'd been a time, long ago, when he had loved his father. But that love slipped away by mistreatment and seeing so many people tortured and murdered by his hand.

"You don't get to speak of my mother. Not ever." He walked to the window and pulled it shut with a slam. "So very cold," he murmured before turning to his father again. "There is a storm coming. Be careful or you might catch your death."

Meserek clutched his lapels closed as if feeling the artic intent and weight of Ian's words in his bones. "Prepare the Kingswatch for war."

"I resign my position. I will not fight the truth seekers. And I certainly will not fight the gods chosen one."

"You're wrong, you headstrong bastard," Meserek said with malice in his voice. "You will be on the front lines, upfront with the Kingswatch where you belong or I will begin slaughtering the units one man at a time. Beginning with your favorites."

Ian silently cursed. He knew his father was well aware of which soldiers had become his closest friends. He'd grown up with them.

"And don't think I'm unaware of Chesla."

Ian's heart dropped. The king had forgotten things like plums and biscuits but remembered the truly important things. His friends and lover. He'd tried diligently to keep Chesla, out of the king's sight and keep their relationship a secret. He wondered before if his father had him watched. Now he was certain.

"Fine. I'll prepare them for war."

He'd only agreed because he didn't want good men to be killed. He bowed half-heartedly and backed up toward the door. He turned, grasped the handle and looked over his shoulder. "And what of Rohen?"

"He is none of your concern. He is a traitor to the crown and will remain in the hands of the punisher."

"You're torturing your own nephew?"

"No. I am torturing a traitor!"

"The crazed look in his father's eyes said all there was to be said. He was gone. Loyal only to the one who sat on the fiery throne in the pits of the underworld.

All I can do now is save as many as I can. Beginning with one. My brother.

His father continued to murmur aimlessly. His mind going in and out of awareness. "Now, be gone! War is on the horizon and I am in need of rest."

Ian left the king. Instead of heading to his room, he made his way to the back stairs leading to the servant's quarters.

There, in the farthest room, was a secret tunnel which led to the prisons below. He'd attempt to make his way to the lower level undetected. Some of the servants might see him but he knew many of them and had even worked on some of their family's homes. No matter, it was time he stepped up his efforts. It was time to see Rohen.

He continued down the stone steps leading to the caverns below, stopping now and then to keep a watchful eye behind him. When he reached the bottom he turned left and saw two guards outside of the prison cell he'd heard Rohen was placed in. He was thankful he recognized one of the solders. Keit. He was more than an exceptional fighter. He was as true of a friend as they came.

"Commander," Keit said, addressing Ian formally as he did when others were around.

"Keit." Ian nodded. "War will soon be upon us. I'm sure you've both heard of the female who claims to be the queen anointed by the gods."

The soldier to the left huffed.

Ian narrowed his eyes. "Nortan, is it?"

"Yes, sir. That's right."

"I thought so." He purposely lightened the tension in his voice. "You've been here since the time of Burdish, haven't you?"

"That's right."

Ian noticed the look. The Kingswatch soldier had been an admirer of the former vile commander. *Gods,* he thought. He knew a few of the bad seeds in the Kingswatch but not all of them. It would take him more time than they had to sift through this many soldiers. But not if he had help. One thing about spending time in training and in battle with other men. You get to know what's in their head and what's not in their heart.

"I'll be gathering men by units. We'll be meeting soon to discuss strategies. For now, you're relieved from duty. Keit, stay. I'll be sending another to keep watch with you."

"Nortan, I want you to get some of the maps together and find Jitzen and the others."

It was a simple task but Ian knew Nortan would be pleased he'd been given attention.

Nortan nodded and started for the stairs.

"So we need to gather the men—" Ian said, trying to keep a conversation vague while Nortan was still within earshot. When he heard a door close, he spoke more openly to Keit.

"What's going on, brother?" Keit asked. "I know you. Something's in the works. You have that look in your eye."

"I'll fill you in soon. How is he?" Ian asked, turning to look inside the cell.

Keit held a torch inside the cell, lighting it up. "He came to about an hour ago but he's in and out. From what I've heard, the punisher tortured him something fierce. His back is pretty ripped up."

The stench of blood clung to the thick air. Bile rose in Ian's throat. He was no stranger to the whip.

Rohen lay on his side, facing the back wall. His shirt was shredded, and his flesh fared no better. His wounds were in bloody streaks, the markings of where the whip had landed numerous times.

Ian clenched his eyes shut as images of what his father had done to him assaulted his mind. Every birthday his father had a punisher string him up and whip him, saying it would make his birthday memorable, reminding him each year how he'd taken a bastard child and given him a home and more.

"No more. Neither the punisher nor my father will ever harm my brother again."

He and Rohen had been at odds with one another. They'd separated early on but he'd secretly admired his older brother. Rumors spread throughout all of Kortah regarding the resistance and the rebellion army, including all the good they were doing with Rohen as their commander. He'd regretted not leaving with him when he had the chance. Later, when his father sent him on a hunt for Rohen, he'd purposely let his brother go free. He'd faced Rohen for the first time in decades and the look of betrayal in his eyes tore at his heart and haunted him these many years. The moment he'd returned to Sandrin, he'd dropped to his knees in front of the sacred cave and vowed to do right, pledged to fight against the evils of this world, knowing Rohen wasn't one of them and his father was.

The king must have known because that was the day he'd given him the command over the Kingswatch. His father thought he stayed all this time because of some high appointment, but no, he stayed because he didn't want to abandon his brothers of the Kingswatch like he felt he had Rohen. He'd taken a hard look at the greater good. What if he could do more from the inside? He hoped he'd pleased the gods when he assisted thousands of refugees wanting to escape Sorrah. He'd even sent a team to Borak, his native land, to help with those in need. Secretly, he'd helped the phantom Murtagh although he'd never met the man in person. He'd funded efforts and turned a blind eye at some of Murtagh's missions. He'd made a mark on a specific boulder in the mountains, signaling to the so called mythical dark knight. In two days' time, at the hour of midnight, he would meet with one of Murtagh's men. It was the time to meet Murtagh face to face. It was time for the uprising to escalate. Perhaps, he could even convince Rohen and his army to join forces with those of the Kingswatch who were honorable, those worthy of remaining a soldier in the kingdom.

"And how are you going to protect the king's prize possession? He's a prisoner."

"You are going to help me hide him, Keit, my friend. Rohen is weak; otherwise he wouldn't let me near him. What my brother doesn't realize, is that I'm going to save his life. Open the cell. We're moving him to the servants' quarters. I know the perfect place."

Chapter twenty five

"Sorrah! Sorrah!" Rohen cried out. His fever had taken him to a place between dreams and delusion. A place where everything blurred, only not nearly enough to forget. The horrific scene of her murder kept playing over and over in his mind. The look in her eyes as Foley thrust his blade into her. He'd been helpless to save her, breaking his promise and vow to protect her. What had he been thinking when he urged her, demanded that she go with Sevin. He'd thought it was for the best, for her well-being but he'd been wrong. Deadly wrong. Dear gods, he wanted the torment to end.

"Numb. Make me numb. I don't want to remember! I don't want to feel anything! Let me die!"

He clenched his eyes shut and clutched what felt like blankets beneath him. But he knew such comforts were far from the stone cell the Kingswatch had thrown him in.

Images of his arms being chained to the ceiling brushed through his mind. He'd been whipped by the punisher, a vile excuse for a man who performed such acts for the king. The punisher's duties were simple. Use whatever means necessary to coerce the captive into telling all. Secrets. That meant, pulling fingernails off, yanking teeth or gouging eyeballs with a nail, anything short of death which by that time, all begged and pleaded for. Only Rohen hadn't been asked questions. He'd been thoroughly whipped with a promise of much more to come. He'd remained conscious for as long as he could. He didn't beg, didn't cry... only scorned himself each time the whip crossed his back and ripped open his skin. He deserved the worst. He was the reason Sorrah was dead.

He opened his eyes finding himself in a room filled with nothing but darkness. A light coming toward him slowly filtered through the narrow window, illuminating his salvation. A rope.

He took a firm hold of the rope, looped it around and tied it as tight as he could get it.

The noose lay loosely in his palm. He stared in wonder at the answer to his plea for deliverance. Living in a world without her was impossible. Dying was easy.

Sorrah is dead.

He recalled the image of his mother on her knees, her hands cupping her face as she cried out in agony over the death of her husband. The image altered, changing her face to his. The pain was now his to bear. He held Sorrah's lifeless body in his arms, tightly against his chest while he rocked back and forth.

He was hot. So very hot. A sharp pain pierced his heart as he recalled her words of love to him before she died. *I should have told her.* "I love you. I love you."

She was dead. Nothing else mattered. His spirit was empty, a sea of endless void.

While a bitter requiem played in the background, he walked to a wooden bench, stood upon it and stared at the dangling rope beckoning for his neck. A light had been taken from this world. *His* world. He placed his hands on his head and pulled at his hair. *I can't feel it. I can't feel anything but the pain. The loss.*

"This isn't the end I wanted for you," a male voice said from the shadows burrowing in the corner. "And I expect it's not the one you want for yourself."

Rohen knew that voice. "Father."

"Listen to me. The future remains and you must face it. You will need to open your heart. You are no coward."

"No. I am not."

For so long Rohen had worked diligently, wanting nothing more than to make his father proud. In his youth, he'd trained harder than most, building himself into a strong enough man to avenge the death of his parents. Only a bitter coldness settled within him and eventually he had shut himself off to the possibility of love.

"All men should die an honorable death. A soldier must have at least that in the end," his father said.

"And what of you? You died in a bloody field fighting a war you were never meant to fight. Your own brother put you in front of the enemy so he could blame them when you died. He did this with no thought of your life or the lives of your family and why? Because he coveted your wife. He killed you."

"You must stop allowing my end to define your life. Hatred burns in your heart like a festering illness. You've allowed it to eat you alive. It has been there for far too long, Son. Such hatred blinds you from the truth."

"Truth?"

"Would you have loved her, had you known she'd be taken from you so soon?"

Rohen cringed. He had fallen for Sorrah when he'd thought himself incapable, when he vowed he would never give his heart to anyone. As if there'd been no other choice, his heart had acted on its own and claimed her. "I would have loved her no matter."

"And has that love died now that she is gone?"

"No. It has not. I still love her." He bit the edges of his lip as tears pooled in his eyes. "I will always love her."

"As I will always love your mother. As I will always love you. Love is not limited by the confines of time or death. Not the kind of love that is pure and all consuming, felt in the very soul of a man."

A ghostly image of his father stepped out from the shadows. "I died among my men. Son, I died a soldier's death. I died with honor."

Rohen's body became increasingly heavy, as though it were being weighed down by boulders. His eyes began to close as weariness overtook him. His father faded away before his eyes. "You're right, Father. I shall not die like this," he muttered.

How preposterous was the idea of a coward's end? The punisher had taken him to the racks and whipped him, yet he had survived. He preferred to die from a cause not of his own, than to push himself into eternity before his destined time. He hadn't known Sorrah for long, but memories had been created with her. They had laughed, they had loved, and they had lived. Traces of Sorrah, her scent and even her taste were forever embedded on his mind and in his heart. They were a part of each other. Two halves of a whole.

Darkness encompassed him once more as the height of his fever peaked before slipping into a downward slope. He drifted off in sleep.

"You've made a very wise choice," the voice of a woman said.

Hours later, Rohen's eyes opened and met with the rich brown eyes of a pale-faced woman. She had long black curly hair and held a tray of food in her hands. He glanced around wondering if he were back inside the dream world. Where was he? He expected to wake inside his cell, or if the gods had shown mercy, up in the heavens above, the place where Sorrah was.

Instead he was lying on his side. He moved his foot feeling a soft pad beneath him. *I'm on a bed.* The room was warm and the smell of the food the woman held caused his hollow stomach to growl. Such comforts would never be given to one destined for endless torture.

"Your fever has broken. The gods have given you to us now," the woman said. "You are safe. My name is Shay."

"Shay," he muttered, his dry mouth and throat a pool of scorching sand.

"Yes. Drink," she said, assisting his head forward to the goblet she held at his mouth.

He took a sip of the cooling water. "I dreamt."

"Did you?"

"Yes."

"You've made a choice to live." She busied herself with the tray. "Smart choice."

"I saw my father. How? Where was I? It seemed so real."

"There is a dark place which exists between consciousness and sleep. As you dream, fragments of your dream are stored there, leaving you with the smallest of details upon awakening. For those who have nightmares, this is a good thing. It is necessary to keep the mind intact. But for those who dream of their lost ones, or lives and worlds far more glorious than their own, awakening is most tragic."

Clearly she was a Hendrin. Most of them knew things that they shouldn't and were known for their deep speech and riddles.

"You've been in my care for four days. Your wounds have been cleaned and dressed. The ointment is my own special blend. Smells heavenly and works magic..." she winked, "but it is likely you won't want to lie on your back for a day or two more."

She lifted a spoonful of soup to his lips and he drank it down.

"Where am I exactly?"

If the dream world seemed so real, was this real?

"You are in Sandrin Castle. In a safe room."

"Who brought me here?"

"That I cannot tell you but rest assured, all shall be revealed to you this day. I have to say, you are a surprise, even to me. My, but the gods have plans for you." She sighed and smiled warmly. "I cannot wait to see your Sorrah. Her mother, Alaina, was so very pretty and had such a kind heart." She clapped her hands together once and smiled widely. "Oh, I remember her wedding day as if it were yesterday. The blue gown, the flowers, the music and dancing. We've yearned for such days to return to us again. Sandrin needs a revival. And soon we will have it!"

His heart lurched. She spoke of Sorrah as if she were alive. "You don't know."

"What is it I am to know? I will tell you if I do or do not."

Rohen sat up, his head pounded. "Sorrah is… Sorrah is dead." He loathed his own words. They cut through the center of his heart and split it in two.

"No, brother. You are wrong. Sorrah lives. I saw her myself. I observed all that she did," Ian pronounced from the doorway.

"I'll leave you two to speak. It is far overdue," Shay said, placing the soup on a table beside the bed.

"And I'm to trust what you say?" Rohen asked, raising his voice as high as he could. The effort made his head ache something fierce.

Ian whispered something to a guard before stepping inside the room and closing the door behind him. "Whether you trust me or not, you're going to hear what I have to say."

Rohen slowly stood but wobbled on his feet. "I don't really have much choice now do I?"

"No. You should probably sit."

"I'll stand."

"Well, then you better stay next to the bed so it catches you when you fall over."

"Gods, just say what it is you have to say, Ian, before my head explodes!"

Ian pulled out a chair from the desk, turned it, and sat.

Rohen stubbornly remained standing.

"Sorrah lives, brother."

"I beg to differ, *brother,*" he mocked. "I watched a blade go clear through her body."

"Then your face was covered and they knocked you out. So, you didn't see what happened afterward."

How could he have known what happened to him? Unless he witnessed it firsthand. Why should he be surprised that Ian was there on the battlefield? He was the commander of the Kingswatch.

"Many men died on the field. I didn't see you there."

"I was near you and kept many from ambushing you. But I left soon after they took you away."

How could that have been? He considered how much Ian had changed in appearance and stature. It was possible he'd been one of the cloaked soldiers who wore their hoods at the back of their heads. It was common practice of some in this day and age.

"There are decent men in the Kingswatch. My father had many of the bad ones accompany the wretched man named Foley. He is dead, by the way. I watched him die."

"Get back to Sorrah. What did you see?" Hope flared within. What if she had miraculously survived? He'd seen what happened in the cave and there was talk of her power. Did he dare believe his brother's words?

"She fell to the ground and remained there for only seconds. Then rose unharmed."

Immediately, Rohen's thoughts went to the tree of life in the drawings. The symbol of infinity. Could his Sorrah be immortal? It was surely one interpretation of the markings. Adrenaline awakened his battered body. He moved his feet and ever so slowly began to pace. He clenched his hands into fists. He needed to get out of there. He needed to find her.

"Sorrah is alive?" he said more to himself than to Ian. The Hendrin must have spoken the truth. It wasn't that she didn't know of Sorrah's death, but that she knew she had survived.

The urgency to get to Sorrah and know for himself she was really all right, surged through him. He had to see her, touch her. He had to beg for forgiveness once more. He should have remained by her side. Was he cursed to live his life in constant regret?

Sorrah lives. The edges of his mouth began to curl in a smile but he held it at bay. Dare he believe it to be true?

He made his way to the window and pushed aside the curtain. A stone wall was on the other side. He could see nothing of the outdoors. "Where am I exactly?"

"In the servants' quarters."

A hard lump formed in his throat. What if this was part of the torture? What if Ian was merely playing a part? "You expect me to believe that Meserek knows I am missing and hasn't checked every inch of this castle?"

"His mind has been touched with craze. He had these, along with all other quarters thoroughly checked; only the guards who went through the castle were ones loyal to me. They never saw you, by the way. Besides, this room is a room behind a room. Beyond the door is yet another door. A false one. A passageway to the real quarters. You are safely hidden."

"Why would you do this for me? Why have you done this? For what purpose does it serve?"

Ian stood and stepped closer to Rohen. They were eye to eye with each other. Rohen had a few more pounds of muscle on him but Ian was no slacker by any means.

Ian sighed. "Even though I have made strides here in Sandrin and in this castle, I have regretted these many years of not knowing you. I have regretted my decision not to leave with you."

It took a few minutes before Rohen could answer.

"You were young and foolish. I'm not sure you grew out of the foolish part."

Ian smiled. "Indeed."

"I gave you numerous opportunities."

"I know. You never gave up on me, for that I am grateful. I hope it's not too late for you to allow me to fight alongside you."

Rohen wasn't sure of any of this. However, Ian could have let him continue with the punisher or have him killed. But he hadn't and to top it off, his eyes were that of his mother. Their mother.

"I want you to know that I have worked to free many Sorriens from my father's evil hands. I have stopped as much as I can. There are many of the Kingswatch who are no longer loyal to the king. They are ready to be counted among the resistance and to be part of your rebellion army. If you let them. Your female, Sorrah, is the chosen of the gods to be sure. I watched as the dark knights and Murtagh himself came to aid her. I left the moment I saw him. I knew she'd be safe. It won't be long before Murtagh and his knights join your men and march on Sandrin. I'm sure of it."

Having some of the Kingswatch on the side of the resistance would certainly give the rebellion forces a greater number of men to combat Meserek's evil regime.

"And you want me to believe you willingly betray your king who is also your father?" Rohen asked, folding his arms over his chest. He regretted his movement two seconds afterwards. It stretched his wounds causing pain to shoot through his body. He forced himself to remain still until he could breathe better.

"He may be my king but he has never behaved like a father. He is wretched on both accounts. His seed conceived me from our mother but he never cared for me."

For all Rohen knew this was just another ploy to give up his men. The king was cunning.

"I can see you question my motives. I cannot blame you for that."

With great ease, Rohen unfolded his arms and shrugged his shoulders. Still, he couldn't help the grimace that came across his face.

"How is your back faring? Feeling any better?" Ian asked.

"My back?" Rohen asked bitterly. "Shredded. But you already knew that. You've lived here, in the highest rooms of Castle Sandrin, living a royal's life while so many are given turns with the punishers below."

Ian began untying his shirt and Rohen wondered why.

"Do not tell me I have been brought up privileged and don't know the pain of the punisher's whip."

He let his shirt fall down his arms then turned his back to Rohen.

His back was covered with several deep, ridged scars. It was clear that Ian had been brutally beaten and whipped many times over. Rohen was instantly filled with rage. He and his brother were not close, even at odds with one another, but this? No one deserved to be treated this way.

"I tried to spare you a life with that mad man!"

"I know."

"Why did you not tell me? Why did you not send word?"

Ian pulled his shirt back up and turned around once more. "Did you need more of a reason to hate him or more of reason to want to kill him?"

Rohen tightened his lips and shook his head. He would kill Meserek for everything he had done. He'd killed his father, laid with his mourning mother and fathered a child. A boy who he had abused. Was there no end to his evil? Were there no limits? The gods only knew all of what Meserek had done in his life. The false king might believe he'd gotten away with it, but he was sorely mistaken. One way or the other he would pay. Recompense would be made if it were possible to atone for such a malevolent life. He'd be held accountable. *Your day is coming, Meserek.* Rohen cleared his throat. "Your father did that." It wasn't a question.

"He was never alone. He'd take turns with his favorite punisher."
Dear gods.

"I bear no love or loyalty toward him. Any hope of that has long since passed. I have stayed this long only to overthrow his dealings where I can. Especially brutality done to the people of Sorrah."

"You took the beatings to help others? Why would you make such a sacrifice?"

"Was your sacrifice any less? Your body has its own scars. You could have gone anywhere but you chose a life of a soldier for the greater good."

Rohen shook off the comment. "I've heard some promising things, rumors really. I knew the good done for the sake of commoners couldn't have come from Meserek. How did you manage to do it without him finding out you were responsible?"

"I am in contact with Murtagh. I have been for a long time."

"You've provided Murtagh with information about your father's dealings?"

"Yes."

"Brave or stupid?"

"A bit of both, I suppose." Ian smirked.

Rohen returned the expression. "You've been a spy all this time."

"As soon as I was old enough to understand how things operated around here and how corrupt my father was. Is. The rumors began to surface about Murtagh and his knights and I saw an opportunity to make a greater impact. I've never met the mysterious man directly, only through correspondence with his knights."

"Yet you saw him on the battlefield only days ago."

"I couldn't risk meeting him there. Your woman allowed many of the Kingswatch to go free. The soldiers loyal to my father returned to Sandrin and would have jumped at the chance to tell the king of my treachery. But the anonymity works both ways. All Murtagh and his men know is that I am an unhappy soldier of the Kingswatch. Murtagh has a small army but their numbers continue to grow. Even some of my men have left the Kingswatch in secret and have joined the knights."

"I'll need to see with my own eyes that Sorrah lives. Before anything is done. That's nonnegotiable."

"I expected as much. I know trust is something earned, Rohen, and maybe one day, we will have it between us. I'm not sure how easy it will be to give you what you want. It is possible Sorrah is being kept in hiding until the time of battle."

"Convenient. Especially for those who claim she is alive. I want to see her."

"She is the queen. Her life is in jeopardy."

"Apparently she has more than one life." *Thank the gods.* "I know more than anyone who she is and the danger she is in but that changes nothing. You've discreetly met with the knights; another meeting can't be out of the question. They need to show me proof that they have her or this goes no further. I can get the word out to my men. They will retreat back to their home should I tell them to do so."

Rohen needed to see her standing, breathing, living before his own eyes in order to wipe out the image of her being stabbed by Foley. But he knew the risk the closer she became to Sandrin. If the knights were hiding her, they wouldn't want to endanger her.

"I have already sent word to Murtagh. The time has come to join efforts. Knowing you'd need proof that Sorrah lives, I've requested they produce something to satisfy you."

Rohen doubted anything other than her would satisfy him. He opened his mouth to tell Ian just that but his brother stopped him, raising his hand out in front of him.

"Temporarily. In time you will see her. A meeting has been set for three days from now. I am to meet Murtagh just beyond Whispering

Peaks."

Whispering Peaks, named for the mysterious airy whispers people have said they've heard, is located at the southern end of Diamond Summit, the mountain ridges which surrounded Sandrin Castle. The whispers of the peaks aren't the only peculiar anomaly around the kingdom. A massive cliff extended outward, suspending high above the valley of Sandrin, while the enormous castle with its high luminescent towers and mystical presence stood nestled in the north side of the mountain. The valley filled with trees and encompassing a wide glade, would soon be filled with war and the blood of men.

"Meet *us*. Make sure Murtagh is the one we meet, not one of his knights, because I'm going with you. I don't care how you pull it off— you're getting me out of here. You want my trust? Then this is how it starts."

"All right."

Rohen couldn't wait to meet this Murtagh person and find out exactly where Sorrah was so he could find her. After the bizarre dream he had of his father, he needed to assure himself that he wasn't still dreaming. He would find his way to her and if she allowed, hell, even if she didn't allow, he was never going to leave her side again.

Chapter twenty six

"I've gotten close twice now," Sorrah said, nearly out of breath. She held her sword tightly in her hand. She knew she was no match for the Kingswatch soldiers in Sandrin, but she was determined to learn how to use a sword. Even a little. This way of life, where people used swords, daggers, battle axes, bows and arrows as their weapons, was now her life. They were rudimentary weapons, yet, affective in war. It was one more thing she needed to get used to, that, and no indoor plumbing. She never wanted to get used to that. One of her first acts as queen was definitely going to include a discussion on the matter. Trivial to some. Important to her.

Overshadowing the seemingly primitive living was the existence of beautiful, living, breathing, interacting trees and bizarre wildlife. Including dragons. She had tried but failed to associate this world with an era or time on Earth. There simply was no comparison. It was partly medieval, a bit renaissance, yet, there was sophistication to its structures and even the clothing had its own unique style. No, the fantasy world of Aaru which included the land of Sorrah, was distinctly its own.

"Your skills are improving quickly, sister," Marcus replied as he sheathed his sword. She did the same, uncasing her sword in a custom made belt at her hip.

For the past couple of days, Sorrah had sparred with Marcus, trained with Sevin and prepared, as much as possible, to go into battle with them, knowing they wouldn't allow her to fight any of the soldiers. They told her as much. She was immortal but no one came back from losing their head and after her miraculous recovery, she was certain Meserek would order his soldiers to do just that. Decapitate her.

"As your powers continue to gain in strength, you will be able to utilize it with greater ease and it won't deplete you of energy as fast."

"How were you able to control the sword and fly it into your hand? By using your power to command it?"

"It was barely a command but rather a mental request made before I even had the chance to think it."

"Before you thought it? How is that possible?"

"The power within is far more attuned to you than you think. Besides, how is anything possible?" He smiled. "Your power is part of who you are and at times can stay ahead of your mind. It rather acts ahead of you, knowing what you are going to do."

"That was intended to make things clear to me?"

Marcus grinned. "You were able to help Sevin. Why do you think that is?"

"Because power is inside me."

"Really? Hmm. Many have power but lack the capability of accessing it."

"The same kind of power we possess? Is that common here?"

"No. Not the same power. You and I are rare indeed. But everyone possesses some form of energy in their minds. Power, intuition, instincts, however it is labeled. You told me you possessed some talent with healing. Like our mother had."

"No. Not the same thing. Not as much as her."

Because while her mother had stayed the course and became a nurse, Sorrah had quit. She was more focused and determined than ever to follow through this time and see this finished. She only hoped she didn't disappoint those who were expecting more than she could give.

"It's going to take a while to get used to speaking about our mother, knowing she was both of ours. I never had any true family."

"You do now," Marcus offered with a smile.

She returned the smile but it quickly slipped away. Marcus was family but Rohen was a part of her. She wasn't herself, her better self, without him.

"So, because I had some medical knowledge, my power was able to be used as a healing tool?"

"Yes. My skill with a sword enables me to combine a talent with the power I have."

"I see. I think. I haven't been able to—I mean, I haven't completed much in my life. I'm not sure how much skill my power can access. I could turn out to be Sandrin's greatest disappointment."

"Don't ever say that." His voice took on a sharper tone. "The

239

people of both Sorrah and Borak, for the most part, loved our Father and they loved our mother too. She was kind and giving, but a strong woman as well. I see those same qualities in you. Even more. Don't underestimate yourself. From what I've seen over the past few days, you are unique in your own right. You're special. You are one with nature. You have an admiration, a natural instinctive love for trees and wildlife and in return it answers to you. That is a great gift. You have gained the loyalty of life itself."

She didn't know about all that but considered her past. "I've loved the outdoors for as long as I can remember. I'd rather be near nature than almost anywhere else. I've enjoyed the company of trees more than the company of people. Especially on cool fall days when a blanket, a thermos of hot chocolate and a book were my best friends."

"I claim little understanding of what you just said." He chuckled then became serious again. "Without you knowing it, I've observed you over the past couple days."

She raised her brows in question.

"From a distance. You were walking through a patch of trees just a few feet inside the forest. Your guards, Sevin and another, were walking near but I don't believe they observed the same thing I did. I watched as the branches of the trees and the foliage near your feet, shifted as you gracefully walked by, almost as if they were reaching out to you. Your mind was elsewhere, preoccupied with other things in the moment, but trust me, the branches and greenery rose and leaned in your direction as if they were begging to follow, longing to go where you were."

Sorrah sighed, her eyes drifting to the woods. "I would be lying if I said I didn't feel a strange connection to this place. All of it. From the moment I rose from the pond, I was awestruck by Sorrah's peculiar beauty but more than that, my spirit was taken captive. This extraordinary world spoke to my soul. It still does."

She scanned the area. Beyond the arena where they stood, was a part of the enormous Silvermist forest and high behind it were glistening, blue-tipped mountains. The landscape was breathtaking. She'd never tire of observing it.

"I first thought Sorrah reminded me of something I read in a book. But really, it's the other way around. I've read so many tales of mystical places. Only this place is nothing like anything written in fiction. This brilliant, colorful, magic-filled world is a place writers attempt to describe in their work but fall short because it's beyond menial descriptions and limited human imaginations."

Marcus seemed to carefully consider her words. "You are unlike me in that way. My imagination reaches no further than the place I am familiar with. You and our mother are from a world I know nothing about. Other than the few things she shared with me." He glanced down then out toward the trees again. "Other worlds exist. How remarkable is that?"

"What did she tell you?"

"Bits and pieces really. I was young and suspect she withheld a lot, believing the truth of her world would frighten me. So many people only see what they want to see inside their own small existence. But in reality every one of us could be surrounded by unseen worlds and magic, and I for one can't help but to be a bit curious about that."

"Well, the world I come from does have its own beauty, if people took the time to appreciate it, but it's nothing like it is here. Nothing like this."

"I may not know much about where you came from. But I do know you fit here, Sorrah. Mother loved it here. She was happy here for a while. I think you'll come to love it just as much. How strange it all must seem."

"It does seem strange but then it doesn't. I've dreamt of fantastical things my entire life, only to wake remembering the smallest fraction. It's very frustrating to wake from a dream and recall some details, while other parts elude you. And deep down you know they were the most important ones. Many of my dreams have been that way. I've only just realized how much it has mirrored my own life. And how ironic is that? Fragments of dreams, pieces and beginnings with no end. No completion. My life has been exactly that. I've always known something was missing."

She glanced to Marcus. "That must sound odd."

Marcus shook his head. "No it doesn't."

"This place is a compilation of all those lost dreams. A magnitude of dreams I wished I'd remembered. Only now I am truly awake for the first time in my life and before me is Sorrah. Bright and in living color."

"She certainly is," Marcus commented as he smiled warmly and placed his hand briefly on her arm.

"There are no more broken pieces. And I'll never have to dream of Sorrah again because now it's my home."

A soft peaceful hum stirred within, comforting her and confirming what she'd said was truth.

She raised her hands in front of her and turned them palm side up. "Ever since the time in the cave, my skin tingles." She rubbed her fingers together before placing her hand over her heart. "And the softest most comforting hum stirs my blood. I don't know how, but I know it's the resounding essence of life around me. This place has ignited something which had lain dormant inside me. It fills what once was empty. But still, a part of me remains unfilled. There is a void that cannot be denied. Won't be denied. I can't be all that I'm supposed to be without Rohen. Thoughts of him—worry consumes me."

"You love him."

"I do."

"Had they wanted to kill him, they would've done so on the battlefield, for all his men to see."

She knew Marcus was trying his best to reassure her. "Yes. But that warrants other concerns, doesn't it? What they might be doing to him. The harm he has to endure."

"He has been a part of the resistance for a long time. As the rebellion leader, he has led many men into battle with the Kingswatch. He's also Meserek's nephew. He's strong but I have to ask—"

"Ask."

"Are you sure you should trust his motives?"

She picked up on the tone in Marcus' voice. He was questioning Rohen's loyalty and that just didn't sit well with her. Her eyes gradually began to glow, her hands curled into tight fists. A heat which began at her center, spread throughout her body. She was seeing red.

"Are you well, Sorrah? You don't look it."

"I know the gods have sanctioned my union with Rohen. He is honorable and loyal. You will never speak otherwise."

She was sure her voice had come straight out of a horror movie. Possibly Cujo. It even gave her the creeps. *Get a hold of yourself.*

242

"Holy crow, Marcus. I'm sorry. I'm not sure why I reacted that way." She visibly relaxed and chuckled. "Sheesh."

Marcus smiled widely. "I know where it came from. Rohen is your destiny. Few are fortunate enough to find such a mate."

"And what about you? You're a fairhead and handsome."

"Perhaps someday the gods will see fit to introduce me to my mate." He changed the subject. "I know you're anxious. We've sent for the rebellion troops in Castlemore and for the women you requested join you. But there's a new development you should know about."

"I'm listening."

"I have someone on the inside of Sandrin. He has repeatedly given me information that has proven reliable and useful. I've tested him. He has no loyalty toward Meserek. He has sent word and requested a meeting. He has many of the Kingswatch on his side, those who are ready to make a change. Meserek's mind grows ill and the time has come to overtake him. This informant also mentioned Rohen."

"Rohen?! Why didn't you tell me?"

"We were sparring. And now that I've seen your anger and heard your fierce voice, I think I made the right choice in waiting until now to tell you," he said in a teasing voice. "Rohen is alive and has been told you are safely with Murtagh." He smiled. "They don't know that Murtagh is in fact your brother so of course Rohen is skeptical you are alive and well. He requests proof."

Sorrah smiled but it quickly faded. "He saw Foley thrust his blade into me. He thought I died."

She'd thought over and over again about what Rohen had to face in Sandrin. Torture. Prison. On top of that, he believed she was dead. What if it had been reversed and Rohen had been killed in front of her? She shuddered at the idea. Hope of a reunion with him surged through her.

"I want to go with you to the meeting. The informant can see with his own eyes that I am alive and pass the news on to Rohen. It will give him hope and strength to survive." She wanted to be there to ask more specifics from this informant. What has Meserek done to him? How do I get to him? These questions and more were troubling her to no end.

"We cannot risk your life, Sorrah. I won't allow it."

"Won't allow it?"

243

"That's right. The informant has been reliable, but he is still close to Meserek. If Meserek has found out what the spy has done, the meeting could be nothing more than a trap. An ambush. He asked to see me, Murtagh, specifically, which makes me question why now. It also tells me this meeting is of greater importance than the others."

She didn't agree or disagree. "Just so you know I won't be kept from going to Sandrin with the army."

"I know. Your powers could be helpful there but not in the middle of the battlefield. You have to know you'll be a target."

"Then hide my hair and cover my clothing so no one will notice me right away."

"Yes. And we will make it our mission to get you inside the castle. Guards will need to accompany you for your protection."

"If it's true that many of the Kingswatch are no longer loyal to Meserek, we'll need to be able to identify those who wish to be loyal to me now." She looked deep in thought.

"Tell me something, Marcus."

"Anything."

"What is the meaning of the emblem you wear? The red-handled sword."

He walked to a stone bench facing the makeshift training arena he and the knights had set up in their camp inside the small rural village of Shendora. He gestured for Sorrah to join him.

"When Father began my sword training, he told me if I won an upcoming sparring quest against my skilled instructors, he would have a special sword forged for me. He knew I had long admired his sword. It was the finest I had ever seen. A true king's sword with jewels embedded in the silver handle."

"And did you win the quest?"

"I did. Those who gathered to watch the match, laughed at the prospect of me getting the better of the men. They believed I'd lose, but I proved them wrong."

"So, how did you win?"

Marcus faced her. "For weeks leading up to the quest, I watched them carefully, observed their moves as they instructed me. I noticed how Garvin's eyebrow twitched before he thrust his blade forward, and how Corvis shifted on his feet before raising his sword to the left. I watched and learned their idiosyncrasies without them knowing what I was doing. When it came time to spar with them, I used intellect and endurance to win."

"And did you receive your sword?"

"Sort of. Father made the presenting of my sword into a presentation in front of the elite Kingswatch. Only minutes into the ceremony, three men of the Kingswatch disrupted us, announcing Meserek and an enormous army of Borakien soldiers were entering the outskirts of Sandrin and war would soon be at our gates."

"How horrible."

"Father instantly ordered Mother and I to get to the lower cavern with the others."

Marcus stood. His fists were clenched. "I wanted to fight alongside him, so badly."

Sorrah stood and touched his arm. "The sword he had made for you had a red handle?"

"Yes. Blood red with flecks of inlaid gold. He said the color will remind me that all life is precious. He had bits of the swords of our ancestors melted down and embedded in the iron. Before we were ushered below, I scrambled looking for it, but some of the servants had already taken it back to Father's chambers with other valuables."

Marcus became silent, his expression pensive.

"Please continue if you can. I want to know what happened. I know very little."

"We went to the caves below. That's where Mother spent time with the Hendrin, Shay. Later, she told me about you. She was so thrilled to be having another baby."

"They loved each other a lot, Mother and Father, didn't they?"

"More than I've ever seen two people." He offered her a comforting smile.

"We waited there for what seemed like hours. Waited for Father to tell us everything was safe and all was well. Only he never returned to us. As the war raged outside, a battle was brewing in my spirit, igniting powers I never knew existed. I had no real control over them back then, not until I aged, but they were a presence in me nevertheless."

"Meserek's men separated you from Mother?"

Marcus smiled wryly. "Not without a fight. I may not have found my sword, but I found another." He unsheathed his sword and flung it up in the air. Closing his eyes he reached out his open hand and the sword, like before, flew impressively into his grasp. He sheathed it once more. "We overheard the rumors that the king had been killed in battle. That meant I was the acting sovereignty and I knew in that moment what Father would do. It was as if he spoke to me, called out his orders in my head. I knew the protection of my mother and unborn sister took precedence over everything else. Me and some of the Kingswatch fought Meserek's men, even killed some."

"You couldn't be killed. You're like me."

"No. I'm sorry to say, I'm not immortal. I bear the same mark as Father and have been told I will live the length of time allotted to those of Aaru. Even though, I have Mother's blood in me. They killed Father and they could've killed me."

"Why didn't they?"

"As I fought, signs of my power involuntarily slipped out but not enough for me to escape. Meserek's men were awestruck and told him what they witnessed. The foul man only saw how he could benefit from my power. When I refused to help him, he ordered me to Bethesda. The walls of the prison are made of special red clay, said to be laced with magic. There, powers are useless."

"He wanted to use you."

"He said time in the vile prison would change my mind and said I'd eventually see things his way. Instead, men loyal to Father broke me out of Bethesda and hid me away in a rural plantation just outside of here, near the eastern mountains. When the new Kingswatch came looking for me and the others, we hid in the caves. Many skilled men, assassins, and Hendrins came to live and train there. We trained together for one purpose. For the future we knew would one day come. For the fulfiller of prophecy. For you, Sorrah."

"Oh, no pressure there."

Marcus smirked. "The Kingswatch didn't want to give their king the news that I escaped, so they faked my death. Brought him the head of another boy and said they burned the body. He was furious, yet relieved, I suppose."

"And Mother?"

"It was chaos in the caverns. We were losing the battle with

Meserek's men. I remember calling out to her, "Return! Go home! She knew what I meant. She'd told no one about how she came to live here in this world. No one except for me and Father. We kept her secret. And I've kept her secret regarding you. She made me promise to not speak of you or your existence. I have kept that promise."

"I know. Thank you."

"She was frantic over my safety, her eyes were pools of tears, but I knew with the new abilities churning inside of me, I could take care of myself. Somehow, I knew deep down, she knew that too. She was the widow of the king and with child. I could think of only one place that would, without question, secure her safety. Where could she go in this world without being found?"

Sadness filled Sorrah. "She loved it here. I know she did it for me but she thought she could return here to this place and to you."

"She would've been killed if she had. It was all meant to be. I told Shay to get her out. Eventually Mother found one of her maidens she'd grown close to. From what I was told, she confided in the maiden, telling her only that she knew a way out. She trusted this woman and the woman's brothers to take her to Castlemore."

"To the pond..." Sorrah added. She could almost feel the fear her mother must have known. "She was ambushed by the Borakien soldiers. The people she trusted betrayed her."

Marcus lifted a brow. "How do you know this?"

"She told me in a letter," Sorrah told him. "I saw her in the cave."

Marcus swallowed deeply and stared into Sorrah's eyes. "She made the only choice she could. I'm glad she chose to keep you safe."

"How long ago did this happen? I mean, you look as old as I do."

"Mother had similar questions in the beginning, at least that's what she told me. I'm sure you've figured out that aging is different here than in your former world."

"I assumed as much."

"What I told you happened a very long time ago. Many of the people here are the same ones who witnessed it all happen first hand. They haven't forgotten and neither have I. Meserek killed our father and I intend on avenging him and our mother for that matter. Had it not been for Meserek, our mother wouldn't have had to flee her home. The fool king has been able to hold onto the throne only because of those whom he has convinced of his divine right."

"That must have been horrible for you."

"I was young. It was traumatic. But think of how horrible it was for our mother. She lost her husband and her son in one day."

"She knew you'd survive."

"Yes. I believe that. I remained in hiding for a very long time. Somehow I knew Mother would not return. I knew she'd die and that you'd come one day. I wasn't the prophecy fulfillment, so you had to be."

Sorrah silently nodded. She couldn't help but consider how things would've been, had she been raised by her father and mother right here in Sorrah. *But then, I wouldn't have met Rohen. Or maybe I would have. If two people were truly destined to meet, they would meet, wouldn't they?* she silently thought. *Yes.* She was certain the gods had bound her soul to Rohen's soul long ago in a pool of fate, so to speak. They were meant for each other. They would've met somehow, but in different circumstances.

"You are pondering fate. Yes? Destiny and the possibility that people might not have complete control over their own lives. Am I right?"

"Something along those lines."

"Many have done the same and drive themselves mad with endless thoughts of what might have been."

"You don't wonder what your life would've been like had those things not transpired?"

"I reached the point where I just had to stop and have faith enough to trust that things happen for a reason. There are so many events that take place in the course of one's life. You never know in the beginning how tragic a new happening will turn out when it's finished running its course or how it will navigate your life, turning you around or pushing you down a different road, altering it completely. Therein lies the thrill. Not knowing what's around the next corner."

"You sound very enlightened."

"Trust me. It took a long time for me to get there. But I *am* sorry we didn't get to grow up together and experience the things siblings get to experience."

"Me too. But we're together now. Oh, that reminds me. Mother gave me a message for you when I saw her in the cave."

Marcus furrowed his brow. "What do you mean? She gave you a—what message?" His voice cracked. He was clearly overwhelmed.

"This." Sorrah placed her arms around Marcus and squeezed. "She told me to give you a hug and said, 'Tell Marcus that I love him. So very much.'"

Marcus threw his arms around Sorrah. "Thank you. It means more than you know."

They took a step back. Marcus cleared his throat and rested his hand on the handle of his sword.

"The meeting is set for tomorrow. With the luck of the gods on our side, you should be on the throne within days."

"Pardon me but… yikes. It is exciting and scary at the same time."

"You wouldn't be human if you weren't a bit nervous. You *are* human, yes?" he joked.

She smiled and teasingly smacked his arm. "Spoken like a true brother."

Marcus became serious once more. "This is huge, Sorrah, but you'll do fine. You'll learn as you go and will surround yourself with those who can help. The people of Sorrah and Borak will all see what I see… an incredibly brave and kind woman who is going to make an incredible queen."

Sorrah smiled at the compliment but her mind was on the meeting. Her wheels were turning.

"In the meantime, keep practicing, Little Warrior." Marcus started to leave.

"I will. And will you tell Sevin I need to speak with him?"

"Of course. You do realize he is never too far away from you, right? He nodded to where Sevin and Demetri stood watching them from a distance. "He is diligent, I'll give him that."

"Yes he is." *Loyal and trustworthy too.*

There was no way she was going to miss out on the meeting. If anyone could get her there, it was her elite Queensguard. It was Sevin.

*****

Sorrah watched from behind thick trees as Marcus, dressed in his Murtagh black garb, including his hood pulled over his hair, approached two men near two large boulders. The man in front wore

Kingswatch armor. The man standing behind and to the side of him was taller and wore a brown cloak with the hood over the back of his head. The front was much like the hood Marcus wore, covering most of the man's face.

"I want to hear what they're saying," she quietly told Sevin.

"Of course you do."

She maneuvered forward through the trees, but kept to the side, trying to stay out of view of the men who were facing Marcus. Sevin and Demetri followed. Even though her brother's back was to her, she could see that his hand was on his sword.

"So you are the infamous Murtagh? I and a few others of the Kingswatch have only dealt with your knights."

Marcus nodded. "I am Murtagh. It is true that my knights have met with Kingswatch soldiers, but now we meet. You are the one providing the information. Yes?"

He's good, Sorrah thought.

"And you seem oddly familiar," Marcus added. His head tipped to the side as he studied the man. "You are no ordinary Kingswatch soldier. "Who are you?"

"I am someone who has a great amount of influence over the entire Kingswatch guard. But before we speak any further, I must have proof the queen is alive and safe."

The man standing behind the soldier, who spoke, tensed with the request. He too had his hand on the handle of his sword and Sorrah could see his fingers tapping anxiously. Apparently these men didn't trust each other very much.

Marcus lowered his head then shifted it over his left shoulder glancing behind.

Sorrah sucked in a breath feeling caught in the act. "I think he knows I'm here," she whispered.

"You've only now realized that?" Sevin asked. "You are connected in some way, yes?"

He was right. "I didn't think about that. He must've known the entire time even as we followed."

Sevin looked at her. "I'm not sure about that. But he knows you're here now."

"He's allowing me to be here," Sorrah stated.

"You are the queen. You can do whatever you want. Just remember that."

"Like make muffins," Demetri chimed in.

Nearly in unison, Sorrah and Sevin looked at him.

"Whaaa-hut?" he asked his eyes on Sevin. "She makes amazing muffins, man. I'm just saying. And I'm not ashamed to say that I kinda wish we had some right about now."

Sevin shot a look to the sky. "Besides, Your Highness, I'm sure your brother doesn't want to notify these men you're here. It's probably why he hasn't brought attention to the fact."

Sorrah's attention returned to Marcus and the men.

Marcus widened his stance. "The queen is alive and safe in my camp. That's all you need to know."

The man who stood farther back, moved fast, withdrawing his sword and placing the tip to Marcus' throat. However, he wasn't the one to speak next, but the Kingswatch soldier.

"I believe my brother, here, would like to obtain further proof," he said, remaining in front of Marcus. "He isn't known for his patience."

With mind-bending speed, Marcus waved his hand in the air. The act invisibly pushed the sword away from his neck. His eyes didn't falter from his focus, remaining forward.

The one wearing the brown cloak still gripped his sword but the tip was lodged in the ground. She could see him struggling to lift it free.

Marcus addressed only the soldier in front of him. "You and I, even though through my knights, have been in league with each other for some time now. I received word that you wanted to speak to me directly about some Kingswatch who want to unite with my knights and subsequently, the rebellion army, who, by the way, are heading this way from Castlemore as we speak."

The blade of the sword broke free from the ground. But the man tossed it and surprisingly reached Marcus and gripped his throat. Beneath the male's grip, a glow came forth, changing from white to red. The man instantly withdrew his hand. It didn't seem to be burnt, but whatever happened had shocked him. Marcus used his power defensively but hadn't retaliated further.

Sorrah took a deep breath. These stubborn males could be at this for hours which didn't get them any closer to a plan, or her any closer to obtaining information about Rohen.

"If she really is alive, you will tell me where I can find her!" the man whose hand had been zapped called out in anger.

I know that voice, Sorrah thought. Her heart raced. She'd know the voice of her wolf anywhere.

"Rohen," she muttered quietly.

"Prove to me that she lives!" Rohen yelled his voice a despairing command.

Before Sevin or Demetri could stop her, she stepped out from behind the trees and stood in plain view.

"She lives," Sorrah cried out. "Although, barely without you."

Sevin and Demetri shook their heads and stood behind her.

Marcus rolled his eyes. "Good gods, Sorrah."

Rohen pushed his hood down, lifted the end of his fisted hand to his mouth and shook his head as if not believing what he was seeing.

"Sorrah."

He bolted toward her, taking large, hard strides.

Tears flowed down her face as they met halfway. "Roh—"

He engulfed her in his massive arms, raising her up and bringing her tightly against him.

She kept her arms around his neck and softened against him as they kissed.

He let out a harsh sigh of relief. "I'm not dreaming. I'm not dreaming. You really are here. You're all right. You're all right." His lips found her again and they continued to kiss over and over. He ran his hands over her, caressing and touching as if making sure she was real. All the while he was moving them toward a small cave around the corner in the mountainside.

"Sorrah," Marcus said in a cautioning tone.

"I'm all right," she managed to say between kisses.

While kissing, Rohen edged her inside and guided her against the wall. They were desperate, needing each other with great fervor.

"I can't believe you're here," she murmured against his lips.

She cupped his face with her hands, and Rohen rested his forehead firmly on hers. "I'm sorry for making you leave. I'm sorry for what I said," he told her. "I should've protected you myself."

She let out a cry as pent up emotion escaped her. "I know you were only thinking of my safety. But no more sacrificing, okay? We stay together."

"I'm not losing you again. Not ever again."

The weight of his body held her securely against the hard formation. He wiped her tears, planting kisses on her cheeks then by-passing her lips, trailed kisses down the column of her neck.

"I need to be inside you. Gods, Fairhead, I need to feel you surrounding me." His words, his voice was like a confession. His lips were frozen in state against the skin of her neck and if she didn't know better, he held his breath, waiting to hear her answer.

Their connection had been broken, the loss devastating, and she knew being with each other intimately would be the confirmation they both needed. Confirmation of their well-being, but mostly of their love not lost.

"I need you too." She placed her hands on his back and he jerked with the touch.

"I'm so sorry. I should've realized—what happened to you? What did he do to you?"

"No. We can't allow Meserek to come between us again. This is about us right now. You. And me."

"Let me help you. I can help heal you, Rohen."

"Later. You need your strength and I'm too hungry for you to worry about my back." His lips came down on hers, engulfing her mouth, dominating her senses. She loved his passion and could feel his need rippling through her.

He lifted her dress hurriedly and with gasps from both of them, was inside her moments later.

Overwhelmed by the feel of him, she briefly lowered her eyelids and leaned her head back.

He said no words but the soft rumble of a growl coming from his chest spoke volumes. Her wolf liked her to look at him.

She returned her gaze to his and instantly saw he was pleased.

He whispered as he moved inside her. "Fairhead. My Fairhead." He slid his lips over hers and she opened for him in every way.

There in the cool air of the mountainside, overtaken with the need of reaffirmation and with the certainty of war looking over them, they made love, bonding together as one, once more. They were lost to the moment and to each other, blocking out everything else for the time being.

When they finished, he kissed her tenderly, lowered her to the ground and helped her straighten her clothing. He pulled himself together and studied her face.

"Words left unspoken," he said softly, repeating what she'd told him a few days ago.

He was recalling her words of love? Suddenly, she felt the need to let him off the hook. Words spoken for the sake of the other person was no way to speak of love. He must believe she'd want to hear certain things. But it had to be genuine. Real. The most important thing was that he had returned to her. He came back and they were together again. What more could she ask for?

"It's all right. Please don't say anything for my sake. I now it's difficult for you after all you've been through."

He stepped back from her. "No. That's just it. It's easy."

Her heart sped up. "What's easy?"

"Loving you. It's been the easiest thing I've ever done. My heart is yours."

Sorrah remained perfectly still. His voice, the words he'd spoken sounded very real. She knew he had feelings for her, but he'd finally said what she longed to hear and the sound was heaven.

"I love you, Sorrah. You must know that, don't you?"

Sorrah smiled. "If I didn't before, if there was the slightest doubt... I know now. But I feel the need to warn you... I don't think I'll ever tire of hearing you say it."

"I'll make sure you'll never have to question it again."

He took her hand in his as they made their way out of the cave and to where the men stood.

She knew she must look somewhat disheveled, a clear indication of what they had been doing but she wasn't embarrassed or ashamed. Being with Rohen was right and as natural and instinctive as breathing.

"Well, I guess this means you have your proof," Marcus joked.

They ignored his comment. Sorrah took a better look at the soldier who had come with Rohen, noticing the man's striking resemblance to her sea captain.

"Sorrah, this is Ian." Rohen made the introduction.

"Your brother."

Ian nodded and bowed. "That I am, Highness."

"You helped Rohen escape?"

"Yes, he did," Rohen answered before Ian could. "He had Shay, the Hendrin, tend to me then he got me out of the castle undetected."

Sorrah placed her hand on Ian's shoulder. "Thank you, Ian."

Marcus cleared his throat.

"Oh!" Sorrah said. "Rohen, this is—"

"Murtagh?" Rohen said.

"No. Well, sort of. This is my brother. This is Marcus."

Marcus lowered his hood, showing his light blond hair.

Rohen stepped in front of Marcus and dipped his head reverently. "Marcus. My gods, you've grown to look much like your father. We believed you dead."

"Apparently there's a lot of that going around." He glanced at Sorrah. "My presumed death and Murtagh persona, allowed me to get around more freely."

Rohen nodded. "Your father was a great man. I can't tell you how pleased the people of Sorrah and Borak will be, knowing that his son lives."

"Thank you. I fully support my sister, the rightful ruler, and the gods chosen one. Celebrations will come in due time."

"I expect so. You helped Sorrah to remain safe and I am grateful. If the rebellion is to unite together with the knights and become the new Queensguard, we have much to discuss."

"Agreed. And your men had something to do with keeping Sorrah safe. She is quite fond of them." Marcus looked over at Sevin and Demetri.

Rohen seemed to notice their presence for the first time and welcomed them with a hit down on their shoulder.

"You did well," he told Sevin. "I expected nothing less from you." He looked at Demetri. "You too."

"Good to have you back, brother," Sevin commented.

"Good to *be* back," Rohen answered.

Soon, they stood together and began discussing the battle ahead.

Sorrah couldn't stop from staring at Rohen. He loved her. They were really together again and joy filled her heart. They kept their hands on each other nearly the entire time. When she moved to step away, Rohen calmly, but firmly, pulled her back to his side again. She didn't mind. She was with the one she loved.

"I have an idea how we can distinguish the good men of the Kingswatch and those who are loyal to Meser—your father," she stated to Ian.

"It's all right, Highness. My father has never been a father to me. My loyalty is to you and to the people of Sorrah and Borak. It's time they had the ruler the gods intended for them. It's time you were on the throne."

Sorrah smiled. "Thank you for that, Ian." She continued, telling him her plan.

"It's a solid idea. I'll make sure it's set in motion immediately." Ian nodded. "This will work. In three days, we'll meet again. I will inform the men and those loyal inside the castle."

"Or you could come with us," Rohen offered. "Get word to those you trust in Sandrin and come with us to Shendora. You could help prepare the men."

Ian shook his head no. "I cannot. My time for leaving with you has long since passed."

"That's in the past, Ian. Join me now."

"I *will* join you, but on the battlefield. You are my brother. But the men of the Kingswatch, those who are loyal to me and to the crown, are my brothers too. I will not abandon them and leave them in the hands of my father. I plan on helping as many as I can. When the horn is sounded, you will see how many of us are on the right side. Your side. The side of the queen."

Rohen held out his arm, and he and Ian gripped forearms. "I'm not feeling good about this. He will suspect you helped me escape. For all you know, he might believe you a spy. You know he won't allow you to live."

"I know."

Rohen didn't release his hold on Ian. "Then take all precautions necessary to stay alive."

"I will. I'll see you soon, brother."

Before Ian could leave, Rohen pulled him into his shoulder and the two quickly hugged.

It tore at Sorrah's heart to see them part. She could see the look of concern on Rohen's face. He worried for his brother. She hoped for the battle to be quick with few losses but inside were echoing whispers and quiet voices telling her contrary.

Chapter twenty seven

Sorrah, with Rohen and Sevin at each side and Marcus with an army of men behind her, rode toward Sandrin. The trees of Silvermist forest spread much farther than she had anticipated providing them with needed coverage, aiding in their approach. They knew Meserek wouldn't be caught unaware and would have an army of the Kingswatch waiting for them.

Rohen placed his hand in the air, signaling to those behind him to stop then dismount.

"We leave the horses here," he told Sorrah.

"Here? We aren't riding in?"

"There is no riding down to the valley. The terrain is far too steep and rugged for the horses. We battle on foot."

"If Meserek is so powerful, why haven't we come up against the Kingswatch yet?"

"Ian sent word that Meserek is waiting to fight us below. Most great wars of Sandrin have been fought in the valley."

Sorrah turned around to see all the men draping their horses' reins around branches.

"Let's have a look," Marcus said, moving forward.

Rohen, Sorrah, Sevin and the elite, discreetly advanced forward. They crouched at the end of the tree line behind some rock formations on a steep ledge overlooking the valley below.

"I didn't know how I expected it to look but I definitely didn't expect this. It's spectacular."

"We are in Sandrin," Rohen answered. "The trees of Silvermist extend down into the valley. The glade, the large clearing beyond the trees is where we meet our enemy and fight."

"Won't they be waiting for us in the trees? I don't see another way to get to the glade."

"The trees are sacred. Especially those which surround the castle.

The caves I told you about in the lower level of the castle?"

"Yes?"

"There are tunnels extending outward from the caves. The heavy roots of the trees cover them, protect them but also prevent escape. There is no way inside the castle other than the front door."

"I see."

"The mountain. Has it always been this way, with the ledge coming so far out from it?"

"Yes, only not as far. It began to extend slowly and has never cracked or broke off."

A long protruding rocky ridge with its own cliff, overhung the valley from above, overshadowing the landscape below. Beneath the strange ledge were roots and trees growing sideways and intertwining vines and limbs which cupped the protrusion in a bizarre fashion. But by far the most surreal thing capturing Sorrah's attention was what stood directly across from the mountainside they were on. Sandrin Castle.

Just as Rohen had described, the back half of the castle was embedded deep within the largest mountain she'd ever seen. She knew he wouldn't have been able to accurately depict its brilliance. The color of the stone castle was an iridescent white, with bits of grayish blue and black near the windows and high steeples on top of what appeared to be massive towers with black iron gates surrounding balconies. When the rays of the sun touched any part of the structure, it shimmered.

"It's magnificent. Even Mickey would be in awe."

"Who is Mickey?"

"A mouse."

"A mouse?" he questioned.

She let out a brief chuckle. "I know it sounds absurd. Trust me, you'd never understand."

Her gaze drifted off the castle to the valley below, noticing not only the trees but the army of Kingswatch soldiers. There was a vast land separating them from the castle. "There's so many of them," she said. "And we have to go down there and fight them?"

"Your Queensguard are doing the fighting. *You* however, are not," Rohen replied.

"I can help."

"Yes. But news of your miraculous survival and your claim as the rightful queen has spread. The Kingswatch loyal to Meserek will be looking to take your head."

Sorrah didn't doubt that. In her mind was the resounding call to finish this. Finish what was started not so long ago when she came into this marvelous world. She would follow through on the love she felt for Rohen. She would have a life with him but first the battle must be fought.

She inhaled and exhaled deeply.

"We stick to the plan and clear a path to the castle. I will remain with you. Sevin, Demetri and Alexander will too. Ian will have left loyal guards just inside the door."

"Do you trust Ian?" She had to ask.

"Yes. I do. As soon as we make our way to the valley, Alexander will sound the horn and signal him and the Kingswatch."

"Hopefully there are many of them willing to pledge their loyalty to you, sister," Marcus said, approaching from the side. "We are all exceptional fighters but their numbers are astounding, are they not?"

"Yes. Astounding."

She couldn't help but be worried. There were just so many of them. Once the war exploded down below, they were trapped in the valley among the trees. Climbing back up in retreat would not be a viable option.

This war was part of the reason for her existence. And hadn't her journey already been filled with surreal moments and miracles? Surely, the gods had more in store for her and her Queensguard. She had hope, now all she needed was faith. There was no escaping, no quitting and she didn't want to. This was her time to finally finish something.

"All right. Scary soldiers with swords, a mad king, impending doom. Not so bad as horror stories go. We have the gods on our side. We got this."

Rohen smirked as he guided her backward toward taller formations of the mountain. "Give me and Sorrah a minute," he told the men around them.

"We know what your minute looks like when you edge my sister toward the rocks," Marcus commented.

Rohen said nothing as he continued to move Sorrah away. When they were alone, he turned to her.

"What is it?"

"I need to speak what's on my mind and in my heart before we descend from this mountain."

"All right."

Wearing a serious and determined expression, he gripped his hands behind his back and paced in front of her.

For a second she wondered if she should worry.

"I've told you that I love you."

That certainly started well. "Yes."

"You are the Queen."

Okay, sure. *Yep, I'm the queen.* She didn't pretend to fully understand the responsibilities she would soon face. "Yes. Rohen, what's this all about? I can see something is bothering you. Just tell me what it is. Say it."

He looked nervous now and doing that weird intense thing with his eyebrows.

"Is this is about the battle? We've discussed this many times—" She started but stopped when he grabbed her hands in his.

"Be quiet for two minutes."

What? Fine. She was a bit of rambler when her nerves kicked up. It was a trait which ordinarily didn't bother many people because most of the time she was alone when it happened. Come to think of it... she was rambling in her own mind now. Gah. She tightened her lips to stifle the nervous laughter rising even now. Laughing when someone in front of you was serious could be misconstrued to say the least.

"I mean to marry you, Sorrah."

Okay, so... she hadn't expected that. "Wh—what?"

His eyebrows furrowed, producing a crease in his skin forged by his stubborn nature.

"Before your somewhat strange appearance here, I had spent a long time swearing, vowing, I'd never take a wife. It's clear to me now why, in part, I've been so determined to remain alone. The gods only meant for me to wait for the right woman; the one who was created for me. They had me wait for you."

She opened her mouth to speak but he raised his hand. "I know there'll be a buffet of options spread out before you. Noblemen who would die for your affections—but I don't care."

"Rohen."

Her mind was being blown. Her alpha male wolf was revealing a side of himself she didn't think he possessed. Vulnerability. Insecurity. Options? Was he serious? And she detested buffets. There was too much cross-contamination. Places like that were literally cesspools of germs.

"You belong to me, Sorrah." He closed his eyes and opened them. "You belong *with* me. Queen or not, you—I,"

Sorrah sucked in her bottom lip and he stopped mid-sentence.

"You laugh?" It wasn't so long ago he did the same to her.

"I believe it's my turn."

"Hmm," he muttered, narrowing his eyes. "I suppose it is."

"And like you, I too laugh only because of the absurdity of what you said."

"Which part?"

"Options?" She stopped him before he could continue. "Now it's your turn to listen. There are no *options*, Rohen. There never will be options. My heart is yours. Forever."

He visibly relaxed. "I'm glad to hear you say that because I think I'd have to kill any male who tried to take you from me."

Sorrah raised her brow. "Really?"

"Yes. I'm very protective of what belongs to me."

"It's… hmm."

"What? What is it?"

"It's just that I've never had any man say these kinds of things to me."

"That's hard to believe. There are so many things I admire and love about you, Fairhead."

She smiled but had a hard time keeping eye contact with him.

"Look at me."

She lifted her gaze to his once more. "It's not easy to hear."

"It's best you get used to it because I won't stop telling you. You have a tender heart. You're giving. Loving."

Sorrah pointed a finger at herself and mouthed the word, 'me.'

He cupped her face, placing his hands on each side. "Yes, you." He kissed her softly. "I love so many things…" he paused. "Like the determination in your eyes when you're being unruly and stubborn."

"Heyyy."

He smiled against her lips and kissed her again, stopping her tease and fake protest. "And the way you look at me with those big blue eyes of yours when you think me insane." He met her gaze. "Ah, yes... just like that."

He kissed her once more, leaving his lips a few inches from hers.

"And I especially love the way you grip my hair tightly when we make love and throw your hands down on the bed and take fists full of blankets in your grip. I love seeing the ache for me in your eyes because I ache for you too. You look at me like I'm a predator and you're waiting for me to pounce but you're ready for it. I can't tell you," he nipped at her lip, "how much that excites me."

He was no slacker in the drumming up excitement area either. In fact, he was heating her up pretty well.

"You dare me with those beautiful eyes. Gods, Fairhead, I'll never have enough of you." He took a step back. "So I must know—Will you take me as your husband? Will you be my wife?"

Her grin began small and spread wide. She nodded as she spoke. "Yes. Of course it's yes."

She threw her arms around his neck and hugged him. "I love you too."

Rohen let out a breath she was sure he'd held for far too long.

"I will get you safely inside the castle and you will gain your throne. We'll have a life together, Sorrah. A real life."

"I have no doubt of that. I trust you."

He kissed her, stirring a fervent heat of passion between them. But before they could get too carried away, they made their way back to the other men.

She'd crossed through a magic mirror, been both a guest and prisoner of the resistance, captured the heart of the alpha hero, obtained her powers and gave herself over to the gods. By her calculations and knowledge of romantic fiction... it was high time she stormed the damn castle and took the crown from the evil king.

Sure. No problem.

*****

"The day has come which is long overdue. Many have suffered at the hands of the false king. But I say… this shall be nevermore," Rohen said in a loud and commanding voice, addressing the army of men in front of him. He raised his voice even louder. "This day, the rightful ruler of Kortah will take her place as queen! She will sit on the silver throne of Sorrah because the gods have chosen her and her alone! We have been the resistance for too long. We have battled for too long! The gods have sent her here and have entrusted her safety to us. They have trusted us to lead her into Sorrah and claim her crown. We are now, and forever shall be her Queensguard! We fight today and then we celebrate together on the morrow!"

The men roared as they lifted their weapons in the air. "Hoah! Hoah! Hoah!" the men chanted in strong, short clips.

"What does that mean?" Sorrah asked Sevin who stood beside her.

"Hoah? It means to fight, to win no matter what the cost."

Rohen spoke to the men again. "Let us go forth as soldiers, as the Queensguard, as one. More importantly, as brothers."

"Rohen really was made to lead, wasn't he?" Sorrah asked Sevin.

"Yes. He is a great commander."

Her eyes remained on Rohen. "He's more than great. "He's magnificent," she corrected.

Sevin smirked.

They'd made it down to the valley but before they advanced further, Rohen nodded to Alexander who stood above them on a tall rock formation. He lifted a horn to his mouth and blew it loudly. The sound carried, echoing throughout the valley and ricocheting off the surrounding mountains.

As planned, the sound of the horn signaled the loyal among the Kingswatch. In unison, the soldiers pulled a small black sash from off their upper arms, revealing an emblem. A silver sword with a red handle, identical to the one Marcus wore.

Rohen released a battle cry as the armies charged forward with weapons in hand. He stood protectively in front of Sorrah, while Sevin, Alexander, Demetri, Revel and Kehgen surrounded her. She held a dagger in her hand and has a sword at her hip but Rohen didn't want anything or anyone close enough for her to have to use it.

The majority of the rebellion army made their way through the trees to the main clearing. Kingswatch soldiers lay in wait for them behind trees, forcing the battle to commence before they'd made it to the glade.

A brute of a Kingswatch soldier wearing armor that barely covered his massive body, headed straight for Sorrah but Rohen placed himself in the executioner's path. The soldier swung an axe at Rohen's head but he pivoted and turned in a semicircle with his blade outright, cutting the soldier on the exposed area of his torso.

The valley was filled with soldiers armed with weapons and the sound of blade clanking against blade while blood spilled at the feet of the valiant. The battle was in full force when they heard yet another horn. This time the sound of the horn was high-pitched and came from an upper tower of the castle.

Within seconds, another army poured out from behind the castle gates. Meserek had no doubt kept these soldiers back until now.

As Rohen took a quick survey of the area, his heart fell. There were many new men who now wore the emblem of loyalty but with Meserek's new reserve of men, they were even more outnumbered. Still, he would never surrender, would never give up. The gods hadn't brought Sorrah all this way, to end her life. She would have her place among the royal and obtain the throne. She would end the war.

Sorrah remained close behind him and together they were slowly making their way to the front of the castle along with Marcus and his knights. Abruptly, however, she stopped dead in her tracks.

"Keep moving forward, Sorrah!" Rohen yelled as he fought off another soldier.

"I hear them," she said, but he could barely hear her above the sound of the battle.

She closed her eyes and lifted her hands to the sky. "It's going to be all right now." She flipped her eyes open and caught Rohen's stare. He came inside the circle of protection while the knights and the elite surrounding them fought to keep them safe.

"Sorrah. Who is it that you hear? The gods?"

Nothing was out of the question at this point.

She smiled faintly but he noticed the far off look in her eyes. Something was happening to her. Were the gods speaking to her?

Two enormous shadows cast a blanket upon the land causing many men to stop and look up. But Sorrah's eyes remained steadfast on

Rohen. Rohen couldn't seem to break away from her mesmerizing eyes. They were bright blue and grew increasingly lighter. A soft aura of light surrounded her.

"I... I can hear them. Feel what they feel."

She placed her hand to her heart.

"Who?" he asked.

"Sacred ones from long ago."

He wasn't sure if she meant the gods or someone else. Instinctively, his first thoughts were to protect her, yet, she didn't seem panicked or frightened by what was happening to her. Nevertheless he watched her closely.

"They've come to help. And I'm not afraid. This is the gods' plan. All of what has happened and will happen, even this moment and time, this place, this battle. The gods have known of us, Rohen. This was all meant to be."

Her voice sounded peculiar. Not fully her own. He didn't know what to do but pray the gods didn't harm her for some greater cause.

When a shadow fell directly over Sorrah, he forced his eyes away from her and frantically raised his to the enormous pair of talons lowering upon her. The Tarrigen.

One of the creatures descended upon her before he could react, lifting her high above the battlefield. The mysterious, yet, vicious creatures had fled their mountain, somehow escaping the curse placed upon them long ago. That meant if the fables and tales were true, the priests had returned to Sandrin to claim their queen and had plucked her away right before his eyes.

"Sorrah!" he thundered, raising his sword as high as he could but it was too late, the Tarrigen had her too high in the air. He followed them with his eyes and watched as the creature carried her to the overreaching ledge and set her upon it.

She was all right.

The Tarrigen beasts left her, flying over the battlefield, circling and crying out with loud screeches.

Rohen was in shock but he wasn't the only one. Most of the fighting stopped around him, but some took the opportunity to kill their opponent while they watched the action.

"Sorrah," he muttered, watching her walk to the very end of the ledge. The wind blew back her hood; her long yellow-white hair blew steadily behind her in billowing waves. The sun caught her as if a stream was sent down by the gods to illuminate her and her alone.

She raised her arms out to her sides and splayed open her fingers. Her brilliant blue eyes nearly glowed and widened as she kept them firmly on the Tarrigen.

The creatures swooped down and pierced the queen's enemies with their sharp talons. Some of the men the Tarrigen gripped with their clawed feet and flung into the side of the great mountain.

Many of the Kingswatch, who wore no emblem of loyalty, either died or threw down their weapons and surrendered on bended knee while they bowed to Sorrah.

When no enemies remained on the battlefield, the Tarrigen circled twice more before landing on the ledge, one at each side of Sorrah. The creatures turned to her and bowed submissively on their hunches as all men remaining on the battleground observed in awe.

Sorrah touched one of the creature's heads, then the other.

One of the Tarrigen kept its head lowered but edged closer to her like a dog crawling on their paws. Sorrah, seeming to know what the action meant, climbed on its back.

Rohen held his breath as the creature lifted in the air and came around in a wide circle, landing in front of the castle doors.

He rushed to her side, along with Marcus and the other men of the elite, reaching her just as she finished climbing off. She touched the Tarrigen's head and weakly smiled before it rose into the air, joining the other and flying off in the direction of the mountain where it had come from.

"Sorrah," Rohen said, taking a firm hold of her shoulders. He looked up and down her body. "Are you?"

"Am I all right?" she asked. She smiled and nodded. "I'm more than all right. I've never been better."

"You heard them?"

Sorrah locked eyes with Rohen. "I didn't have to hear them." She raised her face to the sky and smiled. "They heard me. They heard my plea for help. They heard all of you, all of your silent prayers and pleas. My Queensguard."

As words of reverence came out of their mouths, the men one by one, dropped on bended knee.

"Now, if you will all come with me inside. It's time we kick the false king out, don't you think?"

Roars erupted from behind where they stood.

Rohen led the way. He and his men, pushed open the enormous wooden doors of the castle.

Chapter twenty eight

Meserek was seriously demented. That was Sorrah's first thought when she walked inside the castle. Even though Rohen and Marcus were in front of her, she could clearly see the bodies. And the blood. So much blood. It was everywhere. Men in armor, Kingswatch soldiers, who bore the emblem to the new regime on their sleeve, were sprawled out on the floor of the massive foyer, with their necks sliced open.

The soldiers' mouths were bizarrely cut from the corners of their lips as if it were an afterthought. They were as marionettes, puppets with sagging bloody jaws.

The mad king laughed sadistically. "He is my son. I allowed him to live and..." he sighed before continuing, "I *have* allowed him to die."

Meserek stood on the third step of a long, winding staircase, with a blood-soaked sword in one hand a dripping dagger in the other. He wore a chest plate of armor, ragged pants which were cut off at the knees and a gold crown. He wore no shirt nor did he wear shoes.

"Son? You are speaking about Ian? You're speaking about my brother?! What have you done?!" Rohen roared. His eyes darted in every direction. "Where is he? Where is my brother?"

Sorrah covered her mouth, if the bodies on the ground and the blood-soaked floor weren't enough; Rohen's pain was more than she could bear. He was so much like her. No family other than a brother and now even he might have been taken from him.

He'd told her the story of his father and mother. Would he now have to endure the death of his brother as well?

Meserek was more than just wicked and cruel, he was diabolical. Killing his only son was not out of the question.

Rohen frantically began to pull at the bodies of the soldiers who were layered on top of each other. "Ian!" he called out. "Ian!"

Sevin, Marcus and others did much of the same, trying to aid Rohen in the search while no less than twenty soldiers protected

Sorrah.

"You will pay for this, you bastard!" Rohen hollered.

Meserek whistled and guards came out from the rooms at each side of the vestibule. He must have known the men would soon advance on him.

Rohen, Marcus and the other men went into fighting mode, while still providing a large circle of protection around Sorrah. This time it was Meserek and his men who were outnumbered.

From the corner of her eye, Sorrah saw one of the presumably dead soldiers move.

Could it be Ian? Had he survived what Meserek did to him?

The fighting commenced. She maneuvered closer to the soldier, squeezing between two of the Queensguard to reach him.

"Majesty!" One of Marcus' knights, now a Queensguard knight, called for her to return behind him. She ignored him for the sake of the wounded soldier.

"Make a wider circle and include the soldier along with the queen," Marcus told the soldiers.

The man wasn't Ian but needed her help nonetheless. This man's neck was cut but not as severely as some of the others. His eyes opened and widened when he saw her. He tried to speak but quickly closed his mouth.

"Shhh. Let me help you."

She glanced up to see Rohen fighting one of Meserek's men. As promised, he remained close. Her wolf and his pack of men would protect her.

Rohen fought with remarkable skill, and seemingly effortless, quickly gaining the upper hand and cut into the man's torso with his blade.

She knew he'd be after Meserek's head but so was Marcus. Far beyond the horrific deeds Meserek did while deceitfully reigning as king, they both had personal reasons to end the vile man's life. He had killed her and Marcus' father and presumably Rohen's father as well. Such injustices never go unpunished, if not in this life, than most certainly the next. Sooner or later karma catches up with everyone.

Sorrah placed her hand on the man's wound and closed her eyes, fully trusting in the healing power the gods had given her. She hoped the short amount of time she'd spent practicing her power with Marcus, assisted in helping her heal this man now. With any luck, she wouldn't be too drained from the usage.

Power flowed from deep within in a steady flow down her arm and out through her hand. She opened her eyes, seeing the cut on the soldier's neck mending together. Just as she thought her energy levels were fine, her vision began to blur. She steadied herself and took deep breaths as Marcus had taught her but the soldier's wounds were severe and the effort to heal him was taking its toll.

"Sorrah?" Rohen asked as he glanced behind him while clanking swords with yet another one of Meserek's men.

"I'm all right. I'm fine."

Sevin positioned himself at Sorrah's side with his back to her.

"You're pale," he told her.

"I'm… I'm always pale," she answered, forcing the words out of her mouth.

The now healed soldier abruptly sat up and gasped for air.

"You healed me."

"Yes," she replied as she struggled to stand.

"Highness," Sevin said, helping her.

"It's okay. I'm fine."

Sevin nodded and turned his attention elsewhere.

The soldier scrambled to his feet and held her by the arm as she swayed.

"Thank you. I'm okay now."

His eyes went to where his hand still touched her. He dropped on bended knee. "I beg your pardon, Your Majesty. Thank you for helping me."

Sorrah smiled. "You are quite welcome. Please stand."

The soldier obeyed.

"What is your name?"

"I am Aidan, Your Majesty."

Aidan was tall and thickly built, with straight chestnut brown hair tied low behind his neck and light green eyes. He looked around at his fallen comrades and ground at his jaw. He picked up a sword, grasping it tightly in his hand. "It appears I am in your debt. Would you allow me to join the fight, Highness?"

"Go," she told him. No doubt revenge also burned in Aidan's heart.

"Sevin, stay beside the queen!" Rohen commanded. "Move with us," he told Sorrah as he advanced to the staircase. Her protective shield of men moved in step with her.

"Where could he have gone?" Rohen shouted from the staircase where Meserek had stood moments ago. It was safe to assume that sometime during the heat of battle, Meserek saw he was losing and slipped away in the madness.

"Find him!" Marcus told his knights. They separated into rooms and covered the large entry.

"Rohen!" Demetri yelled.

Rohen followed where Demetri's eyes led, above him on the stairs.

Ian, covered in blood, stood at the top of the staircase. His face was swollen, beaten and bruised, nearly unrecognizable. His body swayed.

Sorrah clasped her hand over her mouth, her heart aching for him and for Rohen. Ian was clearly on the brink of death. "Bring him to me, Rohen, or let me go to him. Let me try to help him."

"Sevin!" Rohen exclaimed but kept his eyes on his brother.

"I have her. Go!" Sevin answered.

Rohen glanced momentarily at Sorrah then back to his brother. "Don't move, Ian! Don't move," Rohen told him as he advanced up the steps, taking two at a time. He reached out to his brother, lifting him into his arms.

Ian sagged in Rohen's arms and closed his eyes.

"Ian," Rohen said. "Concentrate on my voice. Do you hear me? You cannot die! Fight!" He leaned closer to Ian's ear. "He'll die for this." His breathing hitched. "I promise you, my brother. The bastard dies this day."

Rohen placed Ian down on a rug, and Sorrah got to work. She touched his bloodied cheek and then his head. Power radiated from her fingers.

"Sorrah," Marcus said. "Do as we practiced. You've already depleted some of your energy. Take deep breaths and go slowly."

"He... He doesn't have time for me to go slowly. Oh gods, I can see it"—

"See what, Fairhead?" Rohen asked.

"Death. I see death."

"But I think it's working," Demetri commented from off to the side. "He has more color in his face."

"While she continues to have less," Sevin added.

Rohen remained at her side while men surrounded her as she worked.

Marcus touched her arm. "Sister... you must take a break."

Sorrah didn't answer.

"N—no. He—I'm nearly finished." She knew helping Aidan had drained her more than she thought.

"Sorrah..." Rohen cautioned as he took a firm hold of her arm. "Stop," he demanded. "If you won't stop, I'll stop you."

"There," she whispered as she let go of Ian and keeled over on the floor. Her breathing was erratic but she remained conscious.

Rohen held her. "Catch your breath, Sorrah. Breathe in," he said, taking a deep breath with her then continued, "and out."

"Is he all right?" she asked without lifting her head from his shoulder.

"Yes," Ian answered. "Thanks to you." He extended his hand to hers and squeezed. "You are truly blessed by the gods. You will recuperate fully?"

"Yes. Time will allow me to heal." She lifted off of Rohen. "I need some water."

"I'll get it," Sevin offered, already walking off to find some. Many of the men cleared the area, leaving Rohen, Marcus, and the elite.

"Don't try to stand until Sevin gets back with water," Rohen told her.

Sorrah was surprised by Sevin's demeanor the past few days. He gave her the impression that he really cared about her. It was nice. She questioned whether the quiet warrior had been telling the truth when he said he didn't sense a lineage between them.

A few minutes later, Sevin appeared in the doorway of the room to the right, holding a glass of water.

"Sevin. Bring it here. What are you doing?" Rohen said, irritated.

"I'm afraid he cannot answer you right now due to the blade I have piercing his spine," Meserek said, showing himself behind Sevin. "It really is remarkable. The punisher taught me how to do this." He chuckled as he lifted his free hand up and pointed to the blade. "It literally renders the victim helpless."

Sevin's eyes glazed over, his mouth dropped open, and the glass of water slipped from his hand, crashing on the stone floor and breaking into pieces.

Then men instantly moved forward.

"Stop!" Meserek yelled, moving back and using Sevin as a shield.

Marcus edged his way to Rohen's side. "We can get to him."

"Ah. Ah. Ah," Meserek chided. "I'll twist the blade and tear out his esophagus. "There's no power that can heal that." He shot Sorrah a disgusted look.

"Let him go," Rohen said, taking a step forward.

Ian did likewise, showing himself to his father, standing even with Rohen. "Your time as king is over. I warned you. The gods, the ones you said you couldn't hear? They are with us."

"I... I killed you! I saw you die!"

"I live. The gods have made it so. It is you who will die today."

Sorrah could tell Marcus' mind was going wild. And Rohen? Her wolf was ready to tear Meserek to pieces. She also knew Marcus and even Ian in his weakened state, probably wanted to get their hands on the mad man. As for her? She just wanted this all to end without any more losses.

"I am the one in control here! You will let me leave or he dies."

He twisted the blade and Sevin made a horrifying gagging sound. The evil king was killing him.

"If you refuse to listen to me, then listen to your man here. Tell them to step back and allow me to leave," Meserek said near Sevin's ear. He pulled back on his blade.

"Ki... Ki..." Sevin stuttered.

"Out with it!" Meserek demanded. "Tell them!"

"Dah... dah... Don't cah... care—my life! Kill him!" Sevin screamed.

Sorrah's heart clenched. *Sevin. No, you must live!*

"No!" she cried, watching Meserek shove the blade deeper into Sevin's neck just as the men rushed him. She too wanted to run forward, but Ian, who seemed to be gaining in strength by the minute, held her back.

"Do you hear them now, Father?" Ian called out to Meserek. "Do you not hear the gods and taste your death in the air?"

He addressed Sorrah. "They will do what needs to be done. But you cannot be harmed in the process."

Tears fell down Sorrah's face as she watched Sevin fall to the ground with a blade impaled in his neck. "No! No!" She thought to conjure up the invisible force she'd used on the battlefield but she needed to regain her strength. Sevin was going to need her help.

"You can go to him once my father is dead. We must wait."

A sword was lifted in the air seemingly on its own accord, just as Marcus, in a flash of speed, stood before a very shocked and disturbed Meserek. In what seemed like seconds, he raised his hand, the sword appearing magically in his grasp. He plunged the blade forward into Meserek's heart, clear through his body and out his back.

"Move!" Rohen shouted.

Marcus pulled his blade out and stepped back. Before Meserek could fall, Rohen, who was now behind him, raised his blade high, sweeping it sideways, severing the mad king's head.

Both of these brave men had finally received the recompense they had long yearned for. Sorrah was pretty certain, Ian had too.

Rohen threw down his blade, meeting Sorrah at Sevin's side.

Sevin's mouth retracted over and over again, opening and closing as a fish out of water while blood flowed from his neck and mouth.

"Shh. Shh. Sevin." Sorrah wasn't sure if her power had regenerated enough to heal Sevin but she would try her hardest. He'd become more than her friend but her protector and beyond that... he was family. She glanced at Rohen who nodded in encouragement, then placed both of her hands on Sevin's neck and closed her eyes.

"Sister," Marcus said, placing his hand on Sorrah's shoulder. He closed his eyes. "Let me try to assist you," he whispered.

She didn't break concentration to speak to Marcus but she'd take any help she could get. Once again her skin shimmered as power radiated out from her. Even where Marcus' hand rested, her skin illuminated.

In spite of their conjoined efforts, little improvement came to

Sevin. His neck wasn't healing.

"No! This has to work! This has to work! Gods, he's my family. He's my family."

The men, who were nearby watching, looked at each other with curiosity.

"He's family?" Kehgen asked with a low voice. Alexander shrugged his shoulders. "Got me."

"If the queen says it is so, then it is," Demetri added.

Sorrah trembled from the effort.

"Fairhead... gods, what can I do? Tell me how I can help you," Rohen pleaded.

"Touch my arm," she answered.

"I am touching your arm. I'm right here with you." He caressed her skin and she felt it anew. Her mate was beside her and that gave her strength. They really were connected, as were many of the soldiers, connected in some way to this world, the gods and to each other.

Demetri lifted his hand moving it closer to Rohen's shoulder. Before he touched down, Marcus looked at him. "Yes. Let us try."

One by one a train of men linked hand to shoulder. Even the dark knights came behind Marcus and did likewise.

"It's working!" Sorrah exclaimed, opening her eyes briefly to look at the wound. She clenched her eyes shut once more and concentrated harder than she ever had.

After a few minutes, Sevin began to improve. "What's going on?" he muttered with a raspy voice.

The men disengaged and stepped back. Many wore grins on their faces.

Sorrah, however, couldn't seem to pry her eyes open. Within her mind and spirit in the place where her gifts lay, there was a magnificent light but something skidded across the light from a distance. Darkness was mingling with the light. A billowy shadow drifted by once more, then backtracked and moved steadily toward her. She remained paralyzed in the vision, helpless to move or cry out, as the eerie darkness encompassed her. Her hands slipped off of Sevin. As if coming from a deep tunnel, she heard the faint shouts of her sea captain wolf. He was angry—no, concerned. Worried. Sad.

Rohen, she thought as she fell into a dark abyss.

When she finally regained consciousness it was many hours later. She moved her hands, feeling soft blankets beneath her.

I'm on a bed, she thought.

"Yes, you are," Rohen said.

She'd once again said her thoughts out loud. The normality of doing so was comforting. She slowly opened her eyes half expecting to be in her bed chambers at Castlemore. But she wasn't. She was in an enormous room inside of Sandrin Castle, on a four poster bed that had thick, gorgeous tapestry hanging down from all corners. She met Rohen's eyes and smiled. Her mate was at her side.

She heard a male clear his throat and her eyes drifted to the many other formidable looking men surrounding her bed. Brave, gallant men. Her brother and Queensguard were with her.

"Sevin... You're all right."

"Yes," Sevin answered. He gave her a flicker of a smile. "Thank you."

"You are most welcome." She returned the smile.

As was Sevin's way, he looked increasingly uncomfortable by the attention being paid to him and quietly slipped away from the bed and out the door.

"You frightened me, Fairhead," Rohen whispered in her ear before kissing her cheek.

"I get that a lot," she teased, turning her face to kiss him.

One by one, and then all at once, the men left them to their privacy.

Chapter twenty nine

The coronation ceremony took place three days later in the church adjacent to the castle which Meserek had closed off for many years. The church is second in size to the enormous great hall, the place where the wedding celebration would soon take place. Thanks to her new and most trusted handmaiden, Silva, and one very ornery head housekeeper, or castle keeper as the case may be, Gerta, the event came off without a hitch. It was official. She was the Queen of Sorrah. Technically, she was the Queen of Kortah but what did it matter? She had done it. She had seen it through and had obtained the throne. It all had been meant to be.

She had great plans which included the governing of Borak. She would be sending a high governor, a chancellor to the land as overseer. It was long overdue. The Borakien people loved their land as much as Sorriens loved Sorrah. Even though they had a Sorrien queen, they could still have a Borakien leader to guide and unite them. Her father had felt the effects of governing from afar and she pledged not to make the same mistake.

She knew the perfect person which to bestow such a title and responsibility. Rohen's brother, Ian. She'd spoken with Rohen in regards to her idea and he enthusiastically jumped on board. They both agreed, however, that Ian must return to Sorrah at least twice a month to give reports firsthand and visit with them as family should.

Ian humbly accepted the prestigious title and position and quickly began plans to change things in Borak to a more spiritually conscious land. He seemed pleased by the appointment.

The wedding preparations were in full swing and Sorrah was exhausted with the traditions those around her attempted to school her on.

"First order of my Queen-ship is to break traditions!" she exclaimed, tossing aside a peculiar looking black jewelry cuff they meant for her wear. She was pretty sure her hair would be gray before she actually married Rohen. "And why can't I see him?"

"Not until tomorrow. The wedding day," Gerta told her.

Really? She hadn't expected the same superstition to be in this world.

"But he is the high commander of the entire Queensguard. Surely he will come to me if I ask him to."

"Aye, he'd wanna come. And you canna command him to do it, but the people would not be pleased. Best let it lie and argue the larger things, aye?"

Gerta meant well. She knew that. She would have to wait to see her captain, her commander and master of the royal Queensguard. She hadn't seen him in a few days and missed him terribly. However, she'd taken the time apart to work with Marcus. She had a lot to learn especially in the art of dance. Apparently, these people expected her and Rohen to dance at their wedding which seemed simple enough if you didn't have two left feet like she did. The dance was actually a lot of fun and could be very sensual when she danced it with Rohen.

Marcus knew all the ins and outs of the castle and attempted to show her as much as possible. She was on information overload from the past few days and would most likely forget much but thought how extraordinary it would've been to grow up in such a place. It was truly spectacular.

They entered the great hall where she and Rohen, along with guests, would celebrate their wedding. Castle servants and wedding planners were busily working in nearly every corner, transforming the space, decorating and moving tables and chairs. The beauty of the room practically took her breath away as she took it all in. To know this immaculate space had been where her parents had celebrated their wedding was surreal. This room, along with the church and the castle, breathed new life now that she and Rohen were here. You couldn't help but feel small in a place this enormous. It was impressively regal but warm and inviting, with cathedral ceilings, gold etchings and paintings similar to those in Castlemore only much more grandeur in detail. The archangels were depicted here as well, painted in all their celestial glory. She smiled as she recognized the gorgeous angel with pale white skin, black hair and the most alluring piercing blue eyes, the same one she had seen on the ceiling in Castlemore. It was nice to see a familiar face. Marcus must have noticed her attention lingered on the angel.

"His name is Vincent," he said from beside her. "The best artists in the world were commissioned to paint him and the other archangels here."

"Vincent," she repeated softly.

"Yes. He is one of many legendary archangels of Elysian. A great warrior. A protector of the gods."

"Elysian—Heaven," she said more to herself than to him. "He is magnificent. And so is this castle. Thank you for showing me around."

"You are confident in getting around on your own then?"

"I'm confident I'll get lost."

He laughed and she joined in until she remembered her schedule. "Oh no. I have to hurry or I'll miss my appointment with Shay."

"Sister—you are the queen. Shay will be available to you anytime day or night."

"Still, missing the appointment is a bit rude. Besides, I'm anxious to meet her." She bid Marcus a temporary farewell and headed for the corridor, with Silva close behind.

Per her instructions, Sorrah had the Queensguard move Shay and a few select Hendrins back into the castle. Meserek had banished them when he ruled, but during her father's reign, the Hendrins were considered valuable assets. Advisors. Her mother befriended Shay and she hoped to do the same. She too would consider advisement from Hendrins. Many of which, from what she was told, were highly sensitive to the gods bidding. The gods had done well by her and she wouldn't forget that. She would heed their bidding and listen to their direction.

Just as she approached Shay's door, it opened and out walked Sevin. He looked flustered but bowed his head to her. "Majesty."

He started by her but Sorrah stopped him. "Are you feeling well, Sevin?"

She looked over the fine features of his face. *He is related to me.*

He was an attractive man, with his black hair, blue eyes and shadowy beard. His steely demeanor only made him that much more appealing, giving him the look of a rebel. Women in any world would find Sevin appealing, she decided. Especially those who liked the bad boy type. She hoped one day he found his soul mate as she had.

Like most days, Sevin's eyes were intense but she sensed something more. Sadness. Worry. He was worried about something.

"I am well. Thank you."

Clearly, the man was covering up his concern which only fueled her curiosity and need to want to know more.

"I'm pleased to hear it."

Silence fell between them.

He seemed uneasy, restless. Even though Rohen had explained that Sevin was closed off in many ways, she got the impression, in this instance that he wanted to say more.

"What is it?" she asked.

"The Hendrin is strong. Powerful. It's hard to refute her knowledge or accept it." He dragged his hand over his face and exhaled. "It's all so hard to believe." He searched her face and she knew he was thinking about the two of them being related. But when he offered her nothing more in the way of words, Sorrah decided not to press the issue. Later, she would ask Rohen to pry it out of him. Casually of course.

Sevin stared into her eyes for a few seconds longer before nodding and going on his way.

"How odd," she murmured.

His behavior only solidified her belief of their connected ancestry and she was certain Shay had spoken about it. If Sevin was indeed related to her and Marcus, through their mother or otherwise, she needed to hear it for herself.

"I'll return shortly," Sorrah told Silva as she pushed open the door.

"I'll be right here." Silva sat on a bench just outside of Shay's quarters.

"Hello," Sorrah said, extending a hand out to Shay. The woman appeared to be older than her, which for the first time made sense. With the time and age difference she knew the Hendrin must be quite old to show aging features. She had a kind smile and Sorrah liked her right away.

"My goodness, you are a pretty one," Shay said, ignoring her hand and pulling her in for a hug. "I remained in the far back at the coronation. I'm so pleased to meet you. Your mother would be so proud of you. You are a brave soul to have journeyed so far."

Sorrah instantly felt like crying. Her tenderness and soft voice reminded her of her mother.

Shay stepped back. "Let me have a longer look at you." She smiled. "I'll pour us some tea. Thank you for such luxurious accommodations. There is a lot of room for my work and such. This is the exact room I had when your father was king."

"You offered him guidance."

"I did. He would summon me and others to come before him."

"I would like the same. I would like you to counsel me as well. Marcus and Rohen are a great help but I believe it's important to surround oneself with a varying selection of trusted people."

Her confidence and boldness had grown substantially since she had first arrived due mostly in part to her connection to this place and to their gods. She sought their will, and in return, listened carefully to what they told her, where they guided her. Even after all that had happened, she felt at peace and at home in Sorrah. She had been born to find the mirror, to find this place and to find Rohen.

"I would be honored to be your counsellor, as long as you don't mind me going on and on with my speech. I have a tendency to babble."

Sorrah laughed. "Not at all. I welcome the companionship. I'll be working in the gardens soon, much to the dismay of well... everyone. But I insist on being outdoors a lot and indoors baking from time to time."

"You are much like your mother. She too had a desire to do things out of the ordinary of those in her station. But you possess the highest station of all. One that once was filled by your father, the king. The people will look to you from now on."

"My life—"

"Yes?"

"Will Rohen—I mean, I didn't die. And I can't imagine my life without him in it. I don't want to think of it. People live a long time here, but do you know how long I might have with him?"

"You've seen the drawings in the cave, yes?"

Sorrah nodded.

"Then you've seen the representation of the infinity tree."

"I assume it is a symbol of my immortality."

Shay's eyes widened. "Yes. But there was another tree there as well if you recall."

"There were two trees. Yes. Their branches intertwined as one." Sorrah's voice was going higher as excitement stirred.

"Rohen. He is the other tree. My mate," Sorrah stated as absolute truth.

"The legends are true and are as romantic as they come. When you gave your heart to him and the two of you found each other, you shared your immortality with him. But there are small spiritual windows to these things. You need to be aware of this."

"He is not immortal?"

"No. He can die but you can heal wounds, both inside and out, as you have already."

Sorrah knew she spoke of his heart as well as his flesh.

"However, he will remain the age he is now and will flourish as the symbol of the trees with life and vitality. The two of you shall never know the sting of death, as long as you are together."

They would be together always. She couldn't wait to share the news with Rohen.

"Also... May I ask—?"

"You may ask anything at all," Shay answered, setting a tea cup on the table in front of Sorrah.

"Sevin—"

"Ah, yes. That reminds me. Marcus has given me a drop of blood. Sevin has as well. May I ask for a drop of yours?"

For a split second, doubt crept in but quickly fled with an onslaught of surety that Shay was not the enemy.

"You are wise to question. Not all Hendrins are as I." She sighed. "Too many have gone the way of darkness. It is a shame."

"My mother trusted you. My father as well. I too will trust you until it is proven to me otherwise."

"Already she speaks as a queen."

Sorrah lifted her loose sleeve and presented her arm.

"The finger will do nicely."

She poked her finger with a pin. "Hold it over the jar," Shay instructed but didn't pick any particular jar.

There were six jars in a row, each a different color and filled with some kind of liquid.

Sorrah gave them the once over before holding her finger over a green jar. When Shay smiled, Sorrah knew she had chosen well or at the very least, chosen what had been expected.

"There would've been no wrong jar," Shay offered, pinching Sorrah's finger gently. A few drops fell into the water blending with its contents.

"But there was no other option for me but to choose the green one."

Shay smiled widely. "Indeed."

"Yet another," Shay whispered, stirring the contents of the green jar.

"Another? What does my blood tell you?"

"Sevin is part of your mother's ancestry. But of the darkest kind going farther back than you might believe. Still, he is your relative to be sure."

Sorrah's face lit up. She didn't care about the dark comment or how far back the ancestry was. She had found more family and she struggled to hide her pleasure.

She recalled the look on Sevin's face. Had the Hendrin not only divulged to him that he was related but that he had a dark druid ancestry? That could not have been easy to hear.

"Did you tell Sevin?"

"Some he already knew. Dark spirits are potent and have a way of lingering through the blood, disturbing its host's life. He fights his demons. You and your brother bear marks of the bloodlines of your parents. They are symbols of the gods choosing and marks which set you apart from all others."

"And Sevin bears such a mark? How could he of hid it for all this time? I can't imagine the people of Aaru would have kept quiet about such a thing."

"He was watched early on but kept to himself. It is possible he's been able hide it. But it has started to grow."

"Grow?"

"It covers much of his back."

"What is it?"

"Saecular arbor."

"Forever tree? Like the one in my mark and depicted on the cave wall? The infinity tree?"

"His tree is strong and has started to grow. Something has awakened and calls to him. It moves, seeks."

"What does it seek, Shay?"

Shay locked eyes with Sorrah. "It seeks what all seek. Vitality. Life. Fruitfulness. A mate."

"And if he does not find what it seeks? Will it die? Will *he* die?" This was seriously worrying her but explained the look on Sevin's face. He too was worried. She could see it. Sense it.

Shay's expression saddened. "I honestly do not know. But I do know that one day he will find answers and must make difficult choices. Dryads, which provide life to the forests and trees, have existed before any of us. They will help guide him if he opens up his spirit to them."

"Dryads?"

"The spirits of the trees. Few people, druids and such, have a special link to these woodland entities, while others are attuned to darker spirits."

Darker?

"Sevin has, for a better word, linkage to the spirits of the woodlands, as do you. But his spirit battles darker forces. I didn't know that until today. These types hide themselves well. What I've told you does bring light to your connection to the forest, does it not?" She winked but Sorrah could see the concern on Shay's face.

"Yes, it does. I'd really like to learn more."

Shay nodded. "In time. I trust you will not share what I've told you?"

"Of course not. You told Sevin what you could though, didn't you? He needs to know."

"I told him of my suspicions as far as his lineage."

"Does Sevin have abilities like Marcus and I?"

Shay smiled slightly as she stroked the fire burning in the hearth. "If he possesses any power, it will not be made known to him until he unlocks it. Just as you and Marcus have. His bloodline stems farther back than yours but is no less powerful. His journey will be one of temptation, discovery, enlightenment, and even love if he is open to it."

"Was he pleased by anything you told him?"

"He is troubled but healing is on the horizon if he accepts his fate."

"My only hope is of his happiness."

Shay smiled. "My but this world needs more like you. You are a gift to us all. Which reminds me… I have a very special wedding present for you but it won't arrive until later tomorrow, after the ceremony is over."

"That is very thoughtful of you, Shay. You can have it delivered to my quarters. I'll leave word with the guards to bring it to me."

"As you wish." Shay winked. "Now, let's have a looksee into how many children you and Rohen will have, hmm?"

"Oh—okay. I have many questions about my mother, the mirror and more. I also seek your help in finding a specific item that means a lot to someone I love."

Shay nodded. "Let's begin then."

By the time Sorrah left Shay's room, she was beaming with delight. She had found a friend in the Hendrin. She also found her nonappreciation, as it were, for knowing her personal future, especially when it came to children. Apparently, she would be pregnant many times.

This was a fantasy world, so why couldn't these people give birth to litters instead? Get it all over with at one time. She was going to be in serious need of governesses. Many of them. She smiled at the thought of her and Rohen's children running around this enormous castle.

She had entered Shay's quarters not knowing what to expect, and left feeling altered, unburdened and better for having spent time with her. And shouldn't that be the experience when you leave the presence of a friend?

The wedding was set for tomorrow and Sorrah couldn't help the flutter fanning in her stomach at the thought of Rohen and the wedding night. She was marrying the man of her dreams in the land of her dreams. They hadn't been together for what seemed like weeks but she knew their abstinence would only make their reunion all the more sweet.

"Where to now?" Silva asked.

"The kingdom seamstresses. They are having me try on my dress again."

"Your mother wore the same one, I'm told."

"Yes. It's a beautiful blue dress but I had a few embellishments added and some alterations. Some pieces of white added here and there, along with a veil and such. I know my mother would've wanted me to make it my own. I have them making a few other things for me too."

Earlier she had sent her mother's ring to Rohen after Marcus confirmed it was her wedding ring. First, she had offered it to her brother but he blatantly refused, saying it was rightfully hers. She didn't want to force Rohen into using it so she merely sent it to him and gave him the choice. Any ring he chose would be perfect.

The morning came and with it, butterflies in her stomach. Her bed chambers were filled with candles and flowers of various kinds. As instructed her trousseau of customized lingerie, including garters, corsets and panties, were laid out on a large bureau. She wanted Rohen to see her extensive collection and see the approval in his eyes.

She stood in front of her mirror. "Mirror, mirror on the wall—" she muttered as she once more looked at her reflection. She liked what she saw.

"It is time," Silva said, coming to stand beside her.

The other handmaidens who were in the room scurried off.

Sorrah took a deep breath and headed for the door. Marcus was just on the other side, ready to walk her down the aisle.

Chapter thirty

The entry of the church was far away from Rohen but he could tell the moment Sorrah graced its doors. Gasps of awe could be heard echoing off the walls and cathedral ceilings.

As the air filled with the soft sounds of violins, Marcus escorted her up the center aisle, taking slow steps. Heads bowed and subtle intakes of breath accompanied the music.

All Rohen could see was Sorrah. He knew she'd look beautiful but nothing could have prepared him for the exquisite vision before him. She was an angel in shimmering blue and white. Her beaded dress shimmered in the candlelight burning brightly from chandeliers above. Her dress eloquently and seamlessly flowed down her body, accentuating her curves with perfection. A trail of her blue dress extended behind her, along with delicate lace and tulle.

She'd kept her sun-kissed blonde hair down, much to Rohen's delight. Soft curls on the ends, gently bounced and swayed over her breasts. A veil softly streamed down the back of her, joining subtly with the train of her dress. On the very top of her head she wore her sovereign crown, filled with pale jewels of every color. It had been custom made with the finest materials and gems in all of Sandrin, accenting her fair skin and pale blue eyes.

"She is a vision, brother," Ian said, standing beside Rohen.

"That she is." He swallowed deeply. "She's the most beautiful thing I have ever seen. There are none that compare to her."

Marcus placed her hands in Rohen's trembling ones and took a seat in the front row alongside Ian.

Rohen desperately wanted to pull her inside his arms and kiss her but for now he'd wait, at least until the ceremony was over. Which couldn't be soon enough.

The final words were spoken and rings were exchanged. Her ring was the one belonging to her mother, silver with a gorgeous pale blue stone. He knew she loved the ring and it suited her. His ring was equally impressive with silver branches intertwined on the surface. Before she placed it on his finger she tilted it so he could see it was engraved then spoke the words.

"My love. My life. My heart."

They were the identical words of those engraved inside the ring she now wore. The final vows were spoken and he eagerly kissed her.

"You are all mine, wife," he told her, resting his forehead on hers.

"And you are all mine, husband."

Marcus, Ian and the elite of the Queensguard were the first to cheer enthusiastically, followed by the viewing audience.

After greeting their guests, many of which were visiting dignitaries and noblemen, they made their way to the great hall for a night of celebration. Rohen had his own ideas for celebrating but he would wait until she was ready to say her goodnights.

"Rohen, look!" she squealed.

The hall was decorated from ceiling to floor with elements of the outdoors. Even the tables were set with the woodland theme. Berries, vines, and evergreen roping filled the space beautifully. Soft lighting shone from the many candles placed everywhere, including large chandeliers which hung low from the ceiling.

"It is exactly how I would've imagined the perfect wedding reception."

Rohen leaned to her ear. "I'm glad you're pleased." He kissed her and briefly lingered to inhale the sweet scent of her.

The cake was huge, a replica of the castle itself. Wine and champagne cascaded out of waterfalls. Ice sculptures of wildlife and trees were commissioned and many, many trees were brought in, their bases secured so they could be planted afterwards and mini candles lighting them up.

They greeted many of their guests, ate dinner, and drank champagne and ale. The music started and Rohen and Sorrah stood opposite from each other while others did much the same in straight rows beyond them.

They bowed once to each other, joined in the center with their hands raised and touching. Rohen kept one arm behind his back, while Sorrah lifted her dress a few inches with her free hand.

Their eyes were only on each other as they turned in a full circle one way and then the other. They bowed again and this time, the music slowed to a seductive melody. This time his free hand came behind her back and with one arm, lifted her as they slowly turned in a circle formation once more. Their faces were aligned, their lips inches from touching, their hearts pounding in sync.

"There is an enormous table over there filled with gifts," Rohen told her as they whirled around.

"I can see that. Would it be rude to have them brought up to our chamber?"

Rohen smiled and leaned closer to her ear. "You don't think to bed me tonight do you, wife?" he teased, his voice a soft whisper in her ear. He lowered his mouth to her neck and tenderly kissed her.

Sorrah's grin grew wide as she tilted her head into his kiss. "It is my intention, husband and you shall comply."

"Shall I?"

She lowered her voice and shifted her mouth toward his ear. "If you want to see the new trousseau of panties and more I had made to please you, seduce you even, then yes."

Rohen stilled. The images of the few pieces she already owned had him roused in the matter of seconds. To think of her wearing other such feminine things, made his trousers down right uncomfortable. He'd never seen such delicate female undergarments but knew they looked even better on Sorrah. And then off Sorrah.

He growled at her neck and rose to face her. "Do not make me wait any longer. I am ravished for you, Fairhead. My kisses could just as easily turn into bites."

"And I am ravished for you." She gave his bottom lip a playful tug with her teeth, following up with a gentle suck. "I bite too."

"We leave now." He grabbed her hand and led her toward the door while she playfully laughed behind him.

He addressed Marcus on their way out. "The queen has given our guests enough attention. It's my turn to return the favor."

Marcus smiled. "I'll see that things are wrapped up here."

"Oh—I," Sorrah said. "Rohen wait. My gift. My gift to Marcus."

Rohen stopped. He knew how much it meant that she give it to him personally.

He stepped away and spoke to Aiden, the Queensguard who

Sorrah had entrusted to keep the gift a secret and set aside.

Aiden produced a wrapped box and presented it to Sorrah.

"Thank you, Aiden!" Sorrah beamed. She held it out to Marcus.

"You are giving me a gift on your wedding day?" Marcus asked, eyeballing the box.

"Yes. I am the queen and am giving my brother a gift. Now open it. I can't wait for you to see it."

Many of the guests' attention turned toward Sorrah and Marcus. They began to gather around.

Marcus turned to a nearby table and opened the box. Inside was a brilliant silver red-handled sword with flecks of inlaid gold. He picked it up in his hands, his mouth falling open. "How did—Where?"

"I asked a certain Hendrin to help me locate it. It was hidden in a secret hideaway in what was formerly Meserek's bedchamber. He never found Father's hiding place. It remains, I assume, exactly the way you remember it?"

"Yes. Yes it is. Just as the day Father gave it to me." He placed the sword down and lifted Sorrah, embracing her. "Sister. It is the best gift I have ever received. Second to you, of course. But what of your gifts?" He casually gestured to the table of wrapped presents.

"Have them sent to the room adjacent to Her Majesty's handmaiden," Rohen said.

"Yes," Silva added, coming from behind Sorrah. "I will see to it."

Rohen nodded and once again took hold of Sorrah's hand.

"Good night!" Sorrah bid her guests as they made their way to the staircase.

*****

Sorrah felt the ground beneath her disappear as Rohen swooped her up into his arms.

She giggled as he nodded for the guards to open the door to their bedchamber.

"Here too!" Sorrah said, looking around the room at all the decorations. Candles and flowers were in every corner and at each side table of the bed.

The fireplace hearth was lit and a warm glow filled the illustrious space.

Rohen kissed her before setting her on her feet.

"They've really outdone themselves." She skimmed her fingers over a vine and berry candle ring and touched the rim of the wooden bowl filled with fruit, bread and cheeses.

"Yes," Rohen murmured, coming up behind her.

He wrapped his arm around her waist and brought her tightly against the front of him.

"Hmm," she muttered as she rested her head against him and arched her back.

"You know what that does to me." He kissed her neck and trailed his lips toward her shoulder. "You are so beautiful." He cupped her breast and gently caressed. When things became even more heated she stepped away.

"Help me with my dress?" she asked over her shoulder.

He slowly undid the long stream of buttons down the back of her dress.

She let her dress slip slowly down and reveled in Rohen's reaction when he saw what she wore underneath.

She wore a delicate lace corset, a matching white lace thong with a small bow, and a garter and stockings.

"Sorrah. What you do to me—turn so that I can see the front of you."

Her face flushed. No matter how many times they'd been intimate in the past, he had a way of heating her with only his stringent voice. Rohen was a man through and through.

She watched his eyes stream slowly down her body, stopping at her breasts which the corset lifted high. His gaze lowered to her panties and garter straps which hung from clips.

"You had these made?"

"Yes."

"Breathtaking. The idea—"

"Came primarily from—" How did she explain? "From a woman named Victoria."

"I feel the immense desire to thank this woman."

"Trust me, she was paid well, many times over. There is more."

"More?" He wiped his hand over his mouth.

She chuckled. "Yes, here, let me show you."

She took his hand and guided him to the large bureau. On top of it were many of the custom made lingerie she had made.

Rohen skimmed his fingers over the items but his eyes returned to her.

He growled and hoisted her up.

Sorrah straddled him. "You are a wolf."

Rohen's grin grew larger. "A *hungry* wolf," he corrected. "With a particular appetite for one. Only one, Fairhead."

He kissed her, moving his hand in the process to her globe of a behind and caressed.

The heat sizzled in the air between them as they moved to the bed. He laid her down on the blankets and sat on his knees between her legs as he untied the front of her corset.

Her breasts spilled out from the confines and he took his time showing them attention before proceeding to help her out of the rest of her garments, leaving the garter belt and stockings intact.

"Don't hold back," she muttered as he slowly lowered himself on top of her.

"My wife is a bit of a wolf too."

"Yes. And hungry for only one."

They made love slowly, methodically, then fast and eagerly, taking all that the other had to give. Temporarily sated, they lay together on the bed.

Sorrah's stomach growled.

"You need to eat," Rohen said, getting off the bed and going over to the table of food.

When Sorrah thought to get off the bed, he stopped her.

"No. Stay right where you are. Let me feed you."

He grabbed a plate and filled it with fruit, cheese, and bread before returning to bed. He lifted a strawberry to her lips and she bit down. A small squirt of juice rolled off her bottom lip and he lowered his mouth and licked it up.

"Hmm," they murmured in unison. While they talked and laughed, they ate the food.

Sorrah glanced at the now empty plate. "Oh, wait. We have to have wedding cake!" She had commissioned the resident bakers to make something special, even provided them with her own recipe and was more than a little curious on how it turned out.

With a growl of reluctance, Rohen turned to his side so she could get off the bed. "I planned on keeping you in bed indefinitely," he teased.

She smiled then looked over to the food table. "That's odd. I asked for them to bring us a smaller version of the castle cake that I had them make. One only for us. But I don't see it."

"I'll go check. Stay put," he said. He pulled on a pair of loose black pants, kissed her, and then left the room.

She heard him briefly say something to the guards in the hallway as she walked to the large closet and picked out a long white robe.

A knock sounded on the door and she assumed Rohen couldn't turn the enormous handle if he was carrying the cake. *Maybe the guards aren't there to help?*

She swung the door open to see a large object covered with a long, royal blue fabric in front of her and two of the Queensguard standing to each side of it.

"Majesty. My apologies," one of them said.

She recognized him as one of the Queensguard who often patrolled the castle.

"What is this?"

"This is a wedding present from the Hendrin Shay. She insisted I bring it directly to you and that I or no other gaze upon it. She said it's a gift and that she spoke of it to you."

"Oh, yes. Of course. That's fine." Sorrah tugged on her robe, closing it tightly before moving out of the way of the door. She hadn't remembered until now Shay mentioning a gift that wouldn't come until after the wedding. She expected perhaps a box or something but not this huge thing. And what a strange wrapping. It looked like velvet drapery. "Please leave it in the center of the room."

The Queensguard did as she asked and wheeled the item into the room.

"If that will be all, Your Majesty."

"Wait outside the door. I'd like to write a note for the Hendrin and I want you to deliver it."

The men bowed and stepped outside the room.

She headed to her desk at the far side of the room but turned back to the mysterious object when she heard a soft buzzing sound coming out from beneath the fabric.

How strange, she thought.

She was going to wait for Rohen to return but curiosity was getting the better of her.

She pulled the rope off the bottom of the gift and lifted the fabric up and off the object. She stumbled back, nearly falling on her behind. "My gods—the mirror."

It wasn't a replica, or similar. It was the one and only enchanted mirror. What could this mean? Did the gods mean to tempt her? She knew her own heart. She knew Sorrah was the rightful place for her and Rohen the rightful mate.

The conversation she had with Shay, drifted in her mind.

"Tell me about the mirror," she asked Shay. "Tell me why my mother could not return to Sorrah."

"Your mother stepped through the mirror as you did and entered the world you were meant to be born in. However, the gods saw the return she made to her former world as a form of rejection. They had made things right by bringing her through to Sorrah, her rightful home. They had set the universe right—"

Sorrah had understood even though she felt saddened for her mother. "And no matter the reason or desperate necessity, she was unable to make things right again. She warned me."

"What did she say?"

Sorrah said the words from her mother audibly as she stared at the mirror. "Once you step through, there is no going back."

She'd been given a clear warning. A warning from her mother, who had been told the future. Her mother had spent time with the Hendrin and had been told things, Marcus said. She had been told the future. Had she been told of this future? Of this moment? *There's no going back. There's no going back.* The words shot into her mind over and over but things were becoming blurred and her thoughts confusing.

"There are many powers all around us, both good and evil. Good will never disguise itself as evil but you can be sure evil hides itself in the most beautiful way. It's best to know the difference. Recognize the true nature of what is before you. Sense it." Shay had said those words to her right before she left her quarters.

Were evil forces tempting her, seducing her to cross back through the portal of worlds knowing she could never return?

Mesmerized by the mirror and how it now shimmered, she lifted her fingers to the wooden frame. Instantly, a magnetic pull connected her fingers with the symbolic engravings, much like the way the drawings in the cave begged for her touch. The symbols trembled, moved and shifted, and even though a still small voice cried out from her spirit to leave the mirror alone, she couldn't seem to pry them away.

The mirror began to glow and involuntarily her fingers edged their way off the frame and toward the reflective glass. There were only inches separating her fingers from the center when she sensed a malevolent force coming from inside the mirror. She trembled as her soul fought against her body's overwhelming urge to touch the mirror. Her hand shook and her fingers slowly began to splay toward the glass.

No. No. I can't touch it. It will take me. It will take me away.

"Ahhh!" she cried as pain shot through her body.

"No!" A loud booming voice filled her ears, followed by a large crash. In an instant Sorrah's body was tackled and catapulted across the floor, her feet lifting in the air.

Her breathing hitched then left her altogether as the wind was knocked out of her.

The cake went flying through the air and landed on the floor, splattering everywhere. Including her and Rohen.

"Ro—Rohen!" she finally forced out.

Rohen's body jerked and out of his mouth came a loud, agonizing lamentation. Sorrah's heart crushed at the sound as she joined in his sorrowful yet, relief-filled cry.

He grabbed a firm hold of her hair and pulled her face to meet his. He planted kisses on one spot of her face and then another and another as he whispered, "I love you. I love you. You cannot leave me! I will not mourn you! Not ever!"

No. He would not mourn her and she would not mourn him. Just as the branches in the infinity trees, the symbol of eternity, they had a forever.

She shook her head. "No. No mourning. I love you."

With tears trickling down her cheeks, Sorrah leaned slightly over his ear and proceeded to tell him what Shay had said. They would be together for a very long time. Forever. There was no better time that this to tell him the news.

They remained on their sides, tightly clutching one another, knowing some menacing force had seeped into their lives to tempt fate and subsequently taunt the gods who brought them together.

Still, Rohen and Sorrah were destined to be together and they had been saved once more. Fate had to take a bow this day. Had any number of things transpired preventing Rohen from returning to their room that very second, had he not stopped her, lives would've been destroyed. His life. Her life. Possibly more.

Gift, Sorrah thought. Wasn't everything a matter of perspective? Had the mirror truly been the Hendrin's gift or the traumatic event itself? Surely, Shay would've known the outcome if she were as powerful as people say she is.

Time had stood still in that fearful moment. She was sure they both saw their time together thus far, flash before their eyes. All could have been lost. They treasured their time together more than most, but how much more did they now, because of that one solitary event?

Gift indeed.

"Cover it, now!" Rohen yelled to the Queensguard who had stormed inside the room as Rohen shouted and had stood in shock as he charged Sorrah.

The soldier threw the cover back over the mirror and tied the bottom back up with rope.

Rohen stood with his hands clenched at his sides. "Burn that blasted thing to the ground! Crush it. Throw it off the highest peak but it is not allowed back inside these walls!"

"Rohen," Sorrah said. "It's indestructible."

She stood and held onto his arm. She had to touch him and keep touching him for a least a few days.

An idea came to her. "I have a better idea. I believe it to be the right thing." She nodded as specifics flooded her.

Perhaps, the mirror itself wasn't the evil but a way to find one's true self, true purpose. A place where they belong.

"One minute," she told the guards as she went to her desk in a hurry.

Rohen pointed to the door. "Get that wretched thing out of this room and out of my sight." The men obeyed, stopping in the hallway.

Sorrah withdrew the pieces of Sorrien gold she came to Sorrah with, plus a few extras, and began writing frantically on a piece of parchment paper.

"What are you doing?"

"I'm offering a gift to someone who deserves happiness in their life. They don't have to accept, but I'll send a prayer to the gods to oversee his choice and guide him."

"Him? Him who?"

Sorrah smiled.

"Fairhead... what are you up to?"

"Only if you agree. Read this."

She handed him the gold and the letter which included a list of items this male were to take with him. Also, names of her ancestors and addresses for him to find.

Rohen took a deep breath. "I do agree. He needs to find answers. He can return here should he choose to?"

"Yes. Just as my mother was able to return to Earth. But if he does come back to Aaru—"

"He can never return to Earth. I get it. Trust me. I could have lost you forever. Now, don't you move and for crying out loud do not touch any mirrors. No windows either."

"Windows?"

"I'm not taking any chances. You're not getting close to anything that has the slightest reflection."

Rohen took a pouch out of a drawer and placed the items inside. He pulled the strings tight and walked to the door.

"This is very important." He handed the pouch to one of the soldiers. "That bag goes with the mirror. They are a gift. A delivery directly from the queen."

"To whom, sir?"

"Sevin. It goes directly to Sevin. Stop for no one. Tell him if he intends to go on an adventure he will need to speak with me and the queen first."

The men nodded and wheeled the mirror away.

Rohen exhaled hard and gathered Sorrah in his arms.

"The only other action happening tonight is in our bed, wife."

Sorrah kissed him. "Agreed, husband."

He locked the door and carried her to the bed. He leaned down and licked some of the splattered frosting off her shoulder. "This is the best way to have cake."

Sorrah giggled. She had everything she could ever want and more. She lived in the most fantastical place, had the man she loved in her life forever, and children in her future. And cake.

She scooped some cake off his arm and ate it. "This is the best life ever."

~The End

Madison Thorne Grey

For more information regarding other works by Madison Thorne Grey:

http://madisonthornegrey.com

Find me on Facebook
http://facebook/madisonthornegrey

30880947R00191

Made in the USA
Middletown, DE
11 April 2016